J. R. Beckwith

The House Behind the Poplars

A Novel

J. R. Beckwith

The House Behind the Poplars
A Novel

ISBN/EAN: 9783744723558

Printed in Europe, USA, Canada, Australia, Japan

Cover: Foto ©Andreas Hilbeck / pixelio.de

More available books at **www.hansebooks.com**

THE

HOUSE BEHIND THE POPLARS.

A NOVEL.

———

MRS. J. R. BECKWITH,

AUTHOR OF "THE WINTHROPS."

———

"The sins of the parents shall be visited upon the children."

———

NEW YORK:

W. E. HILTON, PUBLISHER,

128 NASSAU STREET.

1871.

THE HOUSE BEHIND THE POPLARS.

CHAPTER I.

THE gray shades of quick coming evening settled over and around the gloomy homestead of Miles Sterling, standing solitary and half shut in from the street behind a row of Lombardy poplars, which lifted their ragged tops toward the lowering sky as if imploringly.

There was a comfortless chill in the late autumn air, and ever and anon scattering hail-stones were whirled against the window-panes, in promise of the wintry storm, whose purple clouds scudded over the horizon.

The bleak hill upon whose crest the house stood, was all unshielded from the forcing blasts which whistled shrill and drearily around the rattling window-panes, and the low, wood-colored building itself, looked as if prematurely hastened to decay by a sense of its own uncared-for position in a bleak world.

Its low windows had never repeated themselves in any second story, but stretched in a row of six along its front, shaded by the melancholy poplars which despised it in summer, and seemingly forsook it in winter, when the heavy, sodden snow of northern Ohio furnished a mantle under which they could screen themselves. Excepting these, the rambling, rail-fenced yard offered no object for the eye to rest upon. Not a flower or shrub broke the tasteless monotony of the tangled weeds and grass which spread down to the sandy road, along which the teams of the neighboring farmers plodded and dragged in a hopeless, weary way, as if no thought of a better foothold beyond, lent vigor to the effort. The uncomfortable aspect of the situation was at this season of the year intensified by the ceaseless plashing of water falling over the dam that enclosed one end of a willow bordered mill-pond, which fed the red grist-mill below, and the whirr of the slowly moving machinery kept up a ceaseless undertone to the wind which whistled over the hill, and around the casements, like the voice of departed hurricanes in purgatorial torments.

Inside the weather-beaten dwelling, known as "the old millhouse," from its proprietary connection with the red mill, everything was even more unattractive than without. The ceilings were low and cracked, and dun colored by the smoke that rose in a persevering cloud from the smouldering faggots laid upon the iron dogs whose faces are ornamented by a hollow ring, looking out like an eye ; and the row of windows impartially divided between the two front rooms, were each one covered to the middle sash by curtains of smoke, discolored paper, torn and fretted into more than one irreparable breach, eked out at the last one in the row, by an old number of the county newspaper, no less stained and battered by misfortune.

A faded rag carpet afforded some pretence of protection to the floor ; but even this spoke of the wasting cares of existence, and illy concealed the traces of its direful throes under the grasp of the destroyer. A few red posted wooden chairs, a rickety-legged table, and a contemporaneous settee, comprised the furniture of the room in which Mrs. Sterling sat silently cowering in front of the cheerless fire, her face at times quite concealed between the hands in which she buried it, as she swayed herself restlessly to and fro as if striving thus to restrain some stronger outburst of impatience. But often she raised it toward the continually fading light yet lingering round the homestead, and despite the half disguise of its usual expression, imparted by a frown born of her present humor, it was a face one turned again and again to study, so contradictory were the lines by which one read it. The low, roundish, unspeaking brow of shallow womanhood, the unnoticeable nose, possessing no particular contour, and the usual vapid expression of the mouth, spoke of a low order of intellect, unredeemed by any saving flashes of a higher genius; and one looked again to discover in what lay the undefined influence exercised by such features. The gray eyes were ever changing, yet seldom brightening, but the occasional oblique glance darting from beneath the depressed eyelids, revealed the first cause for an involuntary distrust, and the peculiar formation of brain evidenced by the contour of skull, might both literally and metaphorically be pronounced "long headed;" a decision confirmed by an occasional expression of the usually placid mouth ; and the deep lines extending downward in a peculiar curve, towards the prominent chin, spoke of a jealous disposition descending into positive selfishness. Her lithe, yet vigorous frame, evidenced strong vitality, and the rather coarse brown hair put tidily enough under the keeping of a horn comb, gave no clue to the ever contradictory conclusions as to her age, which at one moment might have been thirty, and at another seemed at least ten years more, as some internal emotion lined itself strongly upon her face.

The sound of a cough issuing from the adjoining room, roused her from her last resumed cowering posture near the fire ; and with a jerk of the door sticking upon the sill as she essayed to open it, she passed on into the other room, from which a chillier draft of air rushed out to exchange places with the smoky atmosphere of the scarcely more comfortable apartment she had left. The room was so dark that only at a second glance could one perceive the outlines of a bed, from whose occupant the tight, distressing cough continued its appeal.

" What do you want now ?" asked Mrs. Sterling, fretfully, and a child's voice replied,

"Oh, I'm so hot and achey; and I want some water so bad ! my bones shake, and all of me "—

" There, there, that will do. I can't help it, I'm sure! Doctor Kelley han't come yet, and I don't know as he's coming at all. He's too much else to think of."

But despite the complaining tone which seemed to blame the boy for his suffernigs, she brought a dipper of water from the kitchen, and when he had finished his eager draught, bade him "lie down and be patient, for once," and then walked to the window and looked moodily out, while the little fellow crawled back among his pillows and said no more.

Even as the deep lines of discontent grew almost savagely marked between her eyebrows, the sound of wheels grinding through the sand, fell upon her ear, and in an instant more, a doctor's gig stopped at the bars which gave egress from the yard to the street, and without stopping to tie the well trained horse, the doctor ran hastily up the narrow path between the tangled grass, and Mrs. Sterling opened the door, with the not gracious salutation,

" It's well you thought to come, at last ! Time *was*, when I hadn't to wait half a day, and that, too, with the old man every minute likely to come in !"

" There, Lydia, don't scold, it's all thrown away on me, and, besides, quite undeserved. I tried to come at the hour named in your note, but a sad accident at just the last moment detained me, as even a doctor can't be always hard-hearted and put one off with a promise to call to-morrow."

"Not unless there's a woman in the case, and particularly an old one. I scraped the last pound of flour out of the barrel last night, and hid it; and as Sterling's got more corn to grind, now, than he can any way finish by the time he's agreed to, and to-day's Saturday, I knew he'd have to borrow of brother Jonathan, over the hill; and so I had him off out of the way by two o'clock to-day, which is just the time I wrote you to come, and as children have long ears, I made him take the youngest boy with him. I wanted to have a talk with you, and here it is night already, and a bad one at that, so the old man won't wait to eat supper at Jonathan's, even to save the cost of one at home."

"Never mind, Lydia. Any woman who is sharp enough to get her good man out of the way when he isn't wanted, is shrewd enough to dispose of him if he comes back too soon."

"'Good man?' I don't know any," retorted Mrs. Sterling bitterly, as she stirred the fire into something like a blaze, and then silently watched the doctor as he shook his gloves and coat free from the unthawed snow-flakes that covered them.

"Well, how is the boy?" he asked, extending in turn each hand toward the blaze.

"Sick, as usual. He's never seen a well day yet, and I don't suppose he ever will. He's nothing but a trouble to me, and never has been, and I could shake the daylight out of him sometimes, when I think how it was him who brought me into the miserable fix I'm in! Look at my home: ain't it nice, not to say anything of Sterling's addle-headed, or, as *he* calls it, *crazy* old mother, who'll live, and live me into my grave, in spite of everything not good for her health! All my trouble is your fault. Yes, you can't deny it. You croaked "awful exposure," and preached "respectability" at me, till I was scared and wheedled into it, while all you wanted was to get me well off your hands before you married that very virtuous and highly respected lady, who is now Mrs. Kelley, as *I ought* to have been—the more fool I was not to have staid as I was, and let you get along about the brat the best way you could! and you'd have made a good way; for *you* are *respectable*, a saint in the eyes of this world."

Her anger grew fiercer and more bitter as she gave expression to it, and turning, at last, the doctor held her firmly by the shoulders which attempted resentfully to shake off the clasp, and compelling her to face him, said sorrowfully, but unflinchingly:

"Stop there, Lydia! I am not as good as I should be; I acknowledge it with pain, as I recall the past with chagrin! but, Lydia, one thing I *never was*—a betrayer of innocence, or honest affection! You were not unsophisticated when I first met you, *and you know, as I do*, that you are in no way worse than you were, for having known me. I will bear my share of it all, but no more—though I wish to heaven I could suffer all the penalty poor little Lisle will unavoidably have to endure in many ways."

"I don't see how; nor would you, if you could see Sterling fuss over and humor him when he whines, and brag over him when there happens to come a day that the weazen-faced, weak-legged brat can be got out to the mill. If you could hear him cracking up and glorifying "my little son," on all occasions, as I do, as if there was nothing else of any account under the canopy, *you'd* despise him, too, for being such a fool! Sometimes I can't help saying back at him, "*your* son," though it's lucky for us all he don't understand it. If he knew it *wasn't* his son, but *yours*, he'd choke the cub to death, and so save the cost of his bringing up, over which he groans enough, I can tell you. He's stingier than the very marrow in the back bone of poverty!"

"Well, we'll discuss him another time. Give me a light and let me see the little fellow; poor boy!"

Mrs. Sterling took up a pair of unwieldy, iron-handled tongs, with which she lifted a coal from the fireplace, and fanning it into a glow by a few vigorous puffs, lighted by it a tallow candle which wearily tottered over the high neck of an iron candle-stick on the mantel-piece, and resumed her seat before the fire, while the doctor went into the next room, and bent over the bed where the little boy lay in a condition that sent a sudden stab into his heart. Rigid, motionless, the widely open eyes seeing nothing, it seemed at first view that he was really dead; but even as the doctor bent lower and clasped the little wrist with pitying fingers, a long, convulsive shudder shook the child's frame, and the blood leaped with sudden force along the arteries. For one instant the doctor leant over him breathlessly, then turned away and went back to the room where Mrs. Sterling indulged her reverie. Placing the candle back upon the mantlepiece, he leant his forehead on the edge of the shelf, and gazed down into the fire in a perfect silence which caused her to raise her head in curiosity.

"Well, what is it? This isn't the first time you've seen him so, I suppose."

"Yes, the very first time I ever saw him *so;*" then turning suddenly, he asked,

"Lydia, how old is that boy?'

"You've a *happy* memory! I've been the wife of Miles Sterling going on seven miserable years."

"Yes, I remember. For God's sake speak lower, Lydia; for as' we both live, he has heard every word that has passed since I came in! The door was partly open."

"Nonsense! he was asleep, and if he did hear, he couldn't understand—such a mere little pimp!"

"Less a child than you think! Suffering, and—I must say it, Lydia—ill treatment, have made him painfully precocious. The child who bears suffering like an adult, thinks and feels as one. Oh, Lydia, you and I have much to answer for!"

"Speak for yourself, for I'm answering for it, I can tell you! I don't suppose that men ever do answer for things of this kind. It is *women*, only, that are guilty and warned to repent. There; don't you hear the wagon coming through the bars? *my husband* has come! You're a great favorite of his, and he'll be glad to see you— *if you've had your supper*, which is worth twenty-five cents," and her lip curled.

"Lydia, why don't you rectify all this in your home which seems so to embitter you? The only part of any one's nature which you ever cared to learn, is the weakest part; assail your husband in that, and lay your foundation for a new experience, and, what is worth more, a new house. This *is* dull and dreary; but you, alone, can rectify it if you choose to do so."

"Yes, and I suppose I can 'rectify' a disposition so mean and stingy it won't let him put any flesh on his bones—he's thin as a shad—and an old woman who lives only to torment me; and a half 'come-by-chance' child, who, to cap all, is forever sick; and a Sterling brood that are likely to come and come on, lucky if not half of them twins! and perhaps, after all that, I can 'rectify' myself, in some way, into a respected, amiable, never tired woman, 'calculated to make a happy home,' as the wise books have it! Yet, seeing me as you do in all this misery, *you*, who helped to bring it on me, can sit there and roll out pills like a machine, or a—man!"

A little shadow of a smile crossed the doctor's face at this tirade; but it as quickly vanished, and dropping some mixture into a med-

icine glass, he carried it to the sick child; and during his absence
Mr. Sterling came in, leading by one hand a little boy, who, when
unwrapped and set out to warm, proved as chubby and sturdy a
little fellow as four and a half years ever accomplished. Mrs. Sterling herself drew the stout calf-skin shoes off the cold little feet, and
rubbed in her own the fat red hands with a cold dimple on every
knuckle, her every action and expression showing that this was the
mother's favorite, the child *par excellence;* and the hard, dissatisfied
look her face had worn till then, softened into its usual vapid, weak-
minded expression, betokening a character apparently incapable
even of pique or anger. As for the child, he sat patient and undemonstrative under all this manipulating, his wide open gray eyes,
so like his mother's, looking unblinkingly into the blaze, with a
resolute expression of daring and hardihood lighting up the small
round face, almost grotesque to witness.

"How's Lisle?" asked Mr. Sterling briefly, as he drew his own
chair into the warmest corner, and taking out his spectacles, wiped
them on a red silk handkerchief, and then evolved the weekly
newspaper from an obstinately retentive pocket, accompanied by a
grunt of approbation at the success of his efforts.

"I'm sure I don't know. Dr. Kelley never came near him till a
few minutes ago, and he never tells me anything if I ask him. He's
in there with him, now, and maybe he'll tell *you* what ails him.
Have you had your supper?"

"Yes, Jonathan's wife got an early tea for us. She's a smart
woman, but extravagant; and, as I told Jonathan, when they run
through their property they mustn't come upon me."

"Told 'em so, did you? I suppose your tea was too good to be
economical—more's the pity."

"Where's the old lady?"

"In bed, for a mercy. She a'n't the best of company, a'n't the old
lady, so I let her lie. She'll wake up when she gets hungry. Sakes
alive! how the smoke worries my poor eyes! I'd as lives freeze and
done with it."

"Ma, don't Li. freeze, too? a'n't he shivery in there?"

"I suppose so, my son; but sick little Lisle can't stand the smoke
like the rest of us."

Mr. Sterling laid the newspaper across his knee, and looked
thoughtfully into the fire, his pinched and narrow face wearing an
unusually serious expression, which his wife noted in the oblique
outlook from under her brows.

During the silence, Dr. Kelley returned from his visit to the sick boy, and after the usual common-places between Mr. Sterling and himself, he said,

"Mr. Sterling, it is but one degree short of murder to keep that sick boy in this uncomfortable old shell of a house. The smoke, and continual exposure to drafts, of this room, is but little improved upon by the raw dampness of the one where he lies, and, with his feeble constitution, I won't be answerable for the consequences."

"Ahem," began Mr. Sterling in the weak, indistinct voice natural with him: "I meant to have built, this year; but some way the money didn't seem to come. It's a hard world to get along in with a growing family."

"Don't borrow trouble, Mr. Sterling," said his wife mildly. "It may please Providence to take away some of us, and I'm sure you'd ought to be glad it's like to be Lisle, who's more expense to you than all the rest of us put together."

The doctor buttoned his great coat preparatory to going, and Mr. Sterling added, more as if in comment to himself than in answer to the suggestion of another,

"If I thought we'd have an open winter, I'd begin now. I s'pose .I *could* find the money."

"For that matter," said the doctor, cordially, "I will cheerfully lend a hand to help an old friend. I can accommodate you with a loan of a hundred or two, and of course interest is not to be thought of between such old neighbors. Think of it, Sterling, and you'll be ready to commence next spring, at the latest. And now good evening, as Mrs. Kelley will be waiting tea."

A whirl of wind and snow met the doctor as he went out into the street, and the falling water over the dam, added a chill of its own to the surroundings; but scarcely noticing it all, he gathered up the reins and turned his horse's head toward home, both brain and heart absorbed in deep thought. Left to its own guidance, the faithful Pegasus made good time homeward, and the doctor was taken by surprise as the bright light from his own windows shone upon him, and the boy came out to lead the horse to the stable. A warm fire and a cheerful tea table awaited him, and a pleasant looking little woman lingered for one last tucking in of the soft quilt which covered the rosy occupant of a wicker cradle in the warm corner, and then came forward to welcome her husband.

"You are late to-night, William, and I know you must be both cold and hungry. Has old Mr. Higgins an addition to his miseries, or Miss Dobson a relapse of hypo?"

" No, Emily, Mr. Allan's oldest boy fell from the hay loft and broke his arm, which made me late with my other patients, and I am now just from Miles Sterling's."

" Which answers my suggestions that you are neither warmed nor fed. Is little Lisle sick?"

" Yes, poor little fellow, and I'm afraid not too well nursed or cared for. That old house is as cold and cheerless as a barn ; and really, Emily, were it not for overtaxing you, it would be only Christian charity to bring him to our own comfortable home for the winter. I'm afraid he won't live it through, there, and if he does, it will be only at the price of much suffering which ought to be spared him. He is a manly, patient little fellow."

" Yes, he is. Do let us go after him to-morrow. It will not over-task me at all, as Bridget is the best of servants, and baby is quiet as a kitten."

The doctor smoothed the soft brown hair, and kissed the cheek of his wife, and his spirits rose to cheerfulness as they sat at their tea. The troubled expression which had hardened his face, relaxed, and he looked, now, a genial, benevolent gentleman, of about forty years of age. His large, finely-formed head, seemed in perfect harmony with the square, well-made forehead, from which the plentiful locks waved back over the high temples, and his blue eyes had a kindly beam that won their way at once into the hearts of both young and old. His rather large but not unhandsome mouth seemed formed only to utter the kind words, which, accompanied by a still kinder voice, made him beloved by all.

" Oh, Emily, this is what home ought to be," said he, as, tea over, he drew his wife's chair close by his own in front of the bright wood fire. " I never come back to it without feeling that here we do not know what trouble is. To see so many gloomy, comfortless, discontented homes, is enough to give one the horrors on purely scientific principles."

" Speaking of those Sterlings; even to pass their dreary place makes me shiver ; nor could I ever account for the disagreeable feeling so commonplace, not to say silly, a woman gives me! I always feel as if her gray eyes were piercing me through and through in hope to discover some unconfessed unhappiness, or possibly even guilt, though I know she hasn't the penetration to recognize it, if found. I think Fate must have united that couple to punish him for his parsimony and narrow-mindedness, and her for her general disagreeability. How did such a marriage ever come about?"

"An unanswerable question as to most marriages, but not this one. She was a Miss Fitzjames, of good family, I believe—at least their high blood is her constant boast—but impoverished by some unexplained fatality, and being too poor to gratify her ambitions in life, and too proud to marry any one of less noble lineage than herself, she passed her days in a vexed struggle between her pride and poverty, till at twenty-five she was no nearer her goal, and much nearer old maidenhood.

"When I first commenced practice here, she was a rather pretty girl of nineteen or twenty years, whom I often saw at her work in a little dressmaker's shop which she kept for the town; but it was not till two or three years afterward, that I ever formed any personal acquaintance with her. I believe she rather schemed to become acquainted with Sterling, when his father died—leaving him the red mill and the homestead; and he, unsocial, and pre-occupied as much as his illiterate mind could be occupied, was rather astonished, if not really pleased, with the chattiness and energy of the lady whom his friends persuaded him would make just the wife he needed to look after his house, and his mother, who was even then a harmless sort of lunatic.

"Miss Fitzjames consented to overlook his inferior birth, in consideration of his superior property, and married him, to find it above and beyond her reach, and even her feminine aggravations and annoyances in consequence, fell unheeded upon the granite rock of his parsimony and obstinacy. If there ever was anything soft and womanly about her, it has vanished under the certainly not enviable existence she leads with him there in that rickety ' Castle of Despair.' I'm really sorry for her."

" What a pity such a couple should have children ! They certainly will avenge a miserable childhood, by a contemptuous manhood; and justly enough, too, because naturally."

The doctor and his wife sat silently gazing among the glowing cinders, and an occasional quiver of his eyelids evidenced that *his* musings, at least, were not altogether general in their application. Did the thought occur to him that he, too, might fall heir to something of this vengeance for a miserable childhood ?

The subject opened a wide field for conjecture, and if the doctor lost himself among its intricate windings, and vainly sought a reassuring way out, who shall say that his anxiety for the little one over whom he felt a yearning responsibility, almost destitute of power, was not in part a reparation for a wrong long ago committed? Gladly would he have made it so, and he was ever seeking some excuse or pretence to adopt him as his own; but Mr. Sterling felt for the child the first spark of real affection that had ever dawned upon his flinty nature, and in all ways such an act was hedged in by difficulties.

No scandal had ever breathed upon Dr. Kelley's name, and if he bestowed unusual care and attention upon the Sterlings' invalid child, often taking him along upon his country rides, or keeping him whole days at his house, it was accepted by the admiring town-people as only another proof of his kind heartedness, and lauded as such, while his wife vied with him in attention, really feeling for the delicate child a motherly tenderness only second to that she cherished for her own little daughter.

The dread and mysterious Power who presides over matrimonial ventures had vouchsafed the doctor a good wife, and he prized her as she deserved. So they sat there musing and chatting by turns, while the wintry storm raged without, and having vainly beaten at their door, swept on and held high revel on the hill where "the mill-house" stood, breathing a raw chill through each crack between the weather-beaten clap-boards, whistling a general rally of forces as it assailed the loose windows which each rattled and whistled in a voice of its own, and having at last thus fretted itself into quietude, gave place to a grim, relentless cold, which laid a petrifying hand on all things without and within, stopping the noisy murmur of the dam, and sweeping with a frosty breath the upturned faces of the sick boy and his little brother lying side by side upon one pillow, the chubby arms of the younger thrown as if protectingly around the invalid boy, soothed at last into a deep sleep.

CHAPTER II.

WHAT a spirit of squeaking seemed to pervade all inanimate things touched by the breath of winter, as morning succeeded the night's storm carousal. The crisp snow gave way beneath the tread, with only a faint and softened echo of the shriek poured forth by every hinge and crank, and human fingers stuck maliciously to each frosty substance with which they came in contact. Even the old well-pole hung a creaking bucket high in air, all decked with icicles and rime, and one listened expectant of frosty wails issuing from the grinding machinery of the very cows chewing and turning their cuds to warm, in the barn-yard.

They were not early astir in the mill-house on this cold morning. It was Sunday; and even had it been a working day, the voice of the mill was silenced by an icy command, and nothing was to be gained by leaving a comfortable bed for a cheerless territory beyond.

First, the boy who tended the mill, came out; and by dint of much kindling and coaxing, lighted a fire in the kitchen, as a faint promise of breakfast to come.

Then Mr. Sterling seriously emerged to view, rubbing his lean, large hands together, as if hoping one of them might contrive to impart some gleam of comfort to the other, and in course of time Mrs. Sterling followed, twisting up her back hair with benumbed fingers as she came; and from cupboard and pantry, a series of vigorous attacks and hard raps, at length gave place to a more agreeable sound of sputtering and frying, and the odor of forthcoming breakfast called out the remainder of the family. The little boys scampered out to finish dressing by the fire, their stiff little fingers redly tugging at the buttons which persisted in considering themselves off duty, and lastly the door of a small bed room opened, giving egress to a fleshy old woman, who took possession of the high-backed rocking chair in the warmest corner, and wrapping a faded black shawl around her shoulders, bent herself forward so that her knees might afford support to her elbows, as, looking anxiously over into the frying-pan hissing on a shovelfull of coals drawn well out upon the hearth, she began an improvisation in her customary rhyming way, singing the measure in a sort of colloquial tone—

"Poor lady, poor lady; 'tis pity, alas!
That things is come to such terrible pass.
For sleeping all night as slim as a shad,
In lack of full stomach, is awfully bad."

"Hadn't you any supper last night, mother?" asked Mr. Sterling in an injured tone.

"No, thank ye. I was privately informed that Lydy had locked up all the eatables; so I didn't come out."

Mrs. Sterling explained a little irritably—"I didn't cook supper, because there wasn't any body but us two to eat it; but there was victuals and drink enough to be had for the asking, as everybody knows."

"Yes, yes; I know it; but I was privately informed by my heavenly Father, that I wasn't to have any," said the old lady, hurriedly, with a glance over her shoulder; and then resuming with a preferatory "hum, hum," she went on with her rhyming:

"The weather is cold, for winter is come,
It is well if you have a plenty of rum.
But I see by the looks of this scant frying-pan,
There won't be fried apple enough for a man!"

Hem, hem—Lydy, don't you think you might chuck in a quarter or two more o' them greenin's? The family a'n't all small eaters, like me; and a hungry belly makes a cross temper. Here, Pomp (to the dog), get off the harth and let your little brother Lisle come to the fire. He's as pinched and weazen as if he'd just come down out o' the fog."

"I don't want you to tell about folks being made up in the fog, before the children. It ain't scriptcral," said Mr. Sterling reprovingly; and then lifting Lisle upon his knee, he clumsily but kindly finished the task of putting the buttons under subjection, as he asked,

"How do you feel this morning, my little son?"

"I feel better, father; but something hurts me all the time in here," and he pressed a thin little hand over his chest, vainly trying to draw a long breath.

"Yes, and his head goes round, round, round, and his nose wags up at the sky; hem, hum—I think you'd better give him some opium and salts, with a touch o' epicack, and hang him up to dry," suggested the old lady sagely.

"You stop that, you gran'ma," shouted Eddy indignantly. Li. an't going to be bullied by you nor nobody. Don't mind nassy gran'ma; she old—she don't know nothin'. She's a nassy gran'ma all the time."

"Who's that you call grandma, youngster? I'm only nineteen year old, and going to be married:"

"Serve you right if you be," retorted Eddy stoutly, without any definite idea as to in what being married consisted, but believing it some penalty for one's sins.

"Don't be bad to grandma, Eddy," said Lisle, softly drawing him by the sleeve. "She don't mean any harm."

"Come, now draw up; breakfast's all ready," said Mrs. Sterling, shaking out her apron by way of toilet arrangements.

"Ma, give Li gran'ma's warm place to eat in. He's sick now—gran'ma's fat—and give he something nice; will you?" suggested Eddy.

"You make a baby of your big brother, Eddy. He can eat what the rest of us do, I'm thinking. Do you want some johnny cake, Lisle?"

"No, thank you. I don't feel hungry at all."

"I can't help it if you don't; you're going to eat. I won't have any putting on airs at *my* table."

Lisle took the buttered piece thus pressed upon him, and leaning his elbow on the table, supported his pale face in one hand while the other raised the unwelcome morsel to his lips.

"None of that, now! Eat it," commanded Mrs. Sterling, transfixing him with the cold gray eyes that always possessed a kind of terror over him. For the first time in his life, he gave her back a look of defiance, which she read with surprise, and laid the bread resolutely upon his plate. Mrs. Sterling colored in anger; but before a word passed her lips, the child's self-command, singular in one so young and frail, returned, and he made an effort to obey.

Eddy looked wrathfully on; but, warned by former experiences, he waited till his mother's attention was temporarily distracted, and then hastily smuggled away and crammed the offending morsel into his own not unwilling mouth; and when she again looked at the child, she gave expression to the gratified comment,

"I thought you'd find appetite when you found there was to be no titbits for titmen."

"Titman yourself," shouted Eddy in a rage, which, instead of arousing his mother's ire, as might have been expected, seemed to gratify her pride, as she said approvingly,

"He's a real Fitzjames, Eddy is! All my family had that high spirit. There's no *Sterling* in *him!* Here, Lisle, drink this warm milk, one can't let you starve to death, if only for the looks of it."

"Can't you speak kind to the boy when he's sick?" asked Mr. Sterling, interfering for the first time. "What can I give you, my little son?"

"Nothing, thank you, father. It hurts so in here I don't feel like eating."

Mrs. Sterling gave another glance which plainly said, "for shame, baby;" and sliding down from the table, he went back to the fire and sat down by Pompey, who lifted his pitying dog face up at him as if he alone could enter into and appreciate his feelings.

Lisle understood him as if he had spoken, and softly stroked his long, silky ears, trying for his sake to summon up a smile of reassurance.

The old lady came back to her chair in the chimney corner, and resuming her favorite posture, commenced—

> "Poor lady, poor lady, you're always undone!
> When breakfast is over you feel you've had none,
> And if of strong tea you don't have some,
> You'd ought to have a little good o-pi-um."

"Han't you had enough breakfast, mother?" asked Mr. Sterling.

"Oh, yes, yes; I just compose poetry to exercise my mind. In the estate I'm about to enter into, poetry is so soothing to the feelings! I'm privately informed that Lydy, there, was sent down with a gift for making poetry; but it has been took away from her, for some heavy sin she committed agin them as she left behind her in the fog."

"What fog is that you're always telling about?" asked Mrs. Sterling, carefully wiping up with a bit of bread the little patches of fried apple left here and there clinging to the dish, by way of a last saving installment to her already liberal meal.

"Why, the fog we all go floating around in, maybe a thousand year, before we're let down onto the earth. We have to go back into that fog, after we come down the first time, to be superannuated down; you know as fast as we grow old we have to be made down small again. That is, you've been made down small again, superannuated down, three times, because you've been long on the earth."

Mr. Sterling turned his chair slowly around from the table, and said with an unusually severe air, "I've often told you, mother, I wish you wouldn't go over all that nonsense before the children. Human natur is wicked enough without having any such stuff crammed into its head. What it don't study up in the way of unscriptural infidelity, an't necessary to be suggested. Wife, are the boys going to meeting to-day?"

" Yes, of course. Don't they have to go every Sunday, rain or shine? Why not to-day, pray?"

" It's too cold for the horses to stand out, to-day; besides, one of 'em has got a bad cough, now. I don't think Lisle ought to go to-day, anyway."

" Nonsense! He grunts and whines all the time over something or other; and you don't mean to let him grow up a heathen, do you?"

" Fazer, fazer," interrupted Eddy with unusual animation, " what's the use goin' to a cold meetin' to sleep? Don't he hurt you to nod so, and wouldn't you like it, to lie on a nice warm settee to home's house? Li and I'll keep real still, and gran'ma'll preach to you till the nods come. Hello; here's Dr. Kelley come, with lots o' sheeps' skins in his sleigh."

All eyes now turned to the window, and Mrs. Sterling stirred the fire into a brighter blaze, and pushed Pompey unceremoniously from his station by Lisle, to make room for the doctor, who now entered, bright and cheerful from the bracing air through which he had driven half concealed by the warm fur robes Eddy had pronounced " sheeps' skins."

" Good morning, good morning all. Glad to see you, Sterling. How are you, grandmother?"

" He, he, he! I didn't know I had so fine a grandchild," laughed the old lady, and then added seriously, "I 'spose, though, you might o' been down small the last time I saw you, before."

" That's the old lady's way—pretending not to know folks from one day to the next," explained Mrs. Sterling apologetically, as she drew up a chair for the doctor, and thus made an occasion to cast a warning glance upon the old lady, whose loquacity obediently subsided.

" Well, Lisle, how are you to-day. Better, eh?" and he lifted the boy to his knee, and smoothed his hair in the tender way Lisle always loved.

A quick flushing and paling crossed the little face as he glanced up at the doctor, and the dark eyes wore a troubled expression, which, however, soon died out, and he leant his head contentedly against the doctor's breast, and twined his fingers in and out among the little chains which formed the watch-guard decorating his satin vest.

" Always speak when you're spoken to, my son," said Mr. Sterling. " You are better to-day, an't you?"

Thus adjured, Lisle glanced shyly up at the doctor's face and no ided assent.

"What ever ails the boy this morning, that he can't speak!" exclaimed Mrs. Sterling impatiently. "He's generally free enough with his gabble when you come; and now not a word out of him."

A shadow of pain crossed the doctor's face, as in the child's unusual silence he read the strongest confirmation of his fears as to that overheard conversation of the preceding evening; and holding him more closely to his breast, he said,

"Don't worry the boy. His lungs pain him, I am sure. This cold, bleak place will be his death."

"I know it's bad for him," replied Mr. Sterling, "but I don't know what's best to be done. I'd send him to brother Jonathan's, over the hill there; but he's got such a snarl of his own children that his wife's beside herself a'most, and everything's topsy-turvey day and night. I don't know "—

"I'll tell you, then, friend Sterling; let me take him home for the winter. My wife wants him, and it will be much more convenient for me to attend him there. He will need the best of looking after, all winter."

"Why, you see I could eas'er make it all right with Jonathan, when he wants grinding done at the mill. Work an't like paying out cash."

"Don't mention that. We've potatoes enough for the winter, and if we hadn't, the few he will eat wouldn't make any difference. Indeed, my wife will feel hurt if you speak of paying anything for him. What do you say, Lisle? Would you like to live with us?"

A quick, glad light flashed over his face in reply, and again the wistful eyes gazed into the doctor's.

Dr. Kelley's heart beat quicker as he read the look, and involuntarily he bent and kissed the boy's forehead. Mrs. Sterling had furtively watched it all, and with an air of well studied amazement she exclaimed,

"I declare! it's wonderful, the understanding there seems to be between you and that child! I hope you'll make him as good and honest a man as you are, since he takes after you more than he does me, nor yet his father there. You'll lose your boy, Mr. Sterling."

Lisle turned a glance upon the thin figure bent into premature old age, and the narrow, unintellectual face opposite, and then upon the prepossessing exterior of the doctor, in an evident mental comparison which it needed no filial affection to explain, or account for.

Yet Mr. Sterling was, in his weak way, kind to the boy, and, moved by an impulse of gratitude, Lisle slid down from the doctor's knee, and slipping his hand into the hard palm of the young old man, who had not answered his wife's last observation, said gently,

"I won't go away from you at all if you don't like me to. You are always good to me, and I love you."

"Yes, my son I hope so ; but I think you'll be better off at Dr. Kelley's ; so, if your mother thinks best, you may go "

"But I *don't* think best. I don't believe in sending my children away from home to be raised. He'll live it through, here, I'll warrant !"

"Don't mind about your clothes and things to-day. I'll bring them down to you to-morrow, as I'm going by that way," said Mr. Sterling as if his wife had not spoken ; for it was noticeable that though he always asked her opinion, he was never at all influenced by it. Perhaps she herself took advantage of this well known peculiarity, to indulge in a little opposition, not attended with any consequences in the present, and liable to end in a species of triumph if the unlucky hour ever arrived in which she could offer the consolations of "I told you so," for which, like most people, she had a proclivity at proper seasons.

"Hurrah," cried Eddy, tossing his cap in air as the point was thus decided.

"I hope, Eddy, you are not so glad as all that to get rid of your brother," said Mrs. Sterling, vainly striving to suppress a little exultation in her voice.

"Yes I am too! Ma's real mean to poor Li, doctor; she spank him when he sick and can't lie still; don't her, Li? and this last eatin's, didn't her make you eat when you couldn't; and don't like you all the time! Say, Li? now you *run off and never come to home's house any more at all!* I isn't sick, I'll run away for you. Yes, Li!" and the little fists clenched themselves ambitiously over the happy suggestion.

"Only to see how ungrateful children can-be!" sighed Mrs. Sterling, taking Lisle's cloak and cap from the nail where they hung when off duty, and detaching from another a pair of red woollen mittens linked together by a cord made to suspend them round his neck; and he was soon ready for his ride.

"There, that will do nicely," said the doctor, lifting him in his arms to carry him to the sleigh, between which and the house the snow lay heavy and deep. "I've some nice buffalo-robes to wrap him up in, and we shan't be fifteen minutes going home. Let Eddy come down and spend the day with his brother, as often as possible. Well, what is it, little fellow?" for Lisle was pulling at his collar to attract attention.

"Please, sir, mayn't Pompey come with us? See how his face begs; that's the way Pompey talks. He sleeps on my bed all night, and is just like a little brother."

"Yes, of course he may. Come on, brother Pompey."

There was a whole *Gloria in Excelsis* in the glad bark with which Pompey sprang through the open door, never stopping for the good-byes quickly spoken as the cold air rushed in to do battle with the glowing coals, vainly striving to impart a comfortable degree of warmth to the open room.

"Providence grant this freak of yours may turn out well," sighed Mrs. Sterling as the door closed. "It's plain as the day, the boy thinks more of Doctor Kelley now, than he does of his own kin, and the Lord knows how it will all turn out!"

"Yes, he does know, and that's enough for now," replied her husband, as, unfolding last evening's unfinished newspaper, he resumed its perusal, and thinking "discretion the better part of valor," Mrs. Sterling said no more. As for Eddy, unconquered even by his prophetic visions of loneliness, now that both brother and dog were gone, he looked steadfastly into the fire for a musing five minutes, and then fell to *whistling* practice, in his ambition to "do" his first tune.

¡CHAPTER III.

THE events of that winter formed the first real glimpses of sunshine that had ever dawned upon Lisle's little life. Nursed and
cared for by kind Mrs. Kelley, who embodied all his childish ideas
of motherhood, he often wandered among the romantic imaginings
from which no childhood is altogether free, at times quite working
himself up to the conviction that this was his own real mother, who
in some unavoidable and inexplicable manner had been compelled
temporarily to deliver him into the keeping of the woman at the
mill house, who, under the title of his mother, disliked and misused
him; and he quite revelled in the fancy that this, his temporary return to his true home, might grow into a lasting reality.

The little baby who crowed her wildest on his lap, and played for
hours raised to his level by her high chair, at the table so gloriously
stocked with pretty books and pictures, did not she, too, seem to
recognize that they were linked together by kindred blood, and
foreordained for companions ?   Speculative as these musings were,
they were the pleasantest among the many which crowded upon his
brain as he sat meditatively through the days when he was most
free from pain, for, though his health improved under better care,
he was still delicate, and often suffering.

Often and often his mind reverted to that fatal dialogue between
the doctor and his mother, striving to take in and fully comprehend
all it involved of mystery.   The sudden shock of what he did comprehend, had at the time overpowered him ; but in a vague way he
felt that this was not all, and, as if spurred on by a relentless fate,
he thought and thought over it, feeling that inexplicably linked
with it was a something, which if confessed to the world would
make his mother scorned by it, and himself—he knew not what !
Painfully precocious as he was, he thought, too, pityingly of Miles
Sterling, the man whom the world believed and called his father,
and yet whom he now knew held no claim to the name.   An unap-
peasing sense of *wrong* oppressed him, and a feeling that he himself

was an agent in it; fevered him through the restless nights when he was most pressed by it.

Had not his mother, in referring to him, said that if Mr. Sterling knew the truth he would kill him ?   Then was he, too, guilty, and if so, how ?   It was a tangled web.

Then an instinct of profound compassion took possession of him as he thought of this narrow-minded, undemonstrative man, who yet manifested so much parental regard for him, and who, whatever his failings, was an honest man, and uncompromising in his ideas of right and wrong.   He, of all, seemed most to be pitied, yet his own wife had spoken of despising him !

Yet, puzzled and troubled as he was by all this, an unconquerable reserve forbade him to mention it even to the doctor, whom he loved with an all absorbing affection, and not the most remote allusion was made by either, to the topic that was often present in the mind of each.

Often, raising his eyes from his books, the doctor met that troubled, questioning look he so well knew how to interpret dating from the time when he had seen it first, and the sensation it gave him was one of mingled pain and pleasure.   Sincerely attached to the boy, as much for what was really winning and noble in his nature, as from that parental affection, inevitable though unacknowledged, he yearned to clasp him to his heart and feel the tie acknowledged. Yet both judgment and affection restrained him.   It involved too much, and consequences might be endless and fatal.   The boy was so young, there yet remained to him some years of ignorance of all the shameful tale.   When coming years, with their additional knowledge, should tear away the last remnant of the flimsy veil between him and it, then he would tell it all, and plead for such love and respect as extenuating circumstances might award him.

So the doctor braved the searching eyes as he might, or turned away from them, satisfied that the plain path of affection-prompted duty, was sufficient for him to tread, till circumstances should force him into a wider field.   As one standing before an open powder-magazine feels that at any instant a falling spark may launch him into the unknown, the doctor waited for what fate might inflict, confessing that the hand which should drop for him the exploding spark, would perform an act of human justice; and only wishing that with it, the wrong might be wiped out, and his atonement blot from Lisle's life the shame and suffering so unjustly forced upon it. Yet the doctor felt that he himself had been as much sinned against

as sinning. Lydia Fitzjames, when he first met her, was more than
his equal in worldly guile and experience; and while he now made
no attempt to cast his share of responsibility upon her, retrospec-
tion showed him how he had been lured on, step by step, by a designing woman whom self-respect forbade him to make his wife
when circumstances awoke him, too late, to a sense of his situation.

Miles Sterling had entered upon the scene at a propitious moment, and, glad of any loop-hole for escape from impending ruin, he
had helped to influence and accomplish the marriage, with little
pity for the victim thus offered up in his stead.

Never had he forgotten the scene between them when the baffled
woman learned that her scheme to entrap him for a husband had
failed. Plain words were spoken by each, and the conscienceless
character of the woman stood out in characters from which he
turned away, shocked and disgusted. Once for all he taught her
that he recognized it all, and that though he might be her tool, he
would never be her victim; and her upbraidings ceased when she
saw they were vain. But she had never forgiven it, and never would,
and she hated the child who had failed to perform its mission, and
wreaked upon it the wrath that glowed ever in her heart as she realized the utter failure of all which even in her union with Miles
Sterling had seemed alluring.

The first retribution for an unjust act overtook the doctor when
he learned that the man whom he had lured into the breach yawn-
ing for himself, was really worthy of esteem for many qualities which
redeemed his parsimony and narrow mindedness; and coals of fire
seemed heaped upon his head as he saw this man love and care for
his unowned child, and bearing the tender name for which his heart
ached unappeasingly!

Far better for his peace of mind, had he never learned to respect
Miles Sterling; far better had no deep affection thrilled his heart
for the little boy whom he could never claim, and whom he daily
saw suffering for the sins of others—himself among the foremost.
His punishment seemed heavier than he could bear; and it was this
care that had sprinkled his brown locks with gray, as self-respect
felt many a stab of shame and agony under the ever recurring query,
how many who called him "friend," and blessed him for "a truly
good man," would offer him the hand of fellowship did they know
of him what he knew. Conscientious as he was, he felt himself an
impostor, and none guessed how restlessly he goaded himself on to

all good works, as if they could in some way make the balance weigh more evenly between him and the world.

Alas, no! In a small community, where everything is known and discussed, no secret deed remained unapplauded, as even one offset upon the score against him, and strive as he would, he could never set the matter any nearer right with his own conscience. He was the man whom society delighted to honor, and he must go on, feeling himself a hypocrite, to the end of his life. It was a retribution above all others best calculated to oppress the doctor's heart, and at the times when most savagely galled by it, he felt that he thus earned the right to all that was comforting in the interchange of affection between little Lisle and himself. Could he only receive it feeling that the child knew all he was bestowing! Time would soon teach him this; and the doctor waited, making the most of what was his while suffered to retain it, wishing for, yet shrinking from what that future with its revelations might bequeath him as so much belonging to him in free gift from one, at least, to whom he was no hypocrite.

"Really, William," said Mrs. Kelley one day as the doctor sat explaining a large book of pictures to Lisle, "you have petted, and affiliated with that child, till he is growing to look like you! His mouth is the *fac-simile* of yours, and his eyes have the same dark blue; only yours are bright and sparkling, and his are languid and heavy. If his hair were cut and brushed like yours, you would see, too, that your foreheads are not unlike. It strikes me that he may be your twin brother, belated in 'the fog,' or 'superannuated down small,' as old Mrs. Sterling has it," and she laughed at the conceit, and then added in the same tone, "I think I'll call him 'Little Doctor,' after this, in compliment to his having copied so many of your features; and really, now I think of it, why won't it be a good idea to read him up as an M. D.? His father will consent to his pursuing any vocation not likely to levy upon his own purse, and you could do so much for him in this."

"You calculate very confidently my dear. How do you know the boy may not prefer to watch the mill wheel, like his father before him, or even to smite the anvil like many another honest man?"

"How can you suppose it! - *Talent* looks out from every line of his face, and such a head was never meant to be roasted near a blacksmith's forge. I could not love the child better if he were my own, and I want him to become a smart man and a good one, like you."

"But, my little wife, I'm *not* good. This is all a popular delusion. I hope Lisle will shun the pitfalls into which I have stumbled, and be a far better man than I ever was. I have sometimes hoped he may feel a preference for my profession, and if he does I will gladly help him in it. But by-and-bye, when we may have boys of our own, you will become jealous of poor little Lisle, whom you love now for the woman's reason—and it's a good one, too—that you take care of him and feel sorry for him. You'll love him less as he becomes less dependent."

"Why, William! how can you think so? Come here, Little Doctor, and speak for yourself. What will you do when you become a man, like this old croaker in the arm chair who wants to make a blacksmith of you?"

"I'll take care of you, and him, and little sissy, and give Eddy lots of new tops and jack-knives."

"Very right; but Eddy will be too large for tops, then, and you'll have to make the money it requires to take care of sissy and us. Won't you learn to make sick people well again, and keep little children from dying away from their mama's?

"No, I don't think I'll be a doctor. I wouldn't like all the little boys and girls to cry when they see the pill-bags coming; and Jimmy Lucas says the doctor has carried so many babies to his house, that his ' old man '—that's what he calls his pa—swears *awful* every time he comes with another; and Jimmy says he hates a doctor worse than he does a minister, or anything!"

"There," laughed the doctor to his wife. "See what you get by trying to 'bend the twig.' Better let him wait till the spirit moves him; and after all there's time enough, as he has a world of things to learn before he comes to that."

"Then, sir. if you please, why an't I learning some of them? I can stop when my head aches, and I don't think I'll die and cheat you out of all your trouble."

"What put such an idea in your head, child?"

"That's what mother always said. She s id ' what's the use wasting money on a child that'll die and cheat you out of it if he takes the notion?' so, you see, I never asked any more. Fred, in the mill, teached me my a b c's, and I can spell a little. Pompey knows more than I do, though—he's got good dog learning, and I'm just a dunce b y. A'n't that true, Pompey?'

Thus appealed to, Pompey placed his nose c nfidently in his young master's hand, as if obligingly willing to assent to any proposition coming from such a quarter, or, perhaps, grateful for his own reward of merit.

Lisle's evident desire to be upon the road of learning, resulted in Mrs. Kelley installing herself as his preceptress, and few were the days in which he was induced to avow himself too unwell to be taught. Eddy often spent whole days at the doctor's house, upon which occasions he divided his attentions impartially between the baby, whom he christened "Dummy," in compliment to her limited command of speech, and Pompey, who was inseparable from his master, sharing with him, and evidently thinking he bore an equal part of the labor at each lesson, so that it was a juvenile boast that Pomp already knew as much as the village justice, and *would* be run for President if he didn't look sharp—an awful penalty which might well appall any rash adventurer on the highway to knowledge.

Fired by a kindred ambition, Eddy hoarded all stray pennies which fell to his lot in reward for extra chip-basket filling, and when, after some task far too severe for his years, he received a whole sixpence, he was far more cla'ed by it than by the title of "little major" bestowed upon him by his father, who boasted, in the pride of his heart that his son was "no shirk." This hard-earned treasure was expended in the purchase of unlimited "Robin Hoods," and "Punch and Judys," whom he liked all the better after "Dummy" had mussed into a not too dressed up condition; and he really shouted in delight when that bellicose young lady "hit *Punch* a rap in the eye" in return for the one he administered Judy to quench her appetite for pie. Not fully appreciating her own success in meting out justice, "Dummy" opened her mouth and swelled herself out hard in a vigorous shout by way of keeping company, which intellectual feat had an impressive effect upon her admirer, as proof of great juvenile precocity, and if the shake of any dog's tail ever evidenced internal laughter, Pompey, too, was overflowing with appreciation.

The winter passed by all too quickly for the doctor and his family, loth as they were to yield. Lisle up again to his loveless life in the mill-house, and he already shrank with an unuttered, but unconquerable dread, from all he was so soon to resume. Fully appreciating the injustice he suffered from a mother who often declared her hatred of him, he was yet too small and weak openly to rebel against it, and even a remonstrance from his lips increased his suffering.

Shuddering recollections of dark closets in which he had been imprisoned, and once forgotten through a long cold night when Eddy was not at home to champion him, rose again before him, peopled with the myriad horrible images which danced before him in the rayless obscurity, jeering and menacing him till he could endure no more, and was at last taken out in convulsions,—days of semi-starvation which racked the delicate frame totally unfit for any such discipline, but one degree removed from heathenism when practised upon *any* growing child; and, added to all these, blows frequent and severe, of whose very provocation he was often ignorant, yet which a real fear of threatened retaliation forbade him to reveal to his nominal father, who, had he known of them, would have suppressed them with a strong hand, from which even his wife shrank, though her only escape from its power was in Lisle's fear of her. Such were the retrospections which threw an ominous cloud over the future, and preyed upon his delicate health till a real alarm seized upon the doctor's mind, and he made one more effort to get him entirely under his own custody.

But Mr. Sterling was obstinate. The boy should return home when the first warmer days of spring should come; he did not think it right to separate brothers, and he wouldn't have his children burdens upon any one. All this he declared with a determination nothing could alter, but stronger than all, though unexpressed, was a jealous dread, already partly realized, he believed—what would he have felt had he known to what extent—that his child would learn to love another better than himself.

"After all," he concluded, "I don't see why the boy should wish to live away from his own home. His mother is here, and if he had the right kind of a heart, he'd want stay with her, even if he don't think enough of his *father* to want to come back. I don't see why he don't care more for his mother."

"Excuse me, Mr. Sterling," replied the doctor. "It is a delicate subject to mention, but I must say I often think she herself is far from blameless. When a child shows the shrinking fear of a parent which Lisle cannot conceal he feels of her, there is some strong reason for it. He has told me nothing, nor would I encourage him to do so, but if you will accept the suggestion of a friend, you will keep an eye over him, and, above all, prevent a repetition of punishments which he has not the strength to endure."

"I don't think he ever received any such ones. He is most always sulky after any correction, and, as his mother often says, his health won't give out till his temper does. You know what Solomon said."

"Solomon was an old fool," retorted the doctor angrily, then swallowing his ire by an effort, he said more temperately, "you are entirely mistaken as to the child being sulky. He is *reserved*, to a degree I never saw equalled in any child, and in few grown persons. It is this very knowledge of how little even you know the boy, which makes me so anxious to keep him till he is older and stronger, and better able to fight his way among trials of which you do not dream. If you object to separating brothers, let me have Eddy too. I'm much nearer the school-house than you are, and at the summer term they can both commence, and go together. It certainly will be a relief to your wife, who will have her hands full enough without the care of them while you are building."

"No, sir, thank you. The more she has to do, the better for her. If it's so hard for you to give the boy up now, what will it be a year from now? I'll go after him to-morrow and bring him home, where he belongs."

So, instead of carrying his point, the last days of the child's stay were curtailed, and the doctor sat that evening looking gloomily into the fire, with the old pain tugging at his heart against which little Lisle's head was pillowed as upon the only anchor of protection this world held for him. His eyes, too, peered into the flickering firelight, through a long silence employed by Mrs. Kelley in some last stitches upon his wardrobe which she hoped would prove a suggestion to Mrs. Sterling, who neither thought nor cared much for such little details. The doctor roused himself, and smoothing the boy's head, asked cheerfully,

"What are you thinking all this time, little fellow?"

"I don't want to go away from you. Why can't I stay here always? Nobody loves me at home."

"I think your father loves you, Lisle; don't you?"

The child raised his earnest eyes to the doctor's face, and his lips quivered, but not a word passed them. Moved by an irresistible impulse, the doctor with both hands held the flushed little face up toward his own, looked with unutterable affection into the dark blue eyes all swimming in tears, and, covering cheeks and lips with fervent kisses, as suddenly put him down and walked to the door—hesitated there, and then returning laid his hand upon the child's head and said sadly,

"Poor little fellow; this is a hard world for us all—doubly hard for you! Be a man, always, and when you need a friend in anything, come to me. Remember—*always*."

A quick sob, the first he had ever heard from him, fell on the doctor's ear; and turning silently, he left the room.

CHAPTER IV.

THE summer days drew on, and the new house was rapidly progressing. Banks of earth lay in irregular masses where it had been tossed in excavating for a cellar, and long rows of lumber locked fingers over tho rail fence that supported it for a due amount of "seasoning." The "raising day" arrived. They were early astir in the mill-house, and having made a tour of observation to tho pantry filled with the huge loaves of orthodox "raising cake," to make sure it had not been spirited away during the night, Mrs. Sterling hurried breakfast, that it might be over and done with before the neighbors, relations, and friends, should assemble, as in duty bound, to lend a helping hand toward the rearing of the new domicil.

The little boys and Pompey ran busily around the yard, seized by the contagion an important day spreads all through a household, and even the old lady rocked more vigorously in her high-backed chair as she plied the knitting-needles held to unwilling service upon a long-legged cotton stocking grotesquely distorted by sudden and unmistakable cramps relieved by a liberal widening, and evidencing each day's progress in a streak of tight or of loose knitting, according as she had felt the affliction of the family parsimony, or given rein to a liberal fancy.

Mrs. Sterling's restless eyes detected some irregularity in the looping and dropping of the stitches, and possessing herself of the malformation, she exclaimed,

"For the land sake, what are you doing here! The thing is pulled in and let out, and puckered and twisted, till a lawyer's foot couldn't find its way into it!"

"Why ma'am, I was privately informed that I must put a new stitch in the instep, by way of adornment, so I've been contrivin' and practisin' on one, but it don't seem to come. I don't like openwork stockins', they take so much scrubbin' of the feet to set em off well. I widdened too much all day yesterday, what with thinkin' o' the new house and seein' you makin' so much cake; and it seems all the narrowin' in the world won't get it back into genteel shape."

"You'll have to 'superannuate it down small,' so ;" and drawing out the needles, Mrs. Sterling proceeded to unravel the work with a liberal hand, the old lady indignantly protesting till she saw it was useless, and then breaking out with her favorite song under all tribulations—

"Poor lady, poor lady, you're always undone,"

finishing the lament with a statement of the particular grievance in hand. However, upon this exciting day trouble was not to be harbored ; so, philosophically retreating to her own room, she left the knitting to its fate ; and after a vigorous round of shaking and dusting of apparel, she at length reappeared, serene in a flame colored robe kept for state occasions, and an armful of ruffled garments which she shook out one by one and examined not over complacently.

"Now tell me, Lydy, which o' these vandykes do you think 'll be most becomin' to me for this 'casion ? I'm informed that my bridegroom will eat here, to-day, disguised as a laborin' man—though he's a prince of light—and I want him to find me fine and gay."-.

"Oh, clear out with your 'vandykes!' The finer and gayer you are, the worse you look ! All you Sterlings have that peculiarity. You'll be a sight, whatever you put on."

"Envious," whispered the old lady to herself, and retiring with the insulted capes, she made her toilet by the broken bit of mirror in her room, and endured an hour of martyrdom in searching and pulling out the gray hairs mingled with her still well preserved brown ones. It was a tedious operation, though semi-weekly performed with feminine care, and she finished only as the men assembled and commenced work.

Despite the little boys' pleadings for a holiday upon this grand climax of all days, they were driven off to school, where they fell into disgrace in the usual way ; Lisle, for some unknown sin of omission or commission, and Eddy for espousing his cause and resenting the penalty. Little heeding the schoolmistress' threat to follow them home and report them in person to their mother, they ran home the moment school was dismissed, hoping to be "in at the death," if only to see one last beam lifted to its place in the new house—but the frame was up—unromantically complete—and Pompey seemed to deprecate and lament it, as, meek and sympathetic, he came out to meet them. There was nothing for it but resignation ; so, consoling themselves with a huge piece of the "raising cake," they seated themselves on a sill, where they shared it bite for bite with Pompey, who sat genteelly awaiting his turn, and never took greedy mouthfuls.

" Eddy, do you believe the schoolma'am will come to-night, as she said she would ?" asked Lisle, a little troubled.

"I don't know, she's just mean enough to, a'n't she ? If she does, let's play her a trick. By jimminy, don't I wish I could lick her! Schoolma'ams always ought to be licked !"

"I wish they'd baptize her, so she wouldn't be mean to me every time the boys do things. It wasn't me that put the thistle in Sally Beebe's shoe. It was Carry Frink did it. You see she don't like that Beebe girl putting on airs and not going barefooted like the rest of us. Sally, she thinks it's nicer to wear shoes; so she wears them ragged old things with the soles almost clear off, so that when she sits down with her heels a little ways up from the floor you c'n see clean to her toes. Carry put the thistle on 'em, and when she let her heels down, to go into the spelling class,—*plunker!* down she came on it, and didn't she howl   If I'd been Carry, I'd have owned up to it before I'd see a boy whipped that didn't do it; but when she da'sn't tell, I wasn't going to ; and 'cause the schoolma'am saw me laugh—a boy couldn't help it—she whipped me to make it all straight ; and now if she comes and tells, ma'll whip me again, for getting flogged in school.   I can take one licking well enough, but when a boy gets *two* for the same thing *he never done at all*, it's a shame !"

"I don't believe you'll catch it again, this time, 'cause I got it, too, to-day; and ma never licks me.   By jimminy, there comes old Schooley, now, with her yellow sunbonnet flying !"

Through the open bar-way came the teacher with indignant stride, and thinking discretion the better part of valor the boys stole off and did not return till nearly dark, thinking that by that time the coast would be clear of the teacher, and their mother's first wrath abated.   Dire and unwelcome vision !   There on the settee reposed the teacher, quite at home for the night, received as an honored guest and regaled with all the house afforded.

Mrs. Sterling drew the boys forward with no gentle hand, and condemning them to go supperless to bed, dispatched them at once where they lay planning vengeance for the morrow, accompanied by Pompey, who seemed equally interested in their plans, and looked from one to the other as if fully weighing each suggestion from the busy brains that were at last overtaken by sleep, without having settled upon any definite project.   But fresh inspiration came with the morning's opportunity, and the young avengers looked on not uninterestedly, as sundry delicacies were compounded for the noon time delectation of the enemy, who, departing early, left the luncheon to be brought by the boys. It was past the opening school hour when they walked demurely in, but inquiry eliciting the fact that they were detained upon account of the delicacies now delivered to her, they escaped unpunished, and affairs proceeded much as usual, save that Lisle did not once fall into disgrace, and seemed unusually attentive to his books.

The noon intermission came at last, and allowing the other boys to pass out before them, Lisle and Eddy lingered in the entry while the enemy took one by one the articles from the luncheon basket, smiling approvingly at the goodly array; for Mrs. Sterling prided herself upon her culinary skill, and gloried in an opportunity to display it. The fried cakes looked sufficiently tempting, turning one golden side up at her, and she helped herself to a liberal bite of one. An expression of infinite disgust convulsed her face, as the offending, treacherous morsel was ejected. They certainly were flavored with snuff! Yes; she sneezed and strangled again and again ere the suspicion had fairly fixed itself upon her mind. Eddy smothered a laugh with his handkerchief; for his had been the generous hand that lent such piquancy, while Lisle, nearly upsetting a pan of milk in the pantry, had called for maternal aid which he considered cheaply purchased at the price of a boxed ear. With a warning "hush," Lisle checked the threatened explosion, as the teacher cut in half a small pie serenely awaiting her attentions. It proved a heathenish compound of apple, salt, and sulphur, and when she had sufficiently conquered her disgust, she closely examined it. Yes, as she suspected, the upper crust had been separated from the lower one, and carefully replaced, since it left the oven, and a grim smile wreathed her lips as she thus detected the way-side iniquity.

Lisle saw it, and knew the probable penalty, but he had the satisfaction of seeing her compelled to endure a dinnerless day in return for his supperless night.

"There, Eddy," said he as they stole out together, "I did all that, you know, so ma can't whip you for it (the one who *thinks* how to do naughty things, is the bad one), and now all the sulphur is gone, so we shan't have any to take to-morrow morning. I only wish we could have crammed in all the pichra and columbo, too! *That* would have fetched her!"

The brief feeling of triumph he experienced despite the impending and inevitable penalty due, was checked by an unpleasant, if common incident; for as they passed down the steps, Bill Brown, the bully of the school, stepped slily behind him, struck him a blow behind his ear, as severe as unexpected. Stunned for an instant, he leaned against the door-post while the young pugulist made off at the top of his speed, for, like all tyrants, he was a coward. He was the largest boy in the school, and it was useless to attempt wreaking a summary vengeance upon him. Eddy seized a stone which he was whirling round and round to gather impetus, when Lisle looked up.

"Put it down, Eddy. He'd come back and whale us both, now, but I'll do him the first time he an't looking for it."

The opportunity came sooner than he could have hoped.

"Come here, Li Sterling," shouted one of the boys in a knot among whom Bill had run for protection, "make us a board house like the one you had the other day, and I'll give you something. Will you?"

"Yes, I'll make you the house, but you needn't give me anything. I'm willing to do anything if I'm *asked*, but I don't like to be *told*," and throwing off his coat, he went cheerfully to work, and soon finished a sort of commodious pen for a small family, dignified by the name of house.

"Here, Bill Brown, you get in first," said the contractor who had called Lisle, "you are taller than any of us, so if you can stand up in it, we can."

"Oh, Bill is going to live in it too, is he? Then it wants a higher roof," suggested Lisle.

"Of course, booby; and if you don't stand around lively, I'll give you another knock to keep that one company," replied Bill clenching his fist suggestively.

Lisle obligingly and meekly rearranged the board forming the roof, and looked again at the foundation of the structure, with which at last satisfied, he raised the entrance and bade Bill enter. With an air of supercilious triumph at being the commander of such services, Bill entered the trap, when down it came around him, burying him among the ruins, from which uncomfortable situation he bellowed most lustily, while Lisle, in turn, placed a safe distance between himself and the enemy. This was but one instance among many of the daily bullyings visited upon and revenged by Lisle, whose lack of physical strength was taken advantage of by the boys, who, as a class, dislike a sickly companion, and though he seldom failed to reap his revenge, it was done by some strategy which covered it from recognition by others, however satisfactory to himself.

Compelled to perform many tasks distasteful to him, it was useless to refuse, but his services seldom bestowed much felicity where he did not choose that they should do so. His teachers were quick to recognize this avenging talent, and, wholly unheeding the aggravations which stung him thus to wreak out justice upon his persecutors, they considered and treated him as a bad, designing, treacherous boy. Thus with a rankling sense of injustice gnawing ever in his heart, he dragged on his miserable school days, feeling that every one's hand was against him.

From the little girls in the school he received sympathy, and with them might have had companionship, but the natural pride and arrogance of boyhood made him shrink from joining a congregation of girls, and his shabby clothes made him ashamed to do so, quick as they were, by instinct, to observe and remark upon them.

"I'd like you better than any other boy in school, if you wore good clothes," said a little girl to him one day. "Why don't you have nice new clothes, like that hateful Bill? You're a great deal the nicest boy, and your pa is ever so much richer than his."

"I don't want to be a dandy" sneered Lisle, flushing, nevertheless, with shame, and trying to conceal a patched elbow as he spoke.

"Oh, then you aren't so nice as I thought you were! You ought to want to be real nice! I wouldn't go patched nor ragged for anything. Just see your brother Eddy, now don't he look like a little beggar boy? And you look worse than he does, because you're longer and bigger than your clothes, bad as they are!"

In dignified silence he turned and walked away, but once out of sight, he threw himself upon the grass and tore it up by savage handfuls, as tears of rage and bitterness rolled down his cheeks. In all the world there was not one bright spot for him to turn to, and the very heavens seemed to frown upon, or mock him.

He heard the teacher loudly rapping on the window with the back of a book, to summon the scholars to their seats and afternoon exercises, but he did not obey.

Time passed till his class was called, and the noisy summons was repeated, *for him*, as he well knew. An interval passed, then Eddy's voice called him, at first impatiently, then in alarm; and dashing away his tears, he answered and came forward.

"Oh, Li, but an't the schoolma'am mad as hops! and she's cutting notches with her penknife in the butt end of a big switch that won't leave an inch of hide on you! Oh my, but you'll catch it now!"

"No I shan't. I won't catch it any longer! I may as well die now as any time, and I'm going home. Go back and tell the schoolma'am I'm gone home; that's a good boy."

"But, Li, ma's worser than the schoolma'am is."

"I shan't go to her, I'm going straight to pa. Never you mind about me, Eddy. Go back and say your lessons."

He watched him back to the door, and then turned his own steps homeward.

Mr. Sterling was standing in the door of the mill when Lisle reached it, and surprised to see him at such an hour, asked,

"What are you doing here, Lisle? Why an't you in school?"

"Because I an't fit to be there, and I won't go any more! Kill me if you want to; I don't care. I can't stand it and I wont, so there!" and his usually pale face deepened into a more glowing crimson.

"What language is this to use to your father, Lisle?"

"What kind of a father is it to let his children go looking like little beggars? There an't a boy in the school but what hates me, and even a little bit of a girl not *that high*, told me to-day that *she* wouldn't go patched nor ragged for anything! The teacher whips me because I'm 'a mean little chimney sweeper,' and calls me 'vagabond,' and 'rag-a-muffin,' and everything else mean and dirty. I'll go driver on the canal before I'll stand it any longer!"

"Do you know what kind of boys drive horses on the canal?"

"Yes; bad, mean, wicked boys, that swear, and drink whiskey, and play seven up for money. But I don't care, I'd better have a good time like them, and maybe go to hell afterwards, than be miserabler than them all the time and may be go there all the same. I'm going to try it, any way."

Mr. Sterling was shocked beyond measure. That a son of his should not only stoop to be a canal driver, but thus coolly reason upon and accept the penalty, was enough to make him doubt his own existence!

He looked at him in speechless horror. The steadfast, defiant glance which met his own, taught him at once that no moral lecture or parental sternness would conquer the resolution, and taking him silently by the hand, he led him into the mill, away from any chance of interruption, and there lifting him upon his knee, said very seriously, but gently,

"Now my son, tell me what has put all these ideas into your head. Who abuses you? Tell me the whole story, and then we'll see what can be done."

"Every body abuses me! Ma hates me because I was born, and says if you knew as much about me as she does, you'd choke me. I an't a bit like other boys at home, and she never treats me even decently when you're out of sight. Give me your finger a minute. There; don't you feel that dent in my head? That's where I fell out of a high chair and cut my head against the table, once when it turned so dark and dizzy I couldn't stay up any longer, and I hadn't had a thing to eat all day long, and was sick to begin with. That was last year when you were gone off to the turnpike meeting; and I had to wear a patch on it ever so long, where Dr. Kelley sewed it up; and he scolded ma for it, too, you'd better believe!"

"But, my son, why didn't you tell me of it? This is the first word I ever heard about it."

"A pretty time I'd have had in telling you! Ma said if I did it she'd 'lick me out of my skin;' and she would, too! She told Dr. Kelley I hurt myself running in the yard; but he knew it was a big lie."

"Hush, Lisle; you mustn't speak so about your mother. She wasn't to blame for your falling out of your chair."

"Wasn't she, when she tied me up in it all day and starved me into the bargain? Do you think I wanted to stay in it so long?"

"Well, this was a long time ago. What's the matter now?"

With a portentous nodding of his head, Lisle pushed up his coat sleeve, and baring his arm before the old gentleman's eyes, asked bitterly,

"Do you see these little scars—five, six of 'em? That's where the schoolma'am we had before this one, let Tom Crawford bite me, because I bit his fingers when he tried to rub out all the sums I had done on my slate ready to show. I didn't bite him hard, like this, but just some; and when he made a fuss over it, old schooley called us both up, and when she got my hands tied tight behind me, just let him bite my arm as hard as ever he could: and ma said 'good,' when I told her of it. But I paid Tom off for it next day, and let him have with a sharp stone that gave him one big scar for all these little ones. His would swallow all these and never wink at 'em! When I get big enough to lick him, I'm going to tell him it was me give him that (he don't know it yet), and then he'll know what it was for. If he don't I'll show him!"

"Why, Lisle, I'm astonished! I thought you a good boy."

"Well, then—you thought wrong! I'm just as bad as I can be; but I *have* to be bad, or I couldn't live at all. You don't know how bad every body is; and when I come home sometimes and show ma how I'm all purple, she says I'm served just right, and ten to one whips me herself."

Mr. Sterling put the boy suddenly from his knee, and walked agitatedly once or twice across the mill, then came back and looked down upon him where he had seated himself upon a meal sack with his ragged hat pressed low down over his scowling brows, while his breast labored fearfully with the great gasps which seemed all the more startling for his efforts to suppress them. He laid his hand on the boy's head, as he asked in a troubled voice,

"What's the reason for all this, Lisle? What makes them abuse you in school?"

"Because I look like a little beggar," he burst out indignantly, tearing off his battered hat and hurling it across the mill. "Look at that old thing with the brim all torn off on one side, and a hole in the top; and look at this old brown coat, ragged on one elbow and patched with black on the other one; and these breeches so tight and little they can't come down to but just below my knee, and all tagged out at that!" and seizing the covering of the leg held up to view, he rent the worn out fabric its whole length, and smiled bitterly upon the delicate little limb thus exposed; then suddenly raising his bare feet, said savagely, "Look at these, too. Don't you see how they are all chapped till the blood leaks out, because they need shoes to cover 'em this cold weather? See that big toe. It would have cracked clear off by this time if I hadn't tied that bit of woolen yarn around it. I'm a pretty boy to expect to be treated decent, an't I? All the boys call me 'stingy Sterling's hopeful.' I'll tell 'em, sometime, I an't and never was."

"No, my son, never deny your parents. That's like Peter who denied his Lord, and there's teaching against it—special teaching! I'll get you some new clothes right away, and you shall look as well as any of the boys. I've had the cloth a good while, but some way your mother don't seem to put her hand to it, often as I've spoke about it. Go and buy yourself a pair of shoes, now, if you want to, and don't let me hear anything more about canal driving. I suppose Edward wants fixing up, too, don't he?"

"Yes, some; but Ed an't so miserable as I am, because ma never whips and starves him, nor shuts him up in the dark; and the boys don't pitch into him; 'cause he's stout if he is little, and he's a *real* fighter. But he's ragged, and patched, and barefooted, like me. But see here, now; I won't be bought all off with even good clothes, for I hate that school, and I won't go to it any more. *I* an't going to be abused all the time because the schoolma'am is an old maid; she's whipped me for the last time, and I don't care who knows it!"

"Yes, my son, she has; I'll see to all that. You ought to have told me these things long ago."

"I tell you I was *afraid* to! I'll be killed for it now, may be; but a boy can't die more than once; so come on," and taking up his hat, he contemplated it contemptuously for a moment, then shook the meal from it, and tucking it under his arm with a resolute thrust, walked into the house and to his room, put on his Sunday suit, and made ready for town. The wagon was at the door when he came out, and in it sat Mr. Sterling, awaiting him, while Mrs. Sterling stood near, nodding her head, and twitching her mouth from side to side as she had the peculiarity of doing when especially displease l under circumstances when she saw remonstrance would be useless. She darted a glance upon Lisle as he passed her, that was wont to terrify him in his bravest moments; but it fell powerless and unheeded now, and as he climbed up to his seat beside the old gentleman, his heart swelled with the first throb of real exultation it had ever known. He had courted a conflict with paternal authority, and conquered. No penalty, scarcely reproof had followed his rebellion and defiance; and strong in the thus acknowledged virtue of his cause, he felt himself a man.

Preoccupied in mind, and silent, Mr. Sterling drove into town, and as he fastened his horses at the hitching post in front of the "cheap store," said,

"You may run round to the shoe store and let them fit you, and I'll drive around there for you when I'm ready to go home. Tell Fairfield to give you a good strong pair, and mind you get them big enough; because you'll grow into 'em next year if they are a trifle too large now."

Climbing down over the wheel, Lisle waited for no farther bidding, and a short run brought him to the shoe shop.

"Good evening, Mr. Fairfield. I want a good stout pair of boots, if you please, sir. Nice, long-legged, *real men's boots*, with lots of squeak in 'em—you know, don't you?"

"Yes, my lad; here are just the ones you want. You can black them till they'll show you your own face, if you don't grease them first. *I* don't believe in greasing boots to keep out the water—its a humbug—and they never look so nice after it. There, how's that? Rather large, hey?"

They were on by this time, and he rose and walked a step or two in them. They were rather large, but this was a matter of minor importance, possession being the first; so he declined trying another pair, and telling Mr. Fairfield that his father would be in directly to pay for them and get a pair for Eddy, bade him a hasty good evening, and went out. He looked up and down the street; it was in a lamentably good condition—hard and dry, with not a puddle to be seen. With a little sinking at the heart, he turned a corner. Victory! there was what he sought. In the gully by the road-side lay a pool of water, stirred into something like proper consistency by a flock of gabbling geese and a fraternizing pig; and shaping his course for it, he put them ingloriously to flight, and walked resolutely into it, then perambulated its length, breadth, and circumference, with the pride of a second Columbus! And why not? Columbus had merely discovered a new continent—an accident that might have happened to any one—and it was not made his own even by that discovery; but *he* had thus discovered a way to secure his title in a pair of real boots—his first, long coveted ones! The most magnanimous tradesman that ever lived would not take them back after such a wetting as they had now received, and assured that he was unalterably their proprietor, he went back to the wagon still standing by the "cheap store," and resuming his place in it, gathered up the reins in readiness for a start. Mr. Sterling soon came out, and, sensible that he had spent some time in a but half-successful effort to "beat down" an obstinate clerk, made no remark at finding Lisle awaiting him there instead of at the shoe shop. Driving around to the shop, he handed Lisle the reins, and went in. A few moments elapsed, and the door reopened.

"Lisle, come in here," called Mr. Sterling.

With a face serenely unreflecting anything of the triumph below it, Lisle obeyed.

"Take off these boots, Lisle. I can't afford to buy boots for you. Shoes will answer just as well, and don't cost half so much."

Without a word he drew off one, which he felt would be sufficient in the emergency, and handed it up to Mr. Fairfield, who shook his head.

"Couldn't do it, Mr. Sterling. The boots are unsaleable. Look at them."

| Mr. Sterling looked at the soiled boot handed over the counter. "How's this, Lisle? Where did you get into the water? It must have been pure carelessness. Besides, didn't I tell you to wait here?"

"So you did, didn't you? Well, Mr. Fairfield, couldn't you take 'em back if pa paid you damages?"

"Not unless he paid full price. You can see they are unsaleable," and he returned the rejected article whose passably wounded pride Lisle soothed with an affectionate caress as he put it on again, and then contemplated the pair with renewed pride and admiration. Mr. Sterling paid for them, selected some shoes for Eddy, and went out in silence; but as they drove homeward he said offendedly,

"I'll see to your going on in this way, Lisle. I won't send you for anything again, since you can't be trusted."

A hot flush shot up to his eyes, but he steadied his voice and said defiantly,

"I've been barefooted long enough to have a pair of boots now; it an't a bit more than even!" and encouraged by the silence following his reply, he soon after suggested,

"I must have a good hat, now, musn't I? That old torn out straw one don't go very well with real boots."

Mr. Sterling made no reply, and this time considering silence *not* encouraging, he kept farther suggestions for his own edification. It was quite dark when they reached home, and Eddy was waiting on the door-step, impatient to learn what the day's rebellion had accomplished. The unmistakable creak of *boot*-leather saluted his ear as Lisle came in, and bringing the candle, he bent down and examined them, pinching up the leather on the instep with the air of a *connoisseur*.

"I say, Lisle, they're the thing now! Have I got some, too?"

A thrill of compassion made Lisle prevaricate, and he answered, "Pa has a whole lot of things, I don't know what all! He comes down sharp on the 'cheap store,' and went to the shoe shop last. He'll be here in a minute. Wasn't the schoolma'am mad, Eddy?"

"By jingo, you'd better believe! She tanned the hide of most every boy in school, to make up for you. *Ker-whew*, didn't she!"

Mr. Sterling came in and deposited various packages, large and small, upon the settee.

"Where are my boots, pa?" demanded Eddy, seating himself and squaring one foot across the opposite knee preparatory to putting them on. Mr. Sterling tossed him a package, but was suddenly electrified by receiving it broad-side upon his venerable person, while Eddy sent up an indignant howl.

"*Oh-ie-ie!* They're nothing but nasty shoes tied on a string! I won't wear nasty old shoes like a baby! I'm going to have real true boots, like Lisle's."

Mr. Sterling wiped his coat sleeve in silent horror at the sacrilegious offering, and Mrs. Sterling said,

"Oh, Lisle is his *father's* boy, you know! That makes a difference. Take what you can get, and be thankful."

"I wish, wife," said Mr. Sterling, "you'd teach that boy some respect for his father. He threw his new shoes *at me*."

"I'll warrant it! Just the Fitzjames spirit! You won't be able to *snub him* very long, Mr. Sterling. Why hasn't he boots, like Lisle's, there?"

"Because Lisle tricked me out of what I didn't mean to give him. He played me a trick I shan't forget of him."

"How did you do it, Lisle?" asked Eddy in sudden interest, as if a new idea had occurred to him; but before the reply was given, if indeed any would have been ventured, there, Mrs. Sterling said sarcastically,

"What, your model son deceive his father? Impossible!"

Lisle sat regarding his ill-gotten treasures with a look that plainly asked their opinion as to whether he had not paid too dearly for them. Supper soon ended the scene, and Eddy was appeased by his father's promise to exchange the despised shoes for the coveted boots. So quiet descended upon the troubled day.

Thoroughly resolved upon a complete revolution in affairs, Mr. Sterling the next day had a long interview with the schoolmistress, which, as he was one of the directors, had the desired effect; and it was arranged that henceforth any misconduct upon the part of his children was to be *reported to him*, and upon no account punished by herself. The teacher shut up her pen-knife with a little *click*, as Mr. Sterling left her, and her lips closed uncompromisingly. But the flesh of a teacher is weak, and the power of a director is strong.

For a few days the Sterling boys were absent from school; but they reappeared, newly clothed, and looking comparatively elegant, despite the fact that the " Cadet grey " was not a most desirable fit, Mrs. Sterling's labors proving more persevering than successful, nor were the pride and glory pertaining to their proprietorship sensibly abated even by the derisive shouts, "Stingy Sterling has been to a fire! *Lord*, what a haul!"

CHAPTER V.

COULD irritating boys have been brought to terms as easily as frightened parents and unresisting, if unwilling, teachers, Lisk's school-day troubles would have been ended. The mistress of the rod and ferule, now dethroned as far as he was concerned, kept obstinate silence when reports to headquarters were honestly due, determined that if Mr. Sterling wished his boys to go straight to the Great Unmentionable, they should encounter no obstacle in her; and thus assured that no penalty would follow any satisfactory drubbing he might deem it judicious to administer to his enemies, a fair allowance of physical strength would doubtlessly have made him famous, but proper caution in regard to avenging justice kept half his prowess concealed, or only guessed at, and he was never known as the attacking party. Only in self-defence was he ever seen to raise his hand, and then if lack of strength were atoned for in stategic ability, it was excusable, and few were the evil-doers who escaped him, though he was compelled to master his impatience and wait for opportunity, when the first salient point in the enemy's defence was attacked to the lasting remembrance of the discomfited. What an undisguised blow with his own fist failed to perform, was accomplished by a stone tied in the corner of his handkerchief; and the boys fell back astonished that so feeble a child could deal such blows, while skillful concealment of his weapon prevented the patent from being infringed upon. There was glory in being feared, if he had not the pleasure of being loved, and, after all, as fear is the more enduring sentiment, it was well that he went on his conquering way rejoicing.

Only under Dr. Kelley's roof did this feeling of isolation and bitterness cease to oppress him. Here, the same kind smiles forever beamed upon him—here alone was he made to think himself anything but an interloper among the herd of mankind. The one bright spot to which he looked forward, was the Saturday holiday closing the weary week, when he and Eddy went early to the doctor's house, and were carried home at night in the doctor's own carriage.

Little Julie, having long outgrown her sobriquet of "Dummy," was an object of unceasing interest and amusement to them, and each in his peculiar way made her his companion. Eddy was never weary of arousing her indignation, and submitted to be pummelled, or roundly lectured by her, according to the enormity of his offence.

A putty-headed doll of evil countenance and cotton and bran corporosity, was the principal object of their contention, and the victim whose sufferings compelled her to submit to any imposed terms of peace. This infant member of the fraternity was called "Old Kate," and many were the executions she diurnally suffered by hanging from the door-post by her neck, after which she would have been drawn and quartered had not the strength of her consti- tution resisted his inhuman exertions to that effect, through which little Julie screamed till she was purple from her chin to her eyes. Agonized pleadings of "take her down, oh, *do* take her down," often called Lisle's attention to the crucifixion of "Old Kate," whose vivid color and serene countenance under her sufferings, were remarkable. Toward Julie, Lisle was always tenderly protecting, and he never failed to hasten to her relief and reprove Eddy for his cruelty.

Julie herself was not unfrequently false to the instinct of maternal tenderness—if any such instinct there be—though, in justice, it must be conceded that when so, it was from a mistaken sense of duty, how- ever performed with the cheerful alacrity for which many mothers in real life—who are older if not wiser—are remarkable.

Knowing that half-way measures spoil children, and undermine family government, the young maternal martyr to duty seized "Old Kate" by the morocco covered extremities, and beat her putty head upon the wall till divers indentations attested the force of her blows, and in one instance, after an unusual misdemeanor, a broken skull was the consequence, which, after the customary prayer following the chastisement—endured by "Old Kate" as by many a juvenile, with a sense that the worst was over, and this only a sort of "sum- ming up"—she was carried to the doctor to be dressed and plastered in the most approved surgical manner, after which she soothed and rocked her to sleep, with the comforting assertion that "mamma didn't punish her because she liked to, but to make her good;" a declaration which called out a shout of derision from the skeptical Eddy, for which he was seriously reproved by her.

An untimely end befell poor "Old Kate;" for having been left by the road-side "for the pigs to eat up, for her naughtiness," they act- ually came along and did so, much to the horror of the bereaved mother, who mourned for her in a dark wadded hood with a black neckerchief drooping over it for a veil, till a new doll, of waxen complexion, and with real, curling hair, filled the void in her heart, like the advent of a beauty among a family of real children.

All this, which infinitely amused Eddy, was a source of real pain to the ever reflective Lisle, real life in miniature as it seemed; nor was he to be laughed out of it, for which serious way of looking at things he received the title of "deacon." Little Julie's self-defence was plead with a comical mingling of earnestness and affectation, as, uplifting her rosy face and softly stroking his serious one, she reasoned,

"You know, dear deacon, that you can't understand a mother's feelings; no one but a mother can. I had to whip Old Kate and be very strict with her, because she had a bad temper; but I never have to punish little Pet, because she is the sweetest little thing in the world, and never soils her pink silk dress—and—she's *so* pretty; isn't she now, Lisle?"

"Yes, that's just it. And you abused poor Old Kate because she wasn't pretty, though she was just as much your child as Pet is, wasn't she?"

"Hush; she's gone to heaven, now, and I suppose she is a lovely angel, with that black patch off of her head. I shall go there and see her some day."

"I say, little Ju, if she sees you coming there, *won't* she cut and run!" laughed Eddy, holding up his hands to receive the blows he expected she would rain upon him; but to his surprise she walked away with her eyes full of tears, and refused to be comforted short of much repentance and apology, and even then only by degrees. Praises of Pet at last accomplished what protestations had failed to achieve, and her smiles returned. On the whole, their companionship was a very happy one; and time went by only marked by these Saturday periods in the weekly pages.

Thus affairs went on till Lisle attained his fifteenth year, when a new event broke the monotony of existence in the *new* mill-house now standing complete on the hill near where the old one had been. The same Lombardy poplars towered up into the air, but looked less hopeless and forlorn now that the tangled weeds and grass which had choked their roots, had given place to smoothly shaven turf, fenced in from the street by a substantial white railing, and the old bars were succeeded by a double gate, from which a drive led up to the stables in the side yard.

It was a comfortable, rather pretentious farm-house, of solid architecture, and, awakened to something of her old-time ambition by these surroundings, Mrs. Sterling displayed a laudable pride in making continual internal improvements as she could command the means of paying for them. Mr. Sterling glanced silently at these additions to the household furniture, and sometimes adjourned to the bed-room and examined his pockets suspiciously. The amounts thus appropriated were insignificant. in detail, and if questioned about them, she assumed an air of outraged innocence, and then berated his carelessness in losing so much money which he had far better expend upon his family. Then followed an enumeration of the many sacrifices she daily made upon the altar of economy, of the number of pounds of cheese and butter she had contrived to sell from the milk of four cows, and how she had done it, till, glad of escape upon any terms, he said no more of the still unabated suspicion, but went out and left her to finish the harangue at her pleasure.

The mill was doing a good business, and crops had been good despite one or two late frosts; so the Sterlings were prospering, notwithstanding the melancholy addition of three girls and another boy to the household number. Old Mrs. Sterling, meantime, had sung her last. "Poor lady," and departed for the silent land. Her high-backed chair still occupied its accustomed corner; but the old black cat had enthroned herself upon the faded cushion, and the thin, grey-black shawl had been, by the powerful agency of trade, transformed into an indefinite portion of a glass preserve dish. Mrs. Sterling saw that she had been blessed in many ways, and felt the better for it.

Such was the situation of affairs, when the arrival of a bachelor brother of Mrs. Sterling's added a new interest to the life of the family and its neighbors.

Mr. Fitzjames resided in Kentucky, in which state he had "accumulated a fortune in the mule business," as all who were acquainted with Mrs. Sterling were repeatedly informed, and though the intricacies of "the mule business" remained a sealed mystery, the fortune was accepted as a fact, as also her assertion that "her children, being his next of kin, would some day come into it." In her own mind she had become convinced that Edward, now a fine, manly boy, would fall heir to the bulk of this fortune, and she spared no pains to instruct him how he should win and retain his uncle's favor; lessons which fell uselessly upon his ear, for he was as much a Fitzjames as ever, and would neither assume to be what he was not, nor conceal what he really was, from any one, or for any purpose, and when unusually irritated by her teaching, unceremoniously " wished the old cove and his money in Ballahac !" The old gentleman one day chanced to overhear this irreverent consignment of himself and his possessions, and suddenly addressing the discomfited lad, exclaimed,

" You do, do you ! and pray may I ask what for ?"

" I've no objections to you, sir; I presume you're a nice old chap enough ; but it's enough to make a boy swear, to have you and your money thrown in his face every minute !"

" Really, sister Lydia, he doesn't do credit to his training. He might come in for something handsome at my death if he could play hypocrite; eh ? Well, there's plenty of time for him to learn it, yet ! I'm rugged and hearty, and likely to be," and smiling grimly, the old gentleman walked away.

Filled with shame and contrition, Eddy soon followed him. Mr. Fitzjames took no notice of him for a time, but at length turning quickly upon him, he said,

" An ' old cove ' am I ? Wished me—where was it ?"

" Oh, sir, I'm sorry I said that. No; you're the nicest old boy I ever saw, and it wasn't you I was vexed with. If it wasn't for that everlasting ' money,' we'd be real tip-top friends."

" So we are, my boy ! Go off to your play, and don't be sensitive over trifles. I can't see that it's any worse to be an ' old cove' than an ' old chap,' and either name is good enough when a gentleman isn't over particular,' and readjusting his spectacles he went on reading serenely.

" I thought so," commented Mrs. Sterling, nodding her head sagaciously as she retreated from the door crack which had served as her observatory, and returned triumphantly to her pie-crust rolling. " Everything works for the best."

Mr. Fitzjames' visit drew nearly to a close, and no farther manifestation of partiality for the young embodiment of the Fitzjames' virtues and spirits, cheered Mrs. Sterling's watching eyes. Nothing seemed farther from his thoughts than his young nephews and nieces, and if his attention was ever in any way directed toward them, he bestowed it briefly, in an indifferent manner, which might have sprung from pure carelessness, or been only the exercise of a bachelor's privilege, who, owing nothing to posterity, declined being annoyed by it. At least there was no hope for any of them if not for Edward, and Mrs. Sterling felt a dim forboding that the proceeds of the successful "mule business" might not be preserved to the family after all these expectant years.

The thought was not a pleasant one; and raising her eyes from her early apple drying employment, she glanced sharply down upon the busy mill, and the pond sleeping so lazily below the house, undisturbed by the family chatter of a congregation of ducks who were holding a session meeting with much ado.

At the head of the pond, Lisle and Eddy were laboring diligently upon the construction of a raft, their pantaloons rolled compactly up over their knees, and their shirt sleeves similarly elevated above the troubles of life, in the fashion so dear to the hearts of industrious juveniles. Eddy, as the more vigorous of the two, dragged together the planks for the miniature ark, while Lisle officiated as master architect. Mrs. Sterling looked on for awhile, and her lip curled as she mentally commented, "That's always the way it goes! Prince Lisle always plays the fine gentleman, while others obey his bidding. I'll put an end to his domineering for this time," and going to the cradle in which slumbered the youngest representative of the family, she roused to action a pair of lungs which were the terror of the household. The unwelcome summons fell upon the little boys' ears even before Mrs. Sterling called from the door-way,

"Lisle, come right in here and mind the baby. She's screaming herself into fits."

"Let her scream herself out of 'em again, then; and if she don't, there's enough in the family without her!" shouted back Eddy, defiantly, as Lisle commenced rolling down his pantaloons legs preparatory to obeying.

"Don't budge an inch, Lisle; the raft wont be done to-day if you do, and the more you tend and coax that young one, the more you have to. That's just the way of them little she things! Ten to one the old lady made her squall. She never lets you play a minute."

Lisle had his own opinion upon the subject, but he said nothing, and casting one longing, lingering look back upon the raft, went up to the house and seated himself by the huge iron-bound cradle, which had creaked to sleep not only the present generation of Sterlings, but two broods in the ascendant. The more he strove to rock the baby into quietude, the louder she screamed, and administering a box on his ear, Mrs. Sterling bade him take her up. It was a fat, heavy child, nearly a year gone in teething, and Lisle could scarcely lift her, but once having gotten her upon his lap he was rewarded by an instantaneous cessation of the protesting yells, and resting her

head back upon his breast, she fell into a silent and absorbed contemplation of her chubby fists, as if speculating upon the unknown
purpose for which they were made.   Thus relieved from any active
care in her behalf, Lisle fell into a study upon the construction of
the raft, and planned how he should secure possession of a few nails
much needed to make a neat job of it.

"What are you sulking about now, young gentleman?" asked Mrs.
Sterling so suddenly that he came out of his musings with a little
start.

"Nothing; that is—I mean to say"—and at a loss what to reply,
he stopped short.

"Yes, I'll warrant you do! None of your impudence to me, sir."
He raised his eyes deprecatingly, and commenced to reply, but feeling assured that denial of any accusation, however unreasonable, was
worse than useless with her, he closed his lips and said nothing.

"I caught you at it this time, sly as you are! I'll teach you to
think up impudence towards your mother!" and she reached for the
ever-ready rawhide.

"Truly, mother, I wasn't thinking anything saucy at all! It was
only about the raft."

"Now tell a lie about it, will you! Put down the baby and get
up here. I won't leave an inch of skin on your body, you evil boy!"

Lisle placed the baby in the cradle which he took care to interpose between himself and the uplifted whip, and stepped back while
a hot flush dyed his face and as suddenly retreated leaving it like
marble; and there was something ominous in the tone with which
he said,

"No, you won't whip me, mother. You've struck me the last blow
you'll ever give me."

"What's that, you hop of my thumb! *You dare me?*"

"No, I only say I'll never stand it again! *never!*"

Mrs. Sterling took two hasty steps around the cradle.

"Seize her, Pompey," commanded Lisle.

Loth to obey, yet ever faithful, Pompey sprang forward between
them, and showed his teeth savagely. Mrs. Sterling screamed, as
much in anger as in flight. She dared not advance, and after a moment of mutual defiance, through which Lisle stood with eyes ablaze,
she said threateningly,

"I'll have this dog shot within an hour. *Then* we'll see!"

"Lydia, let the boy alone. He is too large for you to manage
now. Turn him over into his father's hands, in future," interposed

the voice of Mr. Fitzjames, who, from the adjoining room had seen and heard all that transpired.

"That I will, Warren, and he shall get such a tanning as he never got yet. Go up to your room, young man, and don't you show your face till you are called. Just make the most of your bones while they're whole, too, I advise you."

Calling Pompey with him for safe-keeping, Lisle obeyed, and remained in his room till Mr. Sterling himself opened the door and came very seriously in.

"What's all this, Lisle? Did you set the dog on your mother?"

"Yes, sir, I hoped he'd kill her if she struck me!"

Mr. Sterling raised his hands in horror, but not a word fell from his lips. Lisle burst out impetuously,—

"I know it. I'll be hanged if I have to stay here, I know I will, and you'll be the one to blame, too, for not letting me go off long ago when I wanted to. I'll go to-morrow if I'm alive."

"To drive horses on the canal?"

"Yes, or anything else. I won't live here. I hate the very sun that shines on this house!"

"Then you ought to be ashamed of yourself. Don't you think it's my duty to whip you for your conduct towards your mother?"

"No, I don't, and I won't take it. She is the one to blame, and I didn't want to quarrel. She's always treated me worse than a dog and always hated me."

"No she hasn't. It an't natural for any mother to hate her child."

"But you, sir, don't know all, and I do. I could make you hate her worse than I do, but I won't. Only let me go away from here forever, and I'll never open my lips against her."

"I'm going to send you away. I've spoken to your uncle Fitz-james about it, and he will take you home with him."

"There, father, that shows I wasn't the one to blame! He heard every word of it, and if I was such an awful boy he would'n't have me near him."

"You are too bad to be allowed among your little brothers and sisters, and with him you can't set a bad example before any children. Come to dinner now, if you think you deserve any; I don't."

Lisle was not in the spirit to accept another's estimate of his merits and deservings, so he took his accustomed place among the servant faces surrounding the dinner table. He cast many a searching glance upon Mr. Fitzjames, hoping to obtain some clue to his opinion of the morning's adventure, but not a responsive glance met his own, and not a word relative to himself was uttered till Mr. Fitzjames finished his meal and shoved back his chair, when he said briefly,

"I hope the boy will be gotten ready to leave next week; I mean to start for home Tuesday."

"A pretty pass it's come to now, young man!" said Mrs. Sterling to Lisle, "I hope your uncle will shut you up in his nigger pen and give you what you deserve. Now go down to Dr. Kelley's and give a report of yourself, and ask Mrs. Kelley if she's likely to get the shirts she's making you done by Tuesday."

Mr. Sterling looked up as the door closed, and said slowly,

"I don't see, wife, why you can't get along with that boy. Every body else seems to like him. I hope no judgment will follow his being sent away from his own home in this way. It seems strange a mother can't live with her own child."

"He's no child of mine! There an't a drop of Fitzjames blood in him, and never was. He's just a mean, tricky, miserable *Sterling*, and won't come to anything better! besides it's none of my notion having him sent away. *I'd* find a way to manage him, if he was kept at home. That dog'll be shot dead enough before he gets back from the doctor's, and he won't have him so handy next time."

Mr. Sterling rubbed his large hands together, and drew a long breath of meek resignation, and the conversation was closed by Eddy making his appearance for his dinner. Tossing his hat in a corner, he waited for no ceremony, and all unwashed as he was since his labors upon the raft, commenced his meal.

"Eddy, why didn't you come when the rest did? Your dinner is all cold, now, and there wasn't any reason for waiting so," said his mother, helping him liberally to what was before him.

"I wasn't ready to come then. Do you want me to do like the pigs, who run squealing and stick their noses in the trough the minute you say 'swill' to 'em? I'm a human boy."

"You'll be a drowned one if you don't keep away from the pond."

"Well, then you'll only have to bury me—that is if pa can be made to shell out the money. I heard you groaning once when you thought Lisle was going dead, because it would 'cost twenty dollars to bury him, and mourning besides.' You can just leave out the mourning, for me, dame; I'll bury just as well without any. Oh give us a hot potato for the love of"—

"Edward," exclaimed his father sternly.

"Well, then, 'Amen!' but it's hard when a fellow can't ask his own blessing. But say, pa, what's the use of asking a blessing over the grub, like you? If the Lord *wants* to bless a fellow, he'll do it, and if he don't, he an't going to be worried into it."

"Let your victuals stop your mouth, sir. You talk too much."

"Won't you let the boy *speak*, Mr. Sterling?" asked his wife querulously. "If it was Lisle, now, you'd think he was pinfeathering out for a philosopher."

Nothing more was said till Eddy finished eating, and took his hat. "Where's Lisle?" he asked, unconscious of the morning's incident. "Gone to Dr. Kelley's, to tell them he's going to be sent away from home next week. He's going away with his uncle, to live in a nigger-pen and get flogged into decency," replied his mother.

"By hoky! If Lisle go s I'll go too. I an't going to stay shut up here alone with the girls. I never could bear girls to play with! They just want to fuss a boy into 'a sick baby' and pull him around in a pinning blanket all the time. They never will learn a decent play! When is Lisle coming back home?"

"Never, I hope, but don't ask me. I'm done with him."

Eddy's loquacity was thoroughly checked, and he went out without another word.

Mrs. Kelley made few comments when Lisle made the announcement of his approaching banishment from home, but taking a more cheerful view of it than had yet occurred to him, felt a real thankfulness that he was to be released from his unhappy situation under the roof of a mother who unnaturally persecuted and disliked him. The doctor's first pang under the impending separation, soon died away as he realized that any change in the boy's life must be for the better; and looking into the future, he thought how naturally a mutual attachment might thus spring up between Lisle and his uncle, which would be a lasting benefit to the son he could never acknowledge and provide for as he so longed to do. The future had looked dark and hopeless, and here was light from a quarter most of all to be desired upon Lisle's own account. Had anything been necessary to reconcile him to the proposed change, this cheerful acquiesence of the doctor and his wife would have effected it, and he turned homeward with elastic step. The report of a gun, as he neared home, stayed his footsteps and brought his heart into his mouth. Pompey! How could he have forgotten him after that threat! Seldom allowed to leave the place, he had seen Lisle depart, without any manifestation; and with his own head full of other thoughts, Lisle had forgotten him. The report of that fatal shot was more bitter than

his own death blow would have been, and choked by grief and passion he stood a moment without power to move.   Poor, faithful
Pompey!   He had died literally *for him*, and wrung anew by the
thought, he turned away and walked into the woods where no eyes
might chance upon his sorrow.

Grief invariably seeks to revenge itself upon some object directly
or indirectly connected with its cause, and if to Lisle's poignant sorrow for his dumb friend and protector, a hatred as bitter succeeded,
and welled up towards his mother, it was only human justice. . She
had wilfully and maliciously caused him this anguish, and he solemnly vowed never to forgive or forget it!

It was nearly dark when he returned home, and merciful hands
had buried Pompey from his eyes, despite Mrs. Sterling's remonstrances, who, thus deprived of half her vengeance, waited exultingly
for the storm of grief she knew must follow the death of the one
staunch friend and playfellow Lisle had ever known, beside his
brother.   But not a trace of emotion was visible upon his face as
she saw him receive the announcement Eddy indignantly poured
forth, and mentally querying " what on earth the boy was made of,"
she felt her victory robbed of all triumph, while her brother out-
spokenly declared it " a mean action of which a Fitzjames should be
ashamed."

CHAPTER VI.

THE hour of departure arrived, and Mr. and Mrs. Sterling drove to down with Lisle for his parting visit to the doctor's family.

Little Julie was inconsolable. Of her two playfellows, he was much the most popular and beloved, and though she had long outgrown the horrible executions of former days, which even the victims themselves some way survived till decayed dollhood finished their earthly career, Eddy was still too tormenting a companion to be as popular as his more gentle brother. She refused to say good bye, but flew to the library, alone, where he found her sobbing with her face bowed upon the table at which so many happy hours had been spent among their books and pictures. ·

Vainly searching for some word of comfort, he laid his hand upon her head. She pushed it off with mingled grief and anger, and refused to look up.

" Well, Julie," he said at last, making a pretence of going; " I'm sorry you won't kiss me good-bye. If I never come back, how will you like to remember that you treated me so the last time you ever saw me ?"

Shoving back her chair, she sprang impulsively into his arms, and covered his face with kisses as she sobbed,

" No, no; I'm not angry with *you*, but I'll hate your old uncle as long as I live, for taking you away ! He don't want you half as much as I do. I haven't *any body* left now !"

" No, I only wish he *did* want me. I'm sent with him, Julie—*sent* away where no body wants me ! It's bad enough without your making it any worse. I'll come back and see you when I'm a man, and that won't be long. You'll write me lots of letters, won't you ?"

" Yes; and I'll tell you all about Eddy, who, though he's a boy, can't write near as well as I can," and she dashed away her tears at the thought that such a link of companionship was yet left them.

" Come, Lisle, we are all waiting for you," said the doctor, opening the door. Tenderly unclasping the arms Julie again threw around him, Lisle pressed back the tears which sprang to his eyes, and slipping his hand within the doctor's, left the room. They stopped in the hall, and raising Lisle's face to his breast the doctor said with a voice he vainly strove to render firm,

"My boy, I believe that you know I am your friend, and that you love me a little—don't you?".

"Yes, yes, I love you very much; you were always my friend."

"Then I want you to promise me that if you are unhappy you will let me know it. I hope you will have a more happy home with your uncle, than you have ever known yet; but if not, and you do not like to stay with him after you have given it a thorough trial, write me so, and something shall be done for you at once. Do you promise me this?"

"Yes, sir, you are *very* kind; but I think I shall like uncle. I know I shall if he will let me, and I think he's a good man—but no one is as good as you are."

"I have no doubt, Lisle, that you will love each other too well ever to part, and I must tell you, that if so, it will be the best that can possibly happen to you. Your troubles would be pretty much over, then, and you would be spared many that you do not know of."

"I can't have any more than I always have had, any way," said Lisle pressing his teeth over the lip that trembled in spite of him; and, warned by a treacherous swelling in his own throat to offer no reply, the doctor convulsively pressed the little hand he held, and led him out to the gate, where the others awaited him.

The coach was waiting to take the travellers to the nearest depot; and Mr. Sterling seriously shook Lisle's hand as he bade him "be a good boy, and keep the fear of the Lord before his eyes," while Mrs. Sterling pressed her apron to her eyes in a theatrical manner, as she sobbed,

"Good-bye, my son, good-bye. Don't forget your poor mother when you are gone. It's very hard to part with children in this way!"

Lisle raised his eyes in surprise, and then, while a hot flush spread up to the very roots of his hair, he turned suddenly and climbed into the coach, without a word.

"What a bad, ungrateful child!" exclaimed an old lady in the coach, throwing an annihilating glance upon him.

The coachman cracked his whip, Mr. Fitzjames raised his hat in parting salute, the horses sprang forward, and they were off. Once more Mrs. Sterling sobbed, and really deceived by her apparent grief, it became contagious, and Mr. Sterling's own eyes grew misty as he unhitched his horses, and with a hasty adieu to the doctor and his wife, they drove homeward.

"What an abominable she-hypocrite that woman is!" commented the doctor as he went back into the house with his wife. "It's a blessing she over-shot the mark, for once, and so let that poor child out of her clutches."

The only real sufferer under this separation was Eddy, who, utterly refusing all consolation, abandoned himself to a grief as profound as it was silent. Lisle had vainly searched the whole premises over, to bid him good-bye, and lingered till the last moment, hoping he would appear; but, carefully hidden on the hay-loft, he heard, unansweringly, Lisle's shouts for him, nor crept forth till the sound of departing wheels told him he was gone. Then, descending, he wandered off by the river, deep into the woods, and throwing himself upon a mossy knoll, gave way to choking sobs and uncontrollable anguish that shook him convulsively. At last his violent emotion exhausted itself, and, wondering at his physical weakness, he thought he might perhaps thus die, and closed his eyes hoping that he should.

Gradually this feeling subsided, and in its place arose an indignant sense of wrong against himself for which he could find no excuse. What right had any one thus to separate him from his brother—to rob him of his most natural and best loved companion! Had any one loved Lisle as he had always done, fighting his battles and avenging his wrongs? Yes, that, was it! Their mother's wrongs against him had caused him to be sent away; and all the force of his resentment was turned upon her. "It was she who had miserabled his life all up for him! and, after all, what right had she to do so; or to abuse Lisle in any way? She was nobody but Lydia Fitzjames till their father married her; and here she was, whipping his children as big as life!" and strong in the justice of his argument, he rose, and crowding his hat combatively down over his brows, went home.

Unfortunately, Mrs. Sterling did not perceive the force of his reasoning when he rather ostentatiously advanced it, and the implied slight towards her family provoked a vigorous and lengthy recital as to their ancient birth and importance, dating back to royalty itself, with the vast estates in England which would in due course of legal proceedings come into the possession of the branch of the family now in America, and an assurance that all the intellect her children possessed, was derived from her side of the paternity, while the Sterlings, as everybody knew, were mere flint skinning nobodies," an assertion under which Mr. Sterling put on his hat and meekly adjourned to more complimentary regions, while Eddy stoutly declared his resolve to run away from the whole tribe of them.

However, time softened and undermined his resolution, and after an interval he returned to school in charge over a younger brother, in whose cause his coat was pulled off so many times a day that he at last left it off altogether, for convenience, and so conquered a place on the play ground for a wee young Sterling who was as ragged and seedy as his brothers ever had been before him. Only on one occasion did his patron saint desert him, and this was doubtless owing to the fact that his opponent was much the larger and stronger; but anger yielding as much temporary vigor as more reliable muscle, Eddy reinforced himself from an unfailing supply, and, having vanquished the enemy, walked off declaring he wasn't going to take all the blows and let the other boy carry off all the glory.

In short, having given him the physique for a champion, nature seemed resolved that the talent should not rust for want of legitimate exercise, and the very excitement of it proved the best diversion from his sorrow.

Meantime Mr. Fitzjames and Lisle were whirling rapidly Southward, and as for the first time in his life Lisle saw houses, woods, and fields, glide away from him as if by magic—felt himself rolling over high bridges with swift, dark water, seemingly miles below as his inexperienced eyes looked down upon it, or caught the earthy smell of swamps decked with myriad strange blossoms and tangled ferns, he felt himself in an unknown and new world.

His uncle, with the *sang froid* of a traveller, had comfortably ensconced himself in one of the car seats which he turned so that Lisle might sit opposite him, and with a book in his hand, which he read or dozed over as inclination prompted, seemed altogether too far off in virtue of such *savoir vivre*, to be addressed by so mere a wight as the boy seemed to himself sitting there in the smallest corner of space he could shrink into, and altogether too much confused and excited by all this novelty to read one word of the book with which he had been advised to amuse himself.

Looking up from time to time, Mr. Fitzjames saw that he was contented, and silently congratulating himself that the boy was quiet, and as genteel as such shyness admitted, he re-addressed himself to his book or his nap. Rousing from one of these, he observed

Lisle fixing a wistful, inexplicable gaze upon some object in the rear of the car, and, having turned his own eyes in the same direction without encountering anything of interest he asked,

"What interests you so much, Lisle? Do you see any one you. know?"

"Oh no, sir. I was only watching that lady over there with the baby. Do you think it's her own, sir?"

"Why, yes, I suppose so. Few ladies care to tote other people's babies around the country. Why do you ask such a question?"

"Because, sir, she seems so fond of it, and I thought people never liked their own very much."

"Singular conclusion, that, for a boy of your age! Who upon earth made you, and aren't you anybody's child, yourself?"

"Oh, sir," he began, but suddenly stopped and colored painfully. Mr. Fitzjames looked at him curiously a moment, and then with an inflation of his cheeks which he reduced with a puffing sort of whistle, said in a mystified tone,

"The child must be illegitimate upon both sides of the family; he isn't a bit like either Lydia or Sterling!"

He turned again to his book, but its interest seemed to have fled, and Lisle became really embarrassed under the frequent scrutinizing reviews he bestowed upon him, painfully conscious as he was of his own sickly physique and almost infantile *tout ensemble*, and experienced a sensation of profound relief when the closing daylight screened him from farther observation.

Two or three melancholy lamps were set to condoling with each other, by the brakeman, one of which glimmered till glimmering ceased to be a virtue, and then resignedly went out altogether, leaving the others to hold its dismal "wake" as best they might, amidst which ceremony Lisle fell asleep.

The train stopped "twenty minutes for refreshments," as every one was informed by somebody, who, after making the announcement, closed the door again with a resounding slam that brought all sleepers to waking consciousness, and grasping Lisle firmly by the hand, his uncle led him into a long dining hall close by the railway, where much scrambling and pushing for places seemed the principal employment in hand, and through which he at last found himself, he hardly knew how, seated at table, where his uncle's voice, sounding very far away and exceedingly cloud-like, said something to him about "oceans of time for all we find here—oceans of time ;" and a waiter fired down a little volley of plates with something edible on them, and hurried off as if hit by his own shot.

Next Lisle sat a fat, puffy-faced, round-eyed, restless-legged boy, who impatient for the arrival of his own supper, laid violent hands upon his, and forthwith commenced a vigorous onslaught, much to the real proprietor's disgust and indignation. A sudden and retaliatory plung from Lisle's fork, which he manipulated under the table, arrested these proceedings, and while his adversary choked over a huge mouthful which was surprised into going down the wrong way, he repossessed himself of his purloined supplies, and went on with his meal as unconcernedly as possible. Having at last found voice, the roars of the fat boy woke the echoes of the room and the anthemas of his listeners.

The old lady in charge of him shook him vigorously, and slapped his back to relieve his coughing, amid a storm of questions as to " whatever ailed him, and what did he mean by it ?" a subject upon which he did not think fit to enlighten her—probably in remembrance of many a previous enforcement of the lesson, " It is a sin to steal a pin," or perhaps unwilling to confess how ingloriously he had been put to flight ; and no one having seemed to notice the affair, or only caring to have the uproar quelled, no explanation was offered, and the arrival of the fat boy's proper supplies restored peace for a moment. Then the fat boy again was heard, bawling in a nassal tone,

" Gran'ma, give me all the sass there is in the deesh ; and tie me up some o' this ere sweet-cake in your han'kercher agin I get hungry. I won't be half full when the cars hoot."

" Hush, sonny, be a little gentleman, like that nice boy t'other side of you. He don't make so much fuss at the table."

" Oh, he's a sly one, he is !" retorted the fat boy, rolling his eyes and nodding his head sagaciously ; and then leaning towards Lisle, he said offensively,

" I say, now, don't you think yourself a pimp ?"

Declining to express his opinion of himself in such an assembly, Lisle appeared not to have heard the invitation, and much to his joy his uncle said,

" Come, Lisle, if you have finished eating, we'll go. Travelling cannibals have no regard for personal property in the way of seats,' and again piloting him through the crowd that now sat scarcely less strongly in the other direction—a sort of gustatory ebb and flow of the human tide—Mr. Fitzjames restored him to his former situation,

near the defunct lamp, once more resurrected and now emitting quite
a glow of complacency.

"Now tell me, Lisle," said his uncle, "what was the trouble between you and that fat boy next you."

"He stole my supper, sir." ·

"And you ?"—

Lisle hung his head, unwilling to reply. The question was repeated.

"What did you do, that he pronounced you 'a sly one?'"

"I jabbed him with my fork, sir, under the table."

"Just enough, my boy ; very just, only never do anything of that
sort on the sly. When a fellow misuses you, just wring his nose
publicly and openly, like a gentleman. Underhanded justice always has a bad look—remember that."

"Feugh!" exclaimed an elderly female sitting near, who overheard
these remarks. "A pretty fellow he is to bring up young boys!
This 'public nose wringing' don't do well in large families."

Mr. Fitzjames turned and politely bowed!

"It won't make any trouble in yours and mine, I conclude, madam," and as she colored up indignantly, he said as if to himself—
"knew she was an old maid, by the snap and snarl in her voice !"
and after an interval of silence he said to Lisle, ·

"It won't do you any harm to recollect—if you remember judiciously—that in this world, he who shows a talent for receiving
kicks, gets favored with all there are going about unclaimed. Turning the other side may do well enough in Paradise, but it's poor
policy in this world, and I wouldn't advise any one to try it."

Not a little surprised by such teaching, Lisle looked upon his
uncle with his admiration so plainly written in his face that the old
gentleman smiled back in return, and a little chat grew up between
them, in the midst of which he was surprised to find it nine o'clock,
and quite delighted, when, laying his hand on his nephew's head the
old gentleman said,

"So, it seems you have a *tongue* as well as a head, after all ! Well,
put it to sleep, that it may run a little—not too much—to-morrow,"
and making a pillow of his extra coat, he gave it to him and bade
him good-night. Lisle obeyed the suggestion with a happier heart
than he had ever felt, and thought that if banishment with *such* a
man were a punishment, he could endure a great deal of it, and with
the rattling and rumbling of the train in his ears, he fell asleep, nor
woke till they rolled noisily into the grand depot.

"Good-morning, Lisle; slept well, did you?" said his uncle cheerfully. "Now let's go and get some breakfast. There's plenty of time, as the boat doesn't leave till ten o'clock."

As they stepped upon the platform, they met the fat, round-eyed boy and his grandam issuing from the adjoining car. The boy raised his fist, which he clenched suggestively at Lisle, and—"remembering judiciously,"—Lisle slightly elevated his chin in a manner which said, "You'd better try it, once," and so each went his way, Lisle hoping it forever.

What, then, was his annoyance, as, breakfast over, they went on board the steamer, to see this awful boy perched upon a dry-goods box from which he was dangling and swinging his legs with a vigor which brought his strong cowhide shoes with a resounding thump against the box end, while a huge piece of gingerbread absorbed his undivided attention, as he bit from it endwise, lengthwise, cornerwise and across, in an impartial endeavor to treat it all alike, fixing his eyes upon it greedily after each attack, while he snuffed to avoid losing time by the use of his coat sleeve, which was quite glazed by previous efforts in that direction.

Lisle's lip curled contemptuously; but the superior charms of ginger-bread kept him unnoticed, and he watched the complete demolition of it, and the smacking and lip-licking operation which followed it, only leaving his post of observation when the sprawled digital members of the two cake-covered hands reached down and wiped themselves upon the gray pantaloons covering the fat legs, and the boy turned round to see what changes had taken place during his recent labors.

Going up the saloon, Lisle there found the old grandam herself, in wofully pinched attire except as regarded her bonnet, which, to make amends, was three times as large as it should have been had it conducted itself with propriety. Sitting upon the extreme edge of the sofa, and quite as if she asked its pardon for taking even that liberty, she was explaining to the patronizing stewardess that she was "going down to Kentuck' to a married darter as lived at Louisville, bringing along a sweet little gran'son as was just left an orfing, and was to live now with Sally Ann."

The warning whistle was given, and there was a general rush of those who were on the levee and meant to come on board, and those who, coming on board for last good-byes, wanted to get off. Another whistle, soon followed by a sort of shudder through the steamer, and a line of water spread between it and the shore. Lisle looked

around for his uncle; but he had not yet come up, and with a sinking heart he queried what if he might have been left.

The fat boy came up, licking his fingers after some farther delectation, and walking up to the sofa where Lisle sat, he stopped and
looked him fully in the face a moment, before he said,

"So, my lark, you're going down the river, too, are you ? See here
now; you just stick that ere fork o' yourn into me agin, and I'll swal-
ler you who'e, I will!"

"As you did 'all the sass in the decsh,' hey ; or that hunk of gingerbread you ate down stairs, and never blowed your nose once the
whole time!"

"You sassy little skeleton, I'd whale you right now if yer bones
wouldn't cut me. Let me ever cetch you sneakin' around my house
down in Kentuck', and I'll have one o' my niggers chaw you into
mince meat, I will!"

Curling his lip contemptuously, Lisle walked away in dignified
silence, glad enough to see his uncle at that moment come up stairs,
and joining him he avoided the round-eyed boy, and so overcame
the temptation which tingled at his skillful finger tips. Mutually
pleased, if silent, they read side by side, or enjoyed the beauty of
the vine-covered hills, below which they passed, and Lisle's imagination wandered off to all the vineyard stories he had ever read, among
which romantic recollections time passed by unheeded till the dinner gong aroused him. Begging his uncle to be sure and not place
him near the awful boy, due care was observed, and no unpleasant
adventure happened to mar the satisfaction he felt with himself despite his being twice enjoined not to say "yes, sir" to the waiters.
His fear of his uncle was gone, and could he only have felt that he
was *wanted* by him, instead of endured as a necessity, he would have
been happy.

He was unfeignedly sorry when the pleasant river journey ended,
and they arrived at Louisville. Mr. Fitzjames resided on his plantation, a few miles from the city, and a carriage was soon engaged
to carry them out to it. A drizzling rain filled the air with gloom,
and the mud spattered upon the windows and dripped from the
wheels in a manner indicative of many days previous drizzle. The
whole scenery seemed painfully destitute of beauty compared with
that he had seen on the river, and, a victim to loneliness for the
hour, Lisle looked out dismally.

"You wish yourself back home ?" asked his uncle having watched
him through a five minutes silence.

"No, sir, not unless you wish I was there."

"And if I did—what then?"

"I'll go away from you, sir, if you don't want me; but I'll never go back there to live as long as the soul of a boy is in me! I'd go to the hottest place the Bible tells of first!"

"Well, it isn't worth while shouldering your knapsack just yet. If I hadn't wanted you I shouldn't have brought you. I may as well tell you now as ever, that I went North this summer just to see my sister's children, and discover whether any one among them would make me a comfortable companion in my old age. I didn't wish any of them to prime and load themselves for the occasion; and that they might not do so, I think I pretty thoroughly snubbed the whole of you. I had about decided to ask for you, when that little family scene occurred which ended in poor Pompey's winning a martyr's crown, and I availed myself of it to seem to be conferring a favor where I did not wish to ask one which would be presumed upon."

"No, sir, I should never do that! I an't mean, if I am sickly!"

"Nonsense, child, no one supposes you would. Don't be egotistical in applying to yourself remarks intended for your elders. I don't think you have been spoiled by favoritism at home, and if you are inclined to make anything of yourself, I'll do my part towards helping you. I suppose the first thing needed is a tutor."

"Oh, I should like it of all things, if it isn't too much trouble."

"Trouble to whom, pray? Not to me, as I shall neither teach nor flog; and if your tutor isn't sufficiently up to his own business not to be troubled by it, we'll find another who esteems it a pleasure. As for me, I shall thus have you conscientiously off my hands."

Lisle turned away with a shadow of the old weight flitting from his heart across his face, and his uncle said more gently,

"You must try to outlive this over-sensitiveness, Lisle. One doesn't know how to talk to such a very serious youth. A most uncomfortable sort of people are those who are always dislocating their spines stretching for insults not intended for them, and accepting literally every word one utters! I mean to do the best I can for you, in all kindness; and if we do not come to like each other, it will not be my fault, but our mutual misfortune."

A delighted smile lit up Lisle's pale face; but it quickly faded out, and he said humbly,

"I'm afraid you don't know how bad I am, sir."

"Well, what mak s you 'bad' if you don't enjoy it? and I really don't see that it has put any flesh on your bones."

"Everybody, most, makes me worse than I want to be. When a boy is half sick all the time, and han't any more strength than a girl, nor so much, all the boys keep putting upon him, and put ing upon him, till he has to find some way to get even, and he can't always stop when he's done just enough; and then the grown-up people kind of shiver at him and s y how bad he is, till his heart gets as heavy as a stone, and harder. It's hard trying to be the only good one there is, and nobody trying to help."

The earnestness with which this was uttered quite repressed his uncle's inclination to smile, and kindly smoothing his head he said,

"Well, let by-gones be by-gones, an I commence again. Here no one will annoy you, and whenever you want anything 'to help,' just let me know it. I'm not accustomed to children and their ways and wants, and may not think of much which I ought to, but, as the French say, 'I shall make mine po s ble.' "

A new order of things dawned upon Lisle's mental vision, and he felt that "being good" would be very easy under such circumstances. Casting a retrospective glance upon his school-day persecutions, he wondered what Bill B.own would say if he could see him now, and thought how astonished he would be in that future now dawning, when he should walk past him in a spirit of mild forgiveness, too genteel even to notice him.

CHAPTER VII.

COLORED by this light from within, the rather lonely house and spacious but unadorned yard looked really cheerful to him as they drove to the door, despite the fine rain that still fell, though now with a misty laziness which veiled everything in sombre shade.

The house itself was completely closed, and the dark figured window shades were lowered to the very sills, as if determined that not even a ray of light should enter during the master's absence; but from the kitchen, standing by itself a little in the rear of the house, several woolly heads protruded to investigate the cause of rolling wheels, and then rushed noisily out till the carriage was surrounded by gesticulating figures, and so many tongues running simultaneously that not a word was intelligible.

"Oh, yes, yes"—exclaimed Mr. Fitzjames, putting both hands to his ears to shut out the din—"very glad to see you, but I pray you won't drive me dis'racted. I'd rather see one housekeeper than the whole of you! Tell Mrs. Drew to let us in, and give us a hot supper!"

Even as he spoke, the door opening upon the front veranda swung back, window-shades were drawn up, and a hasty shaking out of things in general, prepared the room for his reception.

Confused by the noise and novelty around him, Lisle made his way into the house in time to see his uncle shaking hands with a middle-aged person in a housekeeper's apron, of whom "fat, fair and forty" formed a sufficiently accurate description.

"Mrs. Drew, this is my nephew, Master Lisle Sterling. I rely upon you to make him comfortable. Give him the room next mine, up stairs, and see that his sheets are well aired, and all that. He's a little delicate, as you see."

"Which it's not a little, I should say, sir. I shall cuddle and do for him like he was my own child, sir, I'm sure!"

Lisle thought her a decidedly comfortable looking woman as she departed briskly upon her mission, and was privately glad she was not tall, lean, and skinny, with a sharp nose. She returned in a few

minutes, and asking if he would like to see his room, preceded him
through a dark hall, and up a stair-case amid whose windings he
quite lost sight of her, and in one of whose angles he ran full against
a lank, loosely put together girl about his own size, who, finger in
mouth, there lay in wait for him, with her chin dropped into the neck
of her dress, and her white hair quite threatening to frowze entirely
out of the two consumptive braids dangling down her back.

"Drat the boy; han't he got no eyesight?" ejaculated the young
lady, putting herself to rights after the encounter by seizing the
lower part of her dress-waist and giving it a vigorous twist to the
right. Lisle thought this action the most mysterious and eccentric
one he had ever beheld, though he learned afterward, that her dress
waists always persisted in going away either to the right or left of
the centre of gravity, and were never, by any fatality, upright, pro-
erly behaved dress-waists.

"Melissy, stand aside and don't stare at Master Sterling so, and
he all strange like in the house!" called her mother, looking back
from the upper step which she had gained quite out of breath and
red in the face.

With a feeling of annoyance at encountering _girls_ everywhere, who
insulted him with pity, and were so aggravatingly protecting, Lisle
hurried on and was shown into his room.

"You see, sir, your trunk and all's here. Which it's a mere midge
of a trunk, too, to carry all a young gentleman's clothes and thing,
what with the brushes taking up so much room, and the bears-grease
always threatening to get broke. Supper's getting itself ready in
half an hour, sir," with which announcement she left him, no less
out of breath and quite as red in the face.

Much as Lisle had always wished to leave his own home, desperate
as were the resolutions he had many times formed to do so, and glad
as he was to have come with his uncle, it was with a failing heart
that he took in all the strangeness of his room, from the dimity curtains to the white wash bowl and pitcher, with the gay flowers
sprawling over them, and he really felt it quite awful to put a boy
into a bedroom with such articles of state staring him in the face.
Seating himself upon his trunk, he curled his feet up under him, and
made a deliberate survey of his new territory, at last deciding that a
boy _could_ sleep in such a room if he had never done so as yet: after
which conclusion he felt better in spirit. "Brushes and bears- rease"
he had none; but a pair of wooden pocket-combs put his hair in full
dress, after which con-ummation he wondered if he could find his

way down such a very crooked staircase, and whether he should
find the housekeeper's daughter still twisting herself on the step—
both of which results rewarding his efforts, he farther congratulated
himself upon having passed her with an air of perfect unconsciousness of her presence or existence, and rejoined his uncle in the parlor. He was reading the newspaper but just arrived, and did not
look up as Lisle came and took a seat near him.

"Humph—'mules steady'—intelligible that, when a man hasn't
seen the market price in two months. Suppose I've quite a crop, or
what do you call it, on hand now."

He was speaking of "the mule business," Lisle felt sure, though a
"crop" of them was no more intelligible to him than the who e
"business," but as these comments were not addressed to him', he
refrained from interruption. Mr. Fitzjames folded and laid up the
paper.

"Ha, ready for supper are you? Is your room comfortable?"

"Yes, sir, only too nice and—*grown-up like*—I'm sure it's very nice."

"Nothing sure about it unless Mrs. Drew looked after it herself.
When one has to trust to nigger agency, nothing is sure but aggravation. Every arrangement for comfort is slept out of memory. Use
the bell in your room liberally, for the house is full of servants; and
I shall delegate you an especial as soon as I get around to it. I
smell hot coffee from the dining-room, let's see to it."

Not only hot coffee, but an elegant supper, concluding with hot
biscuits, and honey, awaited them; and Mrs. Drew presided over the
whole, while her daughter was quite invisible; and Lisle's content
increased accordingly. The neat colored boy who served the table,
looked bright, and displayed his shining ivory unceasingly, and the
lamp threw its cheerful rays over the glittering service in a most
inspiring fashion, causing Lisle involuntarily to compare all this
with the noisy table at home, at which the children often quarreled
and the baby always cried, and the odor of the guttering tallow-
candle was anything but appetizing to one fastidious by nature and
ill-health, as he was. This was positive luxury in comparison!

"A miserable night this. The corn-fields must be flooded already.
Don't go into the blues, Lisle, things will brighten when this rain
stops," said Mr. Fitzjames, shoving back his chair, and observing
that Lisle had fallen into a reverie.

"Indeed, sir, I haven't thought of the blues! I was just thinking
how nice all this is. I don't mind the rain at all."

"Indeed, all the luckier for you. Now, sir, as I suppose you

don't smoke, just make yourself at home while I do so. The sooner
you feel yourself at home here, the better."

Drawing a chair near the light, Lisle opened his still unfinished
volume of "Nicholas Nickleby," and was soon lost to time and place,
only deliciously enjoying. the perfect quietude to which he had
hitherto been a stranger, and for which he had so often vainly
longed.

The large clock in the adjoining room struck ten, sending its
voice through the stillness with a distinct utterance, that roused
him through all his fascination over the life-like pages ; and looking
around at his uncle, he found him soundly sleeping in his arm-chair,
with spectacles still on duty, and the newspaper spread before him
as it had been when slumber overtook him. The sound of the
clock, and the malicious striking of Lisle's chair against the wall,
which it perpetrated quite on its own responsibility, awoke him ;
and rubbing his eyes, he said,

"I suddenly discovered that sleep was bearing down upon me,
but you seemed so much interested in your book, I didn't like to
disturb you by proposing ' bed time,' and so I kept on with the
paper, which, nevertheless, I see came over bottom end up at the
last turn I gave it. Bolt your bed-room door when you go to bed."

" Oh, I'm not afraid nights."

" Bolt it, all the same. It's a plantation custom whose reason you
will learn soon enough without being told. Good-night."

Wondering that such a caution should be given him in so quiet a
house, he nevertheless obeyed it, and soon ceased to think of anything connectedly, wandering pleasantly into the kingdom of
dreams, which, once having ensnared him, transported him back to
the mill-house and renewed the old-time persecutions and misery,
under which he remembered as a dream his domestication with his
uncle, and the hope of better things it had awakened in him, making the present life of trouble doubly dark by contrast.

The sound of the rising bell mingled first with his dreams, and
then came distinctly out of them, rousing him to waking consciousness, and as he bounded out of bed an unspeakable relief possessed
him. Here he was, after all, and better days were a fixed fact in
his existence. The rain had quite ceased, and the sun was shining
cheerily and warm, as if it had taken a contract on time of drying
the pools of water everywhere smiling complacently, and sparkling
saucily up at his beaming face.

In the field, all afloat from the many days rain, a herd of mules spattered and stamped about fretfully, laying back their huge ears in strong disapproval of the stinging flies, whose appetites seemed enormously sharpened by their long baths, and from the various grades and sizes thus fighting destiny in melancholy companionship, Lisle gleaned his initiation into the mysterious "mule business." They were raised for the market, and this was why his uncle had expressed his contempt for their being "steady." It was a very simple explanation of what had been so long a mystery, and he resolved to enlighten Eddy at once.

There was no one in the breakfast room yet, except Mrs. Drew, who was attending to the laying of the table; and strolling out upon the side gallery, he watched a flock of birds which twittered and chirruped around the yard, evidently complaining that their breakfast was all soaked, and not a bug to be seen. A plate of bread sat upon the breakfast table, Lisle remembered; and going back for a piece, he tossed it in crumbs among the hungry brood.

Unaffrighted at his presence, they gathered them with many chirruping thanks. They were in the height of their enjoyment, when, with a sudden spring, a grey cat, lurking unseen around the corner, pounced upon a lovely sparrow whose courage in never fleeing from the descending crumbs had rendered him an especial favorite with Lisle, and with a cry of pain and terror it was borne off as lawful prize, while its comrades flew frightened away.

With an expression of rage and sorrow, Lisle leaped the railing and gave chase to the cat, who, with her fluttering prey, had retreated to the kitchen, where, totally unapprehensive of any impending vengeance, she was surprised by a vigorous kick which doubled her up with a yell of disapprobation, after which she made the quickest cat time around the corner. The little bird lay in its last death flutter on the kitchen floor, and Lisle raised it pityingly, while a red drop trickled over its delicately tinted breast.

" Lawsee, Master Sterling; what a chicken heart you's got under your han'some face ! " grinned the cook, raising her reeking face over the gridiron.

'I'm not chicken-hearted at all, and I want that cat killed to-day ! Do you hear that ? "

" Lawsee, sir, yes, but dat ar cat belong to Miss Melissa, an' she set a heap by him. No nigga on de place dare to kill he, Master Lisle,—taint right, no way, to kill cats ! " ·

" See here : do you know the look of a two shilling piece ? "

" A what, sir ? "

" A two shilling piece," and he held up a quarter dollar.

" Bless ye,—ye means a two bi's! Yes, I knows him."

" Well take it, and if Melissa's cat don't come in sight again, recollect it's probably run away."

" I understands, young masser, and jes you mind, if de cat neber come round no more, old Phillis neber done heerd nuffin bout her at all,—yah, yah."

He met Melissa in the back hall as he went in, and thinking she might like the bird, he handed it to her, saving,

" Keep it if you think it pretty, and I'll show you how to stuff him so he'll look almost alive. He's a pretty fellow."

" I knows how to stuff him without none of your showing," she replied, grinning; and darting to the door, she called, " here, pu s, puss," and, before he had time to stop her, she had tossed the pretty creature to the cat who came round the corner mewing responsively.

" I stuffs 'em into the cat, I does," she said, putting her arms akimbo and spreading her hands over her hips as she watched the result, and heard its little frame crack under the old cat's cruel teeth.

" What an angel you are, and no mistake!" said Lisle ironically.

" Lord, there h'an't no good along a dead truck like that! I h'an't no white-faced picaninny, I h'an't! Lord, I brings that ere cat all the nests o' little young birds I finds She likes 'em best afore they's got feathers on 'em, they makes her breath sweet. She sleeps with me in the bed every night, puss does."

" A pretty pair of you! I don't envy either of you your company," and turning scornfully, he obeyed the summons of the breakfast bell.

Reassured that he had at last met one girl who would neither pity nor protect him, nor anything else, he was not well pleased with his *rara avis*. His seriousness was not observed, however, as Mrs. Drew herself seemed quite in a flutter this morning, and after various hesitating commencements, at last summoned courage and bolted into the subject which so disquieted her.

" I've something on my mind this day, Mr. Fitzjames, as is altogether upsetting to me, and dretful onexpected, which Lord knows! and I don't know whether or no you'll take kindly to it."

" Ah! then it concerns me, I suppose."

" Which it does after a fashion, being as this house is yours, sir, and not mine. I got a letter from my mother this morning, sir, which it was belated in not getting here two days ago, and the news which are in it are quite upsetting to me, as I said before."

"Well?" said Mr. Fitzjames inquiringly, as she had stopped again.

"If it please you, sir,—and for that matter if it don't," she added after an instant's deliberation, "my sister, which lived out West, has just gone home with fever, which it was typhoid, leaving one child as is an orfing; and being as there's no more relations left as belongs to it, more than me, and being as its grandmother, which is my own bles c l parent, is onable to do for it, as she's a tight squeak to do for herself, she's a bringing of it to me, sir, which is the truth."

"Why isn't it taken home with its mother, if she is able to hire it nursed there. It need not be exposed in any way to the disease."

"Which I was not speaking of any mortal home, Mr. Fitzj mes, but of the home beyond."

"Oh, she is dead? Well"—

"Which being as I'm to bring the child into your house, if at all, and you mightn't hanker after any more children in it, sir, perhaps you'd wish me to leave." .

"Not to be thought of for a moment, Mrs. Drew! I suppose you can keep it in the far end of the house if it's likely to howl all night and cut teeth all day?"

"Which it won't, sir, as, being as its eleven year and more, it's likely as its teeth is all over and done with."

"Well, then put it to sleep with Melissa, in the end room, and say no more about it."

"But, sir, which it don't seem altogether proper, being o' the age it is "—

"Oh, it's a boy is it!"

"Yes, sir, no doubt of it, as he's gone eleven," replied Mrs. Drew, a little assertively as if this were the first time any one had presumed to question it, and quite unobserving the fact that "*it*" gave no clue to sex.

"Oh, bother!" exclaimed Mr. Fitzjames in a tone of annoyance, "stow him away as you best can so that he won't be a nuisance—which. if he is an eleven year old boy, I don't see how it is to be accomplished," he added *sotto voce* as he left the room.

The wet ground without confined Mr. Fitzjames and Lisle to the house that day, so that they witnessed the arrival of the old la y and her grandson, which took place towards noon. Lisle could not altogether conceal a start of surprise and dislike as he thought the two looked familiar to him, and a second glance settled the conviction, which he expressed to his uncle.

"It's that awful, round-eyed, fat boy!"

"Why, so it is! A graceless young cub. Whew! this is worse than I thought!"

In fact no boy could have been more unwelcome to both uncle and nephew, and Lisle's fists clenched themselves involuntarily inside his pockets, as he watched the fat legs clambering down the wheel, guiltless of all knowledge that there were steps by which to descend. In his dirty hand was a large piece of something to eat, which he seemed to have divided impartially between his mouth, and his ears, towards which prominent organs a discolored, lumpy streak extended. Mrs. Drew came out to meet them with more cordiality than Lisle had anticipated from the morning's conversation, and Melissa stared from the step, vainly striving to make her dress-waist stay twisted to the right, while it as perversely insisted upon "dressing left."

"Melissy," called her mother, "let alone twisting of yourself and poking all the whalebones through—which whalebones cuts dresses all out—and come and kiss your relations. Here is your cousin Billy which you've never seen, and you nothing to say to him but a twisting yourself! That's your cousin Melissy, Billy. Won't you let her kiss you?"

"Lord, ma," grinned the young lady, "I don't see no place to kiss, unless its his weskit. He's smutier'n a hog, he is!"

"I don't care if I be; I shan't clean myself till I'm done my sweet-cake, nor then nither, for you," retorted the fat boy, reburying his face in the cake, and smacking his lips audibly.

"Laws," snickered Melissa again. "What a little hog it is, and *so* mannerly!"

Billy drew suddenly near, and for all reply plunged an avenging fist into the pit of her unsuspecting stomach, which caused her to double herself suggestively and retreat, while, whiping his fingers upon his pantaloons after the blow, and snuffing as usual, he crammed another mouthful into his puffy face.

Lisle looked on through the window, with a muttered "dog eat dog," and Mr. Fitzjames laughed, "An amiable pair, truly! No, I don't 'hanker after any more' in the house, as Mrs. Drew suggested."

For a few days no encounter took place between Lisle and the fat boy; for, with the over-strained *regime* usual among females who resolve to bring up a model boy, Mrs. Drew never suffered him from her sight, but kept him sewing pieces for a bed-quilt, this having been the employment of her own juvenile hours, and having, as she remarked more than once, "made an industrious, excellent woman of her." Whether or not Billy took kindly to his needle, Lisle had not yet seen him out of its company and that of the superintending Mrs. Drew, and began to hope he never should. But the old lady took her departure one day, and Mrs. Drew having driven her out to the city, Billy escaped from thraldom.

Lisle was walking in the garden when he first saw Billy approaching in the same path, and scorning any appearance of intentional avoidance, he proceeded, and they met face to face.

"So," exclaimed Billy, "you're the chicken-hearted young chap Melitia tells so much about, are you? Thought I knowd you, 'tother day, when I see you strutting out here by yerself. Ef it wasn't that you're the master's nevvy I'd ker-wallop you till you'd quit lording it around here! I an't forgot, I an't, how you jabbed me with your fork at that ere grub-shop by the railroad, coming down here! but as gran'mam says, if I get turned out o' here I'll have to go to the alms-house, do you say 'friends,' or 'not friends?' Jes say which."

"You'd better go back to your patch-work. I don't make friends with such boys as you. Get out of the path."

"Ef I han't as good as you be, what made you jab your fork into me! If you didn't mean to make friends with me, you needn't a begun the acquaintance. Nobody axed you to."

"I want to go past; will you get out of the path?"

"No, I won't, as long as I've got fists as will help me stay in it, alms-house or no alms-house. Come, now!"

"Then I'll set you the example of a gentleman," said Lisle bowing composedly and stepping one side.

"And you han't going to fight for it?" asked Billy wonderingly.

"Not with a little animal like you. I don't fight with any but my equals," and he walked away while the fat boy looked after him with eyes rounder than ever.

"Ki yi," shouted Melissa from the security of an upper window, "you done cotched it that time, smart as you think yourself! Lord, don't ye look wamble cropped!"

Billy sauntered off, feeling that he was on strange ground with a boy who despised him too much to fight with him for even his rights, and soon was still farther cowed by coming full upon Mr. Fitzjames, who, unseen by both boys, had witnessed their encounter. He laid a heavy hand upon Billy's shoulder, and said sternly,

"Now, see here, youngster, just understand, once for all, that I'll have none of your bullying here. When you meet Master Sterling,

no matter where, nor who else sees you,—raise your hat to him, and
treat him as a young gentleman and my nephew should be treated.
Don't you let me hear of your forcing yourself upon him again in
this manner, or I'll take you in hand, sir."

Billy rubbed his eyes with his dirty fists, and began to whimper,
and Melissa, who had listened to every word, suddenly conceived
an immense respect for Master Lisle, whom Mr. Fitzjames must intend should become his heir, or he never would treat him in this
way; and forthwith she unplaited what remained of the frowzed out
braids of her towey hair, bringing some lard from the kitchen, to
aid the smoothing process, and excepting two snarls behind her ears,
which wouldn't comb out, the whole was more neatly braided, and
put dangling down her back afresh; and she twisted her outer girl
before the glass, for a full half hour, in a last tearful effort to come
straight, after which she sought many expedients to keep as much
in his sight as possible.

Had Lisle dreamed himself the object at which all this care was
aimed, it is probable that some overt act of contempt would have
aroused her enmity at once; but he really thought nothing of it,
nor ever seemed to notice her, however closely he was sometimes
compelled to pass by her, and since the bird-stuffing scene, he had
never once spoken to her. Strange as it was, this deportment only
had raised him in her estimation, and though she shrewdly suspected that he might explain the sudden disappearance of her cat,
and felt that her studies in the science of ornithology were henceforth a dead letter, she held her peace under it, and only queried
how she could conquer the contempt he had ever since exhibited
towards her.

CHAPTER VIII.

In due time, the tutor spoken of by Mr. Fitzjames, arrived; a plausible, self-possessed, rather too handsome young gentleman, Lisle thought; but personal comeliness is a fault easily overlooked, circumstances being not extremely unpropitious; and Louis Hartley soon quite captivated the hearts of the household. Indeed it proved that he was far advanced in its good graces long before thus having domesticated himself as tutor in it, and Mrs. Drew improved the earliest occasion to put Lisle *au fait* in his history.

"It mayn't be just proper that I should give you all the facts in the case," said that conscientious, but rather gossiping lady, "but being as you are Mr. Fitzjames' blood relation, which Mr. Louis is not, being as he had a narrow escape of it, I don't see any harm in it, but to the contra*iry*. Which, then, Mr. Louis being a son of a before-time sweetheart of your uncle, and so being in a way your own cousin, which he might easily have been, he oughtn't to be strange like to you, ought he now?"

"I really don't understand, Mrs. Drew."

"Which I'm going on to tell you, my dear, as Mr. Louis is the oldest son of a lady as your uncle would surely have married lawful, —yes, he'd a done it lawful and honorable—if circumstances hadn't gone the wrong way, as they always does in matermonial cases. Which your uncle at that time being poor but gentlemanly, which gentlemanly he now is, but as to being poor is quite to the contra*iry*-wise, it wasn't to be thought of by her parents; the more so which she being at that time an engaged person,—which his name was, and is, Hartley, as is his son's likewise,—it seemed not right she should recall her vows and promises, but Lord, what is a woman's vows and promises? and so Miss Mary thought, which her parents thought, Mr. Hartley was well to do, and probably a reckoning on her, and so she was obedient to them and married him, though it was no secret as she loved your uncle best, which well he knowed it, poor man! Your uncle danced at the wedding, and

kissed the bride, which he had often kissed before, and she not unwilling, but to the contrairy, and Mr. and Mrs. Hartley was reckoned
a splendid pair of matermonials by them as looked only at the outside. But ill luck being his fortune, a year or two afterwards,
which some of his steamers got snagged in the river, and one was
a-burned, Mr. Hartley took poor, and what with children coming on
him thick and plenty, and Mrs. Hartley being amost always complaining, though she never murmured, poor dear, the property went
to the dogs, and it's well beknowst as they had right smart help
from your uncle, first and last; which he had grown rich as they
grew poor, and he went to her funeral at last as second mourner,
which he ought to have been first by good rights."

"But if the lady was engaged before she knew my uncle?" suggested Lisle inquiringly.

"Which as I said before, what's a woman's vows and promises,
matermonially speaking! Which the poor dears themselves never
considers in the least binding on 'em when they've changed their
minds for another, thank God! Howsoever, Mrs. Hartley died, and
dead she is; and your uncle, of the goodness which is in him, sent
Master Louis, as is the oldest child—and which being born the first
year less two months, is in a manner related to him more than them
as came after, and when he had made up his mind that thus it was
and thus it was to be—to school for a right smart o' time, and then
to college, 'to help him to make his way in life,' which he said, and
being as Mr. Louis hankers after tutoring, tutor he is, and what more
nateral than to Mr. Fitzjames own nevvy?"

"I wonder my uncle does not adopt him, instead."

"Which he thinks it better the young gentleman should depend
upon himself a little, being as them as lives on expectations of what
is coming to them, is generally most ongrateful, if not quite ruinated,
but who knows how much he'll have left to him, nevertheless?
Being, too, as Mr. Fitzjames now has blood relations—which he
might a had all this time unbeknowst to me, dear knows—it an't
just likely he'll leave Mr. Louis all I once expected would go to him.
I've my own ideas, of late; but it an't my place to mention 'em,
leastways he mightn't like it of me, which maybe I've said too much
already, though I only know what I know, and not along of him.
Leastways I wouldn't like which he should know it, sir."

"I shan't allude to it, of course; but I don't want to hear anything
he wouldn't like me to know."

"Laws, but you're different from your neighbors, then! Howsoever, as you are but young now, it's likely you'll think quite to the contrairy as you grow up. Most people set; great store by all they learns as them as it concerns most wishes they shouldn't ever suspect, and I've known people which was most onbearable in all other ways you could mention, hold a high place in society as wouldn't in no other way seem to notice 'em, only for the things they knew as they had no business to know. Howsoever, this as I've told you about your uncle is in no way injuresome to him, but on the contrairy quite to his credit, and it's much to be hoped as Mr. Louis will make out good in the world, which some way tutoring doesn't come up to Mr. Fitzjames' expectations of him, and no wonder!"

Mrs. Drew breathed a long sigh and looked absently out the window, and concluding that her narrative was now complete, Lisle left her, filled with wonder that his uncle should have lived this romantic episode, and shrewdly conjecturing that it accounted for his remaining a bachelor all these years. If he did not accept the laws of relationship quite as liberally as Mrs. Drew, he certainly did feel a more genial, hearty liking for his tutor, since learning how especial an object of his uncle's care he had always been, and resolutely closed his eyes to any short-comings or imperfections in that young gentleman's character, loth as he had been sometimes to fancy that some such existed. Mr. Louis might have his own reasons for an occasional moodiness and seeming lack of candor; doubtless he had, thus dependent upon another's generosity for even the means of earning his livelihood; and Lisle felt that it was not for him to comment even mentally upon it, but rather to become his friend as well as pupil.

So the first year passed very pleasantly, during which Lisle made rapid strides in the field of knowledge, and became more than ever his uncle's friend and companion. Lisle could not fail to see that young Hartley in many ways pained and disappointed his benefactor, and he was more pained than pleased that he himself was often turned to as one who in some way compensated for that other's deficiencies. Not that Hartley was markedly deficient in any overt way, nor openly at discord with anything around him, but a certain undefinable something wanting in his character, for which Mr. Fitzjames vainly hoped and waited, brought a shadow to his brow which was echoed in an audible sigh, when, at the close of this year Hartley suddenly departed without having asked leave or even expressed the intention, and without any explanation save what was contained in a brief note left for Mr. Fitzjames, in which he stated

that a sudden emergency called him. Welcome as he was to any
number of holidays for which he might choose to ask, it was evident
that he had thus claimed one to avoid any possible questions as to
its cause, and while Mr. Fitzjames would have asked none had the
opportunity been offered him, he could not refrain from wondering
at the reason for all this strategy. What was the secret thus im-
pelling the child of his paternal care to distrust him ? What object
could there be in the life of the boy he had reared almost as his own
son, which he would not cheerfully advance by every means within
his power ?

The old gentleman was more grieved than offended; but with a
gentlemanly tolerance rare in one of his age, he received young
Hartley upon his return as though he had departed with a due ob-
servance of all forms and courtesies, and waited patiently for the
time when the confidence he longed for might be voluntarily given
him. However, two years more, which passed quickly away, brought
neither this confidence, nor a repetition of the offence which had
caused Mr. Fitzjames so much uneasiness, and, his own trust in
Hartley thus restored, he concluded this one *escapade* was doubtlessly
connected with the finale of some college embarrassment, probably
a pecuniary one, and satisfied that if he had been so imprudent as
to incur debts, he had improved the first legitimate opportunity to
discharge them, Mr. Fitzjames made no comments which might embarrass him; but meantime increased his salary to one which he
thought commensurate with any possible arrears. Determined to encourage no feeling of dissatisfaction with Hartley, he easily persuaded
himself that there existed no real cause for any, and silently rebuked
his yearning for a more complete interchange of affection as the usual
tyranny of the aged toward the young. Even now he was scarcely
twenty-three years of age, and few were those among Mr. Fitzjames'
acquaintances who were as irreproachably sedate and reliable. That
he was so quiet beyond his years, had doubtless been the very reason his benefactor had expected too much of him, and he generously
determined he would do so no more.

Four years passed over Lisle's head, and he was now nearly nineteen years of age. No pains had been spared by his uncle to improve
him both physically and mentally, and he felt well repaid as he noted
the result. The sickly, sensitive boy had given place to the spirited,
energetic, self-possessed youth whose very features had changed in
unison, and if not positively handsome, he possessed a fine, manly

figure, and a face whose intelligence and dignity of expression amply compensated for any irregularity of outline. Enough of his natural reserve still clung to him to render him usually silent unless expressly drawn into conversation, and a tinge of the misanthropy inseparable from such a life as his, with its ever present shadow clouding his heart, often colored his remarks even when most genial.

Occasional letters from Mrs. Sterling to her brother, had duly inquired after the welfare of her "little boy," but neither of them had deemed it necessary to inform her that he was a little boy no more, and nothing had ever been said relative to his return to the paternal roof. Mr. Fitzjames was as heartily glad of this as was Lisle himself, since it avoided the necessity for the one to prefer any request which might possibly be denied in pure malice, and the other from an open revolt against a government to which he had vowed never more to yield allegiance.

Lisle was now at an age when his business occupation should be decided upon, and his uncle often essayed to surprise him into some expressed predilection upon which he might found his preparations. But one thought kept him mute. The business he would have chosen, required capital, and how could he thus ask more where so much had already been done for him! It was but slightly improving upon it to request as a loan, that which, should he be unsuccessful, as many an earnest struggler always has been, he could not repay.

Still, the impatience he felt to be doing something for himself, left no course open but one of plain speaking, and he frankly explained his difficulty. The old gentleman smiled with pride and satisfaction.

" I knew that something of this kind troubled you, and it is just what I should expect from your head and your heart, but as it seems you haven't a talent for wood-cutting, black-smithing, or any of those non-capital requiring professions, we must just choose another. I didn't bring you up to become that polite vagabond, a gentleman, with no business calling, and if you wont *preach*, or *physic*, I can't in any way be disappointed in you. Disputatious vagabonds are as bad as idle ones, if not worse, and preachers and physic givers are death upon all creeds but their own. I've a mind to open a commission house in the city, and make you and Hartley my partners; I to advance the necessary capital, and you to do the work. I was speaking with him about it only the other day."

" A mode of doing business which reminds me how I used to pocket my chestnut winnings 'when I was young,'" laughed Lisle. "Edly used to represent the whole stock in trade, and I borrowed a certain number of him with which to commence operations, a siege of 'odd and even' usually yielding me the whole, out of which I conscientiously repaid him the loan."

"Why, man alive, I don't propose to let you fleece *me* in that style, you know! Our joint operations are to be directed towards outsiders. This is a game of 'odd and even' in which nothing is to be tweaked out of me, and of course I expect to get my capital back, or I shouldn't advance it, would I?"

Lisle thought this a very doubtful proposition; but Mr. Fitzjames preferred basing all his pecuniary kindnesses upon an apparently selfish object, and shunned a "thank you" in every possible manner, thinking it, in all sincerity, an unjust penalty for a kindness conferred in pure benevolence. So the co-partnership was looked upon as a settled fact, and the household adjourned to a home in the city, over which Mrs. Drew presided as an indispensable adjunct, and Melissa and the lazy, overgrown Billy, were tolerated as necessary evils. In vain had the fat boy been variously located, and, Mr. Fitzjames hoped, disposed of, his chief accomplishment, an improved talent for getting into rows, kept him ever vibrating from place to place, diversified only by the calaboose; till concluding that his presence was preferable to the continual complaints of his employers, Mr. Fitzjames resigned himself to his domiciling under his roof, and had no expectation of ever relieving himself of him except by willing and bequeathing him with the estate.

The busy life which now surrounded them had for the two young gentleman an irresistible charm; and quite giving up the quietude and early hours so prized by most elderly gentlemen, Mr. Fitzjames accompanied them among the gay scenes by which they were so fascinated, introducing them to his large circle of acquaintances, among whom they soon became popular, not less upon their own individual merits than the *prestige* they enjoyed as the probable heirs of a handsome fortune.

Well had it been had this gloss never worn off the fair face of society! But familiarity with it, in time taught Lisle, especially how little sincerity lay beneath, and embittered by his own self-knowledge, and the thought how differently this same smiling society would treat him were it aware of all he knew of himself, the vein of misanthropy underlying his character rose oftener to the surface, and his uncle observed, with pain, that he always seemed searching

for some hidden motive in the conduct of those around him, which
not unfrequently wounded some innocent object of his suspicion.
From hating the world, a misanthrope soon comes to hate himself,
if, indeed, that be not the first step ; and Mr. Fitzjames did not over-
estimate the effect of *personal pride* upon a man's worldly success.
Every other essential to such success, Lisle certainly possessed, and
his industry, and devotion to his business won him the confidence
of business men, who are not averse to mere human machines if well
kept in order. Fathers pronounced him " a good reliable beau for
the girls, though a little too severe and sarcastic to be very popular," and brothers liked him when he was genial, and bore with and
excused him when he was not. Young ladies pronounced him "an
awfully provoking fellow," and were sensible that they were often
entrapped into displaying their real characters and dispositions instead of the ones manufactured for the occasion, and himself in
particular, but he was too eligible to be neglected, nevertheless, and
so remained a favorite.

So affairs glided smoothly and successfully on, till a sudden and
peremptory call homeward, reached him.

Dr. Kelley, feeling that his last illness was upon him, begged to
see him once more ; and amid conflicting emotions he obeyed the
summons. Had not Mr. Fitzjames made it a rule of his life never to
volunteer remarks upon subjects not particularly concerning himself, he would have given some expression to the surprise with
which he heard this announcement, a surprise equalled only by that
with which he saw Lisle prepare to leave his business, just now unusually active, without once seeming to question the possibility of
offering any excuse in his own stead. During all Mr. Fitzjames'
acquaintance with him, this was the first exhibition of any unusually
strong regard for him he had ever witnessed upon the part of any
one, and least of all had he suspected its existence in the heart of
Dr. Kelley, whose letters during Lisle's domestication with himself
had been too unfrequent to attract any attention as indicating a
particular affection.

It was not singular that this apparently late coming regard man-
ifesting itself only in the death hour, should excite Mr. Fitzjames'
surprise, but he did not in any way express it, and only prepared
to himself fill his place during an absence which was indefinite.

Hartley, upon the contrary, gave full vent to his curiosity, and
asked the same questions as many times over as they were skillfully
evaded, till, suspecting—what, he could not exactly have defined—

he kept a stealthy watch upon all Lisle's movements, which became too aggravating to be borne with inward complacency, though Lisle resolutely restrained the often sarcastic rebuke which rose to his lips.

"I'll wager the fortune I expect to make, that you are anticipating a legacy, for all you look so humble and self-righteous ! Lord grant it may be a fat one !" had been Hartley's half laughing, half sincere ejaculation as he shook Lisle's hand at parting.

A legacy ! Yes, one of shame and sorrow, bequeathed by no formal " Will and Testament," which the world might acknowledge ; but a gift which had been his curse from the very threshold of life ; a legacy of a blighted existence whose blossoms were distrust and misanthropy, whose fruit was humiliation and bitter sorrow ! How it was that he did not hate this man for all he had imposed upon him, why he did not curse him from his embittered life, Lisle could not himself decide. Yet often as such feelings arose within him, they were calmed and conquered by the memory of his childhood's days when this man had been his only friend, his kind words and endearments the only blessings of his life. Recollections of his sometimes ineffable tenderness, under which his face softened and glowed with an almost heavenly beauty—of caressing arms which had pressed him to a breast audibly throbbing its love for him—of the ever kind smile and protecting care when he had needed them—all these crowded upon his memory, and pressed back the bitter thoughts in very shame ! Despite all he had suffered, despite the apprehension with which he looked at the future, whose possible revelations might far exceed in humiliation anything he had yet endured, Lisle loved him unconquerably.

Whatever wrongs he suffered had not been intentionally inflicted upon him by this man, at least, who, he felt assured, had suffered scarcely less than he, and though he did not forgive him as the author of his existence, he almost felt that even this was a boon compared to receiving it from the illiterate, narrow-minded, selfish man whom the world called and believed his father.

All these conflicting emotions bore him company upon his journey ; and people wondered at the reserve and silence thus hedging from all chance companionship so young a man, whose brow was at moments seamed with the lines of age.

CHAPTER IX.

IT was a raw spring day, and the twilight was spreading cold and gray when Lisle arrived in his native town, now a station upon one of the many railways intersecting the State; and he looked a second time before quite recognizing his precise location. The old landmarks were soon found, however, and a few moments brought him to Dr. Kelley's door. His ring was answered by Mrs. Kelley herself, who did not recognize the tall figure standing in the uncertain light, nor the voice which, to test her, inquired quietly for the doctor. Mrs. Kelley hesitated, looked again, and then asked,

"What name, sir? The doctor is so ill that he receives none but his most intimate friends."

"Mrs. Kelley, is it possible you do not recognize me!" exclaimed Lisle stepping forward. "I must have changed much more than you have done."

"Lisle Sterling, is it possible!" cried Mrs. Kelley, embracing him warmly, while he returned her caress with the grateful consciousness that absence and time had left her affection for him unimpaired. Had she only been his mother! he mentally ejaculated as he kissed again the kind face beaming into his own. Hers had been the only maternal care he had ever received, hers the thoughtful affection that had thrown some rays of sunshine over even his thorny path, at such times as he could escape his own miserable home and find refuge in hers. Every scheme the doctor had planned for his benefit had been most fully seconded and carried out by her, and he knew that this friendship and care had been equally bestowed upon Eddy, after his own departure. He had been duly apprised that he had become the doctor's pupil, and that from his purse were derived the funds which enabled him to attend the necessary course of lectures to fit him for a physician; upon which subject Edward had poured out a torrent of wordy bitterness over his father's stinginess, in which he accused him of having brought him into a world in which he now begrudged him the means of making a living. Lislo had read his brother's indignant outpouring with feelings scarcely less strong, and, later, had blushed for very shame when he learned that the doctor himself had added this charity to his other benefits.

All this passed rapidly through Lisle's mind as he looked upon the loving face of his more than mother, thinking it the only one he had ever beheld whose every line was goodness.

"And now," she said, at last recalled to the of cares the present, "I must go and tell the doctor you are here. He has for some reason seemed very apprehensive that you would not come. Of course there can be but little here likely to prove pleasant to you from association, but thank Heaven those miserable days are gone forever. In this house, which you must make your home, I hope there linger no unhappy memories. I have always wished you were my own son, and I know the doctor wishes it no less. How glad he will be to see you!"

Lisle awaited her return, imagining how the announcement of his presence there would be received by the doctor, and feeling more than ever his anomalous position under that roof; but he had brief space for such meditations, as Mrs. Kelley returned almost immediately, and showing him to the doctor's room, softly pushed him in and closed the door, feeling instinctively that they would prefer being left alone.

No one interrupted the long interview that followed, nor were any remarks made upon it, Mrs. Kelley feeling more than contented that the doctor was calmer and happier after it, hanging upon Lisle's words with an all-absorbing devotion, and becoming restless if he were ever absent, while Lisle repaid this affection by a thoughtful care and tenderness rivalling Mrs. Kelley's own, and shared her vigils unceasingly.

As for the doctor, he felt that this was the one tribute of respect or affection he had ever received which did not stigmatize him as a hypocrite, and he prized and revelled in it accordingly. Had Mrs. Sterling been other than she was; had she won her son's affection by performing even a mother's *duty* to him; had he for any reason loved her more, he must have loved the doctor less; but since he could remember anything, she had been harsh and unkind towards him, and all he had known of anything approaching parental care had been bestowed upon him by the doctor, who at least loved him as a father, if he could not claim the title. Feeling that the time had now arrived when common justice to himself impelled him to a plain, unvarnished history of his former relationship towards Lydia

Fitzjames, the doctor gave it; and while not attempting to deny his own wrong doing, much appeared in extenuation of his fault. That he had been the too easy victim of a designing, conscienceless woman, was only too evident—generously as he spoke of her when the story was ended, and plead her wifely duty so faithfully performed toward the uncongenial husband she had married in extenuation of the errors of her unmarried life.

But one torturing foreboding oppressed Lisle's thoughts by day, and haunted his pillow by night. Weakened in mind by his illness, and shrinking from carrying his secret unconfessed to the grave, Dr. Kelley longed to express his penitence and remorse to Mr. Sterling, and seek his forgiveness for the part he had acted towards him. Time and again the subject was discussed between them, Lisle's forcible reasoning against it satisfying him only for the time. In vain he acknowledged the domestic misery it must inflict, perhaps even causing a separation between Mr. Sterling and his wife after these years, for which the world would demand the excuse; one day silenced by all this, the next it lost force; and the only restraining influence exercised over him was Lisle's sensitive shrinking from the position it would place him in towards an unjust world who would jeer at him to the very portals of the grave, as though he himself were guilty under the stain put upon him by the sin of others.

The philosophy which had reconciled him to being the illegitimate son of a talented gentleman rather than the honorably-born boor of a vulgar, illiterate father, paled and died out under a penalty thus heavy. Such philosophy is attainable by a proud man only under the world's ignorance of the fact; and Lisle plead this so forcibly that the doctor apparently yielded the point, and he hoped all would yet be well. ·

Even Mrs. Kelley remained in ignorance of this secret which had so long lain buried in her husband's heart, and he shrank from telling it to her after all these years of silence. Most men easily reconcile themselves to the idea that it is useless, if not cruel, to reveal to their wives anything which they will not be the happier for knowing; and had the doctor's conscience been as much at rest toward his fellow-man, Lisle would have felt at ease.

Several days elapsed before Lisle turned his steps homeward—alas! a spot less homelike for him than any the wide world contained beside; and only then in dread of gossiping tongues. Feeling, at length, that it could be postponed no longer, he summoned

Edward to help him bear his cross, and the two sat out upon the inevitable visit, scarcely less distasteful to one than the other of them. It seemed a natural penalty that Mrs. Sterling should have forfeited and forever lost the affection of the one child whom she idolized, by the very injustice she heaped upon the unloved one— a penalty whose keenest sting was derived from her own knowledge that it was precisely thus she had incurred it. Despite the fond partiality she had openly displayed for Edward from his very cradle, he despised her for her very cruelty to his brother, even as that brother had declared his own open enmity! Few ever confess the justice of their punishments, and Mrs. Sterling cried out that she was an injured mother.

During his childhood, the scriptural bear story had failed to make any satisfactory impression upon his sensibilities, though often impressively related by his father; and as he grew older, he with wilful perversity insisted that the prophet was more blame-deserving than the spirited children, and pronounced him "a wicked, malicious old hunks," much to his father's holy horror. Nor did any amount of clerical lecturing at all mitigate this opinion, he avowing in the very clergyman's teeth that a fellow who couldn't take a joke from a few brats was no man at all! If not a prodigal, he was an undutiful son; and he had heard it so many times declared, that he shunned the paternal roof persistently.

It was perhaps the legitimate effect of so many years' separation, that a feeling of constraint had grown up between the brothers, loving each other as they always had done; and each had seen and battled with it but half successfully, as they mutually felt now that they were reunited.

Not that there was any change noticeable to others—far from it. But each felt that invisible barrier springing up between the closest friends during years of absence, and individual cares unshared by the other. Had Lisle returned with the same *physique*, so demanding protection and championship, he would have seemed to Edward the very same brother, and his heart and fists would have been laid a free offering before him; but he smiled at the very idea of protecting the dignified, handsome young man at least a head taller than himself, whose very appearance was a sufficient insurance against any insult or attempt at oppression; and as if in continuation of the thought, he asked, as they rode toward the mill-house,

"What do you suppose the old lady will say of your rather imposing appearance?"

"It is a matter of indifference to me, I assure you. I was at this identical moment rejoicing that I'm now too large to be ' whipped out of my skin.' Almost as large as that marvellous 'Mount Tom' which looms up in so many old women's imaginations when about to perform a disagreeable duty with alacrity. ' I'd whip you if you were as big as Mount Tom!' Do you remember ? "

"*Remember ?* Yes, more than I wish I did. I declare it's hard when a fellow can't drum up even a decent amount of regard for his own parents, isn't it ? One ought to have at least a rag of filial respect left him."

"Those are very fortunate who have. I don't know though but its absence is a curse inflicted upon each new generation; for I know our parents were in a very similar position towards their own. It's enough to make all men and *some women* vow themselves to celibacy, if only to escape becoming ' the old folks' themselves."

"Yes, one might look for something of the kind in men; but women, as they take it, were made for matrimony, instead of matrimony being invented for them—a transposition of the affair like unto the Puritan idea of the Sabbath, but twice as fruitful of trouble. However, it's deuced lucky for them that take to it so kindly."

"It may be lucky—*I dinna ken*—I only know that it's vastly disagreeable to a fellow when forced to understand that he is the intended victim of some matrimonially-inclined feminine taking kindly to it."

"Really, now, Lisle, is that meant as an insinuation that you often suffer in that way ? I'm thankful that I'm not fascinating."

Lisle colored under the raillery, but made no reply; and, repenting the insinuation conveyed in it, Edward said, apologetically,

"Now, Lisle, don't imagine that I meant to dub you a puppy or an imaginary 'lady killer;' but you are handsome and all that, and you must know it, so what's the use of making any bones about it. Any woman in a thoughtful humor, will confess that she fancies a good-looking man, and is less apt to feel her own ' a congenial spirit' with that inhabiting an ugly man's carcass. I'd be jealous of you myself, were it not a shame to enter the lists against my own brother; and of course Julie can't see plain, unpretending me behind your more imposing shadow."

"Julie Kelley ? "

"Yes, why not ? Do you pretend to say that you haven't

observed the admiration she looks, acts, and all but speaks, every time you come near her? "

" Why, Julie is a mere child."

" Something more than sixteen, wh'ch many a woman considers sufficiently aged for matrimonial speculations, as our grandmother could testify."

" Yes, but age depends less upon the number of actual years than many people suppose; and Julie is a child despite her sixteen of them. Not over-burdened with intellect, either, I imagine."

" Lisle," asked his brother, with some vexation, " do you never see anything praiseworthy in anything or any one ? "

" Not much, I must confess, always excepting a *very* few."

" Well; if a young lady is pretty, does it effectually prevent her being anything more."

" Quite the contrary; she is very apt to be artful in due proportion."

" Then what, in your estimation, may an ugly one become ?"

" Spiteful and malicious, to a certainty, nine times in ten, and in the tenth one so unbearably sensitive about her personal plainness, that she is equally as uncomfortable for a companion."

Edward laughed, but Lisle looked as though he wondered at what.

" Then do tell me, Lisle, since men must marry these imperfect creatures, which would you advise him to endure ?"

" Neither, as long as he can avoid it. All fools marry, and now and then a wise man takes leave of his senses and comfort in the same way. My theory is, that if we did nothing in the premises, such of us as are pre-doomed to matrimony would in due time find a double hitched to him, or perhaps take it in the natural way, like measles, and whooping cough, or absorb it in his vaccination, which certainly would have this consolation—that a man wasn't to blame for the misfortune."

Again Edward laughed, this time a little provoked, but Lisle's face, so far from wearing a smile, looked actually bitter, and mentally pronouncing him a strange fellow, Edward did not pursue the topic, and the mill-house soon was within sight, changing the current of their thoughts.

" Does it look natural ?" asked Edward with a faint sigh.

" Painfully so. My very toes tingle now, in memory of the cold which used to tweak them during those long slow rides up from town after the Sunday sermons when it looked ungodly to drive fast, and my jacket itches again under the recollection of the flog-

ging sure to succeed the dismal day, as the old lady's arm always
pined for its customary exercise after such a season of inaction.
Really, Ed, it's no shame to speak the truth at all times—Washing-
ton did—so I outrightly affirm that that old lady up there on the
hill, has more of the very evil one under her silly exterior, than ten
smarter women ever had! Her very shallowness only makes a better
cloak to screen his Satanic Majesty, never for one hour out of her.
Did you ever see such a head as she has, really *long*, almost to deformity?"

"Did *you* ever see a gray-eyed person, male or female, who had
not naturally the very spirit of evil in them? A *good* person with
gray eyes, must verily have triumphed over ' the world, the flesh,
and the devil!' (Dashed if there isn't a little of my catechism! I'd
no idea any of it ever struck in!) It's the strangest thing in life to
me how father ever happened to marry any one—above all, her.
They're as antagonistic as possible. Can you account for it?"

"Most marriages defy all human calculation, and if human calculation were ' a saving grace,' few or none would be perpetrated. The
truth was in this case, though, that she wanted a home and *didn't*
want to be an old maid, which she was near being, and he wanted
some one to look after his crazy old mother. He married a housekeeper and maid of all work, and she married a liquidator of bills
—though, for that matter, few husbands contrive to pay fewer. I
don't believe he ever bought twenty dollars' worth of dry-goods for
her in one year, since she took an altar contract to patch his old
breeches!"

"Do you recollect she always pronounced the Sterlings ' a race of
skin-flints!' (I'd like to see that surgical operation performed), but,
after all, if a woman can't be frank and confidential with her own
husband, to whom shall she pour out her trustful revealings?"

The two brothers indulged in a quiet laugh as they left the carriage
at the gate, and casting a furtive glance toward the house, saw Mrs.
Sterling at the window, as they anticipated, peeping at the new
arrivals, and directly the sound of a hurrying broom, and farther
audible evidence of stray articles tossed hither and thither and
slammed out of sight by conveniently ' on duty' doors, proved that
company was recognized as a forthcoming fact, one at least of whom
was a stranger, for whom things should be put to rights.

"Natural as life!" exclaimed Lisle in recollection of many similar
scenes in which he had contributed his mite of assistance, and Edward nodded and laughed.

"Human nature, the world over, 'puts the best foot foremost,' willing to pass, unblushingly, for a trifle more than circumstances warrant. By the way, who make all the proverbs ?"

"Difficult to say, but the Chinese are credited with one which suits me : 'May I never appear in another life under the form of a woman or a jackall.' Now I think of it, this may be a prayer, but 'nobody here knowing any prayers,' as they say in the Legislature, the mistake doesn't need correction."

As they advanced up the path, Mrs. Sterling threw open the door, exclaiming,

"Why, Edward, my son, is this you ?"

"I'm not at all certain upon that point, but a wise mother knows her own son, I suppose."

"Strange if she didn't !" ejaculated Mrs. Sterling.

"How do you do, mother?" asked Lisle extending his hand not over cordially.

"Why, Lisle Sterling, is that really you ?" exclaimed his mother looking at him more closely, and but half recognizing him yet.

"Strange if she didn't !" retorted Edward laughingly, and thus reassured, she embraced him with much feigned affection, kissing his cheek as she did so. Neither the embrace nor the kiss were returned, nor altogether endured with fortitude. Mrs. Sterling was quick to perceive this fact, politely as it was veiled ; but her duplicity prevented her betraying that she did note it, and she continued reproachfully,

"And never once to write us that you were coming to see us ! Well, such surprises are always pleasant, and I suppose you knew it."

"The fact is, that I intended nothing of the kind. I came suddenly, and to myself quite unexpectedly, as I was sent for."

"I was in hopes you had come home to try and retrieve your credit. You know you didn't go away under the best of circumstances, and it has always been my prayer that you might come to see the error of your ways, and repent. But I forgive you, even while your heart is unsoftened. I suppose Dr. Kelley sent for you. How long have you been here ?"

"About five minutes, I should judge, and you haven't yet asked me to be seated, nor called your liege lord."

"Why so I han't ! Do sit down, and I'll send at once. So it *was* Dr. Kelley that sent for you, was it ? Just like him ! He always took an interest in you."

"That is what few others ever did, then. Is father at the mill ?"

"Yes, I guess so. Nell, run to the mill and tell your father the boys have come; both of 'em."

A shy young girl who had been making observations from behind the screen of a half open door, slipped out and darted swiftly away, and Mrs. Sterling, after a moment's criticism of Lisle's appearance, said,

"Bless me, Lisle, how you have grown; a fine gentleman with moustache and all! You must be about as tall as your father now. Don't you think he's just about your father's size, Edward?"

"He's as big as 'Mount Tom,' now, isn't he, mother?"

"Edward, it's right ungrateful of you to twit me as you always do. I never whipped any of my children much, for I never did approve of whipping, though I sometimes think now that it might have been better if I had."

"Then thank the Lord you have sinned away your day of grace! There never lived the woman who thought she had whipped her children much if they grew up with a whole inch of hide on their backs! Lisle here can tell you whether you used to set the stars dancing before his eyes every hour or so. It was five-and-twenty years ago, and I know his ears ring with it it yet. Confess, Lisle, that nothing of this is figurative language except the 'five-and-twenty years ago.' Subtract a few years, and answer."

"Well, then, I frankly confess that I don't care to be 'superannuated down' for the purpose of re-living any of my juvenile experiences. The less said of them the better, for they are not pleasant reminiscences."

Mrs. Sterling colored slightly, and restlessly pinned and unpinned her sleeve cuffs while making some unintelligible comment upon Mr. Sterling's slowness in coming in.

He came at last, dressed in a suit of faded brown, so much resembling the patched garments of years ago that they seemed the very same; and shuffling in with his usual heavy tread, he shook Lisle's hand from side to side, like the motion of the sieves in a fanning-mill for cleaning grain, while he contemplated the changes time had made in his appearance.

"You've changed a good deal in seven years," said he, at last, slowly. "You don't look so much like my family as I thought you would. I don't see any of the Sterling features about you."

"Don't you think, Mr. Sterling, he looks like his uncle Fitzjames?" asked Mrs. Sterling, insinuatingly. "He is more like my family than he showed out when he was little. There's my sister,

Mrs. Deacon Hendry—Lucy Fitzjames that was—they're as much alike as two peas! I wish he was a woman now, that you might see it as plain as I do."

"Thank the Lord for small favors then! I wouldn't care to be a woman, even to resemble 'Lucy Fitzjames that was.' It is no doubt a most illustrious family; but I should dislike being a twin 'pea' to any of them, always excepting uncle Warren," said Lisle, bitterly.

"Yes, by the way, how is your uncle? Hale and hearty yet; looks as if he might live a good many years yet, don't he?" asked Mrs. Sterling, with a calculating expression upon her face which she meant should be expressive of affectionate interest.

"Yes, I am happy to say his health is excellent. He really looks younger than he did seven years ago when I first saw him."

"Well, I'm glad of it," she replied, looking absently through the window; but her expression of features so belied her words, that Edward irreverently laughed outright, then said, cheerfully and encouragingly,

"That's right and proper, mother. Cultivate Christian patience. There's no chance of anything falling to you from the profits of 'the mule business,' for some time yet. There's money enough in the Fitzjames family, 'first and last;' but they all have such inveterately *childish* habits, that sorry a penny falls to the children of anybody else."

An interruption occurred at this juncture, by the appearance of little Nell, who seemed the universal baby-tender, carrying a fat, bald-headed, toothless youngster of something less than ten months, eccentrically slung across one hip, from which he dangled down in a precarious, irregular manner with which he seemed perfectly familiar, as he offered no protest against it. Little Nell was evidently a poor calculator; as, though she entered the doorway in perfect safety as far as she herself was concerned, the hip-slung baby was one too many, and his bald head came in collision with the post, in a manner suggestive of black and blue bumps to one or both of them.

Mrs. Sterling boxed Nell's ears, and shook the now loudly-protesting baby, after which she shut both of them from the room, and returned to her chair just as Mr. Sterling said to Edward, reprovingly,

"It's very wrong of you to speak to your mother in that way about her family. They were one of the very best families 'in the country, before they scattered off, like; and have better blood in their veins than any other family here about. Even if they hadn't you shouldn't allow yourself to speak so disrespectful."

Mrs. Sterling's usual weapon came to her aid, and raising her apron to her eyes, she sobbed, in an injured tone,

"Oh, I'm used to it. I never did have any respect from my own children, and I never look to have any. But it's hard when I've worked so for 'em all my days, not to get any credit for it now."

"Bah!" exclaimed Edward, impatiently; for though he doubted the reality of her ostentatious grief, having witnessed its hypocritical display on many occasions, it was disagreeable to find himself the object at which it was aimed; and as of all things he hated a family scene in which a crying woman acted a part, he walked off into the yard and deserted it entirely, satisfied that Lisle would prove waterproof.

"How did you happen to come home so sudden, Lisle—come to stay?" asked Mr. Sterling, when quiet was restored.

"I don't know how long, sir. The length of my stay depends entirely upon other persons. I want to return to Louisville as soon as possible."

"Ahem! I suppose you are doing a good business there by this time. About three years ago, I should think, your uncle wrote me that if I was ever going to do anything for you, a little capital would be a seasonable offer on my part. But I hadn't any to spare just then, and so I wrote him. It costs a good deal of money to set boys up in any of them town businesses, and I thought you'd better come home and go into the mill with me. It's a good safe business, and the most nateral one for you, you know. Did Mr. Fitzjames mention it?"

"Not to me, sir. This is the first I ever heard of it."

"I said so!" exclaimed Mrs. Sterling, triumphantly. "I knew *my* brother, with all his money out of twenty years at the mule business, never cared the snap of his thumb for any *Sterling* capital. I knew, and I said so at the time, that it was just a way of feeling around to see what your father meant to do for you in the world; and he's proved it by never telling you a word of it, and going and setting you up himself, in a business that suits his notions. Mr. Sterling thought, perhaps, he had taken offence at his refusal to give; but I'm proud to say no Fitzjames ever yet asked a favor of anybody, and he no doubt had his calculations all made before he wrote that letter. I suppose he took your father's answer for a quit claim deed on you; and no wonder! None of *my* family was ever a miller, thank heaven! But you must have wheedled him some way, *I* can't see into! I suppose you're looking to get all his money by-and-bye, and will set up for a nabob on it; but he ought to *divide* it."

" I have never for one moment calculated upon receiving one dollar from my uncle at his death. He has done more for me already than any man could think of without feeling both gratitude, and a species of humiliation; and if he wills his property to an asylum, or throws it into the sea, I shall never feel that it was any business of mine, nor that I am in any way misused by it. Heaven forbid."

" I suppose he *has* done a good deal for you. He isn't a man to do things by halves; generosity is a real Fitzjames trait. But you'll never make *me* believe you han't an eye to the main chance, if you do preach it up to him. But this I do say; *you* ought to give your brother Edward half of it, if *he* don't."

" For heaven's sake, mother, do wait, with a decent amount of patience, before you administer upon the estate. It isn't worth while to begin to grab for it before he is done with it himself."

"Oh, *I* don't expect any of it; but it's certainly natural that I should look out for one child who han't any show to look out for himself, when the other is having it all his own way. *I* never *expect* to be anything but cramped for money, as I always have been. You all of you know that your father is closer'n the bark to a tree; it's in the Sterling blood, closeness is, and if my family could have seen how I was to be pinched and skimped with him, there'd have been other calculations made about dividing the Fitzjames property, if not about my marriage."

" There was only *too much* ' calculation ' in the marriage, it strikes me. Rather a calculating affair, the whole of it!" exclaimed Lisle, stung by the whole tenor of her remarks, and resenting the injustice heaped upon the old man who sat so meekly under the provocations he recognized, undreaming of the wrongs which lay farther back, in which this woman's calculation had made him the victim. She had little right to upbraid him for anything such a marriage might have imposed upon her, and it angered Lisle to be a witness of it. Rising, he buttoned his coat to go. Mrs. Sterling jealously remonstrated.

· " You don't mean to say you can't stop an hour longer under your parents' roof. It *is* a poor place, an't it?'

" I promised to be back at the doctor's by noon, and I don't wish to disappoint him. Beside, I've a livery horse which is to be at the stable by twelve o'clock to fill an engagement."

"Couldn't you have walked up here just as well as to hire a horse? Law! but money is plenty in your pocket! It is a-coming up in the world since I used to 'give it to you' once an hour for ugliness and lying. You was about the worst child I ever saw."

"Your reminiscences may be very pleasant to you, mother, and if they are I am abundantly willing you should enjoy them; but I confess they are anything but gratifying to me, and the less you refer to them, perhaps the better for us both. I am willing in the future to grant you any measure of respect to which you can establish any claim, but I tell you now that such references to the past are neither pleasurable nor profitable, and I should think *you* would hesitate to make them. If we were to compare recollections of the past, I might possibly recall some which you would be more surprised than gratified to hear; so if you derive any pleasure from recalling the persecutions you used to inflict on me during my defenceless, miserable boyhood, just enjoy it silently, being assured that you will never again possess such power over me. Thank Heaven, I am beyond your reach forever!"

"Lisle, Lisle," interrupted Mr. Sterling, "stop—you are saying too much. Remember she is your mother, and you should respect if you do not love her! She has been a careful mother, a good wife, and a hard-working woman always, and I want you to know that *I* respect her, if you don't." The old man looked really noble as he thus defended his wife, laying his large, coarse hand protectingly upon her shoulder; and, deeply touched by the scene, Lisle turned and went out, hardly knowing whether he most admired or pitied the trusting old man who thus raised his voice in testimony for the woman, half of whose life had been one gross deception toward him. She followed him to the door, and called after him.

"Lisle, you'll come again, won't you? If you're above staying in your own old home, and despise your *mother*, it ain't right of you to despise your father; and he feels it."

"Stop right there, mother. For you I have nothing to say; but I never for one moment despised my father, and he should know it. Good-bye, father, and if I do not come as often as you think I ought, do not construe my absence as a want of respect and regard for you. I wish the world were one-half as honest and true."

Mr. Sterling walked with him to the gate, and said, kindly, "I am sorry this happened to-day, my son. Your mother is getting on in years, and hain't the mind she used to have. I know she never loved you very well; but I always did, my son, and I do now.

If it is wrong to love one child better than another, I confess I do wrong, and I don't feel ashamed of it, when I say you are more to me than all the others. Come into the mill when you want to see me, if you don't like coming to the house; and, my son, let by-gones be by-gones as much as you can towards your mother. Won't you come again?"

"Yes, I will come to see you. I wish, too, that all this had not happened to-day; but her taunts called up so much that was unbearable,—injustice, abuse,—everything pertaining to those wretched years, of which you never knew the half! Good-bye, father, I'll see you again in a few days."

Edward came up from the mill when he saw the good-byes were being spoken, and making his own, briefly, the two brothers turned townward, in a silence which neither felt inclined to break.

"Whew!" exclaimed Edward at last. "Ours is a curious family!"

"I don't know; most families might be pronounced 'curious,' for that matter. If most family history were known, the world would be startled and astonished. It is only a matter of curiosity, that bad, weak women, manifestly their husband's inferiors, acquire such an amount of influence over them. It's only to be accounted for, that it grows up little by little, under a man's yielding point by point to avoid a row. What commences in righteous hypocrisy, grows into a settled habit."

"My opinion is, that the sillier a feminine is, and the more unbearably 'good,' the worse she is to live with. Such women are the devil on husbands."

"Most are, I suppose. The only safe way for a man, is to steer clear of them, and preserve his virtue and dignity. He's in the position of 'Dog Tray,'—if he doesn't merit correction in the first instance, bad company will soon bring him to it. It was a great mistake to get out a supplementary edition to father Adam, and the second error, like unto it, was having Mrs. Noah and her daughters-in-law survive their incarceration and family bickerings in the Ark. I don't envy Noah and the boys the time they must have had of it, however the old lady and the girls were edified; my way would have been to leave Mrs. Noah at home."

"Why, I've yet to learn that the old lady committed any farther mischief in the way of posterity. Better to have left the girls," laughed Edward. "Do tell me what makes you such a woman-hater, Lisle?"

"Oh, I'm not, but I don't care to callous my knees in their service, need I?"

"Well, I'll venture you never kneel very extensively. *Some one* has turned your vein of gallantry, into a circulator of pure *aqua-fortis.*"

"I don't see that it should be 'some one.' I never yet saw the woman I'd like to pin to the skirts of my robe of responsibility. I've pitied that poor old man up at the mill too many years, to wish myself possibly in the same position. Women, during the first twenty years of their existence, are rather ornamental than otherwise, but they make a fellow pay dearly for his admiration, when they come to spin off the next twenty. One doesn't require to have suffered in proper person, to know all this. 'He who hath eyes to see, let him see.' "

Edward made no reply, and the doctor's gate was reached in silence. Mrs. Kelley was looking for their arrival.

"There, at least, is a good woman," said Edward warmly.

"Yes, she is; and for her sake I accept Julie at your estimate of her. Such a mother cannot have a very unworthy daughter, and Julie certainly is as good as she is artless. If she hasn't too much will, all the better; and so let us drop the subject."

Dropped it was, so thoroughly, that it soon seemed forgotten, and Lisle sought her companionship during every leisure hour, with a persistency which led Edward to believe that he was "admiring the ornamental," without due regard for the future penalty, however wisely he had talked of it.

CHAPTER X.

THE last days of May drew to their close, and Lisle sat in the doctor's library absently turning the leaves of a volume he had long ceased to read. The waning daylight lingered just sufficiently to cast gloomy shadows around the objects to which it was bidding farewell, and the chill in the lingering spring atmosphere added to the sense of discomfort which mocked his philosophy. A few faintly tinted flowers filled a vase upon the table, striving in vain to look as if any invigorating warmth had ever breathed upon them, and seemingly repressing the shivering provoked by so many hours standing in cold water. Their evident struggle to keep up appearances was more depressing to witness than their entire absence; and seizing the vase, he tossed its whole contents into the open grate. He was in a gloomy, not to say irritable humor, of which he was ashamed, without really possessing the power to banish it, and sensible that he was no congenial companion for others, he had shut himself up alone, hoping that in time a counter current would set in upon his mental channel. Evidently it was at low-water mark yet, as only the most gloomy and unhappy musings occupied him.

"Yes, an interloper—worse than that, a hypocrite "—he thought impatiently, tossing aside the book with which he had been unconsciously toying. "How long can I go on in this way, when every hour, did people rightly read it, gives some convincing proof that I am not what I seem, that I have no right under this roof—no, nor any other—and every proof of affection I receive from Mrs. Kelley is so much more in the balance against me. God pity a life dragged out under such a curse as mine! Even to that poor old man up at the mill I am a hypocrite! Every time I call him ' father ' my conscience rises up in protest, and his openly declared preference for me beyond his own children, pierces me like a dagger. Yet I am tied, tied! bound hand and foot. Good Heavens! what must my real father have suffered, smothering this plague-spot in his heart through all these years!"

The question was not without some alleviating effect, as it turned his thoughts into a softer channel, and as compassion took the place of bitterness, his brow cleared and a tender melancholy beamed from his eyes.

He did not hear the door so gently opened behind him, nor the footsteps which after a momentary hesitation advanced to his side, and it was only when a soft warm hand was pressed over his eyes, that he knew any one had entered. He was in no mood for play, and taking the hand which obscured his vision, he led its possessor to a seat beside him, and looked in her face with a serious, troubled gaze under which Julie looked up in wonder.

"What ails you, Lisle? You haven't been like yourself all day. What troubles you?"

"Nothing which you can help," he said with a sigh, and turned away his face that she might not read its troubled lines. His voice was sad, but not repelling, and stepping behind his chair she turned his face up toward her own and shook one raised finger at him warningly.

"Now, Lisle, don't be gloomy! You don't know how much we all love you, or you would be happy; for doesn't love make happiness?"

"I can't say. I have known too little of it to tell by experience."

"Is it 'little,' all this we all of us feel for you? Don't you remember how we loved each other when we were children—at least I loved you, and you knew it, then, and didn't think it 'little.' And how good you were to me, never scolding me for anything—excepting my maternal partiality,"—she added with a smile. "Do you recollect all that?"

"I was a boy then, and you liked me because I protected your doll babies."

"Now, Lisle, I won't endure that! It isn't fair. You are so horridly suspicious and distrustful, that I wonder sometimes if you don't doubt the reality of your own existence."

"Seriously, then, I sometimes really do; and I only wish the doubt would resolve itself into a certainty."

"And, pray, Sir Misty, what and where are you when you don't exist exactly to your own satisfaction?"

"A pebble in a stream, a stone by the wayside, or a block of marble."

"Always stone and cold. That at least is in character. But

what do you think of yourself as such, for of course you indulge in reflections ?"

"I wonder why I give myself so much trouble and vexation about a world in which I am only an insensate bit of 'primary,' and why I am cursed with an idea that I 'live, move, and have a being ;' and then I hope, in a dreary way, that some revolution of nature will throw me out of my present sphere, and satisfactorily convince me that I am a stone, and thus forever set my doubts of even that' at rest."

"This literally 'beats the Dutch !' I have heard and read something of German philosophy, and mystification upon scientific principles; but I never before saw a walking epitome of it all. Seriously, Lisle, what ails you ?"

"Chronic morbidness."

"But springing from what cause ? You, of all others, seem to have so little to give you an hour's trouble. Master of your own actions at an age when others are scarcely out of leading-strings, favorite nephew, if not heir, of an uncle who must love you or he wouldn't have done so much for you, well located in business; and, not the least of all blessings, young, talented, and handsome. There !"

"Julie, I am too much out of sorts to bow in acknowledgment, as I ought. I willingly admit that I am blessed in many of the respects you enumerate, nor am I sufficiently egotistical to imagine that I alone of all the world have troubles worthy the name; but I only wish I could exchange with most any one long enough to get a breathing spell. If I could only get my burden off my brain for one blessed hour, I would try and trudge on with it cheerfully forever after."

"I imagine you would plod on with any other life trouble pretty much as you do with your present especial. I'm not versed in the matter, but I don't believe any one was ever yet convinced that his own was the easiest of all possible ones to bear."

"Very likely. But, Julie, I'm in no humor for a fair argument to-night, and I am too savage for any one's society but my own."

"Are you savage toward me ?"

"Yes, I'm afraid so. I don't feel myself a distinguisher of persons to-day; and I don't wish in one bad hour to sacrifice all my previous efforts to make you think me not quite a bear."

"I don't, and I shan't. Swear, now, if it will relieve you—don't mind me, for I heard father once. If you once burst out, or break something, it will make you feel better directly."

She looked perfectly in earnest with this advice, and quickly alive to anything approaching the ludicrous, he stopped and laughed.

"There, that answers the same purpose, doesn't it?" he asked, "and now that I'm ready to be entertained, how do you propose to do it?"

"As ladies usually entertain sick people—tell you all the symptoms of 'brother's last illness,' or how 'sister-in-law was laid out,' etc., or any other funeral-baked history calculated to cheer your spirits."

"No, thank you. I'd rather hear all the little things that have been happening during these years of my absence. I haven't been 'talked up' in them at all."

"Well, then, I'll commence with myself. You left me crying at this very table, do you remember? Well, I shall never cry for you again, nor for any one else; for the more people, especially the masculine half of them, are cried for, the sooner they forget you. I recollect that when you never sent me any messages, I wanted to die, so that you should feel very sorry for your neglect; and, failing in the performance of that melancholy feat, I used to imagine it as happening, and I breathed my last with a reproachful message for you, and attended my funeral, and returned with the mourners to the desolate house, in a manner very beautiful and affecting—to myself —to imagine.

"Ed used to form plans how we two were to run away in sad companionship, from the scenes you had deserted ; but I didn't take as kindly to the scheme as he did, though I maintained the promised secrecy, till once he really did start off alone, long after I supposed he had given up the idea, and it was not till father came home from there one day, and told how alarmed the Sterlings were at his disappearance, that I broke my promise. I was in screaming horror lest he might die by the wayside, and I recollect dancing up and down in a frenzy, at the slownsss of the boy who at last got father's horse all harnessed, when away he went over the hills like mad.

"Eddy hadn't many hours the start, and was overtaken trudging manfully along with a stick across his shoulder, at the end of which he had a few clothes tied up in an apron of his mother's,—I suppose his little old shirt-made handkerchiefs, were too small for his wardrobe,—as veritable a 'tramp' as ever lived! Father thought it

best not to.notice him at first, and drove past; but Ed called out to
him to 'give him a lift if he were going his way,' and father took
him in as innocently as needful, since Ed kept a sharp eye upon
him. So they drove on awhile till they came to a road leading back
toward home, which Ed didn't know, and as they came down it
father got him to tell the story of his wrongs, which was that his
mother was 'a nasty, mean woman, who didn t give him any comfort, and had driven you away and got Pompey shot,' and his father
was 'an old stingy, who made him go raggeder than ever, now,' and
he had concluded to cut their acquaintance, and go out to Toledo
and work on the canal,—an idea that he seemed to have fallen heir
to when you resigned it. Father always did feel sorry for you boys,
you know, and he finally persuaded him that he had better come
back and study with him, and by-and-bye come out an M. D., to
which *I. D.* he cordially consented, and they drove home upon the
best terms with each other. Ed made his own terms about remaining in his native town, and has lived with us nearly ever since."

"Yes, and the doctor is helping him even to lectures. How much
he has done for him, and your mother, too."

"Oh, that's nothing; but ma did get vexed with him sometimes,
and no wonder. She noticed the old cat getting thinner and
thinner, and so weak she could but just walk; and she couldn't imagine what ailed her, till she fairly caught him with the lancet in
his fingers during a bleeding operation, after which he 'proceeded
in the usual manner,' as he affirmed when ma demanded explanations. Of course there was a stop put upon this; and then he went
to practising upon the old rooster, relative to whose adipose tissue,
tendons, and jugular veins, he delivered me a very learned lecture,
which, as old 'Mahomet' was a pet of mine, I didn't duly appreciate, and our first real quarrel arose from my complaining about it
to father; and he said thus depriving him of much useful information, for which humanity would some time inevitably suffer, whether
because he lacked this information, or practised upon them to
obtain it, I don't know; but if people call a doctor, let them take
the consequences. Old 'Mahomet' hadn't, and I rescued him."

They were both laughing as they walked the floor, now socially
arm in arm, unheeding the darkness setting in upon the long struggling twilight, when Mrs. Kelley opened the door, having vainly
sought Lisle elsewhere in response to the doctor's frequent inquiries
for him.

"How selfish I have been. I had no idea time had passed so

rapidly!" exclaimed Lisle, in self-reproach, hastening at once to the doctor's room.

Mrs. Kelley arrived suddenly at a conclusion; and unquestioning its correctness, gave expression to it at once, as laying her gentle hand upon her daughter's head, she said, softly,

"I think I understand, Julie, and it may be a pleasure for you to know that I have always hoped for this. Lisle was always my favorite, and from loving him as a son, I can very easily call him one." And without waiting for a reply, she passed on. .

Left by herself, Julie first paused in astonishment, then the color spread over her neck and brow at her mother's suggestion. Till this moment it had never occurred to her that Lisle regarded her in any other light than that of an old playmate and pleasant companion. Even now, nothing he had said confirmed the idea at this moment awakened, but his manner—had he not sought her constant companionship of late, preferring it even to his brother's—manifested a ceaseless interest in all her occupations and ambitions—and even to-day implied a doubt of the truth and strength of her confessed affection for him through so many years, by accusing her of having liked him from interested motives as a child—as if he questioned whether she really liked him now from any. The more she thought upon it all, the stronger seemed the probability that her mother had been more clear-sighted than she herself; and she acknowledged it with a little fluttering of the heart which certainly did not spring from a spirit of indifference.

A young lady of sixteen readily convinces herself that she loves in return whoever loves her; and it matters little whether this affection is real or imaginary, so long as she believes in its existence. Julie believed that it did exist, and her own sprang into bloom as if by magic. Lisle did not come down to tea, but Edward noted her heightened color and brilliant eyes, and did not fail to connect them with the twilight interview in the library, from which he drew his own conclusions, as Mrs. Kelley had done.

Nothing of this was suspected by Lisle himself, and though he observed a more confidential tenderness in Mrs. Kelley's manner toward him, he was far from understanding it, and attributed it only to her sympathy under his evident gloom, which no efforts that day had been able to conquer or conceal.

Dr. Kelley passed a restless night, and having fallen asleep at last just as day dawned, Lisle stole out for rest and fresh air, just as Edward went into the office. He fancied that his brother's salutation

was cool, and, determined to make a final effort to break down the
invisible barrier between them, he followed him in, and drew a chair
near the table at which Edward moodily seated himself. He looked
anything but genial, and Lisle hesitated for a moment, uncertain
how to approach him in his present humor, and for the instant he
resolved to go away from him and let the estrangement, if such it
really were, take its natural course. But second thought-restrained
him, and casting away all thought of diplomacy, he asked abruptly,

"Edward, what is the matter between us?"

"Nothing worth mentioning," replied Edward as abruptly.

"Yes, there is something, and I want to know what it is. We
have not been just as we should be, any of the time since my return
here, and if I am in any way responsible for it, I shall try to rect fy
it. I have too few friends in this world to be willing to lose the
oldest and dearest among them without an effort to retain him."

"I don't see that you are particularly calculated to awaken confidence, or to retain it; or why you should expect others to be more
steadfast and unselfish than yourself," replied Edward in a tone that
betrayed how much the unkind words cost him, determined as he
was to speak them.

"Ed, I insist that you are unkind and unjust! I know that I am
not as winning as many, and that I make few friends; but this is
my misfortune, and I have not deserved to be taunted with it by you,
of all the world! I am steadfast in my friendships where they once
exist, and God knows I am incapable of being selfish toward you,
whatever you may think me towards others. There has never been
an hour in my life when I would not willingly have died for you,
could such an act in any way benefit you."

Edward turned suddenly in his chair, and faced him.

"Lisle, I believe I am a brute! My 'Fitzjames temper' has always been a curse to me, and it isn't in me to be gentle and sensitive
like you. All my sensations are trubulent ones, I believe. I'm sure
I don't know what it was that first rose up between us two; I suppose it was only the result of our being separated and differently
brought up. I didn't begin to see the extent of this wall of constraint, till you came back; and then your changed and dignified
appearance—so different from what I had ever known you—only
made the matter worse, and I *couldn't* get near you. Your experience in life has made you a polished gentleman, while I am the same
country-bred boy; you have the air of one who knows his own place
in the world, and is sensible of filling it creditably, while I am a

doctor's student, by the charity of one upon whom I have no earthly claim. You may think these considerations should have no effect between two brothers born into the hard luck we were, but if we could exchange places a minute, you'd feel it as I do. It all the time seemed to me that you might put affairs straight between us if you chose—though just now I don't see how—and I came to believe you rather fancied being looked upon as one afar off. But there is another cause for my feeling really unkindly towards you, and you must know it."

"No, I do assure you I can't imagine it. Go on as plainly as you please. Don't stop to choose words."

"I admit, to begin with, that I have no right to complain, nor do I of anything except that you did not deal frankly with me. Knowing what you did, you owed me candor, at least. I don't ask now to be made a confidant in your love affair; but when I recall the terms in which you spoke of Julie while expressing your opinion of her whole sex, I do think you were neither truthful nor honorable, since it isn't supposable that your feelings towards her have undergone any extensive revolution. I thought then there was an understanding between you, and now I know it; but of course it's none of *my* business. *I'm* nobody's heir—unless being the recipient of her father's charity makes me one—and I can't expect to be noticed by her."

"For heaven's sake, Edward, what do you mean? Speak out!"

"Just what I'm doing, I think. I can't well think of it without performing just that ceremony. If I abuse you, 'don't take any pride in what I say,' as boys caution one another upon like occasions."

"Edward, if any woman the sun shines on stands between you and me, out with her; but if it is little Julie Kelley for whom you are cherishing this delusion, do tell me how I have anything to do with it."

"Do you mean to say that you don't wish to marry her yourself?"

"I! How utterly impossible!. You don't know what you are talking."

His look of pain and surprise was too genuine to be doubted, and Edward felt so at once, as he exclaimed, impulsively,

"I'm sure I don't. Do kick some common sense into me. I should feel the better for a good Christian kick or two from you just now. But, Lisle, if you knew how I have loved her all these years, and how I am forever hoping that some day I shall come to something worth noticing, and be noticed by her; for it hasn't come to marrying yet, and I don't suppose ever would. People may laugh about 'puppy love,' and I suppose you think I've got it. Well, perhaps I have; but it's hard, nevertheless, to see some one, particularly a brother, carry her off any way. Money and position make you matrimonially eligible, while I, not two years younger, am but a boy."

"What ever gave you the idea that I wish to marry? Heaven forbid!"

"I got it from pretty near the fountain head, I assure you, since it was from Mrs. Kelley herself, though she didn't intend to say anything, as you may be sure, knowing her as you do. I know *she* thinks so, and if Julie isn't entertaining the same delusion, I'm mistaken. I don't see how you can avoid reading what stands out as clearly as print. How is it you didn't suspect it?"

"Because I never dreamed of the possibility of such a thing. It is really dreadful!"

Edward laughed. "I don't see it in that light. However, since you thus quake at the idea, I suppose I may rest in peace, notwithstanding the uncomplimentary phrase used in connection with the fair Julie."

Lisle was in no humor for jesting, and after a moment of painful silence, he said,

"Don't willfully pervert my remarks, Edward, but understand me for all time, when I say that much as I like Julie upon farther acquaintance (I know I insinuated that she was silly, but I retract it now), she is the best living woman I should ever think of as other than a—*sister*—and nothing could so pain me, as that she should ever care for me beyond a mere brother. It would be the worst possible misfortune that could befall her or me!"

"Well, Lisle, I believe you, and I *will* do so; though how any man not actually her brother, can prefer that position towards her, is more than I can understand. You always were a strange fellow, though! Only tell me now, that you forgive all my hard words and injustice toward you, and I shall be happier than I've been since they crowded their company upon me."

"I certainly do. I am only too well satisfied with anything which may have led to this explanation between us. Do, once for all, put aside all these comparisons and unjust considerations, regarding any of my supposed advantages over yourself, and let us be once more *brothers.* You speak so bitterly of being an object of charity, what else have *I* been all these years? Dr. Kelley has done no more for you than uncle has for me, I don't see in what I can possibly claim any advantage over you."

"Bother! Yes you can, and so do others. However, one enumeration is enough; and you've established a claim upon another, this hour. Had you, or any one else, 'let into me' as I did to you, this morning, I wouldn't have explained nor pardoned him, till the crack of doom! You deserve all the good luck you are heir to; that's one consolation! But Lisle, if you think I have seen more than exists, keep your own eyes open for awhile, and you'll see it, too. It's as plain as poverty on a debtor's face. I don't look out of green eyes, as you'll soon see."

In obedience to the injunction, Lisle did observe Mrs. Kelley and Julie more closely than he had yet done, and either he had been most obtuse, or indications of their belief in the character of his attentions were more open and marked than they had been any time before. Julie manifested a tender consciousness under his every word and glance, which he had never seen in her manner till that day, natural expression as it was of her new conviction concerning him. Edward saw that it was noted by Lisle, with something like real pain; and as they strolled out together in the twilight, he looked up at him inquiringly. Not a word had been spoken upon the subject since the morning's conversation in the office, but Lisle knew the burden of that questioning glance, and answered to it frankly.

"I believe your suspicions were correct, Ed, though it is the strangest fact ever forced upon me. There is just this consolation for us all, these sixteen years' old impressions are fleeting. It seems as though girls of that age are ready primed and loaded with sentimental epidemics, from 'eternal constancy,' down to 'early deaths!' There never was one free from the whole category."

"It's all very well for you to ridicule it in general; but this case, of all others, is anything but laughable to me. I was impatient enough for Julie's arrival from school, I can tell you, and when it was decided to send for her upon account of the doctor's illness, I hurried out to New York for her. The seminary was a regular young lady manufactory, it seemed to me, and *my!* didn't they each and all stare as if they didn't expect to see a young gentleman again till the end of the course,—for it's a regular three years affair. Julie introduced me to several of her friends, pale, round-eyed young feminines, with the usual comp'aint of starvation become chronic.

That didn't matter so much, for young ladies always eat like turkey buzzards, it seems to me; but they forgot even their stomachs when we got ready to leave, and the way they cried was at once aggravating and gratifying. Julie was the only sensible one among them, and if I hadn't been in a bad enough way about her before, I should have been then. I brought her home just a week before you arrived, and *this* is the way I'm repaid for it all."

"Will she go back to the seminary for the remaining two years?"

"Yes, I suppose so. The doctor intended her to have gone through the whole course, and I presume Mrs. Kelley will carry out his wishes, however much she may miss her if left alone. But for her father's illness we should not have seen her at all this year, as she was to have passed the summer vacation at Niagara, with the family of her favorite schoolmate. I'd have fought against it if there had been any use in it, for I'm always fearing some one may see her and speak before I can; for of course I can't say a word till my position in life is assured. I only hope, now, that she will go; for it's plain that till you are out of her head I can't hope to get into it. I wonder if it isn't unfortunate to have known a young lady too long? If we had been as little acquainted since childhood as you and she have been, I should have twice the chance I now have of making any impression. However, two years are something, and if she gets her head full of everything else, to my utter exclusion, so much the better for me when she comes back. It will be a sort of fresh start, you know."

He looked resolute and hopeful even under such a prospect; and looking upon him, Lisle wondered how it is that affection in this world so seldom directs itself into the proper channel, or bestows its treasures where they would be most highly prized. It is a rule, and not its exception, that it is poured out upon some indifferent or unworthy object, while one who would have prized it more than life, plods on in sorrow and neglect, or at best falls heir to but the sorry crumbs of so-called friendship.

Something of the same tenor seemed to have occupied Edward's musings, for he said a little ironically,·

"It's well that married people can't read all the sentimental histories each of them has passed through. If all the disappointments, and unrequited what-you-may-call-ems, were as well known to one as to the other of them, I don't imagine they would prove matrimony sweeteners. However, if there must be a dozen or so of tender passages in each one's existence, he or she is the lucky one who comes last, and I do suppose that if I know Julie to have fancied a round baker's dozen of admirers, I shall hail my turn, when it comes, with no less thankfulness."

" I should hope so, certainly ! The world might well laugh should a man seek to make it believe that he was his wife's first love. No doubt such blessed beings do live ; but the world doesn't believe in them, and I'm sure I don't see why it should, nor why one should care to have it. When real life, and preaching—no matter how pretty and fine—can't get along together consistently, it's time that preaching, as the more artificial, should die out or be made over ; and it's every one's duty to lend a hand toward its demolition. There are so many fine theories which every one admires—*for others' practice !* Any one in this world who cares to be loved, is a fool indeed to cast the gift from him when offered, because another may have gloried in it first. It is curious that both the winner and the loser feel aggrieved ! Some day your 'turn,' as you style it, must and will come, if you continue to wish it, and I hope your present bitterness may then re-assert itself as sound sense ; as I've no doubt it will. Just cast away all care for the ' baker's dozen,' and be thankful if you are the last on the list."

· " When I said I supposed I should, I meant that I have thoroughly resolved to, and I know I shall. Don't I prove the truth of it in your case ? Well, I've no idea I shall be the next favored one, so there's an end to enumeration. And now what do you say to running up to the mill to-morrow ? I won't trust myself in the house, for I believe a careless fellow's words are, among a woman's sensibilities, what a bear is among the gimcracks in a china shop ; and the old lady has cultivated hers into so pugilistic a state that they rush out from the most unexpected corners in a perfectly rampant condition. Those poor youngsters at home are coming up just as we did, and as none of them ' take after the Fitzjames(s,' there is no lucky escaper from the shakings and slappings visited upon the unfortunates who are ' for all the world just like your father.' It is enough to make a pious individual forget all his prayers except the opening address which is jerked right out of him, to see her go on at times ; and the old gentleman won't insist upon justice, because he's too weak to oppose her when he knows she is wrong. Did you see how much afraid of her that very baby was ?"

" I didn't observe, particularly. The truth is, I haven't one feeling of relationship towards any of them up there ; and if it were possible for one to suspect his legitimacy upon his mother's side, I'd challenge mine. It is time I were back by the doctor. I think he is failing, and may go suddenly at most any hour, now. What a shame some rascal doesn't die in his place! I believe it is well established that one scamp outlives ten good men."

" Yes. I don't believe Doctor Kelley ever did a wrong thing in his life, and everybody else says the same. There never has been one breath against him."

" Good night," said Lisle, abruptly; and, leaving Edward, he walked toward the house.

Edward looked after him a moment, then smiled at his eccentricity, and made his own way back to the office alone.

CHAPTER XI.

WARNED by what he had observed, Lisle avoided the former frequent *tête-a-têtes* with Julie, and when they met in the presence of others, was so guarded in his deportment, as to prevent any possible misinterpretation.

Julie often raised her eyes wonderingly to his face, surprised by the reserve he had so suddenly adopted, and missing day after day, the society she had so learned to prize, but blameless in her own conscience of having merited this seeming neglect, she asked no explanation, and silently acquiesced in the new order of affairs, depressing and unaccountable as they were. Heretofore, he had always sought her society as persistently as he now avoided it, and the hour had gone by, when she could frankly have asked the reason for this change in him. There was infinitely more happiness in his society, and more freedom and cordiality existing between them, before this new belief had found place in her heart, and from wishing that it had never come, she began to reason more unprejudicedly as to whether it were well founded. Certainly no kindred delusion could long survive the exterminating treatment hers received, and she awaited the *denonuement* with a real serenity of spirit, which attracted Mrs. Kelly's curiosity, no less than the sudden change in Lisle's deportment had done.

There seemed but one solution to all this, some "lover's quarrel," or temporary misunderstanding, which the false pride of each prevented from being explained away; and regretting that such a shadow should come between them, she at last addressed Julie relative to it.

" What is the trouble between you and Lisle, Julie? Is there any serious misunderstanding that estranges you ?"

" Not that I know of, mother. He is so eccentric; and of late he seems to have taken a new something into his head, which, I suppose, will work itself out after its own fashion. If he chooses us to know what it is, he will tell us."

"I am glad you are so philosophical under it. If you ever are his wife, you will very probably have to cultivate such a spirit under many trying circumstances. This is most wives' experience, and happy is she, who, through all, retains her respect for her husband undiminished. I dare not hope that your life will be as wholly free from such trials as mine has been. Your father has been to me what few husbands ever are in this world, and I can smile upon every act of his noble life and love him the more for having performed it."

Tears born of her sincerity and wifely tenderness trembled in her eyes as she spoke, and a little pause ensued.

"Mother,' said Julie hesitatingly, "it is very possible that we may have been mistaken in supposing that Lisle cares for me—you know what I mean—in a particular way. He never told me that he did, never really uttered one word to such an effect. The more I think of it, the more I am certain he never meant me so to understand him. He really might be my own brother, for any word he ever spoke to me."

"Is this possible? Then I am more in fault than you, and I have felt ever since that evening in the library, that I was too hasty in the words I spoke upon the impulse of the moment, since I would not in any way seek to influence your decision, should he ask you to become his wife. As a counter-balance, I will tell you, now, that when I mentioned the subject to your father he quite opposed the idea; urged that such a marriage would prove most uncongenial, and, in fact, grew so flushed and nervous upon the subject that he excitedly declared it '*impossible*;' at which I could have smiled, as men rarely consider that in such matters nothing is 'impossible,' however ill-advised it may be. I do not see why he should be so much opposed to the marriage, as he has always loved Lisle like his own son."

"Then, mother, that would, under any circumstances end it all. I do not think either that I ever felt towards Lisle that sort of regard which leads people to marry each other. When I thought for a little while that I did, it was more because I fancied he loved me than from any other reason. We were at ease and happy together before such an idea came to me; and we have not seen a comfortable hour together since. I only hope he doesn't imagine how silly I have been. I should die of mortification if he knew it all!" and her face was flushed as she turned it inquiringly upon her mother, as if hoping for reassurance. Much as she wished to give it, Mrs. Kelley felt that she could not do so conscientiously. She could not

hope that he had failed to interpret Julie's manner after that unfortunate library scene, and that he had read it aright, his sudden reserve
was a strong indication.

She maintained a silence therefore under this mute appeal, which
confirmed Julie's worst fears; and humiliated and chagrined, she
suddenly quitted the room. She avoided meeting Lisle for the remainder of the day, and only when twilight deepened and she knew
he was sitting alone, summoned courage to seek him. Her heart
beat suffocatingly as she placed her hand upon the door-knob; but
after an instant's hesitation, she turned it and entered the room.
He was leaning moodily against the window through which he
looked with a troubled gaze, never turning as the door was closed,
though he must have heard it, and laying her hand upon his arm,
Julie spoke but one word, " Brother."

He started and turned his face upon her, dyed almost to crimson,
without daring to ask the meaning of that name. One glance reassured him, even before she continued,

"Do be a brother to me, Lisle, and accept me as a sister. You
are troubled and unhappy, and I fear I have rendered you more so."

Intensely as her approaching greeting had startled him, he was
relieved as he realized that his secret was still his own; nothing
now had power to embarrass him, and all things unconnected with
that one trouble were light in comparison. The discomfort of the
last few days seemed as nothing, and he answered cheerfully,

" Don't mind my gloomy moods, little sister, they are an unfortunate part of me, and I shall doubly regret them if they prove contagious."

"Well, you used to say I was the best antidote for such moods,
and yet for a whole week you have shunned me in every way. Why,
pray?"

He commenced a laughing reply in evasion; but she interrupted
it.

"Don't try to put me off in that way. One of us must speak the
truth, and it had much better be you."

He saw that nothing short of the outspoken truth would content
her; but any words that he could choose seemed all too abrupt for-
utterance, and he hesitated, unable to commence. She spared him
the task.

" You saw that I was silly and vain enough to misunderstand you,
and you could not endure it. I shall never do so again, as my presence here this minute is your best guarantee. You cannot be more

- vexed with my foolishness than I am; but, certainly, very little punishment is justly due me, unless you mean it to be sadly disproportionate to any happiness, or satisfaction I derived from a mistaken idea while I retained it. It was a most uncomfortable delusion, and I only realize how unhappy it made me, now that it has ceased, and I remember how happy we might have remained all this time but for it."

He clasped her little hand with his old cordiality as he said,

"Julie, you are a sensible girl, and an honest one. It is usually quite safe to believe in avowals of *lack* of affection, whatever one may think of declarations of its existence. I believe I shall prove a tolerable brother; but Fate protect the woman destined to receive me as a lover, much more as a 'liege lord!'"

"I can hardly imagine you in either capacity. It seems as ridiculous for you as if you were to dance, sing, play the piano or something, or perform anything in the department of the fine arts. It is very plain that you were never intended for ornament, whether or not you were-for use."

"Use! of course I am, and I shall probably fulfill destiny as some woman's bill-payer and martyr, though heaven postpone the hour! I don't take kindly to matrimony, and if it were not really inevitable, I should have some hope of escape. I shan't look upon the woman who says 'I will' for me, as my friend, though I hope I shall treat her with Christian charity. It is a pity that so many glorious friendships should be brought to an untimely end by the setting in of matrimony. It seems to be a sort of last stage in the diagnosis of the life-fever, and fearfully liable to relapses, circumstances being propitious. Were it as dangerous to life as most people find it disagreeable, there would be such a stampede for vacination against it, as was never yet equalled. Matrimony has slain its thousands, in a mental sense! Watch and pray that it does not engulf you, little sister."

"Lisle, if you really meant one half the abominable heresies you utter, you wouldn't be tolerated in polite society! I wonder who originated the fashion of men aping bears, and crucifying nature! It is all very well to cry out against certain natural results of being human, and divers affectations believed in by humanity at large. They who are most sincere in this cynicism, prove the most striking back-sliders, or, if you will, fallers from imaginary grace. Much as you like to sneer, you are as kind-hearted, yes, and as susceptible, as any one, and it sounds monstrously like affectation, in one so young and fortunate as you are, to be forever hinting of 'dust, ashes,' etc. I hope I shall never live to think nature made a mistake in my manufacture, and so set myself to the task of rectifying her blunders. I would rather one should be even *disagreeably* natural, if it be his misfortune to *be* disagreeable, than to make himself over till nothing appears but affectation. I dislike ' cut and dried' things, especially in the animal kingdom, and I have yet to see a *made-over* person, who isn't stamped with his own handicraft as plainly as if it were chalked on his back."

"Thank you. I think I never saw you so complimentary."

" I was not alluding to you, Lisle, as you would know, did not conscience in some way upbraid you ! Little as you resemble either your father or mother, I never thought that you pretended to be what you are not. You were mentally out of joint when you entered upon life, there is no doubt ; and you had as much right to add to your original allowance of peculiarity as to increase your physical proportions. But don't become bitter in it, Lisle ! It is bad enough for old men to be bitter and biting, but intolerable when young ones adopt it."

They were interrupted by the entrance of Edward, who, overhearing them as he chanced to pass the window, joined them, unfeignedly glad that the uncomfortable constraint which had overshadowed them all for a whole week, had given place to something like geniality once more. It was evident that the understanding between Lisle and Julie was perfect and satisfactory to each ; and his jealous distrust was effectually banished. In Lisle, at least, he · had no rival, and silently hoping he might never encounter a more serious obstacle to his suit, he felt his heart throb more lightly than it had done for many a day. Julie's regard must have been slight and transitory indeed, if it could so soon give place to the calm friendship now so unmistakably existing between them, and he need no longer feel that another was preferred to himself, even if his own prospects were all unassured. He knew that years must elapse before he could hope to claim her, even if she learned to love him, and he resolved to wait patiently and in silence, rather than to inflict upon her those years of hope deferred which would be inevitable, and doubly bitter to him if she, too, suffered. Resolved as he was to leave her free and untrammelled, it became the part of wisdom as well as generosity, not to press a suit which in the chances and changes of those years might be lost beyond recovery ; since it is even more difficult to revive a languishing affection, than to kindle one in the first instance.

It was a patient, all-enduring philosophy little to have been expected in one so impetuous as Edward was by nature; but it formed only one more among many examples of the way in which

"Love works by various ways in different minds."

In his modesty and total lack of egotism, he never once dreamed that Julie might bestow her affection upon him as a voluntary and unsolicited gift. He only hoped to win it, and these years of silent devotion were only one offering at her shrine to be crowned by many. He submitted cheerfully to the prospect of years of careless friendship, but one degree removed from indifference, content if, at last, in Providence's good time, she should come to appreciate him; and he was sincere in the remark he had made to Lisle, that he cared not how many might have been preferred to him, if only she came to love him at last. Tender prepossessions and heart histories were inseparable from her existence as a pretty woman; she would be sought by others, wooed, and perhaps temporarily won—happiness sufficient to him should it prove only temporarily; he would welcome her with his whole soul when and how she might come.

Perfectly unconscious of this chivalrous regard, Julie met him day by day, amid the careless, unthinking interchanges of life's small courtesies; and nothing could have been more distant from her thoughts than that he should ever become more to her, or she to him, than each now was to the other. So intimate from childhood had been their companionship, that he was to her like a brother, and she entertained for him only that lukewarm, passive affection usual between brothers and sisters, whose component parts are toleration and criticism. Had he ever attempted the customary *rôle* of elder brother towards her, even this passive regard would have subsided into indifference; but his ever ready courtesy and complimentary deportment towards her were as unbrother-like as were the sentiments whose only expression they were; and her 'liking' for him was unshadowed by any other sentiment whatever. Separation and worldly experience, in destroying this slight tie, might make way for a nearer one; and upon this hope he relied with cheerful faith.

Through what suffering and disappointment might she one day learn to appreciate him? When, if ever, would she turn to this steadfast love for solace after one of life's battles, where even hope lay wrecked and shattered. Such warfare comes to all earth's children, and blessed are they who gain a peaceful haven, though many a scar and seam tell of the conflict!

Wooed by the sunshine and the singing birds, Lisle strolled aimlessly along the road leading out to the mill. Suddenly realizing that he had accomplished nearly half the distance, he determined to pay Mr. Sterling a visit; and a brisk walk soon brought him to the hill, descending which unseen from the house, he sought the old gentleman at his work.

The water was at its height, and the drooping willow branches lay far out upon the swollen bosom of the pond lying so majestically in sunlight and shade, as if unconscious that its dam was chattering in noisy accompaniment to the softer whirring of the mill-wheel in its busy round. Lisle lingered to look upon the scene as one does upon familiar haunts of one's childhood, even though unendeared by fond recollections. It was painfully familiar, associated as it unavoidably was with his miserable boyhood; and turning away, he abruptly entered the mill. The doors were open for the entrance of the soft summer breeze, for "mild-eyed June" had come with her balmy breath; and looking around in search of Mr. Sterling, Lisle saw him at the far end of the room, covered with the flour that fleeced his coat and battered hat, and heavily powdered his eyebrows. Seeing Lisle in the doorway, he came to meet him, relieving his hat of its fleecy covering by a few well-planted blows, the like of which upon former occasions had rendered it mellow and dejected to the last degree; and dusting his face with his red handkerchief, he merely said, as he shook Lisle's hand with a repetition of the fanning-mill process, "Well, my son." But the satisfaction expressed in his face spoke more than any words could have done, and Lisle answered it accordingly.

"Yes, I have stolen away this morning for an hour or two. I should have visited you sooner, but many things prevented. You seem busy."

"Only tolerable, only tolerable. I don't make money these days. It seems to me there an't as much money made in any business as there used to be. Nobody wants to pay cash for anything now-a-days, and I can't make anything by always putting up with part of the grist. Flour gets lower and lower all the time, with all this Western wheat coming into the market. I don't see how I'm to look out for my family if things don't take a turn by-and-bye."

"Oh, don't take so gloomy a view of things. You are worth

more, to-day, than most of your neighbors. You, needn't care to make money."

"No I an't, Lisle, no I an't. Children always have the idea that old folks are able to '*shell out*' on all occasions, but it takes a' most all an *honest* man can earn, to bring up a family. I couldn't have done anything for Edward if Dr. Kelley hadn't come forward and begged as a favor to take him into his office. He is a proud boy, and didn't take kindly to being a miller like his father. He has his mother's blood more than mine; the Fitzjameses were a proud family, but very upright and honorable. I could have wished Edward had a *little* more Sterling about him though, as he could by this time have carried on the business I'm getting too old to 'tend to. But I suppose Providence will provide."

"Yes, if one never stops working, and continually whittles down ones necessities. I must confess I haven't the sublimest faith in this 'providing of providence.' It seems to me the most unaccountable freak of faith where all is mysterious; and I'm not anxious to bestow upon an imaginary 'providence' the rewards of my own hard work and clear calculation."

"My son," replied the old man seriously, laying his hand upon Lisle's shoulder, to enforce the words, "don't speak lightly of serious things; and beware of taking up any of these infidel doctrines every year spreading round the world. Remember that 'the devil is as a roaring lion.' A good many things seem hard for human natur' to believe; but you'll come easier to believe them, when you consider that if you don't you will enter into everlasting damnation. Think of that, my son: everlasting damnation! It's better to believe in most anything, no matter how hard."

"Well, father, you may well believe 'providence will provide,' since you are well assured of 'peace and plenty' if you never work another day. But how is it men never make the discovery which women are forever announcing—that they have done their share of hard work in this world, and are entitled to rest during the remainder of their natural life."

"I think, my son, that I have known more lazy men than I ever have lazy women. There's your mother, now; a harder working person—man or woman—never lived. She's been just the wife for me, though I don't think she was quite calculated for a mother. The Fitzjames blood is smart and quick, and quickness don't quite agree with children. By the way, did you see your mother when you came up? Suppose you go in and sit awhile. I haven't quite finished my morning work, and Deacon Jones may send round for it any minute, now."

"Don't let me detain you. I'll stroll around till you finish, if it isn't long," and going out he wandered around for a while, in a listless, not altogether happy frame of mind, when the sudden whinnying of a horse at the hitching-post, attracted his attention, and he recognized Dr. Kelley's boy, who walked rapidly to the door with a note visible in his hand, which he delivered to Mrs. Sterling, who came out in response to his knock, and immediately remounted his horse and rode back towards town. Alarmed by what he saw, Lisle conquered his aversion to meeting his mother, and quickly reached the door.

"What is wrong at the doctor's, that the boy was sent up?" he asked abruptly without offering the ordinary salutation.

"Oh, it's you, is it, Lisle! The doctor's boy? Oh, he was coming this way, and Edward remembered I wanted some arnica—it's the best thing in the world for bruises and burns, and all that—so he sent him up with it. I inquired about the doctor, and the boy says he's suddenly worse since morning."

"Then I shall return immediately. Be good enough to explain to father why I don't wait to say good-bye," and he hastened away.

The tearful faces that greeted him as he arrived, confirmed the alarming intelligence, and he at once repaired to the doctor's room. Dr. Kelley turned his eyes eagerly toward the door as he heard it open, and for the first time Lisle missed the usual smile of gratification at his presence. In place of this, a look of pain crossed the doctor's face, and he exclaimed sorrowfully,

"He won't come, then!"

"Who are you expecting? I know nothing of it."

"Miles Sterling. Have not you just come from the mill-house? My note must have reached him. Julie wrote and dispatched it fully one hour ago."

"He may have done so ere this. I had not seen him for some time before I left, nor did I stop to say good-bye when I learned you were worse. I am quite certain the note was then in the house, as I saw mother talking with the probable bearer of it. I am sure the old gentleman will come at once, though it is a busy day at the mill."

"Oh, I cannot die in this way! I must confess the wrong I have done him, unrepaired through all these years. I have sought to quiet conscience by bestowing benefits upon him and his, have reared as my own *his* son, as expiation for putting mine under his name and guardianship—in vain! Even his curse is preferable to carrying this miserable secret to the grave. Hypocrite during my life, I would lie in my grave an honest if a hated man!"

" Do you really feel that such a revelation, involving all that it must, is wise, or that you will be happier for making it?"

" Yes, Lisle, yes! I am done with earthly happiness, and looking at this thing in the light of the other world, I dare not enter it condemned, to bear through eternity the aching burden I have borne in this one. I think you over-estimate the consequences likely to ensue from what I must confess. Miles Sterling respects, and in his own way loves his wife, and he will overlook this one error, when he thinks of all these years of faithful duty to him. His pride will seal his lips, very probably even to her; ánd I am sure *you* will not shrink from so slight a sacrifice as it involves to yourself, when you know that it takes from my last moments the sting I have suffered for so many, many years! Let me at least *die* in peace!"

Pressing down his rebellious feelings, Lisle murmured,

" Do as you will," and only the actual giddiness the effort cost him, evidenced the pang with which the words were wrung from him.

The doctor laid his head back upon its pillow, with a smile of content, and an unconscious interval, half sleep, half waking, succeeded the excitement under which he had labored. Mrs. Kelley looked in, but seeing him quiet as if sleeping, softly withdrew that she might not disturb him. The closing door again aroused him, and seeing that no one had entered, he murmured sorrowfully,

" Not yet, not yet! Is all reparation denied me?" A few inaudible words followed, and then he wearily repeated, " No hypocrite shall enter the kingdom of heaven! Ah, me! Who speaks?"

There was another interval of unconsciousness, during which his head tossed restlessly from side to side; and finding upon a second essay that he was not sleeping, Mrs. Kelly approached and bent over him. He looked wistfully into her face as he asked again,

" Won't he come to me?"

" Who, William! Is it Edward you wish to see, young Sterling?"

" Yes, Sterling, Sterling. It's him I want," murmured the doctor, wearily. Lisle knew not how to interpose, assured as he was that it was only the name of the man whom he had wronged that caught his wandering consciousness. Edward approached and addressed him; but the doctor interrupted querulously,

"Not him, not him. I want Miles Sterling; he who married Lydia Fitzjames, the mother of my—" He checked himself even then, and his wife supplied the word,

"Your pupil. Yes, I understand. He shall be sent for."

"Father was sent for fully three hours ago. Julie handed me the note she had written at her father's request, and I charged the boy to make all possible haste and deliver it to whoever he saw first at the house, as father might be out. He must have been so, or he would have been here long since," Edward said, explanatorily.

The doctor's eyes turned steadily upon him and rested there, plainly evincing that he heard and comprehended every word; and when Edward ceased speaking, he rocked his head to and fro, as he muttered hopelessly, "I see it all ; it's all clear to me now."

His hand dropped heavily upon the bed as he tried to raise it to his brow upon which heavy drops of moisture gathered, and a look of utter wretchedness and disappoinment settled upon his face.

It seemed as though with the death of hope the cords of life had snapped; for moments succeeded when it was impossible to say that he even breathed, and during one of these Lisle bent closely over him to ascertain if he indeed were among the living or the dead, when suddenly the closed eyes looked up, filled with a luminous haze, and the pale lips smiled as they uttered foudly, " *My son !*"

"His mind wanders," said Mrs. Kelley, softly, but even as she spoke, Lisle saw that all was over, and tenderly pressed his hand over the open eyelids in a way that spoke all which words could have told. A few moments of utter silence reigned in the room, when, hearing Julie in the hall upon her way hither, Mrs. Kelley summoned self-command and went out to intercept her, unwilling that she should suffer the shock such a sight must inflict upon her. Taking from her the bowl of nutriment she had just prepared for her fathers's lips, Mrs. Kelley placed it upon a table near, and clasping the hand that had held it kissed it tenderly, and led her away. Not a word was spoken, but Julie knew that kiss was bestowed upon a hand that had performed its last loving office for a living father. Edward saw them weeping in each others arms as he stole past the open door upon his way down stairs, and his heart swelled, as much at the tender sight as under his own bereavement.

Lisle remained alone with the dead. Inexpressibly affected as he was by the death of that father whose error had crushed out the happiness of two lives, he yet felt an actual heart-throb of relief that the hour of his more than mortal peril was over, and the humiliating secret was still his own. It was enough that they two should so have suffered under it, without pressing the draft to the lips of poor, honest old Miles Sterling, even might he have drained it in silence; but knowing, as he did, the old man's keen appreciation of anything approaching to dishonor, he felt assured that he would not have extended toward his erring wife that forgiveness upon which the doc-tor had so firmly counted. It was better for all that the secret and its bitter repentance remained untold, even at the price of trickery in withholding the note which summoned the wronged but unsuspecting old man to the death bed.' That it had been withheld, Lisle was as well assured as the doctor had been when he avowed that he "saw it all," and so resigned the hope for whose fulfillment he seemed to have stayed his steps upon the very threshold of Eternity.

It seemed to Lisle that this escape from the ever impending calamity which rendered his very life a nightmare, was little less than miraculous. A little more caution with that note, and all had fallen in ruin around him! An object of town gossip—a tainted individual from whom men turned away and maidens shrank—a humiliated, wrongfully punished man, whose very tombstone must publish his shame or rear aloft a lie—death, mental and physical, were sweet in comparison! Fate far more bitter than Cain's, in bearing that bitterer sting of injustice!   ·

It had passed by him through a chance as invisible as the thread of fate, and half stunned by the very intensity of this unhoped for relief, Lisle moved and felt like one in a dream.

CHAPTER XII.

Aroused from thoughts of himself by his considerateness and care for others, Lisle took upon himself the necessary direction of affairs, and spared Mrs. Kelley the many harrowing details inseparable from the last offices to the dead; and, from his calm decision of manner, no one would have suspected that any tie of consanguinity existed between him and the friend for whom the whole country round was inconsolable. Few indeed were they who had not some act of kindness to recall, some beneficence of word or deed, whose memory should rise up in blessing whenever Dr. Kelley's name should fall upon their ears.

Ever alert to relieve the wants of the poor, those who suffered in spirit only were the even more blessed recipients of his aid and sympathy; and the tact with which he relieved all suffering, amounted to an inspiration. If Lisle mourned for him in bitterness of spirit, it was a natural and noble testimony to his worth and kindness; and no one criticised it in very sympathy.

Edward was to all outward seeming more inconsolable than he. More demonstrative by nature, and feeling no necessity for the stern control Lisle imposed upon himself, he gave natural expression to his sorrow, feeling that he had lost *a father* more truly than had Miles Sterling himself lain in that silent coffin.

Vain benefaction had Dr. Kelley offered in expiation of his sin since the first-born of the man he had wronged, thus transferred to him all filial allegiance and affection, in very gratitude for the expiatory offering!

Mr. and Mrs. Sterling had offered their services to the doctor's family; but as they were not required, no meeting had occurred between them since his death. They came to the funeral, however, rather earlier than the appointed hour, as behooved such old and intimate friends; and as Mrs. Kelley and Julie were yet invisible, the brothers received them. Mrs. Sterling was uncomfortable and manifestly ill at ease in Lisle's presence, dreading lest he might make some allusion to the errand of the doctor's boy upon the last occasion when they had met ; for she thought it almost an impossibility that so pressing an errand should not have been made known to him upon his return. But he had resolved not to broach the subject, well assured as he was that her cunning had defeated the doctor's intention of a last interview with her husband, and she might have escaped the ordeal, but for a remark of the unsuspecting Edward in reply to some question of his father's relative to Dr. Kelley's last hours.

"He did not seem to suffer very much physically ; but he was very anxious to see you, asking again and again if ' you would not come.' Why *did not* you obey his request, father ? Old friends as you were, I should never have dreamed that you would have delayed for one moment."

"I never knew before that he wanted me. Of course I should have come."

"Then you didn't receive the note Julie wrote at his request, begging you to come to him immediately ? I sent it by the errand-boy, and charged him not to lose a moment on the way. I know he went with it, and he told me upon his return he had delivered it."

"It got lost somewhere, for I never saw it. Did you, Lydia?"

"Why, really ; I remember all about it now. Yes, the boy brought it to the house, and never *dreaming* it was anything pressing, I put it up in the clock to keep till you came in to dinner. It was a real busy day down in the mill, and you didn't stop for your dinner till late in the afternoon, so that with one thing and another, I forgot all about. I'll give it to you as soon as we get back home."

"It ain't much use now. I don't see how you could have forgot it at the time, when you knew the doctor wasn't expected to live many hours more. I thought you set more by your friends than that."

There was reproof, but not suspicion in his voice ; and involuntarily Lisle turned a searching glance upon her. She became slightly disconcerted under his scrutiny, resolutely as she endeavored not to betray it, and he could not resist throwing a certain meaning into his tone as he said, too low for any one but her to understand,

"I am afraid *that ' arnica '* caused forgetfulness. Did you find it equally efficacious with bruises and burns ? You have much to thank it for, truly !"

He regretted the words the moment they were uttered. His only safe-guard now, against the revelation he dreaded, was in this woman's power to keep the secret, and he could illy afford to weaken one of its defences by suspicion. He was, then, relieved as well as rea-sured by the perfect simplicity of manner with which she composedly replied, in a tone audible to all,

"It is very likely as you say. Any woman with a housefull of things to 'tend to, from children up to cooking and dish-washing, has enough to *make* her forgetful! I wouldn't be afraid to make my oath that I'm the first Fitzjames that ever was so put to it to get along. It's only a wonder that I ever think of anything, let alone a miserable little note no larger than my two fingers."

Sick at heart and disgusted at her consummate duplicity, faithfully as it served him even now, Lisle turned away and looked out among the crowd now rapidly assembling. He felt that he had little to fear as long as her mind remained subject to her will; that the secret she had guarded half a lifetime would not escape her control while reason retained its throne; and mentally praying that this might be forever, he threw off the incubus upon his spirit, and fulfilled the duties devolving upon him through the day, with a calm exterior that spoke nothing of the secret torture within.

The feelings with which Mrs. Sterling saw Dr. Kelley lowered to his last earthly home, were known only to herself. She made no pretension to inconsolable grief, nor was it probable that she felt any such, since she had never forgiven him for having married another, and the firm control he had never ceased to exercise over her since one well-remembered scene between them, increasing to outspoken authority wherever Lisle was involved, had stung and galled her since she had felt that as the wife of Miles Sterling she should be free from it. She had endured the continual consciousness that his eye was ever upon her so far as this boy was concerned, and every instance of his protecting affection for him had stung her to active malice where she could elude his observation. Any affection she might ever possibly have felt for him, was long since dead, and indifference had succeeded to the hatred she had once really borne him and outrightly declared.

It was Miles Sterling, the honest, unsuspecting friend of later years, who mourned him most sincerely of the two; and but for the veil which concealed her face, his wife's contempt for this sincerity would have been plainly visible to all observers, despite the expression of sorrow she had forced upon it. Poor, honest old man! Lisle pitied him with his whole soul. The peculiarities and weaknesses which marred his character formed no bar against the sympathy excited by the unmerited wrongs he had suffered from the two persons whom he most trusted and esteemed—his wife, and the benefactor of his son. For all his narrow-mindedness and parsimony, he was strictly just and honorable towards his fellow-men, not one of whom he would thus have betrayed, for life itself. It was an un-·merited insult which his wife now dealt him in her own heart, and Lisle felt it by that intuition which is as strong and unerring in bitter antipathy as under the nearest sympathy.

Impatient as Lisle was to return to his own home, and thus bid adieu, happily if forever, to so much that was painful in all respects amid his present surroundings, it seemed to him little short of heartlessness to leave Mrs. Kelley now, when she more than ever needed his aid and sympathy. Totally unfit to assume the necessary direction of affairs, she clung to him with an affection intensified by the remembrance of how dear he had been to her husband, and relied upon him as entirely as only a woman can. It was worse than useless to think of leaving, till affairs should be smoothly running in their new channel; and to this consummation he bent every energy.

Dr. Kelley, though too generous and uncalculating ever to have accumulated a fortune, had left enough property to secure to his family a comfortable maintenance, and a small legacy was willed to Edward for the purpose of completing the course of lectures already begun. Lisle thoroughly rejoiced that he was thus enabled to secure the advantages which his stubborn independence would never have allowed him to accept as even a brother's gift, and Edward's future thus far provided for, he directed his own immediate attention to other matters. Dr. Kelley had, with the exception of this legacy, willed all his property to his wife in trust for their daughter, associating Lisle as her guardian, by Mrs. Kelley's own request; and in connection with this trust, she one evening sought him, and with more calmness than she had assumed since her husband's death, said kindly,

"I know, Lisle, that you are anxious to return to your own pursuits, and that the weary weeks you have spent here were a sacrifice, however cheerfully yielded. I am going to release you at once."

He would have disclaimed the assertion, but she prevented him.

"It was very kind of you to leave everything and come in response to a wish that must have seemed unreasonable, and wholly unaccountable, as so many years separation tells more upon the unstable remembrance of childhood, than upon such love as the doctor always cherished for you. He always loved whatever he protected, and your delicate, unhappy childhood affected him deeply. I think he had long designed naming you as Julie's guardian, and when I saw how noble and trustworthy you are, I, too, overlooked the objection of your youthfulness, and to spare him the evident em-barrassment under which he labored in naming a request which he feared I might think a singular if not unreasonable one, I requested him to associate you with myself in her guardianship. You were painfully precocious as a child, and young as you yet are in years, mentally you are older than most men who have exceeded them by a third. I rely upon your judgment most implicitly, as I need not assure you. And now, Lisle, promise me that if Julie is ever left alone in the world, you will be a brother to her. I know that as guardian, you would be faithful and kind; but take her to your heart, and—if you have one of your own—your home, as a very sister. At my death she will not have a relative in the wide world."

"Dear Mrs. Kelley, may that time lie far in the future! I do promise, most faithfully, to be a true and loving brother to Julie, in all things; and should she ever be left alone by your death, my uncle will be to her the father he has been to me. I can safely promise that she shall find a home with us."

"She may require it sooner than you think. I am not gloomy or foreboding; but I have long been far from well or strong, and with William's death I have lost the *will* to live which has thus far kept me up. Next month Julie returns to school to finish the course of study her father wished her to pursue; and I am certain that this farewell will be our last. I have not breathed this to her; for, with youth, continual apprehension is more grievous to be endured than the bitterest sorrow falling unannounced. In the hour when this falls upon her, comfort her as you best can. If the love her father and I have always felt for you is thus reflected back upon our little daughter, we shall not have left her unprotected. You and I may never meet again; but I shall die in firm reliance upon your promise. I wish you were her brother in fact as well as in name."

Lisle felt the flush that crept swiftly up to his very forehead, and bending his head, he reverently kissed the hand Mrs. Kelley had placed upon his arm, powerless to utter a word. When he again looked up, she was gone.

The next morning, Lisle commenced his preparations to return home at once, amid which he was interrupted by a startling event. Chancing to be near the door when the bell was hastily wrung, he opened it himself, and received a telegram from the messenger, directed to his address, and with an intuitive sensation of alarm, he tore it open and read. It was from Mr. Fitzjames, and read as follows :

"'L. H.' decamped last night with all the available funds. Have written you full particulars."

For a moment he was stunned beyond all power of motion. Louis Hartley, the companion of seven years, during which not one suspicion had arisen against his honor—the *protégé* of that kind old gentleman who had been his constant friend and protector—whose loving care had raised him to the very position which enabled him to strike such a dastardly blow!

The black ingratitude of Louis' crime gave to it a tinge of positive horror, under which Lisle stood as if spell-bound. Then his thoughts reverted to his uncle. How would he bear this utter disappointment in one upon whom he had bestowed an affection which made each benefit heaped upon him a real pleasure to the donor, this cowardly act of the son of the woman he had loved even beyond the grave, with a fervor and constancy whose light was reflected upon her boy !

Lisle knew not the extent of the business injury thus inflicted—thought not of the possible ruin involving himself as well as his uncle. His one desire was to go to the poor old gentleman at once, and give him such consolation as he could impart; but deeming it only prudence to await the arrival of the letter which might contain something important for him to learn at once, he forced himself to do so with outward calmness. Long as the hours seemed in their progress, the final one was reached, and Mr. Fitzjames' letter was received; a kind, though sorrowful one, in which he merely repeated the announcement contained in the telegram, and remarked that Louis had seemed moody and preoccupied for days before his flight, and was impatient under every effort to win from him the cause of his evident trouble; that on the night he decamped, he had excused himself at an early hour, confessing that he was ill and wretched ; and Mr. Fitzjames reproached himself that he had not then made one more effort to gain his confidence, as he was almost assured that something weighed upon his mind which might even then have been explained, and so averted the commission of the deed. But he had suffered him to depart with a mere good-night, and in the morning he was found not to have occupied his bed at all, while evidence of hasty packing implied that he had gone in accordance with some pre-arranged plan which his early retiring was designed to aid.

The office key was found upon his table; but the safe had been relieved of a considerable sum, in addition to which he was discovered to have borrowed a few hundred dollars for which he had given the obligation of the firm. The missing amounts, in all, made about ten thousand dollars, and the only wonder was that he had not trebled the sum, as he so easily could have done.

Throughout the whole letter there breathed a spirit of patient forbearance which put Lisle's wrath to shame; but the request with which it closed, was more incredible than all that had preceded it.

He asked as a personal favor, that no pursuit should be made after the absconder, no publicity given to the affair in official quarters, and that Lisle himself should bear as little ill-will against the offender as possible; and he added that he had always intended to bequeath to Louis a sum not less than the amount to which he had now helped himself, and that doubtlessly his affairs were desperate and pressing, and he himself was not blameless if he had kept so poor a watch and guard over his necessities. He added that he had already repaid the sums borrowed upon the credit of the firm, that it might stand proud and honorable before the world, and that, after all, ten thousand dollars was not an amount of sufficient importance to cause any great consternation at its loss; it was better to consider it an unfortunate investment, and so let it drop.

Lisle refolded his uncle's letter, with a more genuine respect for him than he had ever experienced, much as he had loved and honored him. Not one reproach had he uttered against the ingrate who thus wounded him; not one regret for the care he had bestowed so unceasingly from his very cradle! Only a self-reproach for his own failure to learn the wants and weaknesses of the nature his fostering affection had matured. Any other man so suffering, would have mourned the ingratitude that thus could rob a benefactor; he only mourned his own short-coming in having rendered it possible for his foster-son thus to betray him! As if his hand had held the temptation up before him! Lisle remembered, if *he* did not, that Louis had never been frank and open in his deportment, and that during those days of his tutorship, this want of candor and manliness had given his benefactor's heart many a stab of cruel pain and disappointment. Lisle had striven to like him, with only partial success at best, and many a time had argued against the constantly recurring presentiment that this man was destined to work him some

deep wrong. Instinctively he had recognized him as an enemy; and
he recalled this, now, with a keen appreciation of the mysterious inward monitor whose voice he had temporarily strangled under what
he deemed the force of reason.

It was, then, with no kind feeling towards Louis Hartley, that he
made his adieus, and started upon his return home.

Mr. Fitzjames received him with more than his usual demonstra-
tion of affection, and assumed a cheerfulness of deportment which
it was plainly to be seen he was far from feeling in his heart. Despite his effort to keep up appearances, he looked more worn and old
than he would have done in ten ordinary years. That he was
cut to the heart by the disgrace Louis had brought upon himself, as
well as wrung by his ingratitude towards him, Lisle could well understand. He had hoped so much for him, believed so entirely in
his honor and rectitude of purpose, even when most disappointed
by that manifest lack of ambition to assume a desirable position in
life, which others had commented upon since he left college. This
radical want in his character, Mr. Fitzjames had obviated by himself
establishing him in a position where with anything like attention to
business, he could not fail of success. All his hopes were shattered
by this fell blow, and in his old age he was doomed to see his years
of loving care brought to worse than nothing, his foster son a repro-
bate. It was no wonder that his kind face grew suddenly aged,
and his frame bent as though under the weight of additional years.

Lisle's eyes grew misty as he looked upon him and realized all he
must be suffering so uncomplainingly; but no allusion to it ever
passed his lips, and only in the unprecedented tenderness of his manner, did he evidence that the subject had attracted an hour's thought.
Day by day the old gentleman leaned more heavily upon his cane,
and from having led a life of unusual activity for one of his years,
he now seldom went out at all, but, seated in his easy chair at home,
bent his eyes for hours upon the unturned page in his book, ever
and anon taking off his spectacles, which were unaccountably blurred
and dimmed, and wiping them with a slow indecision very different
from his former briskness of manner. In vain Lisle strove to re-
awake his interest in outside affairs. The old gentleman shook his
head wearily, as he strove to smile.

"I never felt any sympathy with the dying war horse that pricks
up its ears at the sound of the combat. When nature says 'lie still,
you have done your job sleek and clean,' I don't believe in brushing
around like a distracted comet! I have lost my ambition in accord-

ance with some plan of higher origin than my own will, and if my part in the programme is merely to doze in the chimney corner, it certainly involves no great risk to life or limb, and I'll e'en try it. I believe Bill is making love in a fatty way to 'Militia,' as he calls her, and I'm getting to be quite useful as the receptacle for Mrs. Drew's maternal trouble in consequence. I suppose Bill diurnally over-eats, and imagines his suffering in consequence, to be the pangs of love. I'm at no loss for amusement in my quiet corner here."

It was a cheerful evasion of Lisle's argument, but left him no course save that of submission to the new order of things; and he yielded it, only condensing his business into the briefest possible space of time each day, and spending every leisure hour by the old gentleman's side.

Thus sitting together one evening, they received their letters by a belated post; and fully occupied by his own, Lisle did not look up till a gasp from his uncle caused him to do so in alarm. In his trembling-hand he held a letter of which Lisle only noticed that the caligraphy was fine and clear, like a lady's; and large tears coursed down his furrowed cheeks as he regarded the inanimate sheet in a sad, pitying manner affecting to witness. Rising, Lisle laid his hand tenderly on the old gentleman's head, and for a moment neither uttered a word. Then softly smoothing with his hand the page upon which his eyes yet lingered, as if it some way were sensible of the caress, he said sorrowfully, re-igning it to Lisle,

"There, my boy, burn this, here before my eyes, that nothing may ever bare it to the scrutiny of others. It is a sad, sad world, Lisle, and when one has staggered under as many blows as I have, a light one overcomes, at last. I'm a weak old man now. Ah, me!"

Lisle took the proffered letter, and lighting it at the gas flame, held it till it burned to cinder, and tossed the charred sheet into the yard. His uncle watched it with pitying eyes, and when all was consumed, fell back in his chair, while a spasm of pain swept over his face, followed by a cold rigidity, and his hands groped aimlessly about him. Lisle raised him in his arms and bore him to a sofa. Unclosing his eyes the old gentleman murmured something of "pity and protection," coupled with a name Lisle did not catch. Some unconquerable difficulty obstructed his utterance, for often as he essayed to explain, the words refused obedience to his will, and only a confused murmur succeeded to the effort. Lisle realized then that a paralytic attack had overpowered the poor old man, and that the story he strove to tell might never be related by the lips which no longer yielded their allegiance to his will.

Thus he lingered for days, intelligent as before this misfortune, but utterly powerless physically, and it was grievous to watch the eager expression in his eyes so filled with a sad longing; to realize, at every moment, his useless efforts to relieve his mind of the burden upon it.. In such strength of mind and body as he had yet, to have expected he would not, even to Lisle, have wished to reveal the burden of that fatal letter; his wish that it should be burned, was sufficient evidence of his desire to bury it in his own breast; but with the hand of death upon him, his inability to make known his wishes was a torture, whose expression was promptly lined upon his face.

So he lingered for a few weary days, and death took him, at last, with the mental burden unrelieved—life's closing page a sealed mystery.

So Louis Hartley's crime had done its work upon his benefactor. Whatever had been the final blow, his had weakened and undermined the strength that otherwise had been sufficient to have met it; and Lisle regarded him as his uncle's murderer.

His debt to him was increasing, and he vowed to repay it if ever they crossed each others path. That they should yet do so, he felt an absolute faith. Even though pursuit might not. even now, be fruitless, Lisle yielded his wishes to his uncle's, and firmly resolved never to seek him; but if there were any magnetism in hate, that could lure him within his reach, he would repay at least the last half of his debt of vengeance. The man who could commit such a deed as he had been guilty of, would incur the penalty of the law for others; and in fate's good time he should have him at his mercy. For that hour he would watch and wait. Wait with an ever accumulating hatred "toward him and his," intensified by the utter isolation of heart and sympathy imposed upon him by the death of this one friend and companion, whose love was wholly unmixed with pain, whose kindness and protection had been a free-will offering uninfluenced by a sense of duty.

Lisle pressed his hat over his corrugated brow as he turned from his uncle's grave, and returning to his desolate home, he gave full sway to the torrent of grief and misanthropy which overwhelmed him.

Nature was at last avenging herself for the weeks of stern control that had checked and concealed so many varying emotions; and, completely unmanned, he lay silently upon the sofa where he had thrown himself, neither answering nor hearing Mrs. Drew's repeated appeals to him, from the threshold of the inexorable door he had locked between himself and the outer world.

CHAPTER XII.

"MISTER Sterling, I take it right ongrateful of you to fly in the face of Providence in this way, which it is likewise onaccountable to *man* or woman, and Lord only knows why you're bent on emigrating yourself off to the fur South, where, what with its yaller fevers, and its break-bone fevers, and its fever and agues as is born there, is enough to make ones hair stand on end! What can you be looking to find down there, aside of these, that you haven't in tenfold here?" observed Mrs. Drew, pulling nervously at her cap strings, from her position behind the coffee urn at which she presided during Lisle's now solitary meals.

"I shall provide for you, Mrs. Drew," he replied laconically.

Mrs. Drew resented the insinuation, and replied with feminine spirit,

"It isn't myself which I have in my mind's eye, Mister Sterling, for all you are beset to think that if any one speaks, it must be for himself or herself, as the case may be. Thank fortune, as a respectable woman as knows her duties and is yet young enough to perform 'em —let alone matermony itself—needn't be an object for '*providing*,' to any gentleman, if he have just stepped into a property !"

"I beg your pardon, Mrs. Drew. I only meant to say that I shall not sell this house, and that I shall be obliged if you will remain in it till a suitable tenant can be found, when I will see that you are comfortably located either here or elsewhere. Sometime, and somewhere, I shall have a home of my own, and I shall rely upon you to preside over it as you have done over my uncle's so many years. Will you come to me, then, despite fevers, and other unnamable horrors ?"

"Which I most certainly will ! I'll shake with chills and fever, in *your* cause, with pleasure and heartiness; and why not, being as I've been a sort of lowly mother to you these many years. I was only bemoaning as you should be took with restlessness as you should go running your head into you know nothing whatsever *how* many dangers as is vexing, and may have right smart of ill luck. Why, bless us, with your handsome fortune and good looks, what *couldn't* you marry in the shape of a fine, showy wife, as would make you as lovely a pair of matermonials as eyes ever looked on; and you wouldn't know your own house and home, it would be such a "—

"Pandemonium," interrupted Lisle.

"For all the world!" ejaculated Mrs. Drew; but she uttered the apparent suggestion in quite a different spirit from the one borne upon the face of it, surprise, not unmixed with indignation, having betrayed her into a favorite expression.

"Yes, that's just it," Lisle replied, provokingly pretending to misinterpret the spirit of her remark. "It is bad enough to be turned neck and heels out of the mastery of ones own premises, into which if one henceforth ventures to bring an unexpected friend they both suffer the pricks of figurative pins and needles, with an explosion every moment threatening; but that *the world* should thus come in for a matrimonial share of discomfort, isn't a 'soothing reflection,' as the immortal Pecksniff would have it."

"Whatever is it sets people's brains into such a whirl of contrariness! Far am I from meaning this which you understand! That I, being a woman which has a daughter as is matermonially sought —howsoever troublesome and onsatisfactory to myself—should so go t) testify against the marriage state, which I ought, con*trairy*wise to praise, which I do. Oh, Mr. Sterling, I'm afraid you belong to that misfortunate class as is naturally unmatermonial!"

"I think I do. But to return to the original subject. I do not leave, this place in any spirit of restlessness. It is simply impossible for me to remain in it, changed as everything is to me since uncle's death, and I shall sooner rally to a real interest in life, if I am entirely away from associations which every hour oppress me with unavailing regrets. This house, this whole city, weigh like an incubus upon me, and I can better bear my loneliness anywhere else."

Mrs. Drew was a naturally kind-hearted woman whose sympathies were always keen enough when aroused; though a life of homely duties and narrow experiences had rendered her a little obtuse where the case was not a marked one. She had been sincerely attached to Mr. Fitzjames during the many years she had served him, and from his boyhood Lisle had been a favorite with her, despite the oftentimes sarcastic manner under which he rendered her illy at ease; so she wiped away a few real tears that gathered in her eyes and maintained a little silence before broaching a topic which lay near her heart.

" You know, Mr. Sterling, which though I was your uncle's house-keeper for many years, I am not yet an elderly person ; very far from it, being that my Melissy was born when I was in my seventeenth year, which she is not yet twenty. Being that you are such a *young* gentleman, I will tell you in confidence, begging you won't mention it, I am in my seven-and-thirtieth year, which you wouldn't think it, would you ? The widowed state is a very uncomfortable state for an enterprising woman to submit to, and being that I've sup-ported it for many years, I'm now an engaged person. It is only right you should know it, so I tell you I'm an engaged person."

"Indeed ! Who is the chosen individual ?"

" Being as it is one as is unbeknownst to you, I tell you that he is named Joseph Perkins, which, though somewhat young to be a father to my Melissy, is of no account, being as she is determined to cling to Billy, useless as he is ! Poor girl; my heart aches me as I think how her life will be just cooked and stewed out of her, along of his stomic as is never satisfied. I've never seen him filled up yet, though many is the time I've tried to do it. The hoe-cake, and the gumbo, and the sweet-potatoe pudding that Billy *will* cram into himself is enough to bust an elephant!"

In her excitement Mrs. Drew fanned herself into complete obliv-iousness of anything but Billy and his internal capacities, and Lisle recalled her attention to her own prospects.

" Which sure enough I hadn't gone on to tell you ; and no wonder, what with the state of wonderment that Billy puts me in to. His internal improvements must be made of cast-iron, or they'd certainly give out on him ! Such wear and tear would be death on mere human organs ! About my Joseph, which I'm coming to him. I don't know but we shall be married right away, and I hope as you won't object to take him likewise into your service, with me. He is as en-terprising a young man as you'll see, and has many a year good work in him, being that he is now just one-and-twenty years old."

" Suppose you were to adopt him as a son, instead of accepting so young a man for your husband? It seems to me this would be more suitable in a matron of your years," suggested Lisle.

"And remain in a widowed state fifteen years more ? No. He will make me a very serviceable husband against my old age, being that I can't always work as I do now, and a young partner is better than two which are old and broken down. Adopting and marry-

ing are two different things, which my desire is for matermo·;y.
You'll keep a place open for my Joseph, Mr. Sterling?"

"Yes, but if Bill and Melissa marry, I want it distinctly under·
stood that I have no house-room for them. Bill will come to no good,
and I don't want him around. Besides, your husband should have
none but good examples before him, and Bill would be a bad associate. Perhaps, if you are to be married, you would prefer remaining here altogether, instead of accepting any other situation till I am
ready for you. I will instruct my agent so to arrange for you, if you
wish."

"I make bold enough to say I do wish. As for Bill and Melissy,
I don't care how soon you set them adrift, as it don't seem fitting
which my Joseph should be father-in-lawing them as is so near his
own age. Me and Joseph'll be better off without 'em, and if it is to be
matermony between 'em, why matermony let it be! I've struggled
a many years to keep her and her dresses straight, which crooked
both of them still are, and crooked they'll go on; which I can do no
more!"

"Permit me to wish you all a very happy honeymoon, Mrs.
Drew," and with a rather ironical bow, he took his hat and went
out.

Lisle had, as this conversation implied, decided to dissolve his
business connection with the city of Louisville, and seek a residence
farther South. Of too restless a temperament to be content with a
life of inaction, which his fortune as his uncle's heir by bequest now
enabled him to pursue, had he so chosen, he had arranged a co-partnership with a friend, under the style of Sterling & Bertram, and
the new house was to be opened immediately in the chosen location.
The farewell calls were punctiliously made, the customary, sometimes
sincere expressions of regret received with the degree of acknowledgment to which he considered them entitled, and Lisle was about
to depart from the scene of so many happy hours, the home more
desolate, now, from the very remembrance of all it had been to him
during his uncle's life. Painful as it was to him to remain in it, this
departure was scarcely less so, and he abbreviated it as much as possible. Already his trunk was on the carriage at the door, and he
was gathering the last few articles in a valise, when a rather ostentatious sobbing at the door caused him to turn toward it.

There stood Melissa with her apron to her eyes, her low necked
dress-waist as usual twisted far under one arm, with a protruding
whale-bone threatening her chin, and hair guiltless of comb or brush

for an indefinite period. She had never been a favorite with Lisle, whose first impression of her had proved durable, as first impressions usually are, and annoyed by her proximity he said curtly,

"I have no desire to cut short one snivel which you consider proper under the circumstances, but you will oblige me by airing them out on the gallery. If you want anything, say so."

Melissa assumed an air of injured virtue as she replied, still with her apron before her eyes, but administering a surreptitious push to the pugilistic whalebone.

"You never did give me credit for any decent feelings, and you've never treated me like a human; but I always liked you, and so did Billy, for all you've never quit snubbing him with might and main."

"Oh, I see," Lisle interrupted. "You and the fat boy are going to make a brilliant match, and you want me to give it my protection. Once for all, I will have nothing to do with it. If you marry him despite your mother's good advice, you must accept the consequences. I dare not trust him around the office, and I would not have him under my roof in any capacity. If he loses the place I secured for him when I assumed control here, he will have no one to depend upon in future but himself. You had better listen to your mother, and so avoid trouble; for you will be miserable if you marry the graceless scamp."

"'Listen to mother!' A pretty one she is to listen to, with her head full of Joe Perkins! I an't going to be father-in-lawed around by him, and no more an't Billy. You'd better talk to her about being miserable with a 'graceless scamp.' I'd rather be the missis of a scamp than a lout, any day; and a lout Joe Perkins is, as you'll see. If Billy ever does take to bad ways, I only hope you won't blame yourself for it—a turning of him off after all these years he's done for your uncle as is dead and gone."

"Thank you, I never shall. Be good enough to carry down this valise, and here's a good-bye for you. Don't lay it out upon Billy's 'internal improvements,' but buy yourself a gown with it—your wedding one if you will."

Seeing that nothing more was to be gained, Melissa accepted the gift with a sulky courtesy, and watched the carriage as it rolled away with Lisle sitting sadly upon the cushions by the closed window. Thoughts of his first ride through these streets filled his mind. Then, a timid, feeble boy, he had felt that his very presence in that city was due to a species of banishment from his home, and that he had nothing to hope for beyond his uncle's good will, or possibly friendship, and that he was to be a useless dependent all his lifetime. Now he was a self-assured man, whose position rendered him an object of envy to some, of social machinations to many. Fair laides would accept his name in consideration of his fortune, whatever they might have thought of his individual merits without this assistance into their good graces; and, what was far more to him, the business world now accorded him a respect and confidence based as much upon his well-known probity as upon the tangible funds that supported it. He had gained all to which he could have aspired, yet he was far from happy. Scarcely less lonely and miserable was the little boy who years before had looked out through the dreary rain and spattering mud upon these same streets overlooking the river. What was it which gave other men an object in life—something to hope, to toil, to scheme for? Often as he had queried of himself, the question was no nearer answered. Was every man a hypocrite to his own heart, and to the world, or were there a favored few whose outward deportment was a reflection of the contentment within? Would that man ever be found who had the frankness and fortitude to make a full confession as to how much was real and what was but seeming! Lisle himself would not have done so, and he judged others by himself.

The steamer was ready to leave the levee as he stepped on board, and Mr. and Mrs. Bertram were impatiently awaiting him. Mr. Bertram, Lisle's co-partner, was a reserved gentleman some years his senior, and, anything but a gallant husband, his pretty little wife levied sometimes severe contributions upon her male friends. Lisle liked her truthfulness and freedom from affectation, and as she was attached to many gayeties for which her older and more sedate husband entertained a decided dislike, Lisle had gradually become her reliable escort, much to the satisfaction of both husband and wife. They greeted him, now, as belated fellow-travellers are usually received at the last moment, and Mrs. Bertram had soon made him the repository of her travelling-bag, a heavy shawl, a novel, a parasol, and a few more of those outer defences for feminine travelling, inseparable from the institution.

Mrs. Bertram breathed a little sigh, as she said,

"Dear old Louisville: my heart quite aches at leaving it!"

"Then perhaps it sympathizes with my arms," said Lisle pathetically, looking down upon the burden they supported. "I must look up some able-bodied darkey who will take the contract to carry all these indispensables; for, really, my constitution is delicate!"

Mrs. Bertram received the sally with a laugh; but her husband protested with real impatience,

"Really, Mattie, it is shameful the way in which you ladies impose upon gentleman who are not in a condition to remonstrate against it! A man feels like an idiot, sweating under a load of feminine traps as high as his chin! I'd rather be whipped than to travel with a lady, anyway, but as though forty trunks and band-boxes were not enough, there must always be a miscellaneous collection of small am_ munition, like this. To make a man a *complete* fool, you ought al_ ways to make him carry a bouquet. I've pitched them into the gutter so many times that I've quite worked myself off duty; but Sterling would probably submit indefinitely. Sterling, rise up, once for all time, and dump that load into the river."

Mrs. Bertram directly placed her fan upon the top of the collection in Lisle's custody, and turning toward her husband, playfully retorted,

"That is just the way with you Benedicts. No sooner do you throw off the lingering remains of your gallantry, than you fly to emancipate all your much enduring brothers. I know my rights and privileges, and I don't intend to resign them till I'm thirty at least. I know Sterling is incorruptible even by your bad example."

"Well, if you resign at thirty, Sterling has but one year more of servitude. Doubtlessly he will endure that."

"What a malicious observation," Mrs Bertram exclaimed with some real as well as simulated spirit, for though good-natured, she was a woman. "You know I'm not yet twenty-five; though it may be that matrimonial cares and vexations are prematurely failing me. One thing is very certain, I haven't sunk under the burden of politeness."

"Nonsense, Mattie, be as good as you are beautiful, and relieve Sterling of that ridiculous trumpery. The truth is, Sterling, she meant to have put all that into her trunks; but the hinges began to creak, and she had to call John off the cover; but thank fortune, you've a state-room, Mattie, in which all this outside matter can be safely put to bed."

"Mrs. Bertram, shall I have the felicity of escorting you to your room?" asked Lisle, bowing profoundly as he added a shawl and valise near to the articles he knew were hers, and prepared to carry them all. An old lady sitting near, made a nervous clutch at her personal effects as Lisle thus levied upon them; but without having seen it Mrs. Bertram interposed,

" For pity's sake don't add insult to injury. Those are not mine,
Here, make over my accoutrements, and let me set you an example
in bearing the burdens of life."

Lisle bore them to her state-room door, from which she soon afterward emerged serenely, with no encumbrance excepting the novel,
to which she addressed herself without rejoining her persecutors.
She was very piquant and pretty, and her husband evidently thought
so, despite the abruptness of his manner towards her, and her animation and spirit were quite refreshing compared with the lazy
gentility so many pretty women affect. Lisle liked her beyond any
woman he had ever met; so, having watched her till the air of indifference with which she opened the book had given place to one
of real interest, he approached and interrupted her.

If there is ever a time when one's best friend is *de trop*, it is when
one is absorbed in an interesting book; and, knowing this as well as
most people, Lisle fully expected some intimation of it, whose very
naturalness would amuse him. She did not look up even when he
seated himself near her; but determined to interrupt her, he said,

" I have come to be amused. Your lord is deeply absorbed in
some business discussion out there, and I must offer my condolences
to his neglected wife."

She looked up a little impatiently, as she replied,

" You won't get me to indulge in any heroics upon the score of
neglect. Upon the contrary, I will pardon similar conduct upon
your part, just now, as this book renders me very forgiving."

" Thank you," said Lisle rising and bowing over his hat; " that is
as much as to say, that, having nothing for me to do, you prefer my
absence. You should never tolerate any one near you unless you
intend to render him useful. If you should chance to want me to
swim ashore with your trunks, in case of collision, fire, or snag, do
me the honor to command me."

" There: don't go away. How provoking you masculines are!
You never consider anything, but put on your little airs at a word.
Who tells you that ladies never mind any interruption? You won't
deny that you never lose an opportunity to tease me, and that while
I remain young and comparatively well-looking you never will lose
one! I have borne and forborne, for two all-sufficient reasons: first
because you are a good beau who finds favor in my husband's sight,
while all the young ladies are as jealous and envious of me as any
woman could desire; and secondly, I like you despite your imperfections, which are more numerous than you think. Yes, really;

but if I didn't like you I would cease to cultivate patience towards
you; for I'm quite in earnest when I declare that I wouldn't excuse
in Bertram one half which I do in you."

"That is the penalty one pays for being your husband. There!
isn't that rather pretty, for me? Though, to be frank, I would
rather be the never-so useful friend of any lady, than her husband."

"Ah, but you will come to misfortune yet! Somewhere in this
fabled South, matrimony will swoop down upon you, and thus avenge
the wrongs of my long enduring sex."

"Yes, you do endure a long time; truly said. One woman will
worry a regular series of husbands out of existence. But do promise me that when these evil days come upon me, and I am locked
out for not being in by ' early candle light,' or doomed dinnerless to
the attic, you will give me a hospitable loaf and a lodging corner.
I shall need friends."

"I don't imagine that even your wife would ever venture to take
such liberties with you, nor indeed any others," Mrs. Bertram replied
very seriously.

Lisle laughed, "I wish I thought so too; but, unfortunately, wives
are no respecters of (their husbands') persons, and I've no doubt that
the wife of ' the Father of his Country' gloried in the remembrance
of many a curtain scene in which she had ' done him justice,' (isn't
that the term?) Am I greater than he, greater than Socrates, that I
should escape?"

"Horrible fellow! 'Justice' will be a fearful work in your case!"

"No doubt. But it is a woman's besetting sin to take a man at a
disadvantage, and then glorify over it. Who hasn't heard old ladies
exclaim over some rising genius who was making a noise in the
world, ' Law! I've taken him across my knee no end of times!' Every
one knows what taking across one's knee means—'gentle warmings,'
&c. Is that it?"

"Lisle Sterling, where did you pick up your ideas of women!
Have you no mother or sisters?" Mrs. Bertram asked, reprovingly.

A tinge passed electrically over him, and he replied, gravely,

"I have both; I might add—unfortunately! But must one cultivate no ideas save those that sprout at the domestic hearth? I dare
say, now, that in that modest shade you were meek and lowly, and
never indulged in such sharp words as you keep for me. Who
knows but you even fancied yourself imperfect!"

"And now?—ah yes; thank you."

"Do you know, Mrs. Bertram, that you are really magnanimous?

I wouldn't tease you if there were any one else near me worth that trouble. I will devote some rainy day to finding a substitute, by-and-bye. Go on with your 'Desrues the Poisoner,' or whatever it may be there. There's no amusement since you won't get angry," and taking his hat he sauntered off and left her to the perusal of the interrupted pages.

The journey was completed without his aquatic services being required for the protection of Mrs. Bertram's trunks, and that lady herself entered with her customary zeal into the various amusements by which the passengers enlivened the trip. Mr. Bertram passed the time either serenely dozing, or discussing business topics with a congenial circle on the guards, and Lisle divided his attentions between the two parties, with very little toleration for either. The brain that never relaxes its tension, is but little superior to the one that is never strung up to the pitch of ambition; and thoroughly energetic as Lisle was during business hours, he locked this business into his office at night, and left it behind him when he journeyed. If the reflections which filled its place were not altogether pleasurable or profitable, he felt himself more a man and less a machine for giving leisure to them, and people queried how it was, that, equally well informed upon many subjects, he seemed engrossed by none. He was in all respects mentally as far in advance of his years as he physically appeared, and no one among those who knew him the most intimately, would have correctly estimated his real age by at least ten years; so true is it that the traces which anxiety and mental torture leave upon the features, are far more strongly marked than any left by the mere flight of time.

The residence of the Bertrams had been prepared in advance for their reception, and for the present Lisle was to be domesticated with them. There was something, which every one has experienced, indescribably grateful in the occupancy of large, fresh apartments, and their luxurious solitude, after the crowding and ceaseless clatter of steam-boat existence; and, having completed his toilet, Lisle folded away the inside shutters opening upon the street, and leaning upon the window-sill, gazed idly down upon the passing pedestrians, with that indifference common to strangers in a strange place. An impatient tapping upon his door roused him from his careless pastime, and opening it, he met Mrs. Bertram at the threshold.

"Are you never coming down to the parlor?" she asked impatiently. "Bertram sallied out as soon as he had inducted himself into his best suit, and I've been moping alone these two hours. Do come down and put me out of patience, or pique me into something like life."

"Now you see, Mrs. Bertram, that were I to cease teazing you, it wouldn't be a week before you would upbraid me for barbarous neglect. Whatever ladies may say of their own amiability, they like to display 'temper' upon every excusable occasion."

Together they descended to the parlor, where in due time dinner was announced, and delayed nearly an hour for the dilatory lord of the house, much to his wife's irritation. But he arrived, at last, as husbands for whom dinner is kept waiting sometimes will, much as everything indicates to the contrary; and Mrs. Bertram assailed him with a storm of questions.

"It is useless to declare you were detained by business, this time. You have undisputably been sight-seeing; so what sort of a place is this?"

"It seems a most extraordinary city. It has streets, some of which are numbered, and some named. I am sure I observed such uncommon names as Canal, and Chestnut, among others. It has public squares, and steepled churches, and horse cars. I didn't observe anything else out of the usual course."

"Bertram, why can't you give a satisfactory answer to an intelligible question?" asked his wife in some annoyance.

"I beg your pardon, my dear; I didn't so consider yours. But I'll tell you whom I saw. You remember Jim Venard, who married Em Wilkins, of Louisville, a few years ago?"

"Yes; and kept her on the regular boarding-school allowance of opera—two evenings each month—all through the very season of their marriage; and she so much admired, too, with beaux by the dozen around her although she was married!"

"Well; Venard survived even this, astonishing as it may seem, and avenging justice hasn't annihilated him, despite his cruelty to the lady of the multitudinous admirers; for I met him just now, and he tells me they are near neighbors of ours. He mentioned too, that they are afflicted with a five or six years old boy, though he worded it a little differently, evidently possessing an affinity for small boys."

"Poor Em! I suppose she looks quite the matron and mother, now. She used to be the most dashing, independent, girl in the city, before her marriage, and everybody liked her. 'A five or six year old boy:' just the age to be most provoking?"

"That seems to me a most indefinite period of life, as I haven't survived it yet, neither has Sterling, by your own account. Venard says that if Sterling insists upon organizing a bachelor establishment, he knows just the place for him, fine house, splendid grounds, and all that, 'to be sold for no fault,'—excepting that of its owner's bankruptcy. What do you say. Sterling?"

"That I am much obliged, and that I will look at it to-morrow."

"And *I* say it is all nonsense to think of such a thing," exclaimed Mrs. Bertram, warmly. "Why can't you be contented with a suit of rooms here? I'm sure the house is large enough for us all, and you wont have the fuss and trouble of housekeeping, which I can tell you is unbearable."

"I have engaged my housekeeper, thank you, and have no idea of leavening the dumplings, and beating pie-crust, in proper person."

"'*Leavening dumplings* and *beating pie-crust!*' And yet you gentlemen are always preaching about a lady 'being able to direct household affairs.' You had much better spare yourself impending humiliation, and remain with us. We need you. Bertram is the very best of society with a third person to draw him out; but like most husbands, he is the very essence of stupidity with one legally bound to endure it. The difficulty is, people don't marry each other till they have worn every interesting topic quite threadbare. I'd be willing to make an affidavit that neither Bertram nor I have advanced a new idea to the other, for the last three years. Make him stay with us, Bertram, do."

"Yes, I'll have an iron grating put around him, at once; and in the meantime, just look up your Natural History, and see what caged animals are dieted upon. How you women do tease a man when you set about it. It seems as though you look upon a poor masculine as a sort of pack-horse and victim in general, and as long as his politeness endures, you peg away at him. If Sterling chooses to stay with us, he knows this house is as free to him as it is to me, and quite as much at his service; but if he prefers one of his own, I don't see why he shouldn't be indulged. By the way, I nearly forgot to tell you that Venard wants us all to take seats in his opera-box to-night: I have the tickets somewhere—box 25, no 52—here it is. I knew there was a 2 and a 5 in it somewhere. I can't submit to it, Sterling. The scraping of the fiddles, and the screeching of the victims to popular want-of-taste, raises the deuce with a business man's calculations. I hope you'll escort Mattie, as I've promised Venard as much. *She* likes it, for the same reason all ladies do,—it is expensive.

"My dear, you converse well upon many topics," said his wife good-naturedly; "confine yourself to them, and you will receive it for much good sense, and possibly some taste."

CHAPTER XIV.

A LITTLE time elapsed, during which Lisle purchased and took possession of his new home under the faithful supervision of Mrs. Drew—now Mrs. Perkins—who, with her Joseph, lost no time in obeying his summons. Lisle was not altogether pleased with the "serviceable husband" his housekeeper had taken unto herself, whose unprepossessing appearance formed a topic for much playful banter from Mrs. Bertram, who never lost an opportunity for making a partial payment of the many debts she owed him, relentlessly as Lisle ever persecuted her upon all subjects in which he knew her vulnerable.

There is no surer index to the refinement and gentility of a family, than the appearance made by its domestic retinue ; and fastidious as he was in this respect, he regrrded Joseph Perkins with anything but satisfaction when that individual made his advent into his es-tablishment. Tall and lanky in figure, his thin, long, carrotty locks clung in a weak, dejected way, around his sunken cheeks, unwhole-somely yellow as if in sympathy, and his short-waisted coat, with its long tails dangling round a pair of consumptive pantaloons, led one's observation by discouraging degrees down to his feet, where his personal misfortunes seemed to culminate in a halo of corres-ponding glory. These members seemed quite to have vacated the front premises of his boots, and to have taken up lodgings in the area, so that while the abandoned territory extended indefinitely in a withered, weakly kind of irregular point, the opposite extremity projected far over the boot-heel, in a swollen condition painful to contemplate. Lisle looked ruefully upon the apparition, while Mrs. Bertram, who chanced upon the scene, laughed outright.

" I have heard of shoes being ' picked before they got ripe,' and. I'm sure poor Joe's must have met with a like calamity," laughed Mrs. Bertram when Joseph had been dismissed from inspection. " If you would like me to make a poultice for them, just say so."

' " It's useless," Lisle replied pathetically. " If I had a dozen poul-

tices, I shouldn't know where to apply them. They might draw his
foot out into his boot-toes, or quite out of the whole thing; according to application. There's nothing for it but to make him over entirely. If you insist upon rendering yourself useful, however, you
may put some 'drawing' application near his mustache that will
disperse it. The fellow is quite running to tops. He'd prove a
good useful fellow in a crow country, though, wouldn't he?"

"I think you had better prevail upon the Infant to 'write a bill
of divorcement and put it in-his hand,' according to the scriptural
directions for husbands who wish to relieve themselves of unnecessary wives. Cupid played her a sorry caper this time."

"Upon account of her youth and inexperience; yes. All said,
though, Mrs. Bertram, it isn't fair to name her 'the infant' save in
all due reverence. All feminines are mentally young upon matrimonial subjects; and Mrs. Drew served my uncle many faithful
years. If Joseph Perkins proves to be the rascal he certainly looks,
I shall be truly sorry for her. There's no knowing, though, what
decent clothes may do for him. Any man looks a vagabond when
he is shabby."

"Ah, yes. I think you fancy that a snub; and I'm not sure but
it is. Matrimony might develop considerable snubbing talent in
you! I'll go, now, and tell Bertram you are coming round and may
yet equal him, though no man need hope to excel him. Let us know
how you get on manufacturing servants out of the raw material."

It certainly looked a hopeless task, but mentally hoping for success,
he resolved to make a faithful trial, assured that could he but render
him presentable, Mrs. Perkins would not suffer him to be dishonest,
at least toward himself, without revealing it. She would see that
he was well served, and knowing that he could confide all things to
her honesty, he lost no time in supervising Joseph's outer man, and
hoped for the best.

Thus far no complaints had reached him, and though he sometimes saw that his housekeeper was flurried and anxious, all the
married people he knew, of whatever condition in life, were the
same, and if she was tolerably contented with her lanky Joe, he as
yet saw no reason why he should not be so. After all, he could
prove no worse than Bill, who, now the husband of "Militia," was
left behind to eat his way through life under other auspices than his;
and thus at last relieved of two disagreeable burdens, it would be a
sorry bargain indeed which could prove a worse one.

With his new home and surroundings Lisle became daily more

satisfied. The balmy Southern air seemed insensibly to penetrate his spirit, softening what had been stern and misanthropic, and attuning him to harmony with the peace and beauty around him, and for the first time in his whole existence, he felt that life offers some atoning hours for the many burdens it imposes, even to the most care-worn of earth's children Sitting in a dreamy languor upon his flower-crowned balcony, while the fragrance of his cigar was wafted round him in eddying coils by the scarcely whispering zephyrs, he watched the twilight as it wrapped its fleecy veil over the scene, and its tender brooding hushed him into peace and quietude as a lullaby soothes a restless child. The old anxiety oppressed him less and less frequently, and the sensitive shrinking from companionship, that had rendered him half a hermit in the midst of society, had vanished.

Without one effort upon his part to banish the past from his recollection, it had ceased to taunt and reproach him, and the stain upon his birth was as if wiped away, with the absence of all that heretofore had made it an ever present pain and bitterness.

Deep as had been his regard for Dr. Kelley, each letter received from him had been a probe applied to his proud and sensitive spirit, and each expression of affection they contained seemed a proclamation of the tie that existed between them. He did not admit to himself that their cessation was a relief, but the effect was manifest. It was as if some obliterating hand had wiped out all that was humiliating to his spirit, and levelled the wall of shame that had separated him from the world of his fellows. Into that world he now entered upon equal terms, and it acknowledged and bowed to his position. Mrs. Bertram depended upon him as an escort among the gay scenes she frequented, for she was an inveterate pleasure seeker, while her husband had neither patience nor respect for any world outside his business; and her chattiness diverted many an hour which he would otherwise have spent in loneliness at his own home. It was fortunate for each that they were near neighbors, since both were exacting in their demands, and though he would have protested, had she avowed to him that she was teaching him toleration if not admiration for her whole sex, it was in a measure true.

Lisle entered the Bertram residence one disengaged evening, to perceive an unusual excitement in Mrs. Bertram's manner. She displayed a tiny envelope to his gaze as he closed the parlor door upon his entrance, whose mission was plainly written upon its very exterior, and tapping with it the cheek of her meditating husband, she exclaimed, "There, gentlemen, I must have both of you upon this occasion. Mr. and Mrs. Venard are to be ceremoniously and handsomely 'at home' to-morrow evening, and I've promised Em that you shall both of you enter an appearance. Now, Bertram, you really must, this once. I've kept the card all this time, till Sterling should come, and so add his commands to mine."

"Humph! He won't be under as good subjection when he's been a 'legally responsible' as long as I have. However, he needn't obey this time, as I told Venard, to-day, I'd go if it upset the board of trade. That's the inconvenience of having friends; you can't say no."

"*Tres bien,* and let those return thanks who owe them. Of course you will go, Sterling, and I've a reward of merit to announce you. Em has at last prevailed upon that inexplicable Miss Wakefield to render herself visible. So strangely pretty as she is, it is strange she will forever shut herself up and utterly refuse to know anybody, despite all Em's protests! I don't believe it is all from pure sensitiveness regarding her position as a governess, for she is too proud for any position to humiliate her. She'd queen it, and that too, successfully, were she a nursery-maid instead of an accomplished pianist. I don't suppose you have seen her, Sterling?"

"No, I believe not."

"'*Believe* not;' you may be certain if you ever had, you wouldn't be in any doubt upon the subject."

"Oh, then she is something uncommon, eh?—'stunning' as the English fast ones say."

"Nonsense; that isn't the word for it, and I don't know any that is. She fascinates one from the very first, and then she grows and grows upon one, till"—

"She must be quite enormous then, I should say. Like 'Captain Murderer' in the old story, she must 'reach from floor to ceiling, and from wall to wall,' if she makes many acquaintances. I hope she won't go off in a catastrophe, as the 'bride-pie' eating captain did 'when he had picked the bones of the dark twin.'"

"Oh, Sterling, you are the most provoking! I'd like to see you thoroughly in earnest once, if such a thing is possible!"

"Why, I'm so this moment. How upon earth a young lady can 'grow and grow' without coming to something wonderful in some way, surpasses my comprehension! Well, proceed; what is she like now?"

Mrs. Bertram looked rebellious and flushed, and maintained a mo-

ment's obstinate silence, but seeing that Lisle was amusing himself at
her expense, while even her husband smiled, she said with an effort
which only rendered her words more piquant,

" She is like nothing you ever saw or dreamed of. She's made of
flesh and blood, and as *some* people say, ' she's got a nice head on her,
and a pretty eye in it, and she's a good figured person ;' and to tell
the truth," she said, suddenly brightening into good humor as she
proceeded, " she is marvellously pretty ; handsome, isn't the word
for her. Her eyes are very dark, and soft ; I suppose sentimental
people would describe them as gazelle-like, but I confess I never saw
a gazelle's eyes. And she has the strangest way—not of *blushing*, nor
anything like it—but rather flashing up the most exquisite color
when anything moves her."

" Well, go on ; I'm all attention," said Lisle gravely.

" She is neither tall nor short, but most exquisitely formed, and
she has the most peculiar arch in her neck just where it joins her
perfect little head quite *loaded* with purplish hair."

" Now let me see if I should recognize her by your description.
A schoolmistress with not very large bones in her anatomy ; has a
way of turning red in the face, at pleasure—(holds her breath !) has
one eye, if not two, of some dark color—has a neck with a curve in
it, like a crane's, and patronizes ' switches ;' isn't that what you call
false back hair ?"

" There isn't a switch about it. It is all her own hair, and as soft
and glossy as—I can't compare it."

" Whipped lard scented with bergamot ; half a dollar per bottle."

" Well, have it so if you will. I shall be revenged when you see
her."   .

Mr. Bertram raised his eyes wonderingly. " Really Mattie," said
he, " I don't see why you are so smitten with Miss Wakefield. I
saw her once, and she seemed to me a rather agreeable young lady,
but nothing wonderful. I should never dream of calling her a
beauty, though Venard and his wife do."

" Oh, you don't know a pretty woman when you see one. No
body expects you to testify," retorted his wife. " The truth is, men
and women never do agree in their ideas of beauty. It is singular
that Venard admires her, for Em thinks her wondrous. Aside from
her beauty, she is an actual prodigy."

" Heaven spare us !" ejaculated Lisle in all sincerity.

" *Fi donc !* You ought to be more reasonable ; you so handsome and well grown a lad! But she isn't a lecturess, nor a literary prodigy; her talent is music, and *such* music!"

"And a musical prodigy, of all others! She eats well, and sleeps immensely, doesn't she? Has a face decidedly running to lower jaw, a wide or at least a full mouth, and is sadly fearful of becoming too stout. Isn't it so?"

"Marvellous guess-work!" exclaimed Mrs. Bertram, sarcastically.

"Oh, not at all; most musicians are the same. Music is decidedly an animal instinct."

"Witness, a pig under a gate, or a calf at his matins."

"Well, then, to speak more correctly, the love of music is an animal instinct, and the talent for expressing it depends upon the animal organization, to such an extent that the very grossest persons I ever saw have been the very best singers. Look at the world of fine musicians, and contradict the shocking assertion if you can. It is all well enough, but I don't imagine that I should ever be fascinated with them in any sense save a musical one."

"Well, be satisfied, Miss Wakefield is not an *artiste;* she is simply an exceedingly fine amateur performer, and apparently wholly unconscious of the effect she produces upon her hearers. I have no doubt she would be hissed off the stage, and she will be glad she never practised her profession on it, when she learns that to this fact she is indebted for a lack of jaw and superabundant adipose tissue. She is delicate and *spirituelle.*"

"You surprise me more and more! I've seen many ladies' beauties, and I never saw one who was not more indebted to flesh and muscle for her popularity than to anything else. Fat men and women are disgusting to me, and I never pardon them for being so unless they are sorry for it themselves; and even then, nine times in ten they might have avoided it had they cultivated their heads instead of their stomachs."

"Dear me, 'I never yet heard that people are to blame for their own noses.' Who made constitutions, pray? and if we all had our *choice* in the matter, who knows if they'd turn out as warranted! I'm heartily glad you are satisfied with your own, and certainly I never saw any one more so. Lisle Sterling, you ought to be snubbed!"

"Well, I don't know any one who would take the job more willingly than you. But I'll wait a little, while you tell me more about your new-found goddess. You've told me *what* she is; now tell me *who.*"

"Ah, that's just the mystery. Nobody knows. She came to the

Venards from Judge Wheeler's family, where she had been employed as music-mistress to the young ladies. They knew nothing of her antecedents, as she brought no letters of reference, nor anything, but was engaged solely upon her evident merit. They were all quite fascinated with her from the first, and finding her a true lady, they made her a friend and companion, treating her in all respects as one of themselves."

" And then,"—suggested Lisle, growing interested.

"She remained with them some time, they liking her more and more, till suddenly,—I don't think, Sterling, that I ought to tell you, as Em told me quite in confidence. " •

" All the better : I've quite a feminine capacity for secrets. Go on."

" You mustn't mention it, then. Suddenly she disappeared without a word, and they saw her no more for two whole weeks. At the end of that time she reappeared one morning just as though nothing had happened, and when the Judge demanded an explanation of such mysterious conduct, she refused to give any. In vain Mrs. Wheeler and the young ladies wept and besought her ; she refused, while admitting that the demand was just and reasonable. They 'gave her warning, ' as the phrase goes, and she was weeping and wringing her little hands when Em Venard happened in. Em had taken a great fancy to her, before, and when she learned the cause of all this trouble, she stepped forward at once and championed her, taking her directly to her own house, ostensibly as governess for little Charley, but in reality as her own protegée and friend. Miss Wakefield confirmed every word the Wheelers had said of her, and Em says, quite pathetically avowed that she was not her own mistress in that respect, and might commit the same offence again. Em neither asked nor wished for any promises nor confessions, sensibly declaring that the poor child knew her own business best, and Venard, who is equally independent in his disposition, thought the same, and outrightly told her so. She has been with them now several months, and they both love and respect her. But she never takes either of them into her confidence, and just plods along with that little cub, Charley, who cares no more for ' gamut ' and ' perspective, ' than for the blue-laws and catechism ! The Wheelers had the grace to keep silence over the escapade,—though that is too harsh a name for it,—and she is nearly always invited out with Em and Venard, as she was with the Judge's family ; but she wont often go. Sometimes she does, and then everybody is smitten with her, for which she doesn't in the least seem to care. This is all any one knows about her, and more than any but us could tell."

" A most mysterious young lady, truly ! And she makes no more startling disappearances ? "

" No : and what is the most curious of all things connected with her, she hasn't a correspondent in the world, as far as any one can find out : never was known to receive but one letter, and as that one came the very day of her sudden disappearance from the Wheelers, it increased the mystery."

" But did the post-mark afford no clue as to the probable place of her visit ? Singular that one lady should receive a mysterious letter which half a dozen couldn't learn all about !"

" Of course we all asked everything about it that we could possibly think of; but the mark was so blurred it was illegible, and even the date couldn't be distinguished. There'd have been some comfort in knowing how long it took it to come."

" Poor Miss Wakefield ! I wonder if she knows how many pangs of curiosity her affairs have excited. I'd advise her kind friends to tea-kettle nose, or coffee-pot spout, the next one. Better that one letter should suffer, than that the whole sex perish ! Why *will* women forever fag and bully each other ?."

" *Some won't*, and Em Venard is one of them. She expressed some pretty vigorous sentiments to the Wheelers upon the subject, for which they like her no better to-day."

" If Mrs. Venard ever becomes a widow, she shall have the felicity of refusing me ! A woman who scorns an unfair advantage, is entitled to every legitimate triumph of her sex. And the mysterious young lady will be visible to-morrow evening ?"

" Yes, she told me so to-day ; and we are determined to make her sing, too. Everybody is crazy to hear her. You may make up your mind that when you see and hear Leonore Wakefield, you are for once going to acknowledge my good taste and judgment. I believe Bertram is really sound asleep. What a blessing it is that man has an amiable wife !"

Lisle bade her good night, and hastened homeward, more interested in the evening topic of conversation than he would have cared to own. Superior as he believed himself to the petty curiosity of human nature, he did not affect to be beyond its interests ; and this partial insight into a delicate woman's history affected him as no mere recital ever had done before. It might be that the mystery in her life which she guarded so faithfully—even to the jeopardy of friendship and reputation—excited his sympathy more thoroughly than any openly confessed trouble would have done, recalling, as it did, to his mind, the weary years he had borne his own miserable secret which he would have suffered death itself rather than reveal. Here was another life made wretched by a kindred burden, and that life a tender woman's, bound even by her dependent position to submit to prying curiosity, and to yield to, or openly defy, demands for explanation. A man could answer such demands as they deserved; but a woman, more than that, a young and beautiful one, could offer nothing but tears and protestations, and stagger on amid averted looks or illy-concealed sneers, as best she might.

All that was chivalrous in his soul rose up under this injustice, and he made his way through Mrs. Venard's crowded rooms the following evening, with a heart throbbing with pity and compassion for one whom he had resolved to befriend by every means within his power. Sufficiently interested in Leonore Wakefield to wish to see her before a formal presentation, he looked round for her. There were a number of new faces present, but not one answering to her description had yet met his gaze, and interrupted as he was at each step of his progress by the greetings of his friends, he was about giving up the search in despair, when Mrs. Bertram touched his arm.

"How late you are, Sterling! Can't you be trusted to go anywhere at a seasonable hour if left to yourself? One moment more and you would have been too late to hear Miss Wakefield sing. There is the prelude already. Come."

"I will if you leave a coat on my shoulders to appear in. Don't pinch so; my arm will be quite black-and-blue to-morrow; and it isn't polite to crowd one's neighbors so."

"Don't spare your neighbors, for they won't spare you. Don't you see you won't get near the piano if you dally along in this way? There! Some one has taken the place I had particularly selected for you."

"I'm not deaf, I don't know why any 'deacon's bench' should be reserved for me. Let us stop here."

"Why upon earth didn't you come earlier, so you could have seen her before she is quite monopolized?"

"Because, oh mortal infirmity—*I couldn't get my boot on!* I about concluded I should have to come, at last, like Mother Goose's son John, with a slight difference; one *boot* off and one boot on,

&c. They are what you ladies call 'a capital fit,' which means—you know what."

"Were any one else to hear that, they'd know at once how vain you are. I fancied you had a sanctimonious look to-night, for some reason."

"Don't compliment my extremities at the expense of my head, I beg you. If you think me pretty, say so, but don't accuse me of being vain."

"You are neither one nor the other. There. Just hear her!"

Leaning against the door-case, Lisle commanded a fair view of the lady at the piano. Prepared as he was to find her beautiful, he had never imagined such grace and sweetness united with that beauty. He had expected something rather in the "dashing" style; an air of *aplomb*, with possibly a tinge of self-satisfaction, despite which he had resolved to like her, knowing that beneath it all she concealed some sorrow that merited the sympathy of every heart that had likewise suffered in secret and alone. But the ruling characteristic of Miss Wakefield's beauty was gentleness; not the insipid, appealing air usually recognized by that term when applied to a pretty woman, but an indescribable grace detracting nothing from the dignity of her deportment, while it softened the rather striking style of her beauty of face and figure. The face, of the clearest oval contour, and pale in its complexion, excepting when some mental emotion tinged it with a brighter tint, was quite illumined by the large, almond-shaped eyes, dark and soft, and wondrously expressive; and the symmetrical head, adorned only by the waving coils of that magnificent hair, purplish in its very blackness, which Mrs. Bertram had apostrophised, was borne with an air of pride as instinctive and free from affectation as it was royally beautiful.

"Isn't it lovely!" exclaimed Mrs. Bertram as the music ceased.

"Yes, she is, exquisitely so," Lisle replied with a sigh. Mrs. Bertram laughed.

"Oh, *she* of course is so. I told you that before you came. I spoke of her singing, then. Did you hear it, or were you as absent as you yet seem?"

"I heard it, of course; but I'll set you an example of frankness, and declare, at once, that I was not thinking of it as much as of herself. I shall never again fear Jove's thunderbolts, since one of them failed to do duty when I last evening enumerated the charms of the schoolmistress! I feel as though I ought to ask pardon for it, but I don't know of whom. How insufferable I must be at times!"

"Of course; don't I tell you so? And you didn't 'think of the singing' just now, when everybody else was spell-bound! Her voice is an audible tear; it is so clear, bright, and liquid! Yet, I would be willing to give bonds, that if you ever hear her sing a glee with corresponding expression, you'll refer to the pathos just now displayed, and impatiently assert that it was all acting—that musical tones, like popular morals, are assumed for the occasion, and have no connection with the real character."

"Why, yes, I make that assertion in this moment. He only is the true philosopher, who is entertained without being deluded. If one only acts well and in good taste, no one should complain, though since it is manifestly but an offering to his gratification. No one acts the hypocrite for his own satisfaction. Do you see that Miss Wakefield has again drawn on her gloves, as a signal that she is now to be entertained? I wish you would present me."

"I will, though I'm quite uncertain whether she will be entertained by you." And seeing that she was, by good fortune, disengaged, Mrs. Bertram introduced him with a blended cordiality and playfulness warranted by their mutual intimacy. Lisle smiled at the air with which she complied with his request, while he secretly rejoiced that it was not a formal presentation, placing him socially *de combat* with one for whom he entertained so much sympathy and admiration.

Miss Wakefield raised her eyes mechanically to his face for an instant, and then bowed formally, without the faintest affectation of a smile.

"A most serious young lady, upon my word!" thought Lisle a little chagrined at her coolness, as if, in some way, she owed him more cordiality for the many kind thoughts he had bestowed upon her; but he offered her his arm for a promenade, with as much gentlemanly assurance as he could summon under this mental shower-bath, and they moved away amid a throng that were seeking the galleries. A lady by a miss-step tore Miss Wakefield's trailing dress, and as she apologized and passed on, Lisle said laughingly,

"You ladies seem to be each others predestined enemies. 'See what a rent the envious *lady* made,' if you will permit the paraphrase."

"I think you judge rather harshly," she replied gently.

"Pretty little creature, but not at all brilliant," was Lisle's mental comment; and he proceeded with laudable perseverance in his efforts to amuse and interest her, till, quite discouraged by the brevity of her replies, he asked banteringly,

"Have you a gift for silence, Miss Wakefield?"

"No, I believe not. I will be unnecessarily frank, and tell you that though not insensible of your efforts in my behalf, I was perversely and inexcusably preoccupied. Language is not always at one's command."

She smiled as she made this unique confession, a sad yet tender smile, that fell upon him like an inspiration; and now quite at ease, he said with mock regret,

"And all the wisdom I have been uttering has fallen upon unlistening ears. Ah me! Well, I pardon you, unasked. I'm magnanimous." ·

"Yes, I know you are," she replied earnestly.

"Thank you. I am equally pleased and surprised that I have friends who thus recommend me to your favor. I supposed that if you had heard anything regarding me, it had led you to fancy me an ogre."

"No; it is impossible for me to commit such an error. I know you far better than you imagine."

Lislé bowed, and his eyes asked the question politeness forbade to his lips. She answered it as though he had really spoken, and with a silvery laugh.

"Oh, one cannot express the sentiments you so universally utter, without acquiring some notoriety; and it might be asserted as a a truth, that the most direct road to a lady's interest, is that of systematic detraction of her sex. Very few of us are superior to the weakness of seeking to make converts—particularly of so-called 'women-haters.'"

"But I am not a woman-hater. I believe, in all sincerity, that there are few living beings who more truly sympathize with a woman's existence, cramped and unsatisfactory as it is, than I do. One has a right to laugh at human peccadillos, however manifested ; and if I appear most amused by feminine ones, it is because they are more innocent than those of my own sex. .You are amusing, while we are guilty ; and it is a perverse heart indeed that laughs at guilt. Are you a believer in the philosophy of affinity, Miss Wakefield?"

"Are you quizzing me, Mr. Sterling?"

"Not in the least; because I confess I am a convert to that science, or instinct—for it is both one and the other. I never came in contact with a mental antagonist, without receiving a sort of psycho-

logical telegram announcing it, and I never suffered it to pass unheeded without regretting it.   I suppose every one experiences the
same to some extent; but, unfortunately, the dread of ridicule pre-
vents the confession of many singular premonitions which fall little
short of the miraculous.   Do I seem to you tinctured with German-
ism?"

"Not at all.   I suppose no one accepts or rejects acquaintance-
ship except in obedience to this law, however unconfessed, or un-
recognized even by one's self.   But what led you to make such a remark just now."

"I will tell you when we become better acquainted, if you allow
me that privilege."

She bowed, and smiled assent, and he added more earnestly,

"Please remember that I shall avail myself of your permission.   I
ask, in good faith, that you will allow me to strive for your friend-.
ship and good will."   - ·

"It is but a slight gift for the fortunate Mr. Lisle Sterling to
claim," she replied with a courtesy whose very pride was a reminder
of the difference in their positions in life.   He closed his lips more
firmly, and offered his arm again to escort her to the parlors; for,
tired of the ceaseless promenade, they had lingered by the balustrade.
She thought he was offended, and as she placed her hand upon his
arm, she said more gently,

"If you indeed care to pursue this acquaintance, I shall be only
too happy.

"I certainly do 'care,'" he replied, with a lingering pressure of
the hand she offered him at parting, as he resigned her to fulfill an
engagement with a waiting partner.   He lingered some time, but
seeing her continually surrounded, and having suddenly discovered
that he was tired of remaining, he made his adieux and departed.
Mrs. Bertram shook a warning finger at him as he passed her, hat in
hand, but with a bow of laughing defiance, he passed on.

Mrs. Bertram reserved her comments for her husband's ear, and
as they sat by their own fire while he smoked his good-night cigar,
she said: "Sterling seemed quite interested in Miss Wakefield this
evening.   Did you notice it? I never saw him so manifestly 'smitten,' and it is plain to me that his heart isn't so obdurate for all
his uttered heresies about women.   If he has enough talent to fall
in love with any woman, it certainly will be Leonore Wakefield,
and I hope it will."

"Nonsense, Mattie!   Can't a man admire a pretty woman with-

out taking leave of his good sense at once and forever? I've yet
to learn that running away from a party in the middle of the evening, as he did, is a proof of having been particularly fascinated
by some one present. I hope that your good sense will effectually
prevent you from any effort at match-making; particularly in this instance, where nothing but trouble could ensue from it. Any man
who marries Miss Wakefield, with that mystery in her life unconfessed, will be miserable, depend upon it."

"And why should it be unconfessed, as you seem to suppose?
Every woman who loves any man, is only too willing to give him
unlimited confidence. That is what makes half the trouble between
them. A wife who goes to her husband with every petty difficulty,
keeps him in continual hot water, and it is strange if amid his
writhings she doesn't get liberally bespattered herself. But don't
be uneasy lest I over-exert myself upon Sterling's and Miss Wakefield's account. He is the last man in Christendom I should ever
presume to tamper with, and she is as proud and reserved as she is
beautiful. I don't believe she would marry him were he to ask her,
for the very reason that the world would say she had 'made a good
match.'"

"Humph! I'd advise him not to risk it. It would prove a sorry day
for him and very probably for her, too. I don't know what her story
may be, but I've a suspicion that it is one that she will never confess to
him, nor to any one else. She has an undisputed right to a secret,
or a husband; they don't go well together, as she'd soon discover."

CHAPTER XV.

THE next evening Lisle started " to call upon the Venards," as he stated in reply to Mrs. Bertram's inquiries as to what took him from her house at so early an hour; for as usual he had called in passing. She at once invited herself to accompany him, insisting that a lady friend was invaluable for filling the chinks and crannies in conversation, with some chatty nothing that keeps the whole smooth and complete. He had expected that she would thus volunteer, and he was glad that by doing so she had spared him the necessity for asking her, as, much as he wished for her company, he did not like to incur the banter he knew she would inflict upon him for insinuating it. She knew, as well as he did, that "the Venards" was only a convenient term including the real attraction that led him thither; but she considerately refrained from any such insinuation, and only as they stood at the gate while waiting for the bell to be answered, did she mention Miss Wakefield's name.

"Of course Miss Wakefield is included in this call, Sterling. I don't know that she'll come down to the parlors, but she ought, after having so ungraciously received you last evening! I felt as though she had dashed cold water on me, when she acknowledged the presentation I had so informally made. What did she say to you, afterward, by way of amendment?"

"I can't recall anything worth repeating. She said nothing but 'yes' and 'no' for a while, I remember; and she seemed so completely abstracted, or pre-occupied, that I was afraid she would forget even that. Yet I know she can talk, and that very well, if she chooses. It is a pity such a woman should be a formalist. It seems to me the whole feminine race are on a strife to defeat everything nature tries to do for them! They seem determined to equalize matters in some way, so that ugly or pretty, intelligent or vapid, there's little choice between them. If Miss Wakefield would really utter one half she looks, she would be irresistible. One lady can always unseal another's lips, and I rely upon you to make your 'prodigy' establish some claim upon all your encomiums. You will hardly like to admit that you have mistaken mere stupidity for 'queenly pride,' and all that."

" I don't intend to make any such admission. You masculines are reasonable creatures, really ! If a lady doesn't tell you all she knows in five minutes, she is 'stupid ;' if she does, she is 'a shallow chatter-box !' You never seem to think there may be any difficulty in knowing just how to address *you*. Everybody has seen talented women chattering all sorts of nonsense to some man who would have appreciated her natural sound sense, whereas she the next moment squanders that upon some simpleton who is mentally pronouncing her a blue-stocking. If a lady with two atoms of tact, doesn't entertain each of you according to his own style, I don't see why *she* should bear off the palm for 'stupidity.' Who tells you to assume an impervious exterior, and often enough one exactly the opposite of your real selves ?"

" Mrs. Bertram, I have at this moment fallen heir to an idea ! Thank you."

" Then ring that bell again. Ten to one the old darkey who keeps the key, can't be found. Whoever invented this provocation for gnashing of teeth outside the gates, ought to be indicted ! I declare, I often start out for a little visit in this way, feeling good-natured and animated to the most liberal extent ; but while waiting, and waiting to be admitted, my spirits sink and die out till I am at last let in in a most depressed and irritable condition, and if I were unmarried, so that I dared not exhibit my ill-temper, I should really turn and fly, in defence of my reputation for amiability."

" I never heard that you had any ! It is strange how long one's most intimate friends often remain in ignorance of one's merits and celebrity ! Here comes our Cerberus in ebony ; so don't make your *entrée* this time in a mentally dilapidated condition. I rely upon you to banish the formality of which I feel a dismal foreboding ; for I meekly confess that Miss Wakefield extinguishes all my self-assurance and *modest originality*."

" So ; it seems we are *two* sufferers ! I never suspected 'that *you* had any' of the last named commodity ! Now do let us be polite before people, or they will begin to think we've no respect for each others mental machinery."

Any fears which Lisle might honestly have entertained of a formal visit, were quite put to flight by his first view of the social aspect of the drawing-room, occupied by a full family party of which even

Master Charley formed an integral portion. Mr. Venard's father and sister had that day arrived upon a visit from the country, and after the usual presentations, Lisle found himself without any special effort toward that satisfactory consummation, seated upon the sofa occupied by Miss Wakefield, with only Master Charley sandwiched between them, whose curly little head offered no obstruction in the way of observation or sociability, and she herself, so far from exhibiting anything like constraint, or pre-occupation, was cordial and animated, and her usually rather pale face was now flushed upon either cheek with a delicate color that rendered her more perfectly beautiful. Lisle had admired her before; he yielded his undivided homage now, and was really annoyed when their *tête-à-tête* was broken in upon by Miss Phebe Venard, who drew up her chair with a manifest intention of becoming a permanent addition, as she said with a directness characteristic of her,

"Now, Mr. Sterling, do say something to gratify my curiosity concerning you. They say you are very peculiar in your ideas upon most subjects, and strikingly original and independent in your expression of them. I do so admire originality and independence! don't you?"

Lisle bowed with as much gravity as politeness demanded, and Miss Wakefield turned upon him a glance full of suppressed mirth, under which his usual quickness and tact quite deserted him.

"To whom am I indebted for so favorable a judgment?" he asked with a feeling of secret satisfaction that so far as one brief sentence could impeach the veracity of the testimony, he had succeeded in doing so, since ninety-nine persons in a hundred would have uttered the same to all effect.

"Oh, everybody, for that matter, including Miss Wakefield herself."

Lisle returned the glance he had but the previous instant received, accompanying it with a salutation of mock reverence, under which she colored visibly, despite the frankness with which she turned toward Miss Venard.

"Now, Miss Phebe, do confess that whatever you might have understood me as meaning to express, I did not say just that."

"Oh, of course one is not expected to repeat such things just literally, but I recollect you quite agreed with sister Em when she said something like it, and that you added that 'he is magnanimous as '—*something*, I forget what—as you are so particular about the exact words. Don't you remember that Em asked you how upon earth you made such a discovery in one short evening, when she thought him an absolute cynic after all the time she had known him?"

Master Charley had manifested a growing uneasiness under his own conversational inaction, which here defied all farther restraint ; and suddenly elevating himself to a more satisfactory position, he said sturdily, with a warning finger raised towards his young aunt,

"Come, now, aunt Phebe; if you're to tell tales on everybody else, just tell what *you* said. Don't shirk it off, now !"

" Hush, Charley. ' Little boys should be seen and not heard.' It . is bad enough that they should have ears ; but they *never must* have tongues," and Miss Phebe threw into a warning glance the irritability she contrived to banish from her tone. Charley caught it, and hesitated.

Lisle extended a shining "quarter," and patting his curly head, said encouragingly,

"Here, Charley, if it is worth more, just name your price. Let us have Miss Phebe's remark with the rest."

Charley pressed the quarter with a cordial palm, and stimulated by its comforting contact, braved the gathering displeasure.

" She said she was just out of an engagement, and you were exactly the style of man she wanted for the next one, because, she said, it was so nice to just wind around her finger a man everybody else was afraid of, and so nice to marry *rich !* Yes, you did, aunt Phebe ; I heard you."

" I'm your debtor for another quarter, Charley. That is too cheap at one."

Miss Venard flushed up angrily, and after an instant's unsuccessful struggle to get the better of it, she gave expression to her choler.

" Well, I must say, Mr. Sterling, that you are ' peculiar ' enough, if your idea of politeness is consistent with hiring little boys to tell tales out of the family. If I couldn't find out what people said and thought about me without stooping to that, I'd remain in blissful ignorance. You are as vain as you are malicious. There !"

" I believe I am ; thank you. Does your vacation occur so early in the season, and if so, will you remain here long enough to allow me to retrieve myself in your estimation ?"

" Thank you ; I'm not just from school, though you choose to insinuate it," and she wheeled back her chair and walked away indignantly.

Amused though disapproving, Miss Wakefield toyed with her

watch chain without once lifting her eyes.   A moment's silence succeeded Miss Phebe's retreat, and then Lisle said deprecatingly,

" You think me a savage, Miss Wakefield, I have no doubt.
Granted, but with the addenda that I *know* better, if I don't always
practise it.   But do tell me what one is to do when one is offered the
actual premium for successful torment which Miss Venard holds out.
Besides, you will admit that she received as much consideration and
mercy as she bestowed upon others."

" If none of us ever received more than we bestow, this would be
a most uncharitable world.   We are all of us too apt to choose the
lesser blessing of receiving; particularly where charity and loving
kindness are involved."

" One has the 'inward and spiritual grace' to extend loving kindness only to a certain class of unpretty doers."

She made no reply save what was involuntarily written on her
softly serious face ; and, really wishing her to speak it, Lisle said so.

" Thank you.   I have no gift for lecturing," she replied with a
smile.

" In which very assertion, permit me to say, you utter the strongest
proof to the contrary.   One who distrusts his own talent in any particular field, is little apt to overdo the matter, which is the one error
to be avoided in this species of lecturing.   I rather pride myself
upon my candor ; so I will admit that enjoying another's discomfiture
is a most abominable revelation of character and disposition.   I
haven't even sprouted for a saint ; and I don't repent and sin no
more, from a deadly fear that I should be a loser by the exchange.
Before one turns from the errors of his ways, if he has a turn for
calculation, he will seriously question whether he derives more happiness from his sins than he could do from the contemplated virtues.
Being good must have its rewards, or so many sensible people
wouldn't be so ; but in a business point of view, it isn't well to sacrifice a known advantage to a problematical gain.   Did you really
pronounce me ' magnanimous,' and if so, may I ask upon what you
based such a supposition?"

" Oh fie, to beg for a sugar-plum after such a naughty speech as
that ! Did I not know that you are not one-half as bad as your
declarations would stamp you, I would not admit that I did say so,
and add, as I do, that it is not a mere ' *supposition.*' "

" I must then believe that you are an equal believer with myself
in the correctness of impressions.   You may recollect that we were
speaking upon them last evening.   Sometime, not yet, I am going

to accuse you of having conceived a most unflattering one of me
when I received the honor of a presentation to you."

"I deny the accusation at once and forever."

"Indifference, if not dislike, spoke in your every gesture."

"Oh, Mr. Sterling! how unjustly we comment upon the actions
of others! I had long before last night received my impressions of
you, and I tell you, truly, that if I appeared taciturn and frigid, it
was the sincerest compliment I could have bestowed upon you."

"Thank you; but don't punish me with any more of a similar
kind. I'm not equal to a just appreciation of that school of flattery.
I shall value all manifestations of your good opinion of me more
highly than I can express."

"Do not flatter me, Mr. Sterling, I beg. One expects such language from so-called 'ladies' men ;' but one hopes for other things
from those whose honest opinions and sentiments are more highly
prized than any fictitious ones could be."

There was an unmistakable air of frankness and sincerity in the
utterance of these words, that placed them far above the category
of mere compliment; and Lisle bowed for once in sincere acknowledgment. Miss Venard again approached them, having conquered
her former indignation, and feeling that she owed an apology for the
hasty words she had spoken under its influence. She was not so
really ill-tempered as she was hasty; and with a good-humored laugh
she addressed her late adversary,

"I excuse your insinuation that I am a mere ill-bred school-girl,
without asking you to offer any apology for having provoked me
into such an exhibition of temper ; but weren't *you* taught to make
suitable amends without waiting for them to be demanded? Don't
they teach magnanimity at college?"

"I don't know ; I never was in college. My mental training was
received from a private tutor whose ruling characteristic was not of
the brotherly-love and golden-rule school. I believe I owe you an
apology, and I'd make it, forthwith, were I not morally certain I
should have to repeat the process indefinitely. When one is so well
aware of one's short comings, it is dangerous and inconvenient to establish a precedent to which one is forever after expected to adhere.
Don't look so serious, Miss Wakefield. Do I speak too lightly of
such very weighty matters?"

The unexpected address roused her with a little start from a brief
but absorbing reverie, and, slightly confused, she said,

"I beg your pardon, Mr. Sterling. Were you again nominating me to your evidently vacant censorship?"

"Yes, if you thus choose to define it."

"I beg leave to decline it. I have no ambition to 'set up in life' as an ogress. If, as I believe, Miss Venard makes you sincere overtures of peace, I do not see how you can well refuse to accept them; but if there really exists any insuperable objections, my advice would be as ineffectual as misplaced."

"Oh, I have accepted them; that is not the question as issue. You have evidently repeated the style of compliment I begged to be excused from receiving henceforth. The query is, do I owe Miss Venard an apology."

"Decidedly *yes*, or you will win no laurels for generosity."

"Please consider it made, Miss Venard. Charley, isn't Miss Wakefield very strict and cross, generally?"

"Yes, she scolds me like everthing sometimes. I wish you could hear her once!"

"I wish I could, but as young ladies never scold in the presence of gentlemen, just tell me how she does it. What does she say when she is cross?"

"Oh, she puts her hands up to her temples, so, and draws down her mouth as if it was cram-full of miseries, and kind of whines out 'Oh, Charley, do be good and pay attention now! I'm so miserable, and I want to get these lessons out of the way;' and then when I dig into 'em and get all through, she just leads me out and then locks the door behind me for ever so long, and won't come down to dinner nor anything, and sometimes I hear her just cry and cry! she's so mad about something."

The relation was not as amusing as it promised to have been, and Miss Wakefield's face paled and flushed as she nervously clutched Charley's little hand with her own trembling one, in a mute appeal for silence. Pained by the revelation of suffering his bantering had evoked, Lisle cast one pitying glance upon her half-averted face, and hailed as a god-send Miss Venard's next question, which she had been deliberating in perfect unconsciousness of this little scene and its embarrassing *dénouement*.

"Mr. Sterling, what is the cost of a good, comfortable coffin? Not something handsome, like that a gentleman gets for his first wife; but a plain one—say a mother's-in law, for instance."

"It depends very much upon circumstances. Demand and supply would have something to do with the question; and the place in which it was ordered; in fact, many things render your question difficult to answer."

"Now that's just like a man's answer; always so wrapped up in generalities or exceptions, that there's no satisfaction to be gotten from it. It is important that I should know, for a reason which I may sometime tell you. I·don't want to over-estimate the reasonable cost of the article, as it is to be bought upon subscription, and it wouldn't look well to seem grasping and ambitious."

"It takes no more time to ask for a pound than a penny, and from a certain class one is even more apt to receive it. I will subscribe very cheerfully, if it is an object of such interest to you."

"Oh, you don't understand, of course; so in return for your kind offer, I'll take you into confidence at once. I'm writing a book; and my hero, who is very poor, is obliged to bury his own dead mother by contribution. It will tell well if the details are nicely set forth."

"Accept my best wishes for your success. May I ask when you intend to publish?" said Lisle, with most becoming gravity.

"I can't exactly say. I am already in correspondence upon the subject; but it seems to be a trick with publishers to decline, and decline, till an author is so discouraged and broken-spirited that he will sell his copyright for most anything, and thank Heaven he has at last received an offer for it. Don't you think genius and talent are very poorly rewarded, Mr. Sterling?"

"I believe that is the individual complaint of at least one-half the world. Your opinion is doubtlessly quite correct; but allow me to hope that your own may prove an exception to the general rule."

"Thank you. You can render yourself quite agreeable when you choose, I perceive," said Miss Phebe, entirely mollified by his seeming courtesy.

Miss Wakefield raised her eyes with a deprecating expression; for her tender heart shrank from anything like practising upon another's credulity, however flattering might be the manner that concealed it from its victim. She knew that Lisle had no respect for Miss Venard's shallow intellect, that he was no believer in the genius she assumed to possess; and she could not attribute solely to a spirit of kindness the flattering remarks which had afforded their recipient such entire satisfaction.

Again Lisle met her reproving glance; and, inconsistent as he knew it to be, it increased his admiration and respect for her. He had resolved to win her confidence so far as doing so would enable him more fully to befriend her in her need of protection and trusting kindness under any and all emergencies; he had felt that he was the stronger and more fortunate of the two, but already the spirit in which he had made this resolve was changed.

It no longer depended for its vitality upon a sentiment of unmixed compassion for all who suffered under a heavy if invisible burden of woe; but a thorough respect, mingled with a more tender and intense pity for one so gentle and womanly, who yet struggled under a burden doubly heavy from its attendant humiliations, forced upon him the consciousness that henceforth his mission of mercy and sympathy could claim no credit for personal disinterestedness. It was Leonore Wakefield he would serve—not merely the suffering woman.

Thus far, as if by common consent, they had been left almost uninterrupted in their *tête-à-tête*, Miss Venard being the only one who had disturbed it; but Miss Wakefield was now urged to the piano, and yielding to his own consciousness of propriety under the circumstances, Lisle made no move to accompany her, leaving the office of page turner to whoever might choose to fill it, while he drew near that little circle by the fire. Mrs. Venard and Mrs. Bertram were holding a confidential conversation in a tone too low to disturb those who listened more attentively to the music; and Lisle, who was nearest them, caught only now and then a word. They were speaking of Miss Wakefield, for Mrs. Bertram exclaimed, *sotto voce,*

"How magnificently she does play! Do you suppose it possible that she is some prima donna, *incognito?*"

"Impossible. She hasn't the manner. It is more probable that she is some once fine lady, reduced to support herself by turning her accomplishments to a practical account; but she never utters one sentence upon which to base any tangible suspicion, and it would be a strange person who could presume to ask her a direct question upon the subject. Even Phebe will hardly venture that. It is seldom one sees so much gentleness blended with such perfect self-reliance and reticence. Charley hangs around her unceasingly, and very few young ladies would feel the interest in him she does. She seems fond of children, yet is as judicious with him as any mother could be."

"Don't you fancy Sterling is *not a little* captivated?"

"I don't know. He is such a Mephistopheles, and no ladies' man."

"That is just the point upon which I base my suspicions. Were

he a ladies' man, a manifest interest would be significant of nothing; and as to Mephistophelism, a good wife would soon cure him
of all that."

"Well, this would be a good match, certainly, in all that goes to
constitute really good matches, whatever the world might say of
it. However, it is all nonsense to discuss it, as only this morning
she said very seriously that she should never marry; that she had
seen so many unhappy marriages that nothing could induce her to
run the risk of adding another to the list."

" Wait till she falls in love with some one. No young lady in
such a mental state ever thought that she could be running any such
risk. I don't wish any one any evil; but if they two ever will
marry any one, I hope it will be each other. Does your husband
administer you a matrimonial 'snub' when you canvass matrimonial
possibilities?"

"I don't remember that I ever did so in his hearing. There are
some things that should never be mentioned in the presence of any
masculine, and this is undeniably the chief unmentionable among
them. Is Sterling fastidious in such matters?"

" Not a doubt of it. He entertains some strange ideas connected
with it, though. For instance, he declares that had he a wife who
would under any circumstances deceive him, even in a trifle, he
should lose his respect for her, even if he brought himself ever to forgive her."

The music had ceased while Mrs. Bertram was speaking, and the
sentence that would otherwise have been inaudible to any one save
her to whom it was addressed, was overheard by all. Mrs. Bertram
laughed.

" Yes, Sterling, I admit that I am detected in the very impolite
act of discussing my friends in their very presence—my only excuse
being that I felt assured they would never know it. But since I am
thus far humiliated, do confess that what I accused you of is every
word true."

" Most willingly, and I hereby reassert that very harsh declaration. Women can never understand the perfect dread men have of
domestic intrigue in any degree."

" And men can never understand the impracticability, if not utter
impossibility, of the implicit confidence they exact as an inalienable
right; while, to make matters still worse, they are painfully prone
to see mountains in the veriest molehills upon the domestic territory.
A natural desire to spare him annoyance—a little feeling of pride

which leads one to shrink from making some humiliating revelation perfectly unimportant in itself—these and many kindred reasons for silence are quite ignored, and we are expected to make sacrifices that not one man among you all, could or would offer towards this beautiful so called ' confidence.' "

" With all due respect for your creed, allow me to suggest that much which passes in this world for reason, is only sophistry—a sort of soothing balm for an unwilling mind—and the mountains to which you allude, are less frequently evoked from the metaphorical molehills themselves, than from the screen by which you attempt to conceal their existence. If a husband feels that his own wife stoops to petty trickery against him, where under Heaven is he to expect faith and companionship ?"

Miss Wakefield looked up as if surprised at his earnestness, as indeed were all, little suspecting the bitter school in which he had so early learned to hate and despise woman's treachery. How could they know that his own mother had, for him, cast over her whole sex a pall of aching doubt and suspicion, which had never yet been lifted, perhaps never could be torn wholly away. Miss Venard petulantly exclaimed,

" Bless us and save us ! how many wives must you have had, that you seem to have suffered the whole catalogue of misery ?"

" Probably the whole number destined for me," he replied courteously.

Mrs. Venard said, more seriously, " If you every do marry, your wife will be a most perfect, or most miserable woman. Very few could every attain your standard."

" Any wife I may ever have, will be fully apprised of my peculiar theory—if it is peculiar—after which I shall be hers as she shall decide. I could overlook almost any secret in the past, even if unconfessed ; but one existing in the very present, necessitating daily trickery and deception bordering upon actual falsehood, shutting in the best part of life by an ever visible barrier against which a husband's heart and brain beat themselves to death, purgatory itself can offer nothing equal to it !"

Mr. Venard came to the rescue of the ladies, who were silenced by Lisle's exhibition of feeling. " Don't be unreasonable in your demands upon the sex, Sterling. We all know that a man's brain, wracked with business cares, and preoccupied to positive surliness, is not a gracious receptacle for a woman's ' confidences,' usually necessitated by her own errors in judgment, as she knows well enough, before we so assure her. ' When *we* have committed an error, we go to work to rectify it as silently as may be; and when we have succeeded, not the least part of our satisfaction arises from the fact that no one else knew anything of it. I don't think that husbands, as a class, at all over-rate their wives' soundness of judgment, and they are excusable for believing that next not to having done an ill-judged thing, is its happy concealment. Marry a good, sensible woman, Sterling, and you'll soon be more liberal in your creed. The happiest couple I ever knew was one in which the wife had been divorced from two former husbands previously to having accepted the present one, who, as he had no suspicion of the fact, never thought to *blame her* for all temporary misunderstandings, upon the natural score that no one else had been able to live with her. The poor fellow even conscientiously believed *himself* somtimes imperfect, and honestly confessed it to her!"

There was a general laugh in which all joined but Lisle, who replied very seriously,

"I don't see that her confession of such a fact would materially have altered their relationship as to candor and mutual forbearance, if he could have reconciled his conscience to marrying her under such circumstances. For me, *one* previous husband would have been quite sufficient had I learned his existence from any one save herself, and *too many* were he still alive. I do not believe in the legality of second marriage, where any power save that of death annulled the first one."

A simultaneous ejaculation from all present evinced the unqualified dissent with which this opinion was received; and Mrs. Venard said,

"Mr. Sterling must look upon marriage from a Catholic point of view. It seems to me unreasonable indeed, if the laws which legalize what one considers a mere civil contract, cannot also annul it."

"Mr. Sterlings views and opinions upon the matter are altogether too unimportant to merit farther argument in this assembly; and as he never anticipates being placed in any personal dilemma of the nature thus under discussion, he declines to do battle in their justification," he replied, bowing ceremoniously and with playful gallantry; and while the others laughed, Miss Wakefield silently left the music chair in which she had all this time remained without once having joined in the conversation, and without so much as a smile resumed her place upon the sofa beside Charley, who was rubbing his knuckles into his eyes and faithfully struggling with a crop of persistent yawns. Pillowing his head upon her lap, she twined his curls around her finger, with an air of absent-mindedness under which Lisle experienced the prick of a thorn of vexation with himself. How much of all this conversation, relating to feminine secrets had she understood as practical preaching at, or at least against, herself! He was pained to think how much of it must have seemed directly applicable to herself, and with a woman's instinctive self-depreciation, and proneness to meet every thrust at self-love more than half way, she might have thought the whole especially aimed at her. Vexed that he should have rendered himself liable to such a suspicion, he reclaimed the seat beside her, and waited for her to address him and so give some clue to her feeling.

Master Charley roused himself to utter a remonstrance.

"What makes you all talk such stupid things to-night, Mr. Sterling? It isn't so very pleasant for a boy to sit still under it all, when he knows that if he so much as gapes once, he'll be hustled off to bed in no time! You used to be a glorious funny fellow; but lately you've looked—well—*just as if you'd got to go to church and didn't want to!*"

"Well, I've come back now to be a good fellow again. I didn't fare very well out there, I can tell you, and Miss Wakefield thinks I ought to travel as a Bruin in a menagerie, and wear a shaggy coat."

"No she doesn't. Miss Wakefield never thinks hard things about anybody. She is so soft like, and good; I'm sorry I said she was cross and cried because she got mad. I was mad with Aunt Phebe or I shouldn't have said it; *she's* the one that's got the temper! Grandpa says if she doesn't get married pretty quick, he'll have to put her out to board, because he can't stand it."

"Charley, my child, is it right to speak so of your aunt, or of any one?" asked Miss Wakefield, with gentle reproof.

"Well, why isn't she good like you? Hadn't she a good ma as you had to tell her better?" She made no reply, and Lisle asked with careless politeness,

"Is your own mother living, Miss Wakefield?"

"Not to me," she answered, so low and softly as to be almost inaudible. Unconscious of what he was doing, Lisle pressed with his own the little hand that lay near him across Charley's recumbent figure. The glance of surprise she turned upon his face awoke him to a sense of his misdemeanor. But she was no prude; and, reading in that look that his action was but an involuntary tribute of

sympathy, she checked the apology he promptly commenced, by
saying very gently and simply,

"I accept it as it was meant, and I cannot tell you how much I
thank you for the kind spirit that prompted it. I have often most
bitterly felt the need of friendship, and I should be false indeed to
my own soul, did I affect to resent any involuntary exhibition
of it."

Could anything have increased the respect he had already conceived for her, this unaffected simplicity and frankness would have
done so, and he answered with earnestness,

"If you will honor me with the name of friend, I will deserve the
title if it be possible. I am not altogether harsh and unfeeling, and
your friendship will be as highly prized by me as mine *can* be by
you."

"But not so severely tested. I may try yours more severely than
you think; and I forewarn you that when I seem most unreasonable, I can least explain. Do you withdraw from the compact after
this declaration?"

"Never. The friendship that is untried, is unproven. Besides,
I am not as severe as you have reason to imagine me. I have both
charity and generosity towards my friends, and I am never harsh
and relentless except where another is compelled to suffer for deeds
over which he has not the slightest responsibility. I have served a
bitter apprenticeship at this, and if I sometimes seem unforgiving
and stern, it is no marvel. And now let me show you what shall be
my first act in ratification of our treaty. I'm going home. It was
unconscionable to wait till ten o'clock before announcing such a resolution; but I quite forgot that you indulged in unaccustomed dis-
sipation last night. I hope to be able to win you from such quiet
'paths of pleasantness and peace.' When may I come again?"

"That shall be left for you to determine. I am always at home."

"Thank you; and good-night. Mrs. Bertram, shall I have the
honor, etc.? It is ten o'clock."

"Good-nights" were quickly given and received, and as they
sallied out, Mrs. Bertram said, "I knew it was ten o'clock, but how
did *you* find it out? Now if you've a spark of gratitude in your
bosom, do thank me for assisting you to a pleasant evening. You
know that had you come alone you wouldn't have remained half
an hour, and not that with any satisfaction."

"Liege lady, accept your humble servant's most sincere and reverential thanks. If you are ever left an interesting young widow, I will repay your gracious services in kind and in proportion. May a consciousness of your virtuous action sweeten your sleep; and so I bid you good-night."

CHAPTER XVI.

A MOST unstaisfactory week succeeded this visit to the Venards ; a week of pouring rain or even more dejecting drizzle, during which a cold, gray fog obscured the very sky uninspired by one glimpse of sunshine. Every gutter was swollen to a miniature river, and the paved streets were deeply covered with mud that spattered against the carriage windows and meandered down them grotesquely as Lisle made his daily pilgrimages to and from the office.

The cold dampness without penetrated the very walls of the house and lay glistening and heavy upon them, despite continual fires and oft repeated drying processes, and twice Lisle subjected himself to the war of wind and storm that beat upon his doors in very challenge, in the hope to find at Venard's the cheerfulness that his own gloomy home denied him. The first time he was greeted by the usual family circle, of which Miss Phebe still formed a member, and he waited in momentary expectation of Miss Wakefield's appearance, till despairing at last, and tired of Miss Phebe's chatter, he left, with a merely polite inquiry if she for whom he had vainly waited were well, and receiving an affirmative reply, took his departure with the resolve to ask for her at once should she not be present or sent for upon the occasion of his next visit. He shook the rain from his coat, upon his return home, with a feeling of vexation at himself for having cumulated the expectant bashfulness of a boy, in not having asked for her upon this occasion till the very delay had raised an unsurmountable obstacle ; and his consequent dissatisfaction with every member of the family whom he had seen remained unappeased after the usually soothing oblation of two cigars, whose smoke-wreaths only hovered heavily around him without stilling one irritated pulsation.

Gloomily he betook himself to sleep, and dejectedly arose the next day to pursue the same spiritless round. Ashamed to confess himself so much the creature of circumstances, yet utterly unable to banish the melancholy spirit which possessed him, he shunned the

Bertrams and condemned himself to the solitude which nevertheless weighed upon him dispiritingly, till, yielding to a second temptation, he made another visit to the Venard mansion, and, profiting by his former lesson, asked at once for the lady whom he alone cared to see. The servant hesitated, then said apologetically,

"I beg your pardon, sah, but Miss Leonore te'l me, four days ago, she be at home to *nobody* till farder notice."

Lisle drew a card from his pocket, wrote a few words upon it, and bade the servant hand it to her and wait for an answer ; and refusing to enter the parlor, he waited in the hall, resolved not to endure another evening's martyrdom in family conclave.

The alert waiter sprang up stairs with the card, knocked at Miss Wakefield's door, and when, pale and serious, she opened it, handed her the brief question written over Lisle Sterling's signature.

"Does Miss Wakefield's prohibition include all friends, despite solemn compacts ? and, if so, for how long is it to continue in effect ?"

She walked once or twice across the room, as if in irresolution, and took up a pencil and card, then threw them down again, and at last said briefly to the waiting servant,

"Say to Mr. Sterling—*yes*, and *till Sunday evening*. Nothing more, he will understand. Don't forget."

"No, ma'am. Miss Leonore say—'yes, and till Sunday evening ;' and having thus recited his message, he ran down stairs repeating it to himself parrot-wise, in its to him utter incomprehensibility.

It was sufficiently intelligible to Lisle, if not entirely satisfactory ; and receiving it with such philosophy as he could summon, he slipped the welcome *douceur* into the servant's expectant hand, and turned away.

Tired of the very atmosphere of his silent home, yet in no mood for society, he resolved to go to the theatre in true bachelor style, and was soon seated quite alone in the usually well filled box. The house was not half full, the inclemency of the weather inspiring more worshippers of Morpheus than devotees to Melpomene, and glancing around to mark the few familiar faces present, Lisle's eye descended to the pit, mechanically.

Abstracted as he was, two familiar figures forced themselves upon his attention, and he looked again. That fat, puffy face, with the round, bullet-shaped eyes, and shock of light yellow hair, had written in every line the name of his old affliction, the fat boy Billy; and the bare-headed young woman beside him, with the light colored calico dress twisted in the waist till its long point mounted guard

over one hip, could be none other than Melissa, though the afore
time fringy braids of her thin hair were now confided to the care of
a four-toothed back comb which held them in a weakly, discouraged
twist, no less fringy, with here and there an ambitious strand doing
its best to stand upon end independent of the general frowze.

Whether or not in fulfillment of the maternal prophecy, "her day-
lights had been stewed out of her," she certainly looked in the last
degree dejected and spiritless, and there was a volume of eloquent
history in the very manner in which Billy turned his shoulder upon
her while he sat with both fat red hands thrust deeply into his gray
pantaloons pockets, his head drawn down to the utter exclusion
from sight of anything at all resembling a neck, and a fold of fat
from his triple chin spreading down upon his dingy vest, decidedly
the worse for wear.

Regretting that they had followed in the maternal wake, even
while resolving anew to endure no farther molestation from them,
Lisle dismissed them from his thoughts, and gradually becoming
interested in the play, felt his spirits revive correspondingly.

Determined that nothing should occur to disturb the pleasant
condition of mind in which he found himself at the close of the performance, he went directly home and to sleep, unheeding the pat-
tering rain that still beat its tattoo monotonously. But one busy
day intervened before the evening when Miss Wakefield had sig-
nified that his visit would be received; and, as it drew near, he was
more curious to know the reason for his temporary banishment,
than eager for any charm the visit might contain in itself. It was
useless to ascribe it to any affectation, since she was utterly free from
anything at all resembling it; and satisfied that she was really
present under the Venards' roof, which he had at first doubted, he
repaired there at the time appointed, resolved to claim an explanation, which might very possibly reveal some unpleasant circumstances within his power to remove, as it might be his duty.

He was shown at once into the parlor, and Miss Wakefield advanced to receive him. He had hoped, and some way fully expected, to meet her alone, knowing as she must that her singular
conduct demanded at least a polite excuse; but Miss Phebe was
present, with every indication of intending to remain so, while
Charley did not once resign his station at her side. Both Lisle and
Miss Wakefield were too well-bred to display the restraint each felt,
and totally unconscious of the mental atmosphere by which she was
surrounded, Miss Phebe discoursed in her usual strain, quite mo-

nopolizing the conversation. Her usual absorbing topic soon banished all others, and she asked, abruptly, "What is a good business for a genteel young man, Mr. Sterling?"

"Ten thousand dollars a year net proceeds, according to my estimation, though the never satisfied might demand more."

"No, I don't mean in that sense; I mean as an occupation in life."

"Being an official on the raging canal. I recollect that was my first ambition in life. Say an officer in the cavalry department of it; duties easy, only to follow the tow-path."

"But that is horribly vulgar; a canal driver! I should be ashamed to put such a hero in my book; I want for him some business in which he will come in contact with good society that shall refine and elevate him; for, being poor, he is to be a self-made man."

"Oh, I see. Well, I should think the profession of street boot-blacking would be about it; brings its professor into the very closest contact with the very elite of business society, where he may at any moment be elevated for an unlucky rap on a sensitive member. Not much capital required—only blacking and a brush, and a pair of willing elbows."

"Of all the hateful, provoking specimens of masculinity that I ever saw!" began the young lady indignantly; and fired by a sudden remembrance, Master Charley exclaimed,

"There you go again, Aunt Phebe! and it was only the other day grandpa gave you a good one about your temper. He says he'll give fifty thousand dollars to any man that will marry and live with you, for he's tired out, and pa says—"

Whatever revelation of paternal sentiment might have been made, was prevented by the irate descent made upon him, and his being borne off in a gale, with Miss Phebe at the helm.

"Thank Heaven for all blessings! I thought she'd never leave!" ejaculated Lisle as the door closed upon her exit; and moving his chair so that he faced his companion, he said abruptly,

"Now, Miss Wakefield, in the name of our compact I demand an explanation of my temporary banishment. I flattered myself that I had found one woman above the caprices of her sex; yet one happy evening she enters into a compact of friendship with me, and having authorized my visits, upon the very next occasion absents herself without word or sign. Magnanimously assuming one-half the blame, I call again, inquiring for her alone, and being refused, resolve to avoid all chance of mistake, and so write, that my sentence of banishment may proceed from her own lips if no other answer be vouchsafed. I receive it, but—marvel of marvels—coupled with a promised restoration to her grace, in time, which I await, and am at last once more permitted to approach her, secure behind such fortifications as she can erect around her from the material of a small boy with capacious ears, and his attention-absorbing aunt! In the name of all that is reasonable, you owe me an explanation!"

"Do you think so?" she asked pensively.

The tone, or manner in which she asked the question, jarred upon a sensitive nerve, and he replied bitterly,

"It is most unreasonable that I *should* 'think so,' no doubt. I should know, as well as another, that friendship, however true and sublime, is too worthless a bauble for one to stoop to gather up in the rush of life! What matters it though one offers as a free gift all that he feels is truest and best within his soul! Souls are at best but problematical, doubtlessly mere myths, and if a man who should know better, goes into heroics over such an offering, it is right enough that his altar should perish and bury all beneath its ruins! I have not often thus egotistically erred, Miss Wakefield, nor shall I soon again."

"Stop, Mr. Sterling; for Heaven's sake, stop! You are unjust and ungenerous!"

"Do you really think so? Well, then I obey. But at least, you owe me frankness. Whatever may be the unwelcome truth, you will never know any one who will face it so unshrinkingly. I will speak it for you. You think that you entered into our league without due deliberation; that in the sympathy of the moment, you admitted to a too intimate relationship one of whom you know too little—one who seems to you, in cooler moments, cynical, if not wholly given over to all unamiable heresies. I do confess that I am unfortunate in the phraseolgy which seems to indicate my real character; and it was this very knowledge that gave me so sincere a pleasure in our friendship, since I, too, sometimes dream of one kindred spirit that will not always misunderstand and judge the inner spirit by the surface indications. I am not all harsh and cold, though God only knows how I have escaped becoming so. I know that I have a heart as true and generous as ever beat, and that one who believed in and relied upon it would find it faithful unto death. Leonore Wakefield, you are throwing away a better, truer friend than you ever had or will have in this selfish world!"

"No, no, you are wrong, all wrong! It is not you whom I banish from me, but myself whom I would—if I could—withdraw from you. You do not know, you never can know, what your friendship is to me; and if I voluntarily resign it, it is the most unselfish act of my life. What your regard would be to me, mine never could be to you, and the more sincere you were, the more you would suffer. My miserable life casts its shadow upon all who care for me, and I have no right or wish to suffer it to fall upon *you* of all the world· You I would preserve from it; and from the world, I have no right to expect anything."

" Why no right ?"

" Because I cannot—or, if you choose—*will* not accept it. The world is one's very good friend, when fortune smiles; one's pharisaical exhorter under temporary affliction, but one's tormentor when it fancies itself entitled to explanations and apologies. If I owe it nothing, I shall never feel humbled at any inability to pay."

" You speak in enigmas, Miss Wakefield. Pardon me if I ask how my own private regards are linked with the caprices and self-interes's of the world at large. Will you make a personal application of your remarks, since I confess that I have neither consideration nor respect for the code of the world in general."

" Yes. I mean that one person has no right to accept the tender regard of another except in an equal spirit of confidence and frankness. I will accept nothing under false pretences, and I tell you again, that ours would be a compact in which you had everything to bestow and nothing to receive. Even as my most cherished friend I could not give you that confidence to which the name would entitle you, and you would, mentally, if not audibly, taunt me with having given you only the shadow where you had a right to expect the substance."

" And you really believe that my friendship might become a thraldom from which you would pine to escape ; a source of annoyance unbearable? Oh Leonore Wakefield?"

" Yes, though it is too harshly worded. I tell you there is interwoven with my very life a humiliating secret with which I will suffer no one to become acquainted while I have power to prevent it. It is not a tale of crime, not a story of horror to make young eyes dilate with fear ; better could I tell it if it were, since there *are* things too humiliating to speak of one's self ! This much I confess to you ; more I never can."

" Then, Leonore, let me tell you that because I knew something of this, I first felt that my friendship might be a not unwelcome offering. I know that you need friends who will never doubt nor question you,

and were I not assured that such a friendship I can offer you, I never
should have breathed it, since I am not prone to make such offerings.
Had I the power, as I have the *wish* to shield and protect you, I
should not for one moment admit your right to cast me off; but do
not, in the name of justice, dread me as a persecutor."

"What, and how much, do you know of me?"

"Too little to be worth repeating, merely what is known to a few
in your immediate circle; but I, like them, know that whatever may
be the blight upon your life, it is linked with no unworthiness in
you, and that however inexplicable to others your conduct may sometimes appear, it springs from some all-sufficient reason of which you
alone should be the judge. Do you still distrust and reject me?
What can I say more than that I believe in you implicitly, that I esteem you above all the women I have ever met, and that, come what
may, I will never fail you if you once honor me with your friendship. Command me in all things. I will obey you blindly if thus I
am permitted to serve you!"

He extended his hand toward her in earnest of his proffer. She
clasped it in both her own, and bent her forehead upon it to conceal
the tears that filled her eyes under his generosity and earnestness,
and if, as she had said, *he* of all others should not be admitted to the
companionship he asked, she was powerless to refuse him longer.
The barrier she had interposed between them was broken down by
the deep feeling his words aroused, and Lisle felt that this new compact was thus sealed forever.

Once having yielded, whether in accordance with, or against her
own judgment, Miss Wakefield affected no reserve; claimed his
services whenever she found them convenient, received him with a
frankness and cordiality of manner at which others marvelled
silently even while they rejoiced, and rarely refused to join in any
amusement of which he was the projector. She brightened into new
life and animation under this change in her life, and her former
pensiveness gave place to a piquancy and sparkling vivacity of
manner of which she herself seemed quite unconscious, as well as
of the surprise it awakened in those around her to whom she had
heretofore seemed a cold, incomprehensible being, in whom every
natural impulse had been prematurely strangled to death. If friends
bring happiness, happiness certainly brings apparent friends; and
many who before had indifferently pronounced her "a splendid
woman," now discovered her to be a very attractive one. Lisle had
given her his friendship and vowed himself to her service in a spirit

of pure disinterestedness; but he soon discovered that he was the one chiefly benefited, since her presence supplied the attraction heretofore lacking in his social life, and added a zest to each amusement in which she participated. It might have been but a just reward; but he felt that it made him a debtor where he had aspired to something nobler, and that he admired where he had only wished to protect.

Meanwhile, the visit of Mr. Venard and Miss Phebe, extended far beyond the original intention, drew to a close, and Miss Phebe packed up her still unfinished manuscript, with few thanks for the many suggestions with which Lisle had favored her, though she made a visible effort to leave in peace, which included even him.

"You have been as provoking as possible, you know you have!" she asserted, in extenuation of her many outbreaks upon him; "but I want you to understand that *I* am magnanimous enough to be forgiving. When I become a famous authoress, you'll wish you had helped me when you might have done so as well as not; but I shall send you a copy of my book, to let you see that I succeeded without you. I suppose you will be married by that time; and I'm sure I wish you all happiness. Miss Wakefield isn't such a frump as I used to think her, after all; and though she hasn't as much money as I have—or shall have, it's all the same—I suppose she will make you just as good a wife."

"You are quite mistaken in supposing that I am matrimonially inclined, nor have I the least idea that Miss Wakefield would marry me if I asked her to do so, which, thank Heaven, I am too sincerely her friend to be guilty of."

"Nonsense! Everybody knows how such friendships end. If a young gentleman were to ask me to be his *friend*, I'd say yes, or no, at once, feeling that I was answering the real question under cover; nothing more or less. Talk about Miss Wakefield not marrying you; she'd do it quickly enough, I know. Every woman loves to make a good match; and much as she is inclined to 'queen it' over ordinary mortals, she doesn't try it over you. I wish you would all of you come up to Niagara next summer. I'm going to stay there all summer, and it will be strange enough if my fifty thousand dollars don't help me to a nice husband! I wish I'd some one there to tell people I'm to have that amount. It doesn't sound well from one's self."

"Thank you; but if I can't serve you in that way, just put up some posters, which will do as well. I've no doubt you will be suc-

cessful, for there are more men in this age who want money even
with a wife, than those who want a wife without money."

"Do you really think so? Well, that's encouraging, anyway,
thank you; so just try and forgive my sometimes rather vigorous
expressions of sentiment towards you, won't you?"

"With all my heart, since I always enjoyed the blessed consciousness that they were deserved; but Miss Phebe, take my advice and
never allow yourself to be provoked by any man till you are fairly
married to him. Natural exhibitions of temper are getting to be a
perfect drug in the matrimonial market."

"'Matrimonial market!'"

"Certainly. Doesn't every young lady take herself to market
just as unmistakably as those old women you can see any morning
driving their snub-nosed horses into town, take their loads of veg-
etables? The only difference lies in their wares, and in the style
of vehicle. Go to market with a sweet temper, and some money,
and you'll be bargained for at once. Let me know what price you
bring; and good-bye," and they parted with more good will than
might have been anticipated from their many skirmishes.

Occasional letters from old Mr. Sterling kept Lisle informed of
the few changes taking place in his native town; but as "postage
came very dear," according to the old man's complaint, these un-
scholarly, but kindly written epi-tles, appeared only at long intervals, always ending in a sort of addenda written in Mrs. Sterling's
cramped and wiry-looking chirography, consisting of that curious
jargon of parrot-phrased piety and exhortation so common in the
messages of the old to the young, and from which Lisle turned with
a thrill of disgust. This woman, who had never addressed him one
word of real kindness, never bestowed any attention upon his "per-
ishable body," except in the way of blows and punishments, now
assured him that he had been "the child of many prayers and sacrifices," and exhorted him till it seemed as if she must fancy that
the sins of the parent would be visited upon the child, in accordance with the old orthodox creed—not in this world alone but in
the one to come. Lisle felt that in this world he had already experienced the curse, and had she meant it in this sense, he would
have received it as it merited. Mr. Sterling wrote that her health
seemed failing, and that she was "flighty like in her mind, often
talking strange and unaccountable;" and Lisle shrunk with a real
dread from what she might thus at any hour reveal. [shameful

secret concealed from all suspicion for so many years, might even
yet escape her, and hunt him to his grave with that unjust and cruel
stigma which attaches to such unfortunates as he ! The half-laid
shadows of the past sprang into life again under the sudden fear,
and his life seemed a nightmare of evil forebodings never to be
stilled.

He paced the floor in bitterness of soul as he thought of the
wretched past, the uncertain present. Was his whole life to be but
one long curse for the sins of another ? Could he have felt that he
was the offspring of an ill-starred love, pity for his mother's sufferings would have deadened the sting of his own; but too well he
knew that selfish calculation stood sponsor at his birth, and that
both he and his dead father had been hated as only a baffled, un-
principled woman can hate—with a malice whose very pettiness
rendered it the more fiendish ! There was not one redeeming feature in the whole miserable story, to render it pardonable !

Supposing that all should be reavealed by her own lips, would it
be credited? Here at least was one foundation upon which to build
a hope. Doctor Kelley's venerated name might prove invulnerable
against a half-demented old woman's babbling ; and she herself had
been so well respected, that her own words might not be taken in
evidence against herself. It was a hope that had never dawned
upon his mind before, and Lisle clung to it till it gained sufficient
force to banish the dread that had seized upon him with renewed
vitality.   ˙

At all events, if worse came to worst, the world was large. Should
a too well founded rumor reach him here, he could leave, and no
one would suffer but himself. The hope that the evil might pass by
him, had already made him strong to face its possible coming ; and
banishing the shadows from his mind, he burned the disturbing
letter, and resolved no more to endure the pains of apprehension,
often more severe than any which the reality ever inflicts.

CHAPTER XVII.

LISLE had left the office earlier than usual one day, resolving to dine early, and spend a long social evening with the Venards, at whose house he was now a daily visitor upon one pretence or another. Having made known his wish to Mrs. Perkins, whom he inattentively observed to be in some evident trouble, as she usually was since her marriage with the unprofitable Joe, he stayed for no explanations regarding the present calamity under which she was laboring, but went at once to his room to prepare for dinner. Suddenly over-riding his soft whistling as he proceeded with his toilet, he heard Mrs. Bertram's voice impatiently calling to him from the staircase.

" What will your ladyship ?" he asked opening the door, through whose crack the sound of an industrious brush reached her ears.

" Do come down, Sterling. Be quick; I've something to tell you."

"I shall be at your service in three seconds, ma'am, if you can survive that length of time with something on your mind."

It proved a long three seconds, and he saw that she thought so, when at last he descended to the parlor which she was excitedly pacing to and fro.

" What is it, Mrs. Bertram ? has cook run away with the spoons, or coachee hitched the near horse on the off side, or—"

" Do hush ! I tell you it is no laughing matter ! Oh, it is too bad, just as we were all so hopeful it might not happen again ! The truth is—"

" Bless us, there are murdered chickens in the last purchase of ' new laid eggs ?' I was afraid of it, so late in the spring ! Cruel !"

" Sterling, Leonore Wakefield is missing !"

"Since when is she astray or stolen ?"

" How can you laugh ? Since last night, I suppose, though she was not missed till this morning. Not appearing at breakfast, a servant was sent to her door, and receiving no answer, opened it.

The room was vacant, the bed had not been occupied through the night; in short, she was gone, without a word left for any one, unless you were so favored, which your manner leads me to believe."

"No. This is the first intimation I have received that Miss Wakefield has seen fit to act upon her own discretion, without submitting the affair to a grand jury of her friends and acquaintance! Unexampled temerity! Shocking manifestation of independence!"

"But you must know such conduct has a very mysterious appearance!"

"Were I to leave upon equally brief—that is to say, *no* notice—would you fear my little instinct was to be eternally lost, in consequence?"

"But you are a man. The case would be entirely different. She will be talked about, and that not gently."

"And is it so very awful to be 'talked about?' I thought ladies liked it, since they one and all aim at making a sensation. I never once dreamed that 'modest violet' was their rôle!"

"You might have been married for years, by the way you thrust and parry with such spiteful weapons; yet had you a wife, your very liberal creed for women would soon come down to the every day code, and you too, would cry 'a woman's reputation is her life!'" The world fancies itself entitled to an explanation of every step a woman takes; and to ignore that claim, false as it may be, is to incur its frowns and severest censure. At most any other time this freak of hers might be concealed by a little polite fibbing, &c.; but Em's cards are already half out for Wednesday evening's social, and no amount of conscience racking could cover her non-appearance."

"Do, with your usual and very lovely frankness, confess that your deep regard for public opinion upon this momentous occasion is much intensified by wounded *amour propre*, and that both you and Mrs. Venard think *you* should have been taken into Miss Wakefield's confidence, however uncommunicative she chose to be towards others."

"Something like it I do confess, though not in so mean a spirit. *I* said that she might have mentioned to one of us that she was going away for as long a time as she purposed, that we might be enabled to say when she was to return, in case we were questioned with politely phrased curiosity; and Em replied 'nonsense; we'll tell them, at once, that it is nobody's business,'—which I've no doubt she would, as she is one of those peculiar few who *can* say such things and feel the better for it."

" Rare type of womanhood! But what, then, was her qualifying
'*but?*'"

" Of course there was one, sneerer; but it was a more charitable
one than *you* would ever imagine. Em said she felt sure that Miss
Wakefield has magnified some unpleasant trifle into a real evil that
will kill her if she goes on in this way; but if there is any real
necessity for her presence anywhere, she ought, in justice to herself
and her friends, and *to you*, to surround herself with such defences
as she can by letting it *seem* that she makes no effort at secrecy. Em
has an idea that one who could surprise Miss Wakefield by a knowledge of her secret, would prove an invaluable friend to her, as she
might gladly avail herself of some assistance not involving any explanations upon her part; and I fancy she thinks she has found some
clue to it, already."

" Of all varieties of so called friendship, *officious* friendship is the
least endurable! As though any one were ever gratified by another's
discovery of what one strove to conceal! I gave Mrs. Venard credit
for better judgment, and I shall tell her so. *No man* would suffer
such interference with his own private affairs, and would be very
liable to administer a good dose of kicks to whoever thus merited
it. I would like to know who first discovered that men and women
were so differently constituted that what is unbearable by the one
should be rather agreeable to the other! It is not beautifully consistent with the creed that women are delicate and sensitive in the
proportion of six to one. All thanks to a merciful Creator who
made me not a woman!"

" Lisle Sterling, you talk beautifully now. But tell me; if Leonore Wakefield were your wife, what would you do under circumstances like the present."

" Thrash into his senses any man who dared to *look* his commiser-
ation for me, or his curiosity relative to her."

" Then marry her and do so. There will be ample opportunity,
if she cannot be prevailed upon to change such mysterious deportment. What can be answered when she is missed and inquired for
Wednesday evening?"

" Any answer will do if it be promptly given. Hesitate, and you
kill her. Go to Mrs. Venard and agree upon something—no matter
what—and then tell it boldly. Should she return before then, as she
very probably will, you will be spared one stretch of conscience,
which it is to be hoped will be put down to your credit when your
Great Book account is balanced."

"How quickly your mind does work! Why, of course the first thing Em and I decided upon, was a story to fit the necessity. You stop just where we began."

"Very naturally. The first thing a woman exclaims, is 'what will people say!' while every man knows that the world has many topics of more engrossing interest than some poor woman's merits and demerits. Let me assure you that the great world has something to do besides to wait on a corner with its hands in its pockets, hazarding conjectures on the passers-by. 'Jog along, keep moving,' is the real 'psalm of life;' and when many a rascal goes unwhipped because justice is too busy to attend to him, the feminine fraternity have little to fear outside their own class and clique. Pity they don't know it!"

"I insist that three-quarters of all the gossip is kept alive by your sex."

"Who is in the advance, goading us on with whip and spur? Wives and sisters, and, worse yet than they—mothers! Forever comes the feminine taunt, 'suppose it were me! Your sympathy is all for others,' till a man is frantic enough to cry out anything desired of him. You are nearer perfection than most of your sex; yet you won't deny that you lay awake nights to think up new persecutions for that dashing Mrs. Pomeroy, of whom you were so jealous last winter."

"'Jealous!' No I wasn't! but no woman is delighted to see another practising humbug over her husband. Mrs. Pomeroy, having been relieved of her own husband by a wisely discriminating providence, had no other occupation than making raids upon other people's, which she did in accordance with a woman's tactics, looking out the weak points in the matrimonial constitution, and then *assuming to be so perfect just where the wife fails!* Women read that trick in each other quickly enough, and it doesn't tend to promote sisterly love. Bertram is snubby enough around home, *you* know; yet he played the gallant to that woman all winter long, in a manner that would have made him a household delight, had he let his light *so shine;* and she seemed to know it all, as well as I could tell her! I couldn't endure her—that's the whole of it."

Lisle laughed as he applauded her eloquence; and as the perception dawned upon her that he had called out her tirade for his own amusement, she colored, but joined in the laugh as she said with uplifted finger,

"Wait till you catch some masculine practising his fascinations against your peace of mind! You'll find then, that it is an inspiring topic. I'm going home now; your dinner is ready, and the Infant's face is one red catalogue of domestic calamity. Adieu."

And Mrs. Bertram returned home considerably relieved in her own mind by the equanimity with which Lisle had received her startling announcement, while he, far more pained and surprised than he had allowed himself to appear, went mechanically out to dinner, in a fit of abstraction through which he noted nothing around him till Mrs. Perkins' voice arrested his steps as he was leaving the room.

"If you please, Mr. Sterling, being as I'm that troubled in my mind as is discomfortable and hard to be borne, would you be kind enough to advise a lone woman which has no one else to depend on? Being as I've taken a partner which is unprofitable to himself, which likewise he is to me, please God; which his advice is rather a damage than anything better to them which take it; I make so bold as to trouble you. Which the fact is, Melissy is come a hankering around me, and Billy likewise, a threatening to take to no end of evil ways if something is not done to encourage them; which it's scant enough of encouragement I have to offer to anybody, being that I'm that put to it in my own mind, what with an unprofitable partner and all!"

"Where are they, and what doing? Has Bill any work?"

"Nothing more than of stuffing himself, which it is likely even that will soon see an end for lack of supplies, being as their money is all run out, and the landlord of the Dolphin—which it is there they stop—has pounced down on their luggage and given them notice to quit; and at this blessed minute Melissy is a-crying of herself out on the back gallery and begging you'll give her a word of advice, sir."

"I made her such a donation some time ago. But what do the miserable couple want? Work?"

"Strange if they do. I never knew either of them to have such a hankering."

"Well; to live they must work. I will have neither of them around me, but I will secure employment for Bill once more, for your comfort, after which he must proceed upon his own responsibility, and I advise you to let him and Joseph see as little of each other as possible. You will pardon me for saying that I fear Joseph is not incorruptible."

Mrs. Perkins leant back in her chair and fanned herself excitedly, for a moment, while making an effort to restrain her complaint, which at last escaped her, despite the struggle.

"He's vexatious indeed, is Joseph! What with filching every-thing he can touch finger to, what with never making his accounts come straight if he but buy a picayune's worth—which I can't send him to buy a paper of needles but he gets it divided so as he can make a speculation of half the cost, and likewise pins the same—and what with being beknownst to his hugging the cook behind the pantry door, I'm a sorrowful and beworried woman! Drew wasn't an angel by any manner of means, which I told him maybe oftener than was just good for him—but his very badnesses were far better than Joseph's virtues, which if he has any I don't know it, but quite to the contrairywise. It's a grievous dose of matermony to come upon a respectable woman as has done her duty so many years to them as is dead and them as is likewise living!"

"I am seriously of the opinion, Mrs. Perkins, that most people find matrimony a pretty 'grievous dose,' whether or not they con-fess it, and the wonder is that the warning is not more effectual! I see no way in which I can afford you any relief, unless indeed I turn off cook and supply her place with an ugly old woman, or a mascu-line."

"Which I shall take it very kind of you, and thank you too."

Lisle smiled his comment, as Joseph Perkins' ungainly figure rose mentally before him, but sincerely compassionating his faithful housekeeper's troubles, he gave her money to redeem the effects seized upon by the young people's landlord, renewing his promise to secure employment for Bill, and if possible for Melissa, and gave the rather pretty cook warning at once. The little incident had temporarily banished his own anxiety; but it returned with renewed force as he went out for the first moment alone since the startling intelligence had been given him. Perfectly as he was aware of these events in Leonore Wakefield's life, frankly as she had warned him that she could not explain her conduct to him nor to anyone, this singular deportment exercised upon him all the effect of an un-pleasant surprise; and, quite losing the social enthusiasm which had led him to plan the evening's entertainment, he betook himself to the upper gallery in a most unenviable state of mind.

The next day passed without any intelligence of the missing one; and calling upon the Venards in the evening Lisle found them in a state of mingled anxiety and vexation, which Mrs. Venard made no effort to conceal from him, protesting that at any other time it would have been no one's business, nor should she for one moment have considered it hers; but the next evening was the one appointed for her grand party, and committed by the invitations issued before Leonore's departure, she could by no possibility postpone it, nor resent the inquiries so natural under the circumstances. "Leonore would become the object of remark among all their circle, and those detestable Wheelers would triumph over her so provokingly! They had played the Pharisee toward the poor child for much less than this, since they were in no condition to suffer annoyance upon her account, and at that time she was too little known to become the subject of much remark under any circumstances. Now it was very different," Mrs. Venard declared; "nor could she imagine how Miss Wakefield's affairs could in any way be connected with such a vagabond."

"What vagabond?" Lisle asked.

"Oh, don't you know about it? Then I may as well tell the whole story, since you are her friend no less than we. It was during the twilight, Monday evening, when we were all sauntering around the yard, that, speaking to Miss Wakefield under the impression that she was close beside me, and receiving no reply, I turned to look for her. She could not long have left me; for I saw her just as she reached the gate where a letter was handed her which she slipped hastily into her pocket, not without glancing over her shoulder to see if she were observed. There was nothing mysterious in the mere fact of her receiving a letter outside of the ordinary channel, nor should I have given it a second thought, but for the appearance of the man who brought it. He was a coarse, rough looking fellow, in a battered wool hat, which may sometime have been white and presentable, but was certainly quite the reverse then; and his gray clothes were not only dirty, but ragged. I don't know whether she hurried him off, or he had the sense to go, himself; but he did not stop a second, in all, and was away so soon that I really stopped and questioned whether I had seen any one at the gate excepting Miss Wakefield herself, who remained there for fully five minutes, looking out as if into the street. Of course I avoided every appearance of having seen anything which it was intended I should not see, and after an interval she went up to her own room. I suppose I must have looked the indescribable things I felt; for Venard laughed when I joined him by the steps, and exclaimed, 'well, what of it!' which is just what I should like to know. He had seen the same performance I witnessed, though he conducted himself with equal propriety, which I rather wonder at, as, usually when he wishes to see anything, he looks at it, and that with sufficient directness."

"Of course. Where's the sense in playing hypocrite and pretending you don't see things, when you do and mean to! The poor girl was embarrassed, however she strove to conceal it; and having seen all there was to be seen, I had no call to seem to triumph in it," explained Mr. Venard in self-defence.

"Well, what next?" asked Lisle.

"I don't know that. I only know that we attached no importance to Miss Wakefield remaining in her own room till you called, during the evening, and you know that she appeared exactly as usual when she received you and bade you adieu afterward. When you left, she went directly back to her room, merely bidding us good night, from which we only understood that we should see her no more that evening. Soon afterward Venard went out, and I took up a book to read till bed time, and of course took no heed of anything more. The light was not burning in Miss Wakefield's room when I went up-stairs at about ten o'clock, and thinking her asleep, I went softly past her door, and awoke next morning to learn that she had not stayed in the house through the night. The gate was locked and the key thrown back into the yard, so I suppose she let herself out. The present question is, when will she be let in."

"I think that had she intended to remain long absent, she would have said something about it to some of us. She knows that to-morrow is the day named for your social muster, or whatever it may be called; and it is the best guarantee that she will return before the hour named in your cards."

"But should she not come at all! Who knows if she intends to?"

Lisle left the house an hour afterward with these words ringing in his ears. They awoke a new fear within his heart, oppressed him with a dire foreboding which he could not banish. During these long months in which their friendship had strengthened and grown perfect, frank and communicative as she had been with him upon all subjects unconnected with her own history, upon this one topic a silence as of death had reigned between them, and not even one accidental allusion had informed him of anything relating to her life which was not equally known to others. If she had kindred, no reference to them ever passed her lips; and after that first inquiry relative to her mother, Lisle had displayed an equal reticence. Should she really have disappeared to return no more, he had actually no clue by which to follow her. Why should he wish to do so?

He did not ask himself the question; the suggestion itself awoke him to the truth. He loved her; bestowed upon her an affection as absorbing and devoted as it was boundless in confidence. He realized it to its fullest extent, now that this clueless absence awoke him to the fear that she was lost to him forever, "gone out " from his existence like a lost star from the firmament. " What if she should never come back ?" What indeed! And if she were to come—what then ? Lisle stopped and looked his own life in the face.

What right had he to love any woman, with one thought of making her his wife! He who had not even *a name* to give her, upon whose very life the uplifted threatening hand of relentless fate might at any hour descend, crushing to dust the last remnant of his manhood's pride and dignity. While his mother lived, he had not one moment's security against an exposure that he felt would crush him doubly were another involved in the disgrace, and that other a woman whom he pitied as sincerely as he loved. Leonore Wakefield had in her own life as great a trouble as she could bear, without assuming any portion of another's, nor could he even appeal to her generosity to do so! Dishonorable as he felt it would be to ask her to become his wife with such a story unrevealed to her, confess it he never could to mortal ear. He could die as he was doomed to live—in solitary isolation from all that makes life beautiful or even endurable, with a wealth of tenderest love and pity forever sealed up in the heart a misjudging world would condemn as cold and misanthropic. Was not everything surrounding him unreal—a stupendous fraud upon society ? The very fortune for which many bowed down and courted him, was like the rest, a mistake. The " Lisle Sterling " named in his uncle's will, had no existence, while in his place stood a *Lisle Kelley* whom nobody knew, as was most fortunate for him!

Supposing that, thus accursed, he should stifle the voice of honor, and win the woman he loved for his wife. Would not his whole future life pay the penalty, as with shrinking dread he received each careless word as a barbed arrow of reproach ? Would not his days and nights be haunted by the ceaseless dread of this shameful revelation he was too weak because too proud to make ? He shivered at the mental question ; but having definitely decided it, the fact remained obstinate against his will, persistently tugging at his heart strings; better than life—better than his own honor—he loved Leonore Wakefield !

He did not argue that *she* was mysterious and unknown, to him as to all others—cared not a rush that the busy world might criticise her as it would be madness to a proud man that wife of his should be criticised—asked not if it were pride or necessity that sealed her lips and placed a guard over every action. It was into his own life and soul he looked, of himself alone that he asked one question—how much short of positive crime would it be for him to marry this woman could he win her?—if, indeed, she had not gone from him forever even now! Perhaps in this very way chance had decided the question, and the fierce contest he waged against himself was as vain as the efforts he made to still it.

It seemed to him but little less than mockery to join in the festivity at Mrs. Venard's while such a pall hung heavily over his heart; but social duty, joined with a feverish restlessness and impatience, urged him forward, and he entered the well-filled parlor scarcely later than he was accustomed to appear elsewhere upon similar occasions. Almost the first words which fell upon his ear as he awaited his turn to pay his addresses to his hostess, were those which inquired for Miss Wakefield, whose absence had thus far been easily concealed; and he watched Mrs. Venard with a latent misgiving which the next instant proved groundless, as she turned very composedly toward the inquirer and replied,

"I regret your disappointment, and my own is equally sincere. Miss Wakefield was suddenly summoned, several days since, to the bedside of a sick mother, and it is uncertain when she may return, if at all."

If those who overheard this reply mentally commented that this was the first time they had ever heard that Miss Wakefield *had* a mother, politeness restrained any exhibition of surprise, and, as Lisle had prophesied, no one appeared to think that anything unusual had occurred. Mrs. Wheeler indeed, turned a curious glance upon Mrs. Venard when the intelligence reached her; but that lady's imperturbability under it, revealed nothing—not even her impatience under the silent taunt which thus repaid the indignant words she had uttered when she took Miss Wakefield to her own house.

The latest guest had at length been duly received, and, fatigued by so long and arduous a ceremony, Mrs. Venard had taken a seat near the door, when a message was whispered her by a servant; and rising she immediately left the room. Lisle, who watched her covertly with an expectancy for which he felt that he had very little reason at this late hour, saw her ascend the stairs, but so calmly that he based no new hope upon the action, nor gave it a second thought. Having passed from the sight of her guests, Mrs. Venard's tranquillity gave place to the intensest eagerness, and flying along the upper hall she reached Leonore Wakefield's door, upon which she first impatiently rapped, and then opened it and rushed in unceremoniously.

" Leonore Wakefield !"

" Mrs. Venard."

She stood in the centre of the room, wrapped in her cloak, and with her bonnet unremoved from her head which was deprecatingly bowed, though she offered no word in her own defence.

Mrs. Venard seized upon her wrappings with a hasty hand and tossed them in a pile upon the bed, as she exclaimed,

" For pity's sake don't stand there, since you have come only at the eleventh hour ! make Justine dress you as quickly as possible, and hurry down stairs. Everybody is asking for you," and as she spoke Mrs. Venard pulled the bell-cord vigorously.

Leonore made one step forward, then stopped, and asked with tearful eyes,

" Do you truly thus welcome me back ?"

" Why not, you foolish child ! Did you think me a second Mrs. Wheeler ? In the name of justice and common sense, what right have I or any one else to assume to be your keeper ? Leonore Wakefield, do see and feel that I am your *friend.*"

Leonore threw her arms impetuously around Mrs. Venard, and kissed her again and again, while her own eyes were streaming with tears of love and gratitude.

" God bless you, dear Mrs. Venard ! You must feel and know that I am not the graceless creature I seem. Would to heaven that I could explain all to you ! but my pride is greater than my strength, and I cannot, cannot ! I am unfortunate, miserable, but nothing worse, God knows !"

"Poor child ! There, be still. Bathe your face till you banish its flush, and call back its smiles. You will need all your self possession, despite what I can do to aid you. Here is Justine, in whose hands I shall leave you. Come in, Justine ; your young mistress has returned. Help her to dress as quickly as possible ; do you hear ?"

When Mrs. Venard re-entered the parlor, Lisle chanced to be standing near the door ; and as she passed him she whispered quickly,

" Leonore has come."

He felt actually giddy from the surge of blood which the suddenly bounding heart forced into his brain, and the glad surprise held him for an instant spell-bound.

Turning towards him as she gained the opposite end of the room, Mrs. Venard marked the effect of this intelligence, and like a flash the whole truth dawned upon her. There was no time, now, to pass even a mental comment upon the fact as it stood revealed to her. The first duty was quietly to circulate the fact of Miss Wakefield's return, and announce her forthcoming appearance; and this she did at once. In their own circle Miss Wakefield was known only as a lady and a rare musician ; and as " Mrs. Venard's friend," the fact that she maintained herself by the exercise of her wondrous musical genius, was a matter of no importance even to the most exclusive, while this very accomplishment secured her the fullest amount of admiration and appreciation.

She entered the rooms, at last, beautiful and calm as ever, without one trace of her late emotion visible upon the fair, pale face, or in the lustrous dark eyes, which, like her lips, smiled her acknowledgment of the many congratulations she received. Only one *passé* belle ventured a politely concealed thrust as Miss Wakefield greeted her.

" May I inquire where you left your mother, Miss Wakefield ?"

"Oh, horrors !" exclaimed Mrs. Venard mentally. " I never thought to tell Miss Wakefield what excuse we made for her absence !" She was, then, intensely relieved by the perfect self-possession with which Leonore replied without one trace of anything like surprise at the unexpected question, whose cause she at once divined instinctively.

"Certainly, thank you. She is once more around her room, though I fear she will for some time be confined to it," and, with a bow, she passed on, serene and undisturbed as ever.

Lisle approached and offered her his arm, and as she placed her little gloved hand upon it and passed on with him, he pressed it impulsively upon his heart as one who thus claimed what he had resolved to possess.

She raised her eyes to his face, and the glance that answered her own told her as plainly as words could have done, all that she had become to him. A spasm of actual pain crossed her face—a faint index of the aching heart whose every beat was unmixed agony !

" You are *distraite*, fair Leonore," he said banteringly, as an abso-

lute silence reigned between them after that brief glance. "May I
ask an explanation of this dire-presaging silence?"

"Yes, some other time. Are you going to reproach me as a false,
unsatisfactory sort of friend, as I prophesied?"

"No, I cannot, for I have ceased to think of you as my friend.
Oh, Leonore, Leonore, give me some right to tell you what I must
and will. If you do not speak it I shall assume it, though in penance you banish me from your sight forever after."

"Beware of appropriating what does not belong to you!" she
cautioned him with an effort towards playfulness, which the perceptible paling of her ever clear cheek painfully exposed.

"That was a lesson of my early youth, which, among others, I
am resolved to forget. It would be well for some of us could we
rub out the entire page of these early lessons, even though some
good thus perish with much evil. In *my* youth I learned to distrust everything and everybody. I have unlearned that lesson,
Leonore."

They had wandered out upon the veranda, and stood now near a
trellised vine, through which the starlight fell upon them dimly.
She could not read the expression of his face, but there was a new
tone in his voice which emphasized his words strangely, and, at a
loss for a reply, she stood silently awaiting what was to follow.

"Leonore, is it possible for a woman to be faithful and true? I
am dreaming it for the first time—the very first."

"Be my friend as you have been, and you shall see. *Only remain
my friend.*"

It was perhaps only fancy that imparted a deeper meaning to
these words; but they fell as the knell of hope upon his heart, and
before he recovered from them, voices were heard demanding Miss
Wakefield, whose musical ovations were solicited. They went forward, and Lisle resigned her, while her last words still rang in his
ears and afterward haunted his sleepless hours. How could he for
one moment have fancied any barrier should separate them, save
that of her own will? he asked himself in contempt for his own
former arguments. Had not every living being a right to seek happiness, and win it if possible? "Let those who have wilfully incurred disgrace, bow their necks to the yoke of merited punishment.
I have not, and I will not suffer voluntary penance for the sins of
others, so help me heaven!" A new resolve had strengthened in his
soul, born of that sense of innate justice implanted in every human
breast.

CHAPTER XVIII.

IF the hours succeeding immediately upon Leonore Wakefield's r.-turn were passed by Lisle in unabated mental conflict, they were fraught with agony to her; and, unlike him, she was far from con-quering a peace. The sleepless, tortured night, left her ill and mis-erable; and when, shutting out the morning light by which falling curtains, she paced her chamber to and fro, her hands fiercely clasped behind her, and her head bent upon her breast over thick floated dark and heavy the masses of her disheveled hair, it was evident in her whole appearance, as well as in the impatient manner with which from time to time she dashed aside the scalding tears from her flushed face, that she was racked by one of those fierce rebellions which at times convulse every suffering soul; rebellions in which the stung and tortured spirit turns and looks its author in the face, upbraiding him for the cruel curse of its creation.

To endure, to suffer—brief words for such an eternity of aching misery! a fearful lease of that life whose every hour is a history of suffering and decay uncheered by one real joy worth the having lived to experience! one linked chain of pain and mental torture, over which pride wreaths the concealing lips, and which actual false-hood scarce cloaks from prying eyes! Who or whatever possessed the *right* to inflict existence at such a price! The flimsy veil of orthodox sophistry is rent to atoms and trodden in the dust, in these fearful convulsions through which the writhing soul *will* be heard.

Gentle and yielding as Leonore Wakefield peculiarly was, by na-ture, in this tempestuous hour she seemed transformed into a tortured Pythoness.

Calling back the course of years which formed her life, each one of them rose before her wrapped in its own peculiar bitterness—an unloved childho d, an unguided youth, an isolated womanhood! Such was the retrospect that led her to the miserable present. A generous, fruitful harvest of wrongs and mi fortunes oppressing her like actual sins, was all these weary years seemed to have yielded her.

How long was all this to endure? Was a brighter day never to dawn upon her? Did not the power that called her into being owe her some atonement for the merciless act? or in this life of suffering, would the maddened soul at last lose its claim even to eternal peace when its earthly race was done! Torn and wrung till many a blasphemous seam marred its beauty, would it perhaps be refused a mooring when this tempest-sought haven at last lay fair and balmy before its longing gaze? Fitting, if fearful end, to such a career as human life!

Contemptuous, withering whispers, that left their impress in the swelling veins that rose and fell with every bitter heart-throb, and spoke again in the deafening surge that beat upon her brain!

She heard a rap upon her door, but gave no answer, nor for a moment stayed her steps. It was repeated, and then Mrs. Venard's voice called in alarm,

"Leonore Wakefield, what is the matter? For pity's sake, let me in."

"Wait one moment," she replied; and, schooled by long self-discipline, Leonore forced the quivering features into peace, pressed back the angry lifetide from her swollen temples, and standing mute one instant as if imposing the power of her will over the weak physical frame, she turned the key and admitted Mrs. Venard, who looked upon her for one instant in a startled silence, and then while tears welled up into her usually keen and penetrating eyes, asked tenderly,

"Leonore, dear child, is there *nothing* I can do for you?"

"Nothing at all, thank you; unless, indeed, you will accommodate me with about six feet of earth and a green covering."

"Leonore, you are miserable, wretched! Do not add bitterness to that. *Why won't* you let me be your friend and comforter!"

"Do not distress yourself, my kindest, my best of friends. Let me work out my retribution in my own way, should such a thing be in the keeping of time. *Were I to accept a comforter at the price it would cost me, I should wither and die! In utter silence lies my only strength.* Leave me that, and so prove yourself my friend. My burdens would not be lightened by imposing them upon you, or any one; but quite the reverse."

"I know one who would give much for the right to alleviate them. I refused to have this card sent up to you, declaring that you had remained invisible to all since last night; but I could not resist the pleading eyes with which he still extended it, and as I *would not* have you intruded upon by a servant, I brought it myself."

Leonore received the card, though it needed no glance to assure her that " Lisle Sterling " was the name engraved upon it.

" I am not fit to see any one to-day. Will you be kind enough to tell him— '

" Impossible—write it," interrupted Mrs. Venard.

" No. I have changed my mind. I will see him," and she rang for Justine while hastily gathering up her hair to be bound in its usual classic style.

Mrs. Venard left her, and sensibly leaving the drawing-room when she had announced the success of her mission, she soon afterward heard Leonore enter it and close the door.

Lisle stood gazing out of the window, with his arms folded behind him, but he turned as Leonore entered, and, reading at a glance that she had passed through some storm which yet was scarcely stilled, he clasped both her hands within his own and bent a searching yet unutterably tender look upon her face.

She did not turn it from him, but her eyes drooped while a steady flush crept by degrees up to her very forehead ; and filled with tenderest compassion, he led her to a sofa and seated himself beside her. Still clasping her hands, he raised them to his lips in a manner more pitying than loverlike, then said softly,

" Leonore, you seem even more unhappy than I am. Is it so ?"

" I am more utterly and completely wretched than you can be ! You are not bowed to the very dust by a burden you can no more cast off than you can look up under. I have no right even to friendship, since I cannot openly and frankly receive it, feeling that I am upon equal terms with those who offer it."

" Nor can I, Leonore. Your right in this respect is equal to my own. Here, at least, we can sympathize with and understand each other."

" You ?" she asked wonderingly. "It seems to me that if any mortal ever was truly blessed and fortunate, you are so."

" You know how little one can judge from externals. Leonore, I am not accustomed to enlarge upon my own private affairs, you will bear me witness ; but I came to you to-day expressly to egotize, and I now frankly and truthfully confess to you that I am a species of vagabond in the polite and fastidious world ; that I am an impostor, though God knows a guiltless one—that a cloud hangs over my life from whose shadow I may never escape ; and which for years rendered me misanthropical and distrustful towards all living beings. My first lesson in life was one of suspicion and distrust, and I have, perhaps, no right to offer a heart thus early warped and distorted, to any woman whom the sun shines on. More than this, I can never explain to you or any one. Were you fortunate and happy, as you deserve to be, I should not say to you what I now do; but, situated as you are, my love cannot prove a misfortune to you, since I can and will protect you from much which now oppresses you, and whatever I *cannot* offer you, I can and do offer the sincerest and entire affection of a heart that never before beat one throb the faster for any living woman. We have each a sorrow which we claim the right to preserve inviolate. Respect mine, as I most faithfully will respect yours; and give me the right to shield and protect, as I love you. Leonore, can you, will you accept as a husband such a man as you now know me to be ?"

"I cannot, I cannot. You do not know what you ask, you would not ask it if you did."

" Do you, then, pronounce me quite unworthy ?"

" No, no. It is I who am unworthy. Were I to become your wife, you would hate me should you ever know all which I know !"

" Then may I never learn it. Enough for me that I know you pure and good, that I trust you as I never dreamed I could trust any one, that without you my life is worthless ! Whatever may be the sorrow you conceal from me, if I ever so far forget my manhood as to persecute you upon account of it, remind me that I now and here assumed the full and entire responsibility of its concealment, and shame me for practising toward another the injustice I would not endure myself. Take me upon your own terms, Leonore. I consent to any."

" Do not torture me. This is utterly impossible, and you must not, for your own sake, urge it."

" Tell me, then, that you do not love me ; and I cease forever."

She was silent, and the hands she had withdrawn from his clasp trembled visibly.

" Leonore !"

She turned impulsively toward him, and exclaimed,

" I do love you ! I will not deny it."

" Then why do you banish me ?"

" Your own lips pronounced that sentence months ago."

" Mine ? Then they spoke what my heart and soul protest against."

" Were any other than you to speak those words, if I loved him I should yield. But to you, of all the world, I cannot. As my friend, you will remain unchanged by any revelations; I believe it. But as

my husband, were I to marry you against the voice of my own conscience, you might one day reproach me in a way that would overwhelm me with shame and despair. The very presence of a secret
between us would embitter your life, and your faith and trust in me
would suffer ceaseless martyrdom. If it is ever to be, it cannot be
now."

"Then you do give me a hope that in time you will revoke this
morning's decision?"

"Perhaps. It is possible. but most improbable."

"Then upon that possibility I anchor my hope. Meantime that I
patiently wait, promise me that if you in any way need the services
or protection of one who only asks to bestow them, you will claim
them of me as you would were you in reality my wife. Promise me
this, sacredly."

"I do. I will."

"One thing more, dear Leonore. If the time ever comes when
you feel, that, despite this day's decision, you will be happier as my
wife, freer under my roof than another's, tell me so without one moment's false delicacy. Will you?"

She raised her eyes filled with tears, but smiling through them,
and Lisle clasped her impetuously to his breast.

"There, Leonore, you are the first woman I have ever kissed save
filially, and you shall be the last."

She raised her hands towards him as she said fervently,

"If to be your wife in this world incurred purgatory in the next,
I would cheerfully suffer it!"

He reimprisoned them as he answered smiling and hopefully,

"My wife you certainly will be; it is only a question of time; and
my effort shall be that you suffer not purgatory *here*, as well as in the
future! It were extortion to impose double rates."

"Oh do not speak so confidently; you make me fear I have done
wrongly to offer any hope for the future. Remember I have promised nothing—all is dark and uncertain. Remember it may never
be!"

"Did you fancy I could forget? Much as there is which I long to
h ar you say, what you have spoken, despite its attendant discour-
agements. has made me happy, and in this I may rejoice, even while
I remember that there are more people who love and never marry
each other, than tho e who, marrying, do so because they love. In
this world where so many affairs go perversely wrong, he only is a
philosopher, who, from the least wrong extracts the most enjoy-

ment. My life has not been so overflowing with happiness that I can throw away what is vouchsafed me, because it is all too meagre to satisfy my demands. Come, Leonore; let us emulate Macbeth, and throw *care* to the dogs. Care makes men mad and women old."

An hour after, as Mrs. Venard met Leonore upon the way to her room, the changed aspect of her face and demeanor prompted her to extend her hand with a smile of congratulation.

Leonore raised her own in deprecation, and while the old expression came back over her features, she said in a voice of self-reproach, "Of all the weak acts I ever committed, I have to-day done the very worst, since I have, under an irresistible impulse, held out a hope which I can never realize—*never !*" and without waiting for a reply, she passed quickly up to her room and closed the door.

In the evening Lisle called to attend Mrs. Bertram to the play, as usual, when she wished to attend ; and to his surprise she herself admitted him into the hall. His surprise at her unusual punctuality was quickly dissipated, as with a meaning smile she said,

"Yes, for once I am ready. You see I would not lose one moment before offering my felicitations, and I hope you will for once admit that my promptness is not ill-timed."

"I never thought you so malicious !"

"What upon earth do you mean ! ' *Malicious* '—I ?"

"Sarcastic, then, if the word please you better. Yours is a novel reception of ' a rejected.' Many such would quite overwhelm me."

" ' Rejected !' Do you mean to tell me that Leonore Wakefield has refused you ?"

"She displayed exactly that good sense."

"Astonishing !"

"The only thing astonishing to me is, how you became so well-informed upon the subject as you were. You shall tell me as we go, as there is no time to lose before the curtain rises."

Once in the carriage, Mrs. Bertram laughed. "You wonder how I gained my information, do you ? Well, I had half of it last night, as I saw you when you met Leonore, and on your whole face was written—' I'll certainly propose before another sun goes down !' and if I hadn't seen that, I should have known it all as you passed my house this morning on your way to the Venards. There was a whole Solomon's song in the very tie of your cravat. 'I charge you, oh, daughters, &c., if you see my beloved,' &c., and so on. There never was a plainer shadow of forthcoming events cast over any mortal man's face!"

"Not to mention that Mrs. Venard dropped in to see you in a neighborly way as early as practicable, eh?"

Mrs. Bertram laughed a confession of such an event, and then added with a little manifest pique,

"It is a singular sort of affair, I must admit, that thus leads both Em and me to such false conclusions. One might have known that you couldn't and wouldn't do anything like other people; and the only hope is, that in Leonore Wakefield you've found your match."

"I wish she would think so!" said he lugubriously.

"I'm not punning. If you will stickle for perfect elegance of expression despite one's righteous indignation under such provoking circumstances, correct the sentence, and admit that in Miss Wakefield you have found some one as eccentric and utterly unaccountable as yourself. What upon earth could have led her to refuse you?"

"I don't exactly know; but I'm shrewdly suspicious—that—she *didn't wish to marry me!*"

"Provoking fellow; I really thought you were going to say something! but as you didn't, I will. I think that any woman who ever married any man who could jest over her having refused him, would come to untimely grief!"

"Make a memorandum for your own future guidance. Bertram is looking rather poorly of late!"

"Sterling, you meant to disturb my amiable temper by that sage remark; but upon the contrary, it soothed my ruffled feelings, and in proof of it, I'm going to announce to you, in strict confidence, that any women who has a sufficient quantity of 'treasures upon earth' to support her in comfort, had better defy 'rust and moths,' and trust in oxalic acid and camphor-gum, instead of marrying any man! Matrimony, for a woman who has nothing in her own right, is a sort of genteel, licensed beggary; and one who has enough, is better off without it. Were my husband's wife to perambulate the streets of this fastidious city as she walks through his house, she would be arrested as a vagrant. 'No visible means of support' isn't put down against a marital pensioner; that's the only difference."

"'Soothing reflection!' to be Pecksniffian in my remark. Let me tell you it is something to possess an acknowledged license to beg and pirate. Now don't spoil your amiable expression of countenance just as we are at the door. The rage for 'spirited women' has gone by."

The curtain had just risen as they entered, and Mrs. Bertram forgot her trifling vexation till at the end of the first act it returned with an accession, and turning toward Lisle she said,

" I'm getting disgusted with plays. The most popular ones seem revised editions and imitations of 'Taming the Shrew,' and one grows as much disgusted with the masculine applause which attends this wonderful exhibition of married authority and household snubbing in general, as with the unnatural feminine meekness exhibited—*on the stage only !*"

" Poor creature! losing all the bright illusions of youth, and a positive monomaniac upon the subject of snubbing! 'Sic a wife as Wille had,' &c. I'm afraid Bertram will never look less poorly !"

"Oh, do hush ! Do you suppose one is never serious? I'm cross as a bear now, and I forbid you to speak again to-night."

Quite forgetting this injunction, she turned again to ask some question after a long silence had restored her good nature; but implicitly obeying her command, Lisle would not unseal his lips, and at the close of the play escorted her home in the same unbroken silence. Bowing her in at her own door, he received a parting thrust.

"You are a most unbearably provoking fellow, and I give you fair warning that another time I won't be made a scapegoat for your ill humor! If you must abuse some one's wife, I'm sorry it can't be your own, I'm sure ; but I won't be made to suffer in her stead."

Lisle laughed unrestrainedly; but really feeling that for his own amusement he carried the affair too far, he offered a sincere apology which she interrupted by a curt "good night," and passed along the hall.

There was a light in her room, by which her husband lay reading ; and she interrupted him at once.

"What do you think ! Leonore Wakefield has refused to marry Lisle Sterling."

Mr. Bertram laid aside his book and deliberately lighted a cigar, having achieved which, he made an eloquent remark. "*Humph !*"

" No ' humph ' about it. She has done a most surprising thing, and a foolish one, as it seems to me. Sterling isn't a domestic angel, I grant, as I've sufficient reason to know ; but he is a good match, and she ought to know it. However else is she to get out of her half governess sort of life for which she is about as well fitted by nature as Queen Titania."

Mr. Bertram puffed his cigar in silence, and she continued,

"Now I suppose we are at the end of our pleasant little gatherings. No more cozy family 'at homes' with Leonore's pretty face and delicious music as an attraction, and ten to one Sterling will leave the city, or at least stop visiting at the Venards."

"If he does either, he isn't the man I think him," Mr. Bertram replied, deliberately and carefully closing one eye against the little eddy of smoke curling up towards it. "Why upon earth an ablebodied man should show the white feather, and run, just because a woman happens to say no instead of yes to a foolish request, is more than I ever could see.

"'*Happens* to say no!'"

"Yes; it's all a whim, either way; and if a man receives a lucky answer, he had better not risk anything by repeating the same question five minutes afterward. If a poor fellow had any instinct of self-preservation under such circumstances—which, unfortunately, he hasn't—he would feel that the time to run was when she said yes. Some sense in it, then."

"Bertram, what under heaven induced you ever to marry?"

"Oh bother, Mattie! don't go off on that tack, I beg of you. You are a wonderfully decent wife, as wives go; but it's hard to expect a man to be gallantly devoted when his seven weekly nights are rendered inquisitorial by gouging curl papers, and his days anxious by too much complexion unrubbed in. Vanity, Mattie, vanity ought to be your stand by!"

"It is all snubbed out of me, as it is out of most wives! It is strange that husbands never seem to think why their wives permit some silken little masculine to play the respectfully devoted! It isn't pleasant to be quite upon the retired list, every woman knows!"

"Oh bother! Why don't some genius invent a love-making, compliment-paying machine, for the benefit of the two years married! Think of my making love to you, Mattie! Fie! go to bed, little woman!"

Mr. Bertram's estimate of Lisle, however based upon a misapprehension of the immediate affairs under discussion, proved correct. He neither ceased visiting at the Venards, nor added one element of unpleasantness to the usual little coteries by any manifestation of constraint towards the lady by whom he had avowed himself rejected. Upon the contrary, the two had never seemed upon more kindly terms, or more content under the relationship existing between them ; and, rejoiced as she was under such a state of affairs, Mrs. Bertram silently confirmed the judgment she had at first rendered—that the whole matter was altogether strange and unaccountable !

CHAPTER XIX.

THE summer vacation of —— Seminary was most enthusiastically welcomed by the young ladies within its monotonous walls, and by none more so than by Julie Kelley, and her friend, Rose Sandford, who were to pass the entire season at Niagara, in accordance with the arrangement made for the preceding summer when Julie had been summoned home by the illness of her father.

Young, beautiful, and naturally of a gay disposition, it was not unnatural that she welcomed such a sojourn with delight, as it is only at a more mature age that one reflects how seldom one's bright anticipations are realized.

Stopping at the Clifton House, the very noise and bustle of hotel life during the fashionable season had its charm for the two young girls, just released from the quiet routine of school life, and each intensified the enjoyment of the other by the manifestation of her own.

Despite the sombre hue of the garments she still wore in memory of her father, it would have seemed a want of harmony in one so piquant and pretty not to have joined in the gayety around her; and she did enter into it with all the zest natural to her age and temperament, while Mrs. Sandford rejoiced that she was the chaperone of two young ladies so gay and attractive as her daughter and her friend.

Mr. Sandford, although a business man in the strictest acceptation of the term, was a most genial spectator of the usual watering-place life when he was present; but this was only at stated intervals, and while he was absent superintending his business affairs, his wife remained sole guardian of the two young ladies. Had any one insinuated to Mrs. Sandford that she was not the most judicious guardian possible, she would have resented it as warmly and conscientiously as would Mr. Sandford himself, to whom such an idea had never occurred. Although no longer young, the natural romance of her character warped her judgment in one essential particular, and that the most unfortunate for those committed to her care.

Easily approached under any formality of etiquette, introductions
to her were attainable by any and all who solicited them, and in
each masculine acquaintance she saw one more candidate for the
favor of her protégés, or appreciator of her own sickly sentimentali-
ty and rather faded charms.   Had not Rose possessed more good
sense and discretion than her mother, they would very soon have
become the centre of a circle of such adventurers as always frequent
these places of fashionable resort; and as it was, Mrs. Sandford's
circle was anything but exclusive.

Shrewd as Mr. Sandford was in business affairs, he had no perception of this weakness in his wife's character; but, the rather,
seeing her always surrounded by people of the most fastidious gentility, and the two girls well supplied with partners, he gave her
credit for the greatest amount of tact and good management in social matters, amid which he was totally at sea.

If it ever occurred to him during his visits when he at each time
noted the extension of her circle, that nine in ten of these gallant
young gentlemen were not the most desirable companions for the
young ladies, he banished the fastidious idea, relying upon the good
sense of his daughter and her friend, and reflecting that, after all,
these were but watering-place acquaintances, very unlikely ever to
be met again, and no serious consequences would occur from a few
evenings waltzing with them, if they were not exactly mental New-
tons.   If among them all one should by bare possibility seek a more
lasting companionship, it would be time enough then to canvass his
merits, social and moral; and meantime no one should expect or
wish Rose and Julie to remain mere wall-flowers in such an assemblage.

"School life must be irksome enough to such bright and lively
young things as they; let them make the most of their holidays,"
the kind hearted old gentleman said to himself when these ideas
now and then obtruded themselves upon his mind; and he gave no
utterance to them.

Among the numerous gallants thus admitted into their circle, was
one who attracted particular attention by his handsome exterior and
polished manners, and who, judging from all appearances, was an
especial favorite with Mrs. Sandford, if not with the pretty Julie to
whom he paid most devoted attention upon all occasions.

This gentleman was no longer in the first flush of youth, as was
Julie herself; at the first glance one would have pronounced him
thirty at least, though in reality he was something less; and his

most striking characteristic was a dignified yet half defiant *hauteur*, which in one less thoroughly well-bred and self-possessed would have seemed a sort of recklessness, if not positive impudence. Tall in stature, and possessing a figure of perfect elegance, there was a certain air of assurance accompanying his most trivial actions, that carried with it that social passport inseparable from people of the highest birth and position, which whether false or true, served the purpose for which it was exercised, and what in another might at once have been pronounced intrusion, was from him accepted as a condescension which secured him a welcome into the coteries he chose to favor with his presence.

Thus, though he was upon terms of polite intercourse with most eligible circles in the drawing-room, none could definitely have explained how he became so, nor upon just whose responsibility he was thus received among them; and thus easily admitted into more exclusive circles, it was not surprising that he had gained the entrée to Mrs. Sandford's room soon after that lady established herself in the house, where, from the very first, he allowed it to be seen that Julie Kelley was the object which attracted him and kept him a fixture forever near her.

A younger, less worldly-experienced admirer would delicately have attempted to shield this *penchant* from the gossiping tongues around them; and Julie's sensitive modesty led her more than once to protest against this too publicly offered devotion. But, young and yielding, as is every woman where her heart is interested, she ceased her protests under his earnestly offered excuses plead with that persuasive eloquence natural to such circumstances; and Mrs. Sandford followed it up with encomiums upon his honest, frank manliness of deportment in pursuing so unmistakable a course, till she was convinced that she was most unreasonable in wishing for anything more delicate and in consonance with her own ideas and predilections.

Naturally somewhat coquettish, as is every pretty woman in her early youth, Julie never thought of practising upon the self-assured Leonard Horton the teasing arts and wiles to which she would have subjected a younger and less imposing admirer, but treated him with a tender respect and trusting confidence of manner all the more dangerous for the species of veneration she felt toward him as one so far her superior in worldly tact and experience, and that undefinable fascination he had from the first exercised over her.

There certainly was a nameless something—magnetism perhaps— in the soft black eyes that possessed such a wondrous power of speech, more forcible and persuasive than any eloquence of audible words; and Julie yielded tender allegiance to their commands, while each approving ray from their luminous depths made her heart throb quicker, and the rosy color sprang into her cheek of purest blonde and most exquisite contour. Vivacious and sprightly as she was, this soft obedience to his caprice possessed an irresistible charm for Leonard Horton, and calm as he affected to be under it, he thrilled with exultation and gratified self-love as he noted the change that came over her when he approached her in her most vivacious moments, and how intuitively others felt themselves *de trop*, and dropped away from his all conquering presence.

Not one warning whisper cautioned her against thus admitting into her heart one so utterly unknown; for, exultant at thus having secured "a settlement" in prospective for her temporary protegée, Mrs. Sandford did not, herself, once question its perfect desirability, and enjoyed in anticipation the felicitations to which she deemed such chaperoneship entitled her. Of course, should Julie's mother and guardians be foolishly exigent upon matters of which society takes little or no cognizance, they must satisfy themselves relative to his moral qualifications. Her agency extended no farther than in bringing affairs on to this *denouement*, and she prided herself upon the rapidity with which it had been accomplished. In her estimation, Leonard Horton was by far the most eligible *parti* she had met —handsome, accomplished, and reported wealthy, and it had been the desire of her heart to secure him for her daughter. But Rose was refractory, and pronounced him disagreeable, utterly refusing to make one effort to attract him; and as he himself had preferred to bestow his attentions upon Julie, it only remained to glory in this as the next desirable consummation. Plainly perceiving these mental self-congratulations, Leonard Horton skillfully pandered to the spirit that conceived them, till, from having favored the marriage, she openly encouraged it; and her opinion was not without its influence over Julie, pre-disposed as she was to suspend her judgment and listen only to feeling.

Thus satisfactory to all parties interested, were affairs progressing, when a disturbing element appeared upon the scene, in the form of Miss Phebe Venard, who, with a party of her southern friends, arrived to spend the fashionable season at the Falls. Directly it became noised about that this not too personally attractive young lady was an heiress, rumor increasing and exaggerating the sum of her possessions, as rumor is famous for doing, till it reached a most fabulous amount. Under this *prestige*, Miss Phebe's rather stout, short figure, appeared only desirably "plump," her foolish twaddle was only "*naiveté*," and her frequent outbreaks of ill-temper were only "spirited and refreshing;" as all her satellites declared. From her own confessions, people soon learned that she was an authoress, and as she modestly refused naming and enumerating her literary productions. curiosity became vividly excited, and all the assembled anonymous novels were industriously read and interchanged, in the hope of stumbling upon something that should identify them as hers. An heiress and an authoress, Miss Phebe's notoriety was established at once, and she reigned triumphant. Admirers gathered around her, ceaseless ovations were offered up to her.

For the first time Leonard Horton's attentions were divided between Julie and another, and he, too, followed the new star. Too proud to manifest the uneasiness and misery it caused her, Julie smiled upon others in his absence, and the immediate accession to the number of aspirants for his favor, evidenced how significant Mr. Horton's heretofore exclusive addresses had been considered.

One evening soon after Miss Phebe's arrival, Rose Sandford watched her opportunity and whispered to Julie.

"I have been presented to the heiress. 'Beauty, talent, *and* money,' you must make her acquaintance."

There was a mirthful glitter in Rose's eyes, that uttered its own comment, and with a smile Julie shook her head. Rose expostulated more earnestly, "Oh, I don't see how you are to avoid it. Mr. Horton has promised to introduce you since I was condemned to go through the operation. It is 'Beauty's request of the Beast,' whom I suppose she feels guilty for appropriating, or perhaps she wants to snap your head off and so make a clean job of it. She has a temper of her own, I can tell you."

"Memorandum—make her exhibit it upon the first mal-apropos occasion. Tell me something more," laughed Julie.

"Hush, here comes Mr. Horton. Don't be overwhelmed, now, by the brilliant scintillations of this renowned damsel's wit. My opinion is that her gold is the only bright thing about her, and I don't believe there's too much of that to be scoured every day by what she calls her ' niggers.' "

Mr. Horton approached with Mrs. Sandford simpering upon his arm, and with bland courtesy addressed Julie.

"I want to present you to Miss Venard, Julie. I am about to in-

troduce Mrs. Sandford, as she particularly wishes to know you all.
She asserts, Julie, that you bear an actual resemblance to a very dear
friend of hers in the South, to whom she insists you must be related."

"Oh, don't take me relation hunting, I beg of you! I should be
quite frightened at the very idea, did I not know that beside my
dear mother I have not a relative in existence. Please tell her so,
and spare me the trouble. I want to dance this next polka."

"I hope, Julie, you do not refuse to receive an introduction I expressly wish you to grant, and have even promised in your name,"
he said reproachfully. She colored slightly, but made no gesture of
compliance; and extending her hand Mrs. Sandford said with mild
authority,

"Of course she does not refuse. That would be unpardonable
under the circumstances, and quite ill-advised. Besides, it is always
well to know people who are *distingué*. It gives one social importance. Come, my dear."

Thus adjured, Julie arose, and in some pique accepted Mr. Horton's disengaged arm. Miss Phebe was impatiently awaiting them.

Mrs. Sandford graced her presentation with one of her set complimentary speeches, which Miss Phebe received with a stare of blank
amazement, and then turned abruptly to Julie.

"Do tell me, Miss Kelley, are you any way related to Lisle Sterling,
formerly of Louisville? You look enough like him to be his sister."

"He is my guardian, but I had no idea there existed any resemblance between us, till Mr. Horton informed me that you had discovered one."

"I didn't say anything of the sort to him. I never once mentioned
Lisle Sterling's name, did I Mr. Horton? I merely said you looked
like a ' friend.' "

" ' A *very dear* friend,' corrected Mr. Horton with a visible effort
to appear careless and only playfully interested. Julie observed
his changing color, and attributed it to a real uneasiness at Miss
Venard having thus familiarly spoken of one who might possibly be
a rival in the young lady's interest; and the same thought occurred
to Miss Phebe herself, very evidently; for playfully tapping his arm
with her fan she said,

"How you gentlemen all do love each other! A lady can't speak
to one of you about another, without pitting you against each other
at once."

"Dear me, what else can be expected," simpered Mrs. Sandford
sentimentally. "I recollect how poor dear Mr. Sandford, the most

amiable man that ever lived, used to frown and make himself look ugly if I so much as smiled upon any other gentlemen ; and if I went so far as to waltz with one, dear me how he would go on ! They are all alike, Miss Venard, and all quite tyrannical before marriage, whatever they may become afterward. To be sure, you are not Mr. Horton's *fiancée*; so he has no occasion to be jealous of your ' very dear' gentlemen friends."

Mr. Horton turned toward Julie whose impatience was manifest. "I think you told me you intended to dance this polka. Shall I take you to your partner ? Miss Venard will excuse us."

"I have no partner; it was a mere excuse," she rather curtly explained as they moved away; but without heeding the assertion he said,

" So this Mr. Lisle Sterling, of whom Miss Venard speaks, is your guardian? I fancied you the ward of Mrs. Sandford."

"Oh, no. She was kind enough to ask me to accompany Rose here this summer ; that is all. We were to have come last year, but poor pa's sickness and death prevented me, and I feel quite guilty now, when I think how lonely ma must be without me, and Edward with her but little of the time."

" And who is ' Edward ?' Your brother ?"

" In a manner, as he has lived with us for years. He is my guardian's brother, Edward Sterling, and both brothers were great favorites of pa's."

" And do you really resemble this Lisle Sterling, as Miss Venard says ?"

" Nonsense. Descriptions of all persons with dark blue eyes, chestnut hair, &c., sound so nearly alike, that it is nothing strange if the owners of them now and then look not unlike. I fancy the lady's only apology for so astonishing a discovery, was her wish to render you uneasy about her ' very dear' acquaintance."

" Julie, I don't think you care to dance, in such a humor. Shall we go out upon the veranda ?" he asked, seeing that she was really piqued.

She assented, and as they passed near Miss Venard she caught a glance from that young lady, for which she was prepared, as she had marked a rising frown upon her face when she and Mr. Horton had turned away.

" I think Miss Venard would like a partner," she said, calling his attention to that lady's manifest displeasure, and not unwilling to show her own indifference to his society at that moment. He laughed.

"I think I should not like to be that partner for a round dance. She weighs too much by a cool fifty."

"How hypocritical gentlemen are. I dare say you have complimented her forty times upon the possession of that same 'cool fifty!'"

"Julie, you are piqued—may I even say *jealous*, I wonder?"

"I see nothing for you to wonder at. I never professed to be anything more or less than human," she replied with a total lack of that tender veneration she had ever before manifested toward him.

He was both surprised and amused at the change, as a touch of feminine spirit was not distasteful to him; and he bent his eyes admiringly upon her, to the evident heightening of her color. But both her shame of herself, and her resentment against him, were soon lost to him under a stronger emotion which found expression in a query whose troubled tone aroused her.

"This guardian of yours, Julie, will he come here this summer during your stay, perhaps carry you off with him where you will be lost to familiar eyes—at least mine—forever?"

"Hardly possible. He is so complete a Southerner that I doubt if he will ever come north again. He made such a vow, and frequently repeated it the last time he was here; and certainly his own home is too uncongenial to attract him. None of his letters indicate that he has changed his mind upon the subject. As for my going to him, guardian as he is, the idea is preposterous, unless, indeed, he should marry, which is quite improbable."

"I don't know that. These cynical, affected woman-haters, are even more liable to be entrapped by most any woman with tact enough to seem a *rara avis* among her sex. Who knows but that may be you, Julie?"

The memory of her own delusion upon this point lent a convincing earnestness to the tone in which she replied,

"No, quite impossible. We have always been more like brother and sister, and always must be. But who told you he is a woman-hater."

"To tell you the truth, years ago I knew him; and I don't suppose he has very much changed. He is not one of the kind who do change."

"You knew him? Where?" She asked the question with surprise as well as curiosity, and he could not conceal that it troubled him. However, sooner or later she must know the whole; self-interest demanded it; and he resolved not to lose so good an opportunity. Throwing into his voice and whole manner a soft melancholy well calculated to excite compassion in a heart that loved him, he sighed,

"It is a piteous story, little Julie. I dare not tell it even to you, lest you too, turn against me."

"Never," she uttered earnestly with a closer clasp of the arm upon which she leaned as they slowly promenaded the veranda.

He looked in her face with feigned incredulity.

"Not even though that tale affix its share of blame and folly upon me—a blame not so deep as it at first appears, a folly of which I repent as sincerely as ineffectually? Oh, impossible! This world has no forgiving pity for the unfortunate who brings his own suffering upon himself, however goaded by circumstances. A life of sorrowing repentance cannot wipe out an error committed in a misguided moment; not even gentle hearts like yours ever excuse his error, despite all the atonement he can offer! Oh, Julie, pity me, for I need all your sweet compassion."

"It is yours, dear Leonard, be assured. But trust me with this sorrowful story, will you not? I do not ask it in mere curiosity, as you must know."

"Do you then love me—a *little*—miserable that I am? Under brighter circumstances would you have been, perhaps, my wife? Tell me this, Julie."

"Not 'under brighter circumstances,' Leonard, but under any, all."

He pressed her hand with rapturous fervor, as he exclaimed,

"Dear little comforter! But first let me tell this sad story—a confession, as it is, which I never could humiliate myself enough to make to any mortal but yourself. Oh, Julie,—listen—two words will tell it all—I am not 'Leonard Horton'—but—"

"But who?" she asked in breathless eagerness.

"Louis Hartley."

She stopped, aghast at the revelation, and he continued bitterly,

"Yes, he whom you have heard denounced as a swindler, an ingrate, a thief who fled at night from the coffer he had robbed! I can imagine all the vituperations heaped upon my head. Lisle Sterling never failed to mete out justice according to his own idea of it, and Christian charity isn't a weakness of his!"

"Oh, unjust, cruel to yourself! I never heard him utter one such bitter word of you! He left us immediately upon the receipt of his uncle's letter detailing the affair, and your name scarcely passed his

lips. Even Mr. Fitzjames forgave you, and in his will, made about
that time, bequeathed you the amount you had—*appropriated*—that
so the matter might be forever set at rest. I suppose you know this
and that Lisle was made heir to all the rest of his uncle's property ?
I believe it was established that you had acquired possession."

"Oh yes. All due formalities were observed—as I said, Sterling
always administers justice according to his idea of it. I did not care
to 'enter an appearance' in accordance with the published citation,
and so submit myself to the chances of a prosecution to gratify the
defrauded heir's private malice. I needed the sum thus ensured to
me, and I kept it; but I always intended to refund his half of that
which I had appropriated from the profits of our co-partnership, and
I still do so intend. More than ever, now that I know he is your
guardian, I will leave him no reason to complain of me. I shall repay as a loan that of which the whole might have been as much
mine as his, had a formal settlement been made between us. After
all, the whole capital belonged to Mr. Fitzjames, since neither Sterling nor I had a dollar to invest; but as he is left sole heir, I have
no doubt he looks upon the bequest left me as so much taken from
himself, and I will keep only my business share of it."

"But since it is really yours by bequest—"

"I tell you no. I know just what proportion of it is mine by the
terms of that co-partnership existing when I took it, and the rest
shall be returned to him. I should have restored it ere this, but one
hope after another has mocked my efforts, and I am still his debtor.
Now tell me, Julie; when I shall have made this atonement, will you
forgive the weakness of which I was guilty under a temptation too
strong to be resisted ?"

"That temptation—what can it have been ?"

"Do not ask me that. You can never know. There are events
in my life that I cannot tell even you. I have confessed my wrong
doing, and avowed my penitence. Is not that enough ? Forgive
me all, Julie."

"I have nothing to forgive. Heaven forbid that I should judge
you."

"And your love, Julie—can you tell me that it still is mine, that
you will under *these* circumstances become my wife, as you were ready
to promise so short a time since."

"Yes, I will. I do believe that you are truly repentant, that you
wish to make a most generous atonement for your error, and that
you deserve not only pardon for it, but sympathy for the suffering i

has caused you. How could you fear that I might be ungenerous—worse, unjust—toward you!"

"Disappointment has been my lot all through my life. It is enough that I dare *hope* for anything, to make it fail me. So will you, yet, Julie, despite your present thought. The very idea that you are the the *fiancée* of one who dare not claim his own name lest public disgrace befall him, will weary and harass you; yet I must endure this burden, and inflict it upon you, till all danger of prosecution from Lisle Sterling is over. I must trust to you to soften his heart toward me, for I am powerless. He never liked me, from the very first, and it was our mutual rivalry for Mr. Fitzjames' favor, that made me fear to trust the old gentleman with the trouble that goaded me on to the deed by which I lost it forever. Sterling has triumphed over me; he stands to day in the place I should have occupied but for him and his scheming; and for that very thing he will be relentless toward me. Suppose, Julie, that as your guardian he forbids our marriage!"

She did not immediately reply, and he made a gesture of impatience as he said bitterly,

"So, wavering already! You will sacrifice yourself and me to the 'duty' of blind obedience; or, hearing me unceasingly denounced by those whom it is more natural that you should trust, you will tell me that you were 'mistaken in your sentiments, did not know your own heart,' and all the rest of the feminine excuses for broken faith. I prophesy it all."

"I never break faith. My promise once given is sacred forever," she answered quietly and with dignified reproach for his taunting words.

"Forever, come what may. Shall *nothing* cause you to violate it ?"

"How little you trust and believe in me !"

"But, Julie, swear it. Swear it and I shall trust in you to the death !"

"Well, I swear it. Foolish doubter, be content !"

"I am, I am ! Oh, Julie, love makes me a skeptic, bear with me; But if your guardian oppose us——"

"I will give him no opportunity, if he remain unjust and relentless toward you, after you have made him every reparation possible. What you propose is more than justice towards him, it is magnanimity; and if, after that, he continues obdurate, as you prophesy, I will fulfill my promise though I walk through fire to accomplish it.

Nothing short of crime shall separate us. Do you see that it is fixed?"

"Oh, Julie, what can I say to you? Wait patiently, dear girl, till I can make this restoration as the starting point to win his approbation. Give me time."

"Ah, indeed; if I were rich, now, like Miss Venard! She would never miss so small a sum, while it would more than swallow my worldly possessions were I even yet mistress of them. Five thousand dollars! I have not so much in the world! Oh, if Lisle only will forgive and understand you!"

"He never will, I tell you. My heart sank when I heard you speak his name."

Mrs. Sandford appeared upon the veranda in search of them.

"Oh, Mr. Horton, you thoughtless man, to keep this dear child out so long, after dancing! You will have her in a consumption at this rate."

"I will take her directly in, Mrs. Sandford. She has just given me a right to watch over and protect her. Give me your congratulations."

They were rapturously uttered; and when he left them for the night he said exultingly, "So far, so good! Eventually she must have known it all, and there is everything in a first hearing. Henceforth any denunciations Lisle Sterling may utter against me, will seem so much persecution. Strange that he is her guardian!"

CHAPTER XX.

"I DECLARE, Julia, if I were you I'd put a stop to Leonard Horton's flirtation with Miss Venard," exclaimed Rose Sandford resentfully, as the two were seated one morning tête à tête over their embroidery. "I never liked him, at best, with his fine and mighty assumption of superiority, and lord knows what not of 'little story' stamped all over him; but if he is going to turn gay Lothario, he will be more unendurable than ever. He neglects you most shamefully for her benefit, and you are a goose to suffer it. Everybody can see that she is perfectly befooled after him, and if I were you I'd kuow why!"

"Oh, Rose, don't speak so hastily about what you don't understand. See how easy it is to misjudge one's most generous actions. Since he learned that your father and mother are not my legal guardians, as he first very naturally supposed, he feels that it would be very wrong to compromise me by such public and exclusive attentions as he had offered me when he supposed their saction was sufficient to authorize it."

"So he fancies that he betters it by leading every one to think that he has deserted you, and that for a silly heiress with not so much brains as my thimble! She kept me in a rage all last evening by her ostentatious assumption of triumph over you, and the malicious glances of exultation she kept turning upon you where you were pining in a most romantic, and to me vexatious style. What did possess you? Every one remarked it all."

"I didn't feel like dancing, and I wouldn't; that is all. I care very little what these people say of us so long as we feel that we are doing right.

"'We feel!' say rather that *Horton* prefers a certain line of deportment, and that you obediently assent. The truth is, that now he thinks he has you all safe under the keeping of an 'engagement,' he wants a chance at the heiress; and you meekly walk into the trap. It may all be very amusing to him, but for my life I can't see

where your share of the sport comes in. How upon earth any girl
as sensible as you are upon most subjects, can be such a simpleton
where he is concerned, is a mystery! If he but looks a sovereign
command, you obey, while his airs would set every drop of blood in
my veins tingling with rebellion; but this last concession, just as
you have the *right* to interfere, strikes me dumb."

"I think, rather, it unlocks your native eloquence. If this is a
fair specimen of your dumbness, fate forbid you should burst into
speech!" Julie retorted laughingly.

"Confess now, are you perfectly contented under this state of affairs?"

She did not immediately reply, but it was evident from her look
and manner, that however loth she might be to admit it, she was
learning the truth that however a woman may feel constrained to
assent to the wisdom or policy of her lover confining his attentions
within the strict bounds of worldly prudence, she is never pleased
to see him bestow any portion of them upon her rival, or one who
may by any possibility become so.

Rose saw that her words had struck a sensitive cord; and added
more gently,

"It wouldn't so much matter, if he hadn't been so distressingly
demonstrative up to the present, that every one formed the only
natural conclusion; but as he can't rub out this conclusion by establishing one of a later date, it would be better to go consistently
and quietly on. A fiddlestick for all these fine points of so called
honor, and the rest of the clap trap! If you are positively in love
with each other—as I suppose you are or you wouldn't be engaged
—what do you care for the ' *sanction* ' of all the guardians you could
cram between here and the south sea islands! Nobody ever stops
for that, if they once really make up their minds, however they may
properly affect to. Besides, it would be a short-sighted guardian
who would advise such proceedings as these under the present circumstances, whether or not he intended to 'give his consent' in the
future. Nobody feels either compassion or respect for ' a deserted.'
Do show some independence, Julie!"

"I intend to when the proper time comes."

"Oh, of course you'll come out a tartar when you are really married; that's expected, always! But what I mean is, tell Horton
you've a decided objection to being made to ' wear the willow ' in
everybody's estimation, and that if he is tired of playing the devoted

to you, he shan't play it to any one else, at least in your very presence. That's what *I'd* do!"

Julie laughed. " Well, Rose, you never will have to reproach yourself with having preached ' obedience ' and the rest of it. It is no match of your making."

" No ; it is a specimen of ma's talent in that direction. Someway she has settled in her own mind that this Leonard Horton is a great catch, and she's preached it to pa, till he, dear man, has come to believe it too. But even poor ma has the sense to see that this sudden ' falling off' isn't the proper thing, and she has told everybody she knows, that it is only a ruse to cover an engagement which *you* don't wish to have suspected."

"Oh, Rose ; how could she! Why won't she allow us to manage our own affairs."

" *You* never *have*, poor child ! Ma made the match from the beginning, ane you have only been walking lady through the whole programme, though you are now and then indulged by being allowed to believe that *he* consults your wishes ; that is, he tells you his, and you fancy that the same."

For the first time Julie became angry, and she exclaimed with spirit,

"Rose, hush! I won't endure it. Why don't you call me an idiot, and so have done with it! That is the whole tenor of it, and you'd better out with it."

Rose caught her in her arms, and returned good humoredly,

" I know you are *not* an idiot, much as you act like one sometimes. I suppose this is the natural consequence of being in love, as everybody I've seen so, cuts up in about the same fashion. But you must know *I* am your real guardian here ; not ma, who needs a mentor herself; and if you become unmanageable, I *shall* be in ill-luck. I'm sure this is your first real lover—you take it so very seriously!"

"And you, madame Mentor. Do you relate your experience," said Julie, laughing again at what seemed a ludicrous assumption of maturity and consequent authority. A shade of vexation darkened Rose's face as she answered,

"Mere school girl as I am, this is the third season I've been put up, like a turkey at a raffle, for whoever chose to take a chance for ma's favor, and should ere this have been ' madam' had I not proved that *I* had some voice in the matter. It is all very well to appreciate the pretty things said to you, but to turn ' spooney ' under it, and go off in a fit of matrimony, is a sorry consequence, from which I pray to be delivered! I wouldn't marry the King of the Cannibal Islands, even to be Queen and dine off baby roast every day: I'm sick of the very word 'matrimony'—for which let all men give thanks! Dear me, there's some one at the door, and late as it is, I'm not dressed!"

It was only a letter for Julie; but warned by the alarm, Rose commenced rapidly to make her toilet, and did not look around till a sob from Julie, who was reading her letter, arrested her.

"Oh, Rose, Rose. My mother is dead—dead and buried! And no one sent for me, or even wrote me she was sick!"

Surprised and startled by the abrupt intelligence, Rose stood without the power to offer one word of sympathy or consolation, and Julie wept on convulsively. At length a feeling of anger checked her grief, and springing to her feet she tore Edward's letter in pieces and threw them upon the floor, as she exclaimed,

"Cruel, heartless! to leave me here in ignorance that my own mother was dying before his eyes. I never will forgive him, never!"

"Oh, Julie, don't be unjust; there may have been some good reason for it."

"Yes, a beautiful reason; that she had been ailing for more than a year—not to have told me even this till now—and so felt no alarm when she became worse, and would not allow my enjoyment to be destroyed by it. Edward, who is a sprouting doctor, must have known how very ill she was, though he says not. Here is his letter; read it for yourself. I'll fit the pieces."

Rose read the letter thus torn and fragmentary as it was; and deeply as she felt for Julie in her sorrow, she saw nothing in it but the most tender consideration. Edward tenderly spoke of Mrs. Kelley's last illness, which no one but herself had considered dangerous till the very last, and even then, when he would have summoned Julie, she had forbidden him to do so, urging that the blow would be more easily endured at a distance, and enjoining that the harrowing details of a funeral should also be spared her.

It was a only proof of the most tender and protecting love for the poor child, who in witnessing a parent's suffering would have been all powerless to save; and Mrs. Kelley had sacrificed her own desire to see her, for Julia's own peace. Edward added that he should immediately follow his letter, to be of any service to her that she might command, as his one wish was to aid and console her in their mutual sorrow.

Rose gently folded the fragments of the letter, and handed them back in silence. Julie looked up for some manifestation of her own resentment, but met only a glance of pity mingled with reproof.

" Would you have wished your mother's last request to have been unheeded ? " she asked gently; and then left Julie to a silence during which she was sure the voice of reason would be heard.

Utterly at a loss what to do under her present circumstances, Julie waited for Edward to arrive, before even attempting to decide. Her one overpowering desire was to leave this place, whose gayety jarred upon her very heartstrings; but where could she go ? Not back to the desolate home, all hushed and silent with a loneliness that would be insupportable in all the newness of her bereavement, —not to her guardian, whose wifeless home offered her no asylum which the critical in matters of social propriety might not cavil at, young as they both were,—for, even to herself, that secret tie of relationship was a sealed and unsuspected mystery. In all the wide world nothing like a home seemed open to her, and a feeling of utter desolation took possession of her. The very loneliness of her position made her anger against Edward forgotten the moment he appeared, and she turned to him as the one hope and reliance left her. For him, far as he was from mistaking the nature of her emotions and sentiments toward him, this was a blissful foretaste of that future to which he trustingly looked forward, resolved to be discouraged at nothing however threatening to his hopes ; and he took her, unresisting, under his protection.

He had lost no time in writing to Lisle of this fresh bereavement, and had briefly called his attention to Julie's desolate position without so much as a living relative to offer her the consolation and substantial comfort she so much required ; and he felt assured that he would at once enter upon the discharge of his duties as her guardian, heretofore only a nominal title. Mrs. Kelley had told him of the solemn promise Lisle had given her to do by her as by a sister, and the one ray of comfort he gave to Julie for the future, was the hope that a new home would be provided for her far from the scenes to which she felt she could not return.

Totally unfitted for study as she was, it was worse than useless to return to school ; nor would Mrs. Sandford consent to Rose's proposition to take her at once to their own home. Fortifying her position toward Julie with the reflection that she had done her duty by her as chaperone, Mrs. Sandford reminded her daughter that her own settlement had yet to be secured, and indulged in so many reproaches against her refractoriness in refusing to allow the affair to be arranged, that Rose in very indignation became silent.

The one thing that remained was to take Julie to his own paternal home, where at least she could remain in quiet till Lisle should be heard from; and, she assenting to this as to all other propositions advanced by him, they commenced preparations to leave at once.

The last evening of her stay was spent with her *fiancée*, who was at once inconsolable and resentful under her departure, and urged their immediate marriage as most judicious, and excusable by circumstances. She refused, and when he insisted with more than due authority, told him as firmly as gently, that until he was reinstated as a man of honor who dared bear his own name in any place the sun shone on, and in every presence, even Lisle's, her promise could never be ratified; that when his atonement had been fully made, should her guardian refuse to accept it, and still persecute him with unmerited prejudice, then, indeed, the whole affair would be merely a matter of personal feeling, in which her own was entitled to as much consideration as any other.

Louis Hartley really loved Julie with the one ardent passion of his life; and as he realized the severe test her affection must sustain, if, living under Lisle's roof, she should daily hear the adverse opinion he knew Lisle entertained toward him, expressed with that force and emphasis for which he was so remarkable, he suffered perhaps the severest penalty possible for his wrong doing. It seemed impossible that her affection for him could survive such a test, linked to Lisle as she was by every tie of old companionship and affection, ·added to that relationship of guardian and ward which *should* render his opinions of even more weight and importance to her. The very knowledge of his own unworthiness forbade him a hope that Lisle would ever accord him the hand-grasp of fellowship, still less approve his suit to his ward; and his heart fainted within him as he saw that Julie, heretofore so flexible and yielding, was upon this point immovable.

The fine sentiment he had expressed relative to reparation and atonement, which had dawned upon his mind only in the moment he had uttered it, was then a fixed fact to be literally accomplished, without which he could hope nothing even from Julie herself, who displayed so unexpected a distinction between words and deeds. How was he to accomplish that which it had cost him nothing to declare, while he exulted in the feeling of conscious honor such nebility of purpose imparted, assumed only for a purpose, as it was. As the problem occurred to him, he cast resentfully aside the little hand he had clasped in his pleading, and said bitterly,

"Like all your sex, you are cruel and pitiless! If, under one impulse, you with seeming generosity cast a word of mercy to a poor wretch who humbles himself to supplicate for it, it is only that in the rebound it may crush him completely. There is always some impossibility to be accomplished, as a passport to your favor."

"You are cruel and unjust."

"In which I trespass upon your exclusive prerogative! See now what a hope you offer me for the future, what encouragement to humble myself before a proud interloper who came between me and a fortune, and skillfully supplanted me in the favor of one who was my benefactor and friend long before he ever became his. He tricked me out of all this, and now I am to cringe to him lest he also deprive me of you."

His injustice banished from her the tender veneration which had been so marked a feature in her regard for him. He was tearing away the veil which had heretofore concealed his real self from her eyes; and she looked up at him with her proud spirit flashing in her eyes.

"You forget, sir, to whom you are speaking, when you utter such words of Lisle Sterling! Understand once for all time, that I never offered you any inducement to seek to retrieve your fair name, never named any reward for a course of conduct which *honor* should inspire, as I believed it did. I would not turn one glance upon a man whom I had *persuaded to act honorably.*"

"Oh, Julie, Julie, have mercy upon me! You torture me till I am not master of myself. I am teaching you to despise me—Lisle Sterling will finish what I have begun. If you go to him I shall lose you forever. Kill me, then, at once; and not by aching inches."

He sank down beside her with an air of such complete dejection and despair, that her heart was torn with tenderest pity, and laying her hand upon his bowed head, she said,

"Do not let us add to our unhappiness by unkind words. If I am firm upon this one subject where you are concerned, it is that I will have the man I call husband deserve the respect of the world, as well as my own, and merit, whether or not he receive, the good will of those whom in a misguided moment he wronged. When you shall have effected this, I will not stop to think whose personal pique may still be unallayed, even if Lisle himself may be unjust

enough to cherish one,—which I cannot anticipate. Beside nothing
binds me to wait upon his consent to my marriage; it is only my
wish to do so. which proper circumstances could quite change.
When I am satisfied with you, I will fulfill my promise: rely upon
this."

"Ah, Julie, you think so now, but gradually you will grow indifferent and cold. I shall forget all else to follow you, and so rush
headlong into ruin. Your guardian will assume authority to ban'sh
me,—I am impulsive and violent,—who knows what may ensue?"

"You must not follow me;—I forbid it most emphatically. If
under any circumstances I can grow 'indifferent and cold,' accept
it as a proof of my utter worthlessness, and leave me to my fate."

"Oh, yes, and mine,—you do not think of that when you speak
so slightingly of your own! There is a bare hope that you may not
go where I am looked upon in such a hateful light, and to it I will
cling. But if you go, and sometimes find me near you, in mercy
think what leads me there, and do not annihilate me for having
disobeyed so relentless a command. Swear to me once more, that
if in what even you must pronounce a reasonable time, and after all
I can do in my own behalf, Lisle remains inflexible, you will nevertheless ratify the engagement you have made."

"Determined *misérable*, once more I swear!" she smilingly returned,
and then rising, she added, "And now I must say good-night. Edward will be looking for me, as he is quite alone."

She held out her hand to him, but pushing it aside, he caught her
in his arms, and as he rained his farewell kisses upon cheek, brow,
and neck, he murmured passionately,

"Oh, Julie, Julie—if need be, crime itself shall help to make you
mine! Nothing shall separate us—nothing!"

Turning to leave him, she opened the door just as Edward reached
it in search of her, having vainly looked everywhere else, and at last
been apprised by Mrs. Sandford that she was in their private parlor.

He drew back a step as he saw how nearly he had intruded upon
" a scene," and said apologetically,

"I was told that I should find you here, but I thought you alone."

"She would have been, in one moment. I am just taking leave,"
Hartley replied bowing over his hat.

The two had been presented by Mrs. Sandford the preceding day,
and had several times passed each other with only such polite acknowledgment as is usually displayed by gentlemen quite indifferent to each other. But in this moment each intuitively recognized

in the other a rival, and after one brief but expressive glance, Hartley made a second bow not altogether humble, as his triumphant smile testified, and returning it with grave politeness, Edward closed the door upon his exit. Julie stood in some embarrassment near the threshold, waiting for Edward to break the silence.

"So," he soliloquized as he turned away. "The list increases! Verily my name will have a goodly number of predecessors, if even at last it be granted a place upon the list!"

Before he had conquered his impatience, he heard the door open and close. Julie had left him without a word! and audibly pronouncing himself "a fool," he too left the room.

The next morning they started homeward, and after a weary journey arrived at the familiar mill-house, where Mrs. Sterling was expecting them. She came out to the gate to receive them, serene in a new bobinet cap and black silk apron; and as it was a sort of state occasion, Mr. Sterling followed, not quite at ease in his best coat, donned in their honor, but to which he had quite failed, after many efforts, to add a hat yet in its pristine newness, and so wore in its stead his battered old "beaver," only half bereft of the flour which from long occupation had assumed the right to resist his most vigorous efforts at banishment.

"A perfect Sterling to the last!" exclaimed his wife contemptuously, as she cast one last glance over his ungainly figure and unique dress, and then, determined to exhibit the Fitzjames native superiority, hastened out to offer her greetings first, leaving him to follow at his own pace.

"I do declare, my son, this is a bright day on which you have come home quite of your own accord," exclaimed Mrs. Sterling as she reached out her hand to Edward. "I was sure you'd bring Julie, too; and she's as welcome as can be, though she'll find it hard to put up with our plain ways. Here's Mr. Sterling will tell you how welcome the daughter of his old friend is. Here, Mr. Sterling; this is Dr. Kelley's daughter Julie. You remember little Julie Kelley?"

"Ahem,—why of course Lydia! and I'm sure she is welcome. Your father and me was old friends, Julie, old and kind friends for many a year, and a good man he was! How do you do, Edward?"

Mrs. Sterling turned again to Julie, whom she surveyed with a critical eye. "You are a wonderfully grown girl now,—I suppose I ought to say *young lady*, as you come from a Seminary, and the Falls, and what not. Dr. Kelley had mighty grand notions of his

own and your mother wasn't a whit better ; but you're young yet,
and you'll come down to common folk's life, I'll warrant."

Julie conquered her indignation at this implied criticism of her
dead parents, but Mr. Sterling uttered his mild protest against the
remark.

" You don't mean just what it sounds as if you did, Lydia. It is
well known as Dr. Kelley was forehanded in the world, and able to
live as he thought best, and his wife was a mild-tempered, slim little
creetur whose equal couldn't be found for kind-heartedness. I never
have forgot how she nursed up Lisle that winter he was so ailing—
just as if he was her own child ! I'm glad to do by you what your
father and mother have done by my boys, Julie, and I will as far as
I'm able. Edward will be a brother to you, and so will Lisle, too,
I'm sure."

" Who says Lisle is her brother ?" exclaimed the old lady, fiercely
turning upon him as he uttered the last words.

" There, Lydia, there," said the old gentleman laying his hand
upon her shoulder soothingly. She shook it off resentfully.

" Don't paw me over after such a speech as that ! Always twitting, twitting, about something or other !"

Julie heard in astonishment ; and taking her arm Edward led her
forward to the house, as he said apologetically,   .

" Poor old lady, she is quite losing her mind, and talks much of
the very wildest nonsense. She never had much mind, as you know ;
but it was enough to make its wreck lamentable. To notice what
she says, only makes her worse. I hope you will soon have a pleas-
anter home."

When Mrs. Sterling reached the door, she seemed quite to have
forgotten her ebullition of temper, and insisted upon showing Jul e
to the room assigned her, though she would much have preferred
being left alone to remove her travel-stained apparel.

Mrs. Sterling showed no intention of leaving her, but lifting the ·
bonnet Julie removed from her aching head, turned it round and
round upon the hand she inserted in its crown, to observe its shape
and style.

" I don't suppose you've bought your mourning things yet. Young
people mostly put it off longer'n is decent. But now you're left to
your own property, like, for support, you'll find mourning costs less
than most anything else that's as elegant, because you won't need so
many changes of it. It's true you are in half mourning all this time ;
but of course you'll have to go into bombazine and crape again.

There's your mother's crape things, every bit as good as new, can be made over for you. Lucky, ain't it—only one year's careful wear out of them! I'm famous at managing—all my family was the same!"

Julie struggled against her rising sobs, and when she could find voice to speak, said faintly,

"Please be kind enough to leave me alone for awhile. I am tired, and half sick; and not fit to see any one."

"Hoity toity; turns me out of my own rooms! But I won't bear malice. I'll go right down and make you some bonese tea for your head. Nobody shall say I bore malice towards Mrs. Kelley's daughter!" and she left her, much to Julie's relief.

Julie soon discovered that nothing like the worldless quiet for which she longed could be found under Mrs. Sterling's roof, unceasingly as Edward strove to secure it; and both waited impatiently for the arrival of Lisle's letter, now daily expected. Edward himself not unfrequently fell a victim to his mother's displeasure for some fancied slight or innuendo of which he was wholly guiltless. A chance word, a misinterpreted look, awoke her ire and suspicion, and with patient meekness Mr. Sterling bent his energies upon the task of soothing and quieting her, in a way that was really affecting to witness.

Edward's patient devotion of his time and talents to Julie's comfort met with some species of reward in the continually recurring amusing remembrances awakened by surroundings familiar to his own and Lisle's boyhood,—incidents not particularly amusing at the time, but borrowing a ludicrous tint from the light of the present; and as he laughingly recalled them in family conclave, Mr. Sterling's grim visage even relaxed, though he never had been heard to laugh. Usually Mrs. Sterling quite exulted in these reminiscences, illustrative as many of them were of that talent for management, and a faculty for securing whatever was desirable, which she boasted was handed down to them from their Fritzjam s progenitors; but upon one unlucky day the conversation took a turn that came more nearly causing a rupture between the old couple, than anything that had heretofore occurred.

Coming late to his dinner, Edward offered his apology to the family.

"I have been looking over a collection of old-time treasures stored away and seemingly forgotten; and the old fascination they

had for me, quite came back again. Father, do you remember that
old buffalo robe Lisle and I so used to covet?"

"Yes, I hid it away, as I never believed in leading any one in'o
temptation, and there's scripter against covetousness. I recollect
you were bent on trading it off; and it was worth more to throw
over the wagon seat."

"Well, I will confess, now, that we hunted it up, and really
should have sold it one day to an itinerant dealer in pelts, had we
not come to an unfortunate impediment in the shape of the last sixpence necessary to close the bargain, which he wouldn't give, and
we wouldn't throw off; and priding ourselves upon our uncompromising firmness, we put it back where we found it, and consoled ourselves with the idea of our sharpness, in place of the money we hoped
to have gained. Lisle and I were hard pressed for money in those
days, and quite envied the maternal privilege of picking off guard
pockets."

Mrs. Sterling bridled up indignantly, and said in severe reproof,

"Edward, confess as many of your and Lisle's dishonest tricks as
you please; but don't drag me into the catalogue. I pick your father's pockets! I think I see myself at such a caper!"

"Very likely, with memory's eye. But you had a right to do it;
so you needn't wish to forget nor deny it. No one would dispute
your right to 'one third,' even if you did take it a little in advance of the calamity for which the law offers that consolation. If
it required strategy to get at it, that was your misfortune," Edward
returned good-humoredly.

"Now tell the truth, Edward. Did you ever see me take one
cent of your father's money, without his knowledge?"

"Did not I? Why, don't you remember how you used to tug
away at the heavy weights father used to pile upon the chest where
he kept his money bag, by way of lock and key? and how you
called Lisle, one day, to have him show you how that strange knot
was tied in the string that served as a patent seal for the little canvas bag itself. He had seen it done so many times that he had
learned it, and he tied it for you exactly as it was before, so that no
tales were told."

Mr. Sterling laid down his knife and fork, looked hard at his
wife who struggled to appear undisturbed; and then rising with an
air of alarm, he went to the chest alluded to, opened it with trembling hands, and evolving the identical canvas bag, weighed it with

a reverent oscillation, first in one hand and then in the other, suspiciously, as though even yet it might disclose some ancient depletion, or effect of more recent depredation; and at last putting it deep in his capacious pocket, he buttoned it carefully in, slapping it a time or two afterward to assure himself that it was really there, and then returned to his unfinished dinner with an increased gravity of manner through which he took no farther notice of anything around him. Mrs. Sterling sobbed theatrically, and as she swayed to and fro she exclaimed,

"Oh dear, oh dear! If it has come to this after all these years, I'd better leave a house where I'm looked on as a thief! I've put up with a good deal in my time, but th's beats all. I'll leave to-morrow, if I have to go to the county poor-house."

Mr. Sterling made no reply to the threat, and with an abrupt change of manner she ceased sobbing, and said contemptuously,

"Thank fortune none of *my* family were skinflints! Among all the Fitzjameses—and their name was legion—there never was a stingy one known! It's hard enough being wife and mother to a race of mean-spirited Sterlings, without being called a thief! You were a real Fitzjames when you were little, Edward, and I did think there'd be one decent one among the snarl. Dear me, Lisle is all Kelley, and you are all Kelley too!"

"The effect of early training, mother. The doctor took us young, and treated us like a real father."

"He wasn't *your* father!" retorted Mrs. Sterling curtly, the one idea forever haunting her and called up by a word.

No reply was offered; and as Mr. Sterling left the table, his wife fixed her eyes with a half vacant stare upon Julie's face, muttering to herself, "They are something like—something like—and both of them all Kelley!" and still muttering, she slowly shoved back her chair and left the room.

"How strangely she does act!" Julie exclaimed half in horror.

"Yes, she is becoming quite demented. She doesn't seem to know what she says half the time. You ought to feel quite flattered, little Kelley, for your name is forever on her lips. Poor old mother!"

CHAPTER XXI

Four months had elapsed since Lisle Sterling plead his suit with Leonore Wakefield with only such success as was embodied in the indefinite hope vouchsafed him for the future—four months of uninterrupted harmony in the friendly relationship established between them, which no engagement, however definite, could have increased —when Edward's letter announcing Mrs. Kelley's death, was received.

This intelligence did not cause him the shock of surprise it had occasioned to others who loved her; for he had never ceased to remember her own forebodings, so freely expressed to him upon the occasion of their last confidential interview, in which she had begged him when they should be fulfilled to be not only a guardian, but a brother, to the daughter thus bereft of her last relative. He had given her this promise, and he would sacredly fulfill it.

Susceptible as was he himself to mental suffering, it needed no enumeration of Julie's woes and perplexities, to spur him to immediate action.

She was, in truth, his half sister, however little the fact might be suspected by others, and his home was her proper asylum ; but the world, so virtuously proper in its requirements of others, would stickle for the decorum of a female companion, even if it forbore to animadvert upon the circumstance of so young a gentleman being the legal guardian of so engaging a creature as Julie, and he at once sat about the task of providing for her a suitable companion.

Here again difficulties beset him. Old ladies were generally disagreeable companions—a young one would scarcely improve matters, unless, indeed, she were his wife—and armed with this apology for again pressing a suit that might be rejected, he bent his steps to the little parlor where he knew Leonore was to be found.

He had always believed that her former rejection, or what was virtually such, was based upon some over-sensitiveness which, if critically examined would vanish, and resolved to convince her how lightly he regarded such an obstacle, and how little he cared to investigate its cause, he felt one of those premonitions of success which seldom betrayed him.

Leonore was sitting quite alone in the luxurious twilight which even upon this glowing August morning rendered cool the pretty parlor shaded by the broad banana leaves, with their varied tints of green spread broadly to the sun, or broken into fringe by the fresh breeze, that, sweeping in at the open window, played fantastic capers with the fleecy curtains, and coquetted with the light morning robe in which she was arrayed, ever and anon revealing, by a fresher eddy, one tiny slippered foot, and lifting little tresses from her forhead with a jaunty freedom which imparted a new charm to her usually rather severe and classic style of beauty.

She beckoned Lisle to an ottoman beside her, and with the unconstraint of intimate friendship, continued the light, ormental employment with which she was busy when he was shown in. In her whole demeanor there was something so indescribably gentle and tender, despite its airy piquancy and half careless abandon, that Lisle was fascinated anew, and forgetting the earnest arguments he had resolved to urge with all the formal logic of which he was master, he poured out the torrent of feeling that rushed and surged through his heart, with a simple, natural eloquence that swept all resistance before it.

She looked into his face for one whole moment without offering one word in reply; but the changing lights and shadows upon her own face, rendered that silence eloquent,—a speechless revelation of the struggle going on within both brain and heart, no less engrossing than the undivided passion he had plead. At length the troubled expression of her glance gave way to one more softly serene, and folding both her hands upon his shoulder, she said with some vague air of indecision in her whole manner, to which she was still reluctant to give rein,

"Now Lisle, rehearse to me without one softening clause or fastidious choice of expression, the whole case as it stands between us. I want to hear, in plain words, all that is translatable of a matter over which I have thought and thought, forever arguing against my own inclinations, till I have lost the very power to see it in an unbiassed light. Recite."

"In very truth, I comprehend it too little to do so! I only know that you refuse to grant my prayer forever offered in one form or another, because you say you cannot, must not, and that *for my own sake*, and you affirm that my lips uttered such a decision—heaven knows how or when ! If they ever did utter it, I retract it a thousand times."

" Yes. Go on, I want to hear more."

" There is no more. The rest, if more there be despite my convictions, lies somewhere in the unexplored region between your heart and lips, and I have no mental compass to guide my investigations. Keep it to yourself, Leonore, guard as jealously as you will this something that thus far has rendered you inexorable ; I do not ask to know it, I never will. All I ask is that you will no longer sacrifice our happiness to it. Be merciful to me, if you are relentless toward yourself."

She did not speak or move ; but her eyes turned from his, and fixed themselves upon the floor unrevealingly.

A sudden fear darted into his heart, and convulsively grasping the hands still folded upon his shoulder, he asked,

" Leonore, is there any legal impediment to our marriage—are you, perhaps, already married ?"

She turned a glance of reproach upon him which her words did not belie, proudly as they were spoken.

" There exists no legal impediment. Were I the wife of another, do you think I would thus listen to you ? I am legally free to wed whomsoever I will. It is only against yourself that even a moral objection exists—a mere conscientious scruple."

" Forgive me, Leonore ; but banish this scruple. I will absolve you."

" You do not know how I am tempted to do so ! You do not imagine the price it costs me to remain true to my own sense of honor and right."

" Then forget 'honor and right' toward me. I plead rather for happiness, and grant you an unlimited dispensation to sin against me. If I choose to endure it, no one else has the right to protest or object. Dismiss this chimera that separates us ! Oh, Leonore, you will, you will ; but speak it."

She uttered not a word, but a soft flush of unspeakable love suffused her face and brow, and her lips smiled the welcome reply.

Lisle caught her to his breast, ecstatically murmuring,

" At last, at last ! *my* Leonore ! God bless you !"

After one moment's unresisting surrender to the happiness that possessed her, she raised her face, and said with earnest tenderness,

" Lisle, Lisle, if the hour ever come when you are tempted to reproach me for this weakness, remember how I loved you, and in mercy restrain the words. I am sacrificing my sense of honor toward you, to our mutual happiness. God grant it may ensure it!"

At length the little feminine task was brokenly resumed, and Lisle, seated quietly near her, with a look of intensest happiness upon his usually grave face which quite transformed it, toyed as one who now possessed the right, with the silken tresses tossed more liberally by the breeze to the threatened peril of the whole mass being decoyed away in kindred dancing streamers. Edward's letter had remained quite forgotten till now, when it suddenly recurred to memory, and taking it from his memorandum book, he spread it upon Leonore's lap, as he said, smiling,

"See, Leonore. Here is a letter upon which I had based more moving arguments than I could have uttered in a day ; not one of which was pressed into service, after all my mental labor! Most well-merited fate of all argument, where only feeling should reign supreme ! Will you listen while I read, and afterward give me your sovereign decision. I am, as it were, a family man already, and, as you will see, am called upon to fulfill an urgent duty !" and he read her the letter, explaining as he proceeded.

She looked up in smiling amazement when he concluded.

"You the guardian of a young lady quite of marriageable age ! How did you establish a claim to sufficient wisdom and most sage decorum, to tempt Doctor Kelley thus to endow you with the honors of age and experience ? Six whole years her senior, and not yet quite gray !"

"I never was young, Leonore, and Doctor Kelley, better than any one else, knew this. His daughter is like a sister to me, as well she may be, reared up together as we were ! The doctor loved me as his own child, and was more than a father to Edward ,who owes him all he is or ever will be. The story of my childhood is a sad one, Leonore ; one that I never can bear to repeat, or even remember." His face clouded, and his voice was at once both sad and bitter.

She hastened to divert his thoughts from such disturbing reminiscences, and succeeded.

"Poor little Julie, how utterly alone she is. She will come to you at once, Lisle ?"

"She will come to us, if you consent. I should have sent for her at once had you proved relentless this morning; how much more, then, since I can offer her a companion and a sister."

"Oh, Lisle, stop. Don't say ' a sister.' All that I can do to make

her happy, I will do with a cheerful heart. But I have no right to
'a sister,' still less one who is such to you. If I won her love, I
should, in pure generosity, regret it. It is enough that I should accept yours!"

"Most humble little saint; you shall be canonized in time, be patient yet a little! But don't, like Lady Macbeth, say a word about
'perfumes of Arabia,' for the Arabian trade isn't what it was."

"I forewarn you, jeerer, that I sha l levy heavy contributions upon
your purse. Firstly, my salary as housekeeper,"—she suggested
with an evident effort to appear as playfully at ease as her words
indicated.

"Oh, no, Mrs. Perkins is all sufficient in that capacity," he
answered lightly.

"Well, then, some sinecure for which I shall receive, in current
coin of the republic, not less than I now receive for professional
services."

"Do you in fancy endow me with the talent of stinginess, that
you thus seek to drive a bargain with me? Not a dime! You
must rely upon my generosity,—an unknown quantity, I confess.
So pretty and so calculating! Fie, Leonore!"

She became grave at once, and there was an audible tremulousness
in the voice with which she replied,

"I *must have* a sum of my own, free from any questioning as to
how I expend it. As your wife you will not wish me to earn it by
my own exertions, as now; but I must, if you refuse me."

He realized that she was painfully in earnest, and wishing to
divert even while he gratified her, he took out his pencil and
formally began, despite the laughing tone he assumed, -

"*Memorandum, not to 'forget to remember,'* that one of the terms
of the bargain this day made, is as follows: A good fat salary
monthly paid in hand, in current funds, to be the unquestioned
property of Leonore Sterling, and to be by the said L. S. expended
in whatever manner she may decide; marital grumbling quite forbidden, and sky blue wigs tolerated and admired, should the lady
so enjoin! So, Leonore, are these terms sufficiently liberal?"

"Yes, if you offer them in good faith," she answered seriously.

"Mercenary wretch, will you turn tyrant, too? Suppose I am
remiss in making payments—will you 'bone' me for the cash?"

"Yes, probably."

"Will you, whenever you presume to desire anything under the
sun, compel me to pronounce absolution and forgiveness for such
temerity?"

" Possibly."

" Well, if I'm to go upon my knees everytime I wish you to accept 'a little pecuniary aid' outside this wonderful salary, I'll be-
speak a buckskin suit at once. I decidedly object to perambulate
the streets looking like a dissenting clergyman after a severe season
of 'revival.' I don't know, either, how much of such wear and tear
my physical constitution can endure; and so I advocate a community
of property as far as we two are concerned. When I say 'with all
my worldly goods I thee endow,' I shan't mean the legally understood dower of the use of one-third after my demise—the usual matrimonial rendering of the phrase, if one may judge by appearances."

Her smiles returned under his good humor and characteristic sarcasm ; and the point for which she had stipulated thus playfully settled to her satisfaction, no farther allusion was made to it, nor did
Lisle himself mentally comment upon its strangeness, excepting to
wonder if she really had believed him possibly penurious, and so
wished to avoid future inconvenience. It was not a flattering infer-
ence, but happiness soon banished its sting from his mind.

Once having won Leonore's promise to become his wife, patient
waiting with no definite purpose was not in his nature. At this
season of the year most of their social circle were absent from the
city, and those who remained felt no ambition for merry-making.
Lisle heartily rejoiced at this, averse to wedding parties as he was,
where the principal actors are at best but self constituted spectacles,
to be scanned and criticised as never before, by those for whose
gratification the whole proceeding is endured. Altogether wrong
as such a prejudice may have been, Leonore herself shared it, and
despite the remonstrances of Mrs. Venard and Mrs. Bertram, who
asserted that it looked like a deliberate social swindle, a quiet wedding was arranged to take place at once.

" Only to think how venerably Venard would have given away
the bride in the presence of an admiring assemblage," laughed Mrs.
Bertram.

" No thanks for his liberality with what would not have been his
own to give," Lisle retorted. " I wonder when people will become
sensible enough to do away with that antediluvian farce, even if
they will keep the rest of the absurd rigmarole ! The idea of
'giving the bride' as one would make over the kitchen caudlesticks,
or any other article of household stuff! I'm only surprised that
those who fancy it, don't insist upon the 'rod of correction' that

used to accompany it, and still does in some countries. Who shall
say that we have no need of missionaries."

"Oh, it's only mere form; like the 'obey' and the rest of it. Nobody ever intends quite to bid adieu to their senses," said Mrs. Bertram.

"Yes; the whole affair is too much 'mere form,' married to-day,
divorced to-morrow, and ten to one *re*-married to a new candidate
for earthly purgatory, long before the real wife or husband is decently dead and buried."

"'*Real* wife or husband!' Mrs. Bertram exclaimed dissentingly.
"Of course the *real* one is she or he whom the law so recognizes."

"Blessed are they who so feel and believe, if it chance to be their
position! As for me, had I married the veriest vixen the sun shines
on, I should feel and consider that she was indissolubly my wife;
and were I to marry another by any permission of 'the law,' I
should deserve arrest as a bigamist," Lisle replied with some
warmth.

"Oh, we have all heard your sentiments upon the subject, before," retorted Mrs. Bertram. "This is the one hobby of your
otherwise quite sensible and steady-going mentality. 'The law is
powerful to bind, but not to unloose!' strange creed, for which, if
you received your just deserts, you'd be incontinently 'gobbled up'
by some grass-widow! If you were to be so, and tried to get the
marriage set aside upon that score, you'd soon find whether the
law were on your side of the question, and what is received as law,
might as well be so for all practical purposes in life."

Lisle turned to Leonore and made her a salutation of mock
reverence.

"Deign, fair lady, to accept your humble servant's most grateful
thanks. Inflict, oh gracious deity, whatever of matrimonial pains
and penalties thou may'st see fit, and thou shalt find me thankful, to
the last, that even thus I escape so horrible a 'gobbling up,'—all
innocent and unoffending as I am. All hail, thou, who savest a
virtuous citizen from the fangs of the grass-widow!"

The others received this invocation merrily; but, pale and grave,
Leonore struggled briefly with some strong emotion before replying,

"Thank me for nothing, Lisle, till you see whether or not I merit
thanks. 'Matrimonial pains and penalties' may prove more grievous than you think; but God knows my first wish is to make you
happy."

Reproaching himself for so thoughtfully having struck upon

what he knew was a sensitive nerve, Lisle drew her arm within his own, and led her out upon the gallery, away from the glances of involuntary astonishment bent upon her.

"There, dear child, you see how often I shall thoughtlessly give you pain if you do not conquer this morbid sensitiveness! What can I do in expiation of my sins?"

"Release me from this engagement I ought never to have made."

"Leonore!"

"Not for my sake, but for your own."

"So help me heaven, I never will! Nor will I be condemned to fight this battle over and over again. Receive now, my just sentence for such a demand. At this hour to-morrow, you at once and forever resign the power to speak such words to me. You talked of 'a week' and I was foolish enough to assent. Not two days, dear Leonore! You force me to be tyrannical, but pleadingly, you know."

"Oh, Lisle, I cannot, must not become your wife. I *will* tell you all my shameful story, though I perish for it,—as I shall."

"No, I will not hear it. It is at best a loss of time, and it is flying. When you are really and irrevocably mine, I will listen to whatever you choose to tell, and shrive you after. But not now."

"Now or never, Lisle."

"Then *never*, and a thousand times never! I tell you, Leonore, that nothing shall come between us! I cannot, will not suffer it! The very recounting those once conquered obstacles, would reinvigorate them; and I cannot endure these struggles for more than life. Oh, Leonore, you do not know what it is to fix one's life hope upon a coveted object, and see it forever just beyond one's reach! Sick, sorrowing, and humiliated, I have struggled into manhood to catch one first glimpse of possible happiness, and I will attain it. Hourly, waking and sleeping alike, I am tortured with the fear and dread of losing you,—you, the one object I have ever cherished or desired; and I cannot resign you even at your own bidding. Without you I am lost, annihilated,—with you, whatever may betide, I cannot suffer more. Keep your revelation, and give me yourself,—*yourself!* I cannot give you up."

"Then you shall not. Oh, Lisle, such passion frightens me!"

"Well, it *is* frightful,—it frightens me, too; but I cannot conquer it. I tried to, long ago, and *it conquered me*, and holds me."

"Lisle, you will never forget that in this hour I tried to tell you that which I must henceforth forever conceal, and that you would not listen to it. Promise me this, for the time *may* come when I shall remind you of it, in very self-defence."

"Against whom?"

"Yourself, and the withering justice you will pour out upon me."

"Never, never! Since I know that all this is but a mere 'moral obstacle,' 'a scruple of conscience,' as your lips declared one blessed hour; I have no care for anything more. I make any promise that leaves you mine, bind myself to anything you desire, so that I do not lose you!"

"Oh, Lisle, if to lose what you love is thus unendurable to you, proud, fortunate, blessed as you are, what must it be to me, who in all this world have only you to turn to. I love you—worship you; and you do not know the struggle each word of renunciation costs me!"

He looked at her one eloquent moment as the tears brimmed up in her eyes and threatened to overflow, and then seizing her hand impetuously, led her back to the parlor they had quitted, where the two ladies still discussed the ruling topic.

"If you have plans all laid, unlay them now, or change. To-morrow I claim Leonore for my wife, however you may wail; and lest she herself turn traitor to the project, lock her into her room at twilight, and bar the window against all escape. It is my sovereign will and pleasure," he said imperatively though laughing.

Mrs. Venard raised her hands in deprecation.

"But the wedding-dress, and 'the bride's loaf!' Impossible!"

"The dress she has on is clean and whole—that's enough; and as for bride's-loaf, bread and butter is far more wholesome if one must eat anything—which I don't see."

"And won't see in my house, and I don't know how you'll manage such a ceremony without. Was ever, ever, such an unreasonable man! Leonore, assert your own will upon this occasion, or forever after don't expect to be allowed any!"

"It is useless. I have been most summarily silenced."

"You've learned the whole duty of woman, in one easy lesson, eh? Well, get yourselves married at once, then, and as shabbily as you please. There's no bread in the house, and won't be; but it is nobody's business, thank fortune!" and half vexed, despite her laughing philosophy, Mrs. Venard locked her arm through Mrs. Bertram's and led her away for a secret council.

Tortured as Lisle was by the ceaseless fear that something would prevent this marriage even at the last hour, it was with an audible sigh of relief that he clasped Leonore's hand more closely at the conclusion of the ceremony which made her irrevocably his, and the sweetest words he had ever heard were those which addressed her as "Mrs. Sterling." Each repetition of that name sent a thrill to his heart, audible confirmation, as it was, of a happiness which even yet seemed unreal and illusory. But for the merriment of the little circle around them, the wedding would have been a solemn affair indeed, deeply moved as were both Lisle and Leonore by secret emotions but half confessed by either; hers, at least, bordering closely upon the tragical, by the very circumstances she had defied in thus becoming his wife against what she had declared her own sense of honor, while his own felicity was disturbed by the thought that thus he had brought her under the shadow of the curse overhanging his life, wholly unconscious of it as she was.

By some enchantment a wedding-dress had been evoked, and even the bride's loaf entered a beautiful appearance at the proper time, in utter refutation of Mrs. Venard's seeming inhospitality in exulting that there was "no bread" with which to honor the occasion. It seems a sort of righteous vengeance upon the lords of creation for so universally eschewing cake and comfits, that they are politely compelled to do honor to them upon their wedding-day, and Lisle was more liberally helped, for the vivid remembrance that he had expressed a preference for bread and butter upon this occasion.

Only Mr. Bertram, by his taciturn deportment, seemed to regard the occasion as anything but a family merry-making; and for his unpopular reproof, silent as it was, he was compelled to suffer penance, and even to be wrapped in a winding-sheet as a fitting accompaniment to his "graveyard face," as it was irreverently termed.

"He always would look, upon wedding occasions, as though he were beholding a second Daniel called to judgment,—or, more properly, cast into a lion's den," his wife declared; and thus compelled in very self-defence to put a better face upon the matter, he reserved his serious one to grace the comments in which he indulged in the privacy of his hearthstone.

"'When a man marries, he sees the end of his troubles,—but one doesn't say which end,'" he quoted with proper emphasis and expression to his wife, who, not captivated by the quotation already worn quite threadbare by former applications, offered no reply, and he continued more seriously but with equal emphasis.

"Lisle Sterling has this day entered into a contract for the making and enduring of more misery than often falls to the lot of two individ-

uals, married or single. Mark my words, Mattie Bertram! He
will kill Leonore by ceaseless suspicion if not downright injustice,
and she will drag his life and pride out of him by torturing inches!
Of all the marriages I ever was doomed to witness, this is the most
positively fearful. I really wished, for both their sakes, that the
winding-sheet in which you thought it such sport to wrap me, had
been needed for them; and as surely as you live, one or both of them
will sigh for it before three years pass over their heads."

" Oh, Bertram; what a kind of evil omen you do make yourself!
You will fall into the clutches of some ornithologist, yet, and I shall
live to see you stuffed and put up in a museum.

'Said I to the man what conducted the show,
Is this the individual called'—"

Before the " William Barlow" could be added, her husband
checked her by an exclamation not amiably uttered.

" Are women possessed by the very demon of malice, or what is it
sets every mother's daughter among them quite demented at the
very name of a wedding! No matter how selfish she may have been
all her life—she will sacrifice the last rag off her back and go petti-
coatless to bed, if 'the *bride*' has need of it! *You* ought to have
more sense, admiration-struck as you have always been with Leonore,
and friend, as you profess to be, to Lisle himself!"

"Don't croak any more to-night, there's a good f llow! I'm decidedly in good spirits, and would like to go to sleep so, just for the
curiosity of the thing. Variety is a spice of which I see so little in
this respect; and it is said to be excellent," returned his wife good
humoredly.

"Humph!" rejoined Mr. Bertram with his usual brief eloquence;
but she did not rally at the sound, battle cry as it was, and actually
laughed in her sleep, after it !

CHAPTER XXII.

"WELL, mother, Lisle is married," announced Edward as he and Julie returned from their drive to the post-office, with the expected letter.

"What! Lisle married?" ejaculated the old lady placing her spectacles high upon her forehead and fixing her eyes upon Edward incredulously.

"I don't wonder you are unbelieving—such a woman-hater 'as he was by instinct—excuse me, Julie; I mean by *nature*. Many is the time I have seen him climb the fence and make a detour through the bushes to avoid meeting in the road a well-behaved, inoffensive sunbonnet! I thought he'd go into fits once when he got hung by his little breeches to a rail, and couldn't get down till the old feminine was fairly upon him, a decent old party who merely ejaculated ' massy sakes !' as the sound of ripping and tearing saluted her ears in Lisle's last desperate struggle to get a clearance. He seemed to think old women perambulated the country, upon spanking tours; and the girls shamed him by making him play light infantry parts, long after he was too large to be carried ' visiting ' and have his gums felt of relatively to ' teething.' Thus he owed a grudge to the whole sex."

"He was the merest sneak of a child; that's true ;" affirmed Mrs. Sterling scornfully ; " a perfect girl-baby that all the boys despised, and no wonder. Nobody knows the cross he was to me! Precious little Fitzjames there is in him !"

"Why, mother, the last time he was here you insisted that he was the living image of some feminine Fitzjames now invisible to mortal ken ! I really fancied you were going to take him into favor for his foresight and self-providence in the matter."

"I never said he was like, for I never thought it," asserted Mrs. Sterling stoutly. "He is his father all over again, as I knew he would be."

"Well, he certainly is as gifted in personal resemblances as a cat

is said to be in lives. Father will be glad to know he's all 'Sterling,' at last—though only yesterday you said he was 'all Kelley,' as
you often do."

"Well, I say so now, don't I? And he's married, is he?"

"Yes, and I'm to be adopted into his family. He writes me that
he has it all arranged, and *will have it* so; and I'm very sure he will
encounter no opposition from me. I never did fancy being a mere
pill-peddler in a country town."

"What, Edward! go away, and your uncle Jonathan's whole
family down with the measles!" said Mrs. Sterling with surprised
reproof.

"Yes, it is an extensive practice, I know; but I'm not sure I
should earn either fortune or fame out of it, if I remained. There's
a very good boil and rheumatism run of custom, too, that I'll make
over, gratis, to whoever will take my place here."

"But you've got all Doctor Kelley's old practice, I'm sure."

"No, mother, I've put most of it under ground, and it doesn't
seem to sprout up again. Someway modern practice doesn't seem to
agree with ancient constitutions. It is like putting new wine into
old bottles, and, as father would say, 'there's scripter against it.'
I must seek a new field where constitutions are less cranky and set
in their way."

"Who on earth ever would marry Lisle? She can't be much,"
said the old lady abruptly returning to the subject.

"That a mother-in-law's welcome, I'm sure," laughed Edward,
vexed as he was by her life-long detraction of Lisle for whom she
had never shown anything like maternal affection. "I'll take the
news to father, who will give it a warmer welcome."

"What is it to him?" demanded the old lady irately.

"A new daughter at least, if not that perpetuity of the family
name, so dear to most old people. Mr. and Mrs. Lisle Sterling
ought at once to be introduced to the second page of the family
record in the big Bible still guiltless of anything better than a
suggestive arrays of blanks after the important babel 'married.'
Father will record it before he eats his dinner."

"What did you say her name is, Edward?"

"Leonore Wakefield 'that was,' as old ladies have it, is Leonore
Sterling."

"Leonore Wakefield, that is to say—Leonore Kelley—wife of William Kelley, deceased—and Julie his half sister," murmured Mrs.
Sterling incoherently, as the vacant look so familiar to her face,

came over it again; and having swayed herself to and fro in momentary silence, she sprang up exclaiming angrily, "It's all a lie, a base lie, I don't care who says it. The doctor was a hypocrite, but he's still looke l on as a saint. Who'll believe it?"

She looked upon her auditors in angry questioning; but no reply being given to so strange a salutation, she turned and walked abruptly away.

Julie turned a half terrified glance toward Edward, who said with something like grim satisfaction,

"Oh, Lord, thy judgments are just! It verily seems like a retribution upon her, that all her mental trouble is suffered for Lisle's sake. Do you remark that it is only when his name is mentioned that these freaks come over her? One would really think that the sound of it is a maddening reproach which she cannot endure. She has hated him from his birth, but he is avenged."

"Oh, Edward, I am so glad you will go away with me! Every thing here is so dreary and horrible; while you and Lisle will be so happy together again."

"I don't know; he is married now, and matrimony changes every one, however unconsciously to himself. I could feel jealous of his wife for coming between us, did I not know how unreasonable it would be."

"Lisle is married, and you may be. When you find some one who cares for you more than a brother ever could, you will make the exchange with full as little compunction, without asking if you are wronging him."

"Do you think that is possible, Julie? Would any one care that much for me, even if I had hung their doll-babies and bled their old 'Mahomets' in my less well-behaved days?"

She colored under the peculiar look he bent upon her as he asked the laughing question, and the suspicion seized her that a deeper meaning lay beneath—a thought for which she the next instant reproved herself. Over one year ago she had made the same mistake in regard to Lisle, she would never be so foolish again. It was still less probably that Edward regarded her as anything dearer than a friend and companion, reared together as they had been, often enough seriously at variance when she resented his boyish cruelty to her pets. She was only the well-grown "dummy" of his childhood, whom Punch and Judy had ceased to amuse, and toward whom he was merely "varying his treatment," as he doubtlessly mentally commented. The long and repeated separations between them had quite destroyed the old time tie of brother and sister, as she felt while blaming herself for being obliged to confess; and their mutual relationship was altogether free from the careless freedom of fraternal intercourse.

Edward noted the fact before she fairly admitted it to herself, and he secretly rejoiced at it, first step in his progress as it was. Better for him that she should regard him with utter indifference, than that she should love him only as a brother and so mock him with a species of affection he could not tolerate from her. He had now as much in his favor as any stranger; he would win or lose in a fair field; and his heart gave one exulting bound as he marked the blush his words had called up. It was the first gleam of real encouragement that had dawned upon him; and he treasured it accordingly.

Unhesitatingly, joyfully adopting Lisle's project for his change of residence, he set about it at once, despite his father's weak-minded opposition. Mr. Sterling had always considered a city as the very sink of iniquity, and its people utterly given over to ungodliness and evil-doing; and the idea of his sons thus being given over to the power of the tempter, was a horrible one. The awful story of Sodom and Gomorrah was hourly repeated as a warning against all cities, and when it was disregarded, he proceeded to personal protest.

"I never approved of Lisle's deserting his own country and going off to the southern one to live; but he was out from under my guardianship, as he had so long looked only to his uncle. He always was a proud boy, and not enough like the Sterlings to heed any warning or advice when he'd got his mind set on a thing. Don't you rush headlong into destruction by flying against the wishes of them that are placed over you by an all-wise and merciful Providence."

"I don't know whether my being ' *let down* ' at the mill house, as grandmother used to have it, is altogether a striking proof of wisdom and mercy. I used even to doubt it, as you may remember. Whatever you may call it, I'm sure I can improve upon the idea, and I claim the privilege."

"' Honor your father and your mother, that your days may be long in the land,'" said the old gentleman impressively. "In my day children were respectful to their parents. I never thought of setting up my will against that of my father, nor of my mother while she kept her reason."

Mrs. Sterling took up the reply. Whatever her wishes might have been, uninfluenced by her husband's opinion, his disapprobation of any project was always sufficient reason for her advocating it; and she came to Edward's defence with her usual system of tactics.

"And who are you, or your parents, that you should set yourself up to judge a real Fitzjames like Edward? You Sterlings always were a slow thinking, bat-like lot, a hundred years behind the times; and the old woman, crazy as she was, had more sense left in her than all the rest of you put together ever had. *You* know how much that was. You ought to know that them that has plenty of spirit, and an ambition to get to be something in the world, can't go maudling through life like you Sterlings."

Mr. Sterling looked up meekly, yet with some honest pride, as he answered,

"I know, Lydia, we ain't so brilliant as some, and never were; but we are honest, hard-working, God-fearing people, and I never knew any one of the name to do a mean or low thing. We deserve respect, at least."

"Well, for my part I don't know what's meaner and lower than stinginess," retorted his wife bitterly. "It mayn't take a man to the gallows, but it ought to. Lisle may have hitched a decent reputation to the name, and Edward is right to go where he'll have the benefit of it."

The old man moved uneasily in his chair, and rubbed his large red knuckles with the palm of each hand alternately, as if fancying that, like the Wonderful Lamp of Aladdin, they were capable of vast resources under judicious friction, but no satisfactory logic having been derived from the process, he deposited them in a heap upon his knee, and said in a cowed manner,

"I ain't finding fault with our boys, Lydia. They are good boys, and I'm thankful they are smarter than their father; but it's natural, and it's right, for parents to want to keep their children at home."

"'Children!' One of 'em is married, and the other old enough to be. You'll never realize it till you see a snarl of grandchildren around under foot."

Silenced but not convinced, he said no more, only shaking his head seriously from time to time as preparations for the departure were completed. Separation usually opens wide the heart before closing it forever, and Mrs. Sterling grew quite cordial toward Julie, in its bare contemplation, making a last effort even at compliment.

"I expect the next I hear of you, will be that you are a married lady *ever* so fine and gay! There ain't many any prettier than you are. The Kelleys must have been a handsome race, for your father was something wonderful here among these common people. Common folks will look common, and you can't beat it out of 'em!"

Edward laughed. "That's a clencher, mother, for you know what '*can't be beaten* out,' won't come out at all. There's nothing like maternal experience!"

"One thing I wish could be beaten *into* you, even yet. You've no more gallantry in you than an off ox! I don't believe you ever said boo to a girl, or ever will."

"The fact is, when I was young enough to have used so persuasive a word of endearment as 'boo,' I was so ragged or bepatched that the girls wouldn't listen to me. The idea of a fellow being in love with a patch on his breeches! Julie, were you ever in love?"

She looked embarrassed and self-conscious, but gayly replied,

"Why, to be sure! Didn't half my candy money go for sentimental cards, which, as everybody who ever had an attack of 'first affection,' knows are most indispensable accompaniments! As long ago, too, as I can remember, some youngster whose very name I have forgotten, gave me a gold washed ring with an emblematical heart on it, which I verily thought, for ever so long, was a flat iron! and as I remember it now, it certainly did more resemble one!'

"If you don't go through anything more serious than that, you'll never know what trouble is," ejaculated Mrs. Sterling oracularly. "Think if you should get married to find yourself tied to a skinflint! *That's* trouble."

Mr. Sterling raised his head with something like spirit.

"Seems to me you are talking awful foolish. The troubles as come through courting and such nonsense, are all imagination; nothing else. Wait till the potatoes get the rot in spite of a merciful Providence, and the very horse you drive to meeting eats himself up twice over every year, what with the high price of feed, and you'll begin to see facts instead of imagination. I shan't have anything to leave you, Edward, and it's right you should be told it in time to calculate according."

"I thought it would bring up in money," sneered Mrs. Sterling; "but it was going a long way round to tell you, Edward, that he never intends to give you a cent after you go away."

"I never did have so many that I shall miss them. I don't want any, father."

Mrs. Sterling pulled her son by the sleeve, and whispered,

"Your father is richer than you think, and I'll see that you get your share when he's done with it. Lisle shan't walk off with all this, as I've no doubt your father would like; he ain't entitled to a dollar of it, and he shan't have it. You are the only one of my children I ever cared for, and I'll look out for you—see if I don't. When will you come to see me?"

"Whenever you want me, if I can. I'm not going to the Pole, mother."

They were ready for a start, at last, and leaving his wife sobbing in the door, Mr. Sterling followed them to the carriage.

"Don't lay up anything against your mother, Edward, neither on your own account or Lisle's. She's had a hard, dull life of it, and is failing fast in her mind. I never was the kind of husband she ought to have married, and I've often wondered how she come to take up with me. I ain't in any way her equal, and it's maybe nateral she should kind of despise me. I don't mind it of her. She's always been a good wife to me; I'll say that."

There was a mistiness in his eyes, and he spoke the last words kindly, even tenderly for him. Edward shook the hand his father extended him in parting, and, little reverent as he was by nature, a something that was more than admiration of the patient, faithful old man, blended with the compassion he felt for him.

What would have been his emotions toward him, had he known, as did Lisle, that this to him incomprehensible marriage in which the poor victim felt himself so honored, was a shameful story beginning in dishonor and ending in contempt, heaped upon him by the unscrupulous woman in whose praise he always testified, and to whose children he appealed to judge her tenderly? Edward might do so; but Lisle never could find one pleading voice for her in the heart she had outraged from the time of its earliest throb. More than suspecting that he knew the miserable secret of his birth, she had watched him with a jealous eye from the hour that made it known to him, and, callous against the contempt she knew he must feel toward her, she gloried in the consciousness that he must suffer every pang a spirit so proud could suffer under such a load of shame. Young as he had learned it, pride and natural reserve had prevented him from lisping one word, as she knew it would. Mr. Sterling still clung to him with that partiality over his other children that had followed him from his childhood, and his wife was too calculating and ungenerous to see that in very pity Lisle returned

him an affection and tender respect that he might never otherwise
have conceived for him.

They were separated now, it was true, and her own favorite
would soon be far from her sight. Let the old man doat on his
false son whom he doubtless meant to make his heir; she would, if
necessary, defy Lisle to accept such a benefaction from one upon
whom he had no claim, or to share one dollar of the estate left by
the old man who owed it to *his children*. It never occurred to her
that Lisle himself would adopt such a view of the affair; judging
him by herself, as she did, he would take all that was offered him,
and feel a real triumph over her that he had secured it; and she
planned and schemed in her busy brain over the old man's death,
with a malice that increasing years had done nothing to deaden. It
was as if the whole strength of her nature found expression in three
sentiments; affection for her second born, hatred of Lisle, and contempt for her husband. It was not so much the voice of conscience,
as this ever present hatred and contempt, that kept her secret forever
on her lips and caused her so nearly to reveal it   In the days of her
strength, she had kept it under by force of will; but her strength
and her will were leaving her now, and she never seemed to realize
the danger that menaced her from her own lips and deportment,
protected as she was only by the unsuspecting minds around her,
which attributed her words to a disordered intellect, rather than
recognized them as the revelations of a weakened one.

After Edward's and Julie's departure, the ripple their presence
had created upon the monotonous surface of life at the mill-house
gave place once more to the old time dreariness.   The very mirrors,
unpretending and ambitionless as they were, grew weary of the un-
varying reflections to which they were condemned, while the old
eight-day clock seemed to grow taller and narrower, day by day, in
its shadowed niche where it swung a ponderous pendulum in air
with a never ceasing " tick-tack " whose complaining voice drearily
chronicled the hours as they went dragging by.

Loveless and cheerless as the old place ever had been, Edward
turned hopefully to the new life that beckoned him on, strong in
will *to do*, and joyful in heart that thus he was to be reunited to the
brother whose exile years before had snapped the last natural fibre
that bound his heart to their boyhood's home.

———

" What limb of the evil one is that who serves you as gardener,
Lisle ?" asked Edward the morning after his arrival, as he came in from

a tour of the grounds whose beauty had attracted him from his pillow long before the household was astir. With imperturbable gravity, Lisle replied,

"That is the 'unprofitable partner' of my worthy housekeeper; and he rejoices in the name of Joseph—commonly styled Joe."

"Well, it is a shame to obscure his brilliant talents under so humble a calling. He would make a splendid politician; he has every requisite for that protean and devious calling."

"Yes, I flatter myself that he has talents of a rather uncommon order. Has he already revealed them to your admiration?"

"I may say he has dimly foreshadowed them, though he would doubtlessly do himself and your choice more credit under more favorable auspices. He was hampered by a limited field for operations."

"Been 'speculating,' as he calls it, I presume. Were you so unsophisticated as to entrust him with money?"

"Not much. I sent him for some cigars, as he was seemingly overburdened with leisure. The dozen turned out only ten, and the change was as short as it well could be and be any. I didn't accuse him, for he looked so sanctimonious I really couldn't; but I admire his talent."

"And his assurance, you will add when you have seen it. We'll have him in when breakfast is over. He is a cool genius."

When breakfast was served and dispatched, Lisle touched the bell, and the dismissed waiter reappeared.

"Send Joseph to me," he said briefly; and Leonore raised the morning paper, that she might at least seemingly be interested in its contents, and so avoid the appealing looks she knew Joseph would turn upon her if he were severely quizzed; or even justly reproved. After a brief interval his lagging footsteps were heard approaching, and in due time he appeared in the doorway, bowing subduedly over his rather mature hat into whose crown his eyes remained devoutly bent.

"Did you buy some cigars this morning for Doctor Sterling?"

"Yes, sir. It wasn't, strictly speaking, my business, but I did it cheerfully."

"I've no doubt; but you brought only ten instead of twelve. How is this?"

Joseph moved uneasily from one foot to the other, and lifted a glance of profound reproach to Edward's face, before replying in a melancholy tone, "I was obleeged to give back two, because the boy couldn't make even change for a dozen. Small change is getting tremendous scarce, sir."

"Just so the doctor thought this morning Now, Joseph, make up the account."

With another reproachful glance around him which no one responded to, he with a sigh of wordless complaint slowly turned one of his pockets inside out, and evolved from its deepest corner a picayune which he placed near Edward's cup.

"Well, go on," said Lisle encouragingly, as Joseph hesitated.

Another profound sigh accompanied a similar experiment upon the other pocket, and a dime reluctantly appeared and was laid beside the picayune.

"Go on, Joseph; be honest, for once, if it takes a limb!" Lisle again exhorted ; and too much depressed even to sigh, Joseph pulled forward one of his coat-tails, from which he dragged forth a quarter, bent on it a most affectionate gaze, and retained it in his not fastidious palm.

"Well, proceed. You improve with every effort."

Throwing back the coat-tail he had retained between his thumb and finger, Joseph tapped his reversed hat upon the crown, shook his coat by the collar and his pantaloons by the legs, then raised his empty hands in testimony that nothing more was to be found. The comically serious expression of his lantern-jawed face effected Edward's risibles, and Julie echoed the laugh. Lisle looked still incredulous, and reading the injurious doubt of his innocence, Joseph raised his eyes and hands toward the ceiling in solemn attestation, as he dolefully exclaimed,

"In the name of my mother and my unknown father, I've stole only one little, sad, miserable picayune! It's little enough, lord knows!"

"So it is," laughed Edward, "and since you confess that you did steal it, nothing more is necessary. Accept my blessing, oh, Joseph, and the quarter with it; and may the reward of a virtuous conscience go with you."

With a gesture of virtuous resignation, Joseph placed upon the table the coin he had heretofore been unable to release, saying with an air of pious dignity,

"No, sir, I couldn't bring myself to keep what is plain enough begrudged me. That as I isn't welcome to, I couldn't take from any body. There is them as ain't dead set agin a poor fellow making a little something by way of speculation ; but from them as is, I don't want a cent," and turning away he awaited Lisle's dismissing signal. A general laugh followed his retreating figure, to which he stopped in the hall to listen.

"I wish I knew if the madam laughs, too," he muttered to himself as he resumed his retreat, shaking his head with a sinister look.

"Is the fellow idiotic, or a sanctimonious hypocrite?" Edward ejaculated when the merriment had subsided.

"How can you fancy him one or the other, after such a manifestation of his peculiar talent? He is merely an advocate for community of property, though, like most disciples of that school of politics, he approves of others dividing with him, as he has nothing to divide. He certainly is the coolest dog I ever knew, and I have to keep a continual watch over him to restrain his friendly overtures to my guests whom he is always encountering in the grounds. He was about proffering a handshake to the governor the other day, and when by any chance he goes with the carriage, he always has to be told to sit with the coachman, or he'd take first-class passage. If he doesn't sit in the high places of this world, it won't be for want of pushing himself into them."

"What induces you to keep the fellow? It can't be his beauty."

"Well, no; not altogether that, though it has its weight. I must confess that the ruling motive, is his legally acquired prerogative of keeping my worthy old housekeeper in grief and affliction. While he is in my service I can restrain him within certain limits and I feel bound to do it in return for the years of faithful service the old dame has rendered me, and uncle before me. Beside, Leonore has taken such a fancy to him that nothing could induce me to deprive her of him."

"I!" Leonore exclaimed in utter surprise.

"Yes I think so. Don't you exercise the most saint-like patience and forbearance toward him upon all occasions, even interposing between him and my sometimes righteous indignation? If it isn't admiration, what it is?"

She colored, but replied carelessly,

"Oh, one doesn't like to live under a continual régime of arrest and dealing out judgment. It seems to me better to resign one's self to a certain degree of victimizing, without seeming to see it. I should not regret Joseph's absence, but I do protest against repeated skirmishes on the moral field, in which it o ten happens that you come off less than victorious."

Lisle laughed. "Truth to confess, one does feel a certain sense,

of humiliation while looking upon so sanctimonious and melancholy
a phiz and preferring charges of rascality against its owner. I don't
like to feel uncomfortable, and I certainly prefer kicking the rascal
out of my service! I told you why I don't. The poor old woman
seems fated to be tied to some crying torment. In uncle's time, it
was the fat boy Billy, who took to wife the crooked-waisted Melissa,
and is scarcely abated as a nuisance even yet. I suppose all such
nuisances should be kept in the family, and I some way feel as
though I fell heir to them with the estate."

"By the way," asked Edward, "have you ever heard anything of
that graceless Louis Hartley, since he decamped?"

"No. I never made any effort to find him, because uncle expressly enjoined that he was to go unwhipped by justice. I don't
care anything for the sum he stolen; but if I ever meet him I will
hold him responsible for his shameful ingratitude to uncle, whose
death he caused as effectually as if he had stabbed him to the heart
with a visible weapon. He is literally and truly his murderer."

"Poor old gentleman, he deserved a better return for his goodness."

Julie felt the hot blood rush to her temples as Lisle's words fell
upon her ear, and could hardly summon courage to speak the words
she resolved to utter; but making an effort, she asked as composedly as possible,

"How can you make so fearful a charge against him. No one
can doubt that Mr. Fitzjames must have been grieved by the seeming ingratitude of his protegé, but 'murderer' is a hard word."

"Could you have seen poor Uncle after Louis robbed him and
fled, you would not wonder that I apply harsh names to him!
Uncle loved him better than he might have loved an own son, and
he never held up his head after what you term Louis' 'seeming
ingratitude.' He was slowly and surely dying under it, when a
second but mysterious shock completed his work; not from Louis,
I am almost convinced, though he may have been implicated in it.
I never have told this to any one; but as we are a family party, strictly,
and the subject has come up, I will tell you something that always
perplexes me when I think of it, without furnishing the least clue
to an explanation.

Just before uncle was attacked by the paralytic stroke which
ended his life, he received a letter to the effect of which there is no
doubt that stroke was attributable weak and enfeebled as he was
by trouble. I myself gave him the letter as I selected my own

from the number brought in, and I remarked nothing in particular concerning it, except that it was evidently a lady's letter, of which I had never known him receive any before. Occupied with my own correspondence, I paid no attention to anything else till a gasp that was more like a sob startled me, and I looked up to see the old gentleman bending forward over the arms of his chair, with a look of utter sorrow and pain upon his kind old face. Alarmed at this expression, I spoke to him. He smiled sadly as his brimming eyes met mine, and made an evident effort to rise, which was ineffectual. Seeing that he wanted something, I rose to assist him; but he merely handed me the letter begging me to burn it, and I did so while his eyes watched the process with a wistful expression impossible to describe. My curiosity quite aroused, I observed the writing more closely as it shrivelled up before my eyes, and was convinced then, as I am now, that it was unmistakably a lady's, as I had first thought.

"Directly afterward uncle was seized with the illness of which he died, and as he remained speechless to the very last, the mystery never was explained, though I am convinced that his inability to do so added anguish to his last hours. What he would have asked of me, I cannot imagine; but he had some important charge to give me which tortured him unceasingly, and he died with the burden unrelieved. This much is certain, that that letter, whatever it contained, troubled his last hours, and as he had no troubles unconnected with Louis Hartley, I laid it, directly or indirectly, at his door. I do not know, though; the whole thing is as mysterious to-day as it was then, and no light will probably ever be thrown upon it."

All three of his listeners exhibited the deepest interest in this recital, but Leonore, especially, was strangely excited by it. Leaning forward upon the table, she had clasped her hands together with a force that rendered them quite bloodless and cold, and her eyes did not once remove their eager gaze from her husband's face. She drew a deep breath as he finished, and then asked hurriedly,

"But the envelope—the envelope! did you burn it with the letter? Did it furnish no clue of any kind?"

"To what, dear child?. There was indeed a postmark, with its date; but it was one of those common names found in every State, and the State initials were quite obscure and illegible. Here, you can see; for I have preserved it as a souvenir of the scene. I found it the next morning where it had fallen beside his chair, and with a feeling for which even now I cannot account, I folded it in my pocket-book. Here it is."

He handed it to her across the table. She took it with trembling fingers, scrutinized it eagerly, and finding it indeed as he had said, dropped it with a nerveless motion quite involuntary. Edward took it up.

"A most peculiar style of penmanship," he commented as he passed it on.

"Yes," said Lisle emphatically. "Were I to see it fifty years from now, I should recognize it. It is very peculiar, and the hand that wrote it is incapable of disguising its work if it would. Do you know it is one of my many impressions that I shall yet discover the writer, by this little relic?"

Leonore abruptly arose, and the others followed her out upon the gallery. An idea seized upon Julie as she meditated, and she said,

"Who knows but it may have been from Louis, after all; that unaccountable letter! It is not impossible that he should have repented—perhaps proffered restitution."

"Quite impossible," replied Lisle confidently. "I know him too well."

"But, Lisle, there may have existed extenuating circumstances of which you do not know; urgent need, which he dared not confess after Mr. Fitzjames' generosity to him; and he may merely have enforced a loan which he means honestly to repay. This is not impossible."

"Even if supposable, it does not better matters. It was cowardly at best, and what can be said for a man who prefers robb_ry to temporary self-humiliation? Don't plead for him, Julie, I've no patience to listen. Why is it that women as a class plead all sorts of extenuation of man's crime, yet have not a breath of charity for their own sex! I am often vexed at their defence of men who deserve thrice hanging, were it possible, while they turn their virtuous faces from the very shadow of a woman suspected of the slightest dereliction! Come, Leonore, lift up your voice in support of Julie's hypothesis, and let us have a worthy catalogue of supposititious extenuations."

She turned with a scornful bitterness of manner quite unprecedented in his previous knowledge of her, and curtly exclaimed,

"I have no sympathy to waste upon this tiresome fellow! Hang him if you will; but in mercy's name, let me hear no more of him!"

Julie looked after her as she walked impatiently down the

gallery, and feeling that her first effort in Louis' behalf held out no very flattering prospect for the future, she closed her lips with a silent resolution. A slightly perceptible quivering of her eyelids evidenced her disappointment and chagrin under the turn affairs had taken; and her grieved expression smote upon Leonore's heart like a reproach against her, as she noted it from where she stood. Returning she laid her hand upon Julie's shoulder in a wordless apology more eloquent than speech,—an apology that was received with a bright smile as Julie clasped the caressing hand with her own.

Surprised by her capricious demeanor, Lisle looked at her earnestly. She was first disturbed, than annoyed by his questioning eyes, and lifting her head a little impetuously, she ejaculated questioningly,

"Well ?"

Lisle drew her arm within his own, and said,

"I was querying how we could spend the day most agreeably. "Sunday is a weary day, at best. Shall we all ride out to the lake ?"

She answered with a smile of gratitude, perhaps of relief; for she dreaded his divining eye with a kind of superstitious awe. Her customary serenity soon returned. And the day passed by with only one disturbing event to mar its peace. This was after their return from their drive, and but just before dispersing for the night, and Edward was its sole spectator. Leonore had gone to the housekeeper's room to give some direction for the ensuing morning, and upon her return found her progress impeded by the improfitable Joseph, just as Edward, quite unobserved by either, chanced upon the scene. Edward heard her say,

"Why do you stand in the door, sir ? Step one side; I wish to pass."

"Not till I speaks a word or two, ma'am," Joseph replied impertinently.

"Speak quickly, then. What is it you wish ?"

"I wants several things, ma'am ! First of all I wants you to put a stop to this making game of me in the parlor. Doctor Sterling has begun by insulting me, and I won't stand it peaceable. I told you the first day I see you here, that things must be altered in this yere house if me and you was to stay friends, and it's only fair to say you've altered 'em along as you could. But since there's new comers here now, some things as I was about shut of is being repeated, and I looks to you to put a stop to 'em ; hey ?"

"It is your own fault, Joseph. If you will persist in getting into such foolish trouble, you must suffer the consequences."

"No, ma'am. I warns you me and you can't stay friends that way."

"Joseph, I warn *you* that I am tired of all this, and I shall insist upon Mr. Sterling's discharging you if it is continued. I will not be annoyed in my own house by you or any servant."

Joseph laughed ironically, and she continued with the same dignity of tone and manner,

"It is only from kindness that I have sometimes endeavored to shield you from the consequences of your own errors—a kindness upon which you have no real claim, and which will be withdrawn from you if you trespass upon it too far. I warn you that it has its limit."

"Only kindness, hey? So you wasn't one bit afeard all this time, oh no!"

"Stand aside, sir. I have no more time to waste upon you."

"So; you don't want to stay friends with me? Suppose I go away and leave my absence behind me, *not* friends! What then?"

"You are a servant whose place will be readily supplied. What should I care for the likes or dislikes of such as you—since you seem to imply a threat."

"He, he: you're a plucky one, you are, but it won't go down with me. I warns you that dodge won't work. I ain't such a fool as p ople mostly thinks me, and you'd ought to know it by this time. Come now; to put it in plain words like the friends we'd ought to be and I'm willing to be, wouldn't you squirm if I was to let out on you, as you know I might if I was drove on to it?"

She kept silence, though her large eyes fairly blazed upon him, and he continued persuasively,

"Come. now; I know you hain't forgot them old days up yonder" (with a jerk of his thumb over his shoulder), "and one or two more little things that a 'ristocrat' like you are now, wouldn't just like to see give to the public. I knowed you the minute I set eyes on you again, and said I, 'lord a massy if it an't the same one.' Come now, quit putting on airs, and let's be friends again, just for old acquaintance's sake. There an't nothing to be made by bullying *me*, as you'll find."

His persuasive eloquence was cut short by a sudden and unexpected blow that sent him headlong down the steps upon whose landing he stood; and taking her hand Edward led the astonished

Leonore toward the parlor, without speaking a word. She stopped
as they gained the hall, loth to reappear before her husband with
her excitement burning so revealingly upon her cheeks. Edward
turned to leave her, but she laid a detaining grasp upon his arm,
while her eyes asked the question her lips hesitated to frame. He
answered it with careless reassurance.

"If I owe you an apology for having so rudely terminated a conversation in which you were engaged, please consider it made.
Coming along the hall, I chanced to look out where you were standing, and from Joseph's impudent attitude I fancied he was barring
your passage-way, or at least annoying you; and, with my usual
hastiness, I waited for no deliberation before administering what I
thought justice."

"Oh, what have you done!" she exclaimed, as, her first fear thus
calmed, her mind reverted to the possible consequences of this ad-
ministration of justice.

"Kicked a born rascal down the area, where he belonged. Nothing more."

"You must think me wofully lacking in dignity to submit to the
insolence you rightly punished—but—much must be excused in
Joseph, as you see. Please do me the favor not to repeat all this to
Lisle. It is better not; and after all, the affair was not serious."

"I have no wish to get myself into hot water by making a report
to *pater familias*, who may prefer to follow his own domestic system
of rewards and punishment, without my valuable assistance," laughed
Edward, as he made his good-night bow and sprang up the stair-
case.   .

But long after others were asleep, this scene, which had surprised
him out of the very consciousness that he had no right to witness it,
and which had transfixed him where he stood, repeated itself again
and again in his memory, and deeply as he pondered over its sig-
nificance, the unanswered query remained,

"What, and from whence derived, was this mysterious power
which the rascal Joseph exercised over Lisle's well-born and beautiful wife?"

CHAPTER XXIII.

THE breezy days and pale golden sunshine of the delicious southern autumn brought back the scattered denizens of the city from
their summer wanderings, and the accustomed gayeties were at once
restored in place of the monotonous quiet that had reigned in their
absence. If many professed to be delighted with the marriage that
had been consummated during their absence, few were surprised,
for society possesses a marvellous instinct for foretelling such events
within its radius, and Lisle had too unaffectedly manifested his regard for Miss Wakefield, to have left any observer in ignorance of it.
Naturally, the admiration that had been generously bestowed upon
the almost unknown Miss Wakefield, increased in corresponding
ratio for Mrs. Lisle Sterling, whose social position was now not only
assured, but enviable, and the conservative few who had heretofore
remained half aloof, in that merciless stickling for "birth" and "antecedents," relative to which they had received no satisfaction,
hastened to atone for past coldness, by present cordiality and em-
pressement.

Fully appreciating the influencing cause for this change in their
deportment, Leonore herself remained perfectly unchanged toward
all, with a calm disdain of owing anything to an eligible marriage,
which would not have been accorded her upon her individual merits; and though gracefully courteous to all, she dignifiedly repressed
this newly conceived cordiality, by seeming utterly unconscious that
it had sprung into existence. Lisle watched her with silent but approving admiration, for, like most who assume the prerogative of
thinking for themselves, he had little sympathy for those who bow
only to position, and discover merit only when joined with eclat.

As for Julie, naturally refined and graceful as she was piquant and
pretty, the circle by which she was surrounded, while it cheered and
enlivened her, imparted to her manner that indescribable charm and
polish acquired only by familiar intimacy with the highest society;
and Lisle regarded with excusable pride the wife and ward who

formed an unfailing attraction to any vicinity or circle they chanced to be in.

Despite Mr. Bertram's repeated prophecies and forebodings, not a cloud was as yet visible in their domestic horizon; and if Mrs. Bertram indeed had in any way lent her assistance at matchmaking, as he had accused her from the first, she was not yet threatened with a matchmaker's remorse, nor did she feel any premonition of the reproaches usually visited upon this dubious class of friends. Upon the contrary, the mutual friendship existing between herself and Leonore was invigorated and brightened by the familiarity which had been established between them since Mrs. Sterling felt that she was giving as much as she received in a social point of view, and she no longer complained of the unapproachableness which had before continually chilled her in their intercourse.

Leonore appeared, as she was, unfeignedly happy; and if the old familiar shadows still lowered above her, they were invisible even to the penetrating eyes of Mrs. Venard, who, better than any other, knew that they were banished only for the time. Leonore's struggles against the love that had conquered her at last, proved that the troubles surrounding and oppressing her were not thus easily surmountable. What these troubles were, remained an unrevealed mystery,—the past as much unguessed as what the future held in store; and Mrs. Venard looked upon the smiling present with eyes that forever dreaded the approach of evil, she knew not in what form to appear. It seemed to her that Leonore herself luxuriated in her present happiness as one who feared that at any moment it might be snatched away, that at times she shrank with a visible shudder from a spectral hand that threatened her,— with what? She queried in vain, not in idle curiosity, but from that real and lasting affection which had never wavered since she first clasped Leonore's hand protectingly.

She saw without one sensitive feeling, that now, during these hours in which she seemed *determined* to be happy, Leonore avoided her ever tenderly watchful eyes, and seemed more thoroughly at ease with Mrs. Bertram, whose unsuspecting cheerfulness and chatty gayety reassured her; for she knew that should real trouble again darken her life, *her own* would be the heart to which Leonore would turn for aid and comfort, could such be afforded her.

Whatever may be the skeptical creed of the world relative to "society friendships," that such friendship does exist, pure, generous, and devoted, among the many "summer-day" professions

of it, is a holy truth. Strange, indeed, should the influences which
soften and brighten life itself, render the heart cold and calculating! It is experience with the harsh, bitter side of life, not its
sunny one, that makes us cold and selfish, and misanthropical.

Scarcely a day passed without that interchange of courtesy and
companionship which so brighten the links of the most casual
friendship, between the little *coterie* that was almost a family one
from its long and close intimacy ; and Mrs. Bertram's unceremoni-
ous entrance into the Sterling parlor upon one particular morning,
awoke no surprise in its two lady occupants, nor did the characteristic explosion to which she treated them awoke more than a smile,
as, tossing her hat into the farthest corner, she exclaimed,

"This is one of my bad days at home ; so I have come visiting,
in search of a cure for 'spells.' Not that like Mrs. Gummidge I'm
'thinking of the old ' un ;' it is pure wilful depravity,—a *bona
fide* ' *spell* ' of the most aggravating variety. Do you ever have
them ?"

Leonore smiled as she wheeled forward a chair for her friend.

" How can you ask such a question, when to answer it involves
either a fib or a humiliating confession ? But to be frank, I fancy that I
really possess capabilities that way, that might, under evoking circumstances, yield me considerable notoriety. Ask Julie. She has had
enough experience with me in more than three months, to judge."

" Well, if I am desired to answer truthfully, I must say that I
thought you decidedly gifted in that way the day after my arrival.
Do you remember how unceremoniously you treated me to a mental
shower-bath ?"

"It was amply excusable ! Be careful not to deserve another
now, as you will if you enter into particulars," Leonore replied, with
a finger raised warningly. Julie hastened to make amends, and
said earnestly,

"Oh, that is the one time, Leonore, that I have ever had reason
to think you hasty or inconsiderate. But I was so much interested
in the subject that day discussed, and the right arguments *wouldn't*
come to me ; while Lisle was so unmerciful that I wanted your
help."

"It was not a case for argument. None would have helped the
affair."

Mrs. Bertram smiled approvingly. "Sensible woman, to have
learned that a cause had better be left to stand on its own merits,
than to be afflicted with a tottering argument. So few ever learn

this, that it ought to be taught with one's alphabet, **that** the only excuse there is for talking at all, is that one has something either forcible or original to say. It really seems as if originality were secured to a favored few by patent right, or something equally unin-fringable."

Julie smiled. " That remark savors of aspiring authorship. It really quite reminds me, by affinity, of a lady aspirant for literary honors whom I met last summer at Niagara, and who, now I think of it, may be some relative of these Venards, as that was her name. I make my bow to you for the insinuation, Mrs. Bertram, but this young lady of whom you reminded me, is more direct than always polite or flattering in her remarks. ʼShe spoke of knowing your liege lord, Leonore."

" Miss Phebe, by all that is probable!'" exclaimed Mrs. Bertram, " So that wonderful *book* is out, is it ?"

" I never heard what one, but she passed for an authoress, as well as an heiress. Is she either, or both ?"

" Oh, yes, to a certain extent. She writes love stories, if that is to be an 'authoress'—a huge name for a small business—and she has some property in her own right, by her mother, and will have more as a reward for getting married, when she thus lets her father out of purgatory."

" Such young ladies are more to be pitied than ridiculed," said Leonore gently. " Miss Phebe was not overburdened with sound sense, and she was too little of a hypocrite to conceal of deficiences. But she was not bad-hearted, or she never would have forgiven Lisle for his merciless quizzing. I used often to feel sorry for her."

" By the way," asked Mrs. Bertram, " didn't we hear that she was married, some time last summer ?"

" Yes, but I quite forget the name of the happy man. It was no one I ever heard of before, and I doubt if Mrs. Venard, herself, could tell it now without referring to the letter. A Mr.—*somebody*, whom she met at the Falls, I believe. Have you any idea who it was, Julie ?"

"Not the least. She had quite an assortment of beaux, of all styles and description ; but no one seemed especially favored when I left. She had not the best reputation for amiability among those who care for that old-fashioned virtue.'

"Oh, she is abundantly equipped with the side arms of matrimony—temper and a good will of her own ! She'll never die from being over-snubbed," laughed Mrs. Bertram.

Leonore gave an arch glance at her friend, as she said with playful railery,

"Julie, let me tell you that one of Mrs. Bertram's striking peculiarities is keeping a keen look-out for what sh; styles 'snubs,' or 'snubbing,'—a production of social and domestic life, which, as I understand it, yields more fruit than flowers. Deal gently with her monomania."

"Oh, it's very well to style it monomania! You and Lisle haven't been married long enough yet for him to be anything but perfection ; but he'll come to it in time. Julie, if you wish to retain a favorable opinion of yourself, don't marry."

"I won't this year, thank you."

The three ladies laughed ; but Mrs. Bertram piquantly rejoined,

"He who has never been snubbed, has a sensation in reserve, and I'd advise him to keep it in an anticipatory condition as long as possible. Make the most of your last year of grace, Julie, if you are really bent upon a 'love match,' as at your precious age I suppose you are."

"I don't know. Lisle's theory is that love and good sense seldom go together—that is, they don't 'hunt in pairs;' and I am prosaical enough to prefer more sense, even at the cost of less love."

"Well, don't look for too much, which is equally to be dreaded. A husband with *some* sense is inclined to give his wife credit for possessing a little; but one with too much, can never be brought to belive that she has any ! Unfortunately, sense and egotism go hand in hand, paradoxical as it seems."

Leonore pressed her hands laughingly upon her temples, as she exclaimed,

"Ah me! Poor Mrs. Wragg's unfortunate head was never in such a whirl, with her omelette, as is mine with your matrimonial ethics! People never did marry by rule, and they never will ; so where is the use of trying to make them?"

"There is none at all ; so, to change the subject, how is the Infant?"

"I regret to tell you that the Infant is in a melancholy condition. Her son-in-law, whom Lisle styles 'the fat boy,' last night regaled himself with the luxury of a lodging in the 'lock up.' It may be a comfortable haven of rest, but it isn't aristocratic, and Mrs. Perkins bemoans it accordingly. Moreover, Melissa his wife, has an heir, who is to be measled, and whooping-coughed, and have his or her teeth umbrella knobed into existence, under the auspices of the old lady herself, as babies don't seem to flourish upon _nothing_, to which this one is heir. I daren't tell Lisle the afflictions of his household, nor that I this hour paid the vagrant's fine, to enable him to go home and make the acquaintance of his family."

"I wonder if it was the persuasive Joe who moved you to that act of compassion," said Julie. "He must be most eloquent in his frequent appeals to your generosity, if one can judge by their success."

"Yes, I'm most tender hearted; and Joseph has had the penetration to perceive, and the talent to avail himself of the fact."

The reply was laughingly made, but there was a spasmodic movement of the hand lying idly upon her lap, that belied the lightness of her manner.

As if the very allusion to him were sufficient to invoke his presence, at that instant Joseph himself appeared in the doorway, and mutely beckoned Leonore toward him. Wondering what could be his mission, she approached him, and with an air of sanctimonious astuteness he placed a tiny envelope in her hand half concealed among the folds of her dress. Raising her hand with an impulsive movement, she read the inscription, and then asked in surprise,

"Why do you deliver to others the messages not intended for them? Did you not see that this letter is for Miss Julie?"

"Oh, ma'm, it's all right then, is it? The thing looked strange like, being as the cove what give it to me told me over and over again to 'give it into Miss Kelley's own hand;' so says I to myself, 'don't you do it, Joe; don't you do no such thing. Just you give it to the madam, instead;' and then says I, 'that's what I will;' and if you'll take my advice, you'll read it. It couldn't do no harm, you know."

"Joseph, you are incorrigible. Keep your lips closed, and in future do exactly as you are bidden," and with a dismissing gesture, she turned, and as she passed the two ladies who in their conversation had heard nothing that had passed beyond it, she laid the letter in Julie's lap, and re-seated herself without a word. But silent as were her lips, her face was eloquent. Surprise, pain, grief, and something of incredulity, lined itself upon her features, and she bent upon Julie a glance of piercing penetration that was almost fierce.

Unconscious of the glance, Julie opened the letter, and her color changed visibly as she read:

"Dearest, I am here. Do not be offended with me for having

disobeyed you; I could not remain away from you! Do in pity's name, give me an interview somewhere, this evening, or I shall seek you at your home, whatever may be the consequences. For myself I do not fear them, and it is only my love for you that makes me prudent. Send me one word by my messenger who awaits it.

Yours devotedly,
LEONARD."

He had followed her, then, as he threatened. Well, she had forbidden him to do so, she would not receive him. She had never pledged herself to receive him till that reparation he had promised, should have been made. She owed him no obligation as yet, doubted even her right to do so, under the ban as he was. She was about to write him this, as she ascended to her room; but second thought restrained her. What if he were to come to the house, as he threatened! Above all things she must prevent a collision between him and Lisle; and seizing her pencil she hastily wrote,

"I will meet you in the summerhouse at eight o'clock. Enter by the garden gate, which you will find unlocked."

Carrying the brief reply herself, she gave it to the messenger, and with all the self-possession she could summon returned to the parlor. She felt that the duplicity of her conduct must be stamped upon her face; but to her relief, Leonore, who seemed struggling against her mental pre-occupation, did not look up, and Mrs. Bertram was chatting fluently as ever. So she continued to do until suddenly the fact appeared to strike her that she received few responses.

"What has happened to both of you?" she exclaimed, making a stop in the middle of a sentence. "One would really imagine, Julie, that the aforesaid husband had made his appearance in *propria persona*, much to the objection of the family, as usual—families always do object, it's their mission! When is it to be?"

Julie forced herself to make a playful reply to this sally so accidentally direct, while Leonore, much to her surprise, said nothing, if indeed she heard what was passing. Illy at ease as she was, Julie felt herself an object of suspicion, if not of displeasure; and, cut to the heart by the seeming coldness, she impulsively bent forward and clasped Leonore's hand in her own. The action aroused her, and but half comprehending it, she started violently; then with a contemptuous smile she said,

"What strange freaks fancy plays with us! I have been dull and uninteresting indeed, and you are right, Julie, to reproach me. I trust your letter was a pleasant one, Julie. It was an example of Joseph's usual stupidity, bringing it to me."

It was not a pleasant letter, nor had it been gladly received.

But for the presence of Mrs. Bertram, Julie would have told her so. As it was, she said nothing beyond a mere word of thanks for the interest displayed ; but the affectionate glance which accompanied it restored Leonore's serenity, and gradually the shadows cleared from her face. Whatever had been the source of her discomfort and alarm, she had reasoned against it successfully, and resumed her part in the conversation with her customary spirit long before Lisle's step in the hall reminded them how the hours were passing.

"Our liege lords have come home for dinner!" exclaimed Mrs. Bertram, hastily scrambling her worsteds together preparatory for flight.

"You needn't be frightened at *my* husband. He is always amiable," said Leonore, amused by Mrs. Bertram's precipitation.

At that moment Lisle threw open the door and entered. He was flushed and excited, evidently not pleasantly ; for at the first glimpse of his face, Mrs. Bertram exclaimed,

"'*Amiable !'* A fond wife's delusion ! May I never see a thunder-cloud !"

Scarcely acknowledging the satirical salutation, Lisle handed his wife a latter already unfolded for perusal, and said imperatively,

"Read that, Leonore ; read it aloud."

She took it mechanically ; but whether his manner had startled her, or sudden illness overwhelmed her, the page swam before her eyes, and when she would have spoken, her lips were mutely white and trembling. Seeing her agitation, Julie reached forward and took the letter from her, together with a folded enclosure which had fallen from it. "Let me read it, Leonore. My eyes are younger than yours, if you won't resent the assertion."

Her smile gave place to a look of surprise and attention as the first words caught her eye ; a glad surprise, a pleased interest ; and in a voice which no effort could quite render firm, she said,

"LISLE STERLING, ESQ.,

SIR,—Enclosed please find a draft on the Bank of Commerce, for the amount of which you have doubtless considered yourself *robbed,* since I had an imperative necessity for it which brooked no delay nor ceremony. Although a portion of this sum is justly mine, as a share of the profits of our co-partnership which at that time existed,

I refund the whole amount taken, with interest to date; that, so far from having any just cause of complaint against me, you may be satisfied that your money was profitably invested.

I believe, sir, that I am no longer under obligation to you; and should we meet, as very probably we often may, I shall consider myself entitled to.that courtesy from you which one gentleman extends to another. My misfortune—*fault*, if you please—proved your gain, since by it you enjoy a fortune of which one-half would otherwise have been mine; in consideration of which, you may well sacrifice personal enmity if you yet cherish it, and allow me to subscribe myself,   .   ·   Yours most obliged,

LOUIS HARTLEY."

A profound silence succeeded to the last word, during which Julie absently toyed with the draft she had not unfolded.

A strange smile wreathed Leonore's lips, as, extending her hand, she took the paper and ran her glance over it.

"Do you imagine this is genuine—that it is collectable?" she asked. ·

" I did not till I tested it, but it is good as the gold itself."

His lips were compressed, and he paced the floor as if struggling to suppress his excitement.

" That is the only surprising part of it," Leonore rejoined, tossing the scrap upon the carpet with a disdainful gesture.

"How did you receive it?" Julie asked, prompted by an unrestrainable curiosity to know if Lisle and Hartley had met.   ·

" From my Post Office box; *dropped*, as you see by the envelope. The rascal must be in the city, or his emissaries are near. I would give half my life to encounter him!"

" For what, Lisle?"

" To see if he has the physical capacity to swallow both the draft and his insulting letter! By Heaven, he shall do it!"

" Lisle, Lisle, in the name of justice, stop!" Julie exclaimed.

" Who speaks of justice and that man? 'Justice!' It would hang him higher than Haman! Julie, Louis Hartley *murdered* my old uncle! do you understand? Murdered him!'

Both Julie and Leonore were struck speechless; and pitying the emotion exhibited by all, Mrs. Bertram ventured an expostulation.

" Don't be unreasonable in your anger, Lisle. Mr. Fitzjames was an old gentleman, already feeble and quite broken. How can you say that Hartley's crime, with all its stinging ingratitude, hastened his death by an hour? It is only your supposition."

" Whatever it be, whether fact or supposition, I hold him responsible; and what the law in its technicalities, will never give me, my right arm shall exact of him. , There *are* wrongs for which the law offers no redress. Who, *then*, should be judge and jury ?"

" What would you do ?" asked Julie, pale and trembling.

" ' Do ?' Horsewhip him to begin with, as a dog who had bitten me—and after—well, words are meaningless."

" Lisle, you are cruel and unjust. What are you made of that you are so implacable ? What reparation would you have ?"

" I don't know what I would have ! I never asked myself upon what terms I would forgive him. *I hate* him ; that is all ! He can make no reparation satisfactory to such a feeling."

" Lisle, Lisle, you were always stern and bitter ! You never were like others, even as a child. From disliking and distrusting the world, you have come to hate it. Is there no mercy in your nature ? Leonore, dear Leonore, speak to him,—you who are so gentle and full of pity."

" Don't appeal to me ; I have neither gentleness nor pity for this contemptible wretch," she replied with an expression of real loathing.

Lisle softly stroked her hair. " Your sympathy is most welcome, Leonore. I believe you are that rare treasure among women, ' a good hater.' Thank you, dear."

Mrs. Bertram arose and drew her mantle around her.

" Don't go, Mrs. Bertram," said Lisle cordially. " We have not been entertaining, I confess. See now how amicably we will adjust affairs. Here, Leonore. I endow you with this draft to do with it just whatever you may decide. I never will touch it again, nor will I accept one dollar from the coward, by what ever name he calls it ; restitution, reparation, or peace offering ! Take it, Leonore."

"Not for anything under heaven ! I would starve or beg first."

" Here, then, Julie ; some one may as well have the benefit of it. No ? Then expend it in charity."

"Not that either, Lisle. Place one-half of this amount to Louis Hartley's credit, since, as he says, it is justly his. With the other half I'll buy me a wedding *trousseau* and a husband, thank you."

" ' What comes over the devil's back,' eh, you remember the adage, Julie ?" Lisle said warn ngly.

" Don't begin to croak now, Lisle. You will have to be very amiable to drive away the impression you have created. Poor Leonore looks quite worn out."

So she did, with the hectic flush of excitement in her usually

colorless cheeks; and there was more of languor than of affection in
the poise of her head as it rested against her husband's shoulder,
where he had drawn it with a caressing hand.

The announcement of dinner was welcome to all, and utterly refusing to remain, Mrs. Bertram departed with the laughing assertion that she expected to be discharged by her cook for having delayed the hour of that ceremony in her own establishment.

Edward intuitively felt that something had disturbed the serenity
with which the family sat down to dine, and as he took his place
opposite Julie, he bent an inquiring glance upon her.

Why was it that her color would so provokingly rise whenever
she most wished to seem at ease! She could have smitten her tell-
tale face in vexation as she asked herself the question. However,
no suspicion could be so embarrassing as the truth, and hardly caring what he might fancy, she hastened what was but the bare ceremony of dining, and shut herself into her own room. It was really
the first moment she had had in which calmly to think over the position in which she was placed. "So, she had acted rightly in
granting Louis an interview! He had the right to claim it since he
had made the only reparation within his power for that error which
Lisle so implacably refused to forgive. Suppose he never were to
forgive it, should refuse his consent to their marriage! Was she to
bow to his decision and forego the fulfillment of her promise so
solemnly made? Was not he alone to blame for the undignified
secrecy of the interview she had arranged for this very evening?
It was foreign to her wishes, foreign to her nature thus to cover
with the veil of secrecy any act which she might commit, and her
spirit rose in rebellion against the circumstances which influenced
her.

It was then no longer with a timid shrinking that she descended to
the garden and carefully assured herself that as usual the side gate was
yet unlocked, and that Joseph, whose peculiar care it was, yet remained
invisible. Satisfied that she was unobserved, she went directly to the
summerhouse, and seated herself to await Louis's coming. The evening was cold and gray, and the rising wind heralded a wintry storm;
but scarcely feeling the chill in the air, she waited with a breathless
impatience which made every moment seem an hour. She heard
the nearest city clock strike eight, and started up impatiently. Suppose she were to be missed, sought for! She had already waited
here a quarter of hour, as impatience had led her out before the
hour she herself had named, she would remain no longer, but avert

the threatened danger. She turned to put the resolution into effect,
but Louis himself arrested her steps in the doorway. His presence
revived her courage, and with an exclamation of joy she threw herself into his outstretched arms. The moments flew unheeded, now.
Had time really stopped in its flight, it would not have been more
unquestioned. Where now were all the reproaches she had prepared for him for having thus pursued her despite her prohibition?
Forgotten in the joy of his presence, as contentedly she listened to
his voice, and felt the happiness of being beloved. Only when the
morning's events were rehearsed in answer to his queries, did that
voice lose its sweetness, and jar upon her ear.

"So;" said he contemptuously, "this immaculate and all-perfect
Lisle Sterling assumes the right to sit in judgment upon me even yet.
What more does he demand? What more can he wish of me?"

"Nothing, oh nothing! He himself admits that you can do nothing more. Time will lead him to realize his injustice; he must relent
and soften toward you!"

"Never, Julie. He always suspected and disliked me, he is incapable of anything soft or merciful. He was, as a boy, cold, calculating, and distrustful; thus will he be to the end of his life. His
vaunted affection for old Mr. Fitzjames was only another example
of his calculation—a most politic and profitable one, as it proved.
You speak of his wife, so I suppose some woman has been found
with enough hardihood to marry him—for his fortune I imagine,
since I do not see what other attraction he possesses."

"No, skeptic. It was a love-match. She doesn't care for his fortune; I believe she would prefer him without it; and if ever husband idolized a wife, he idolizes Leonore."

"Leonore—who?"

"Why his wife, of course—a Miss Leonore Wakefield, I believe,
before she consented to become Mrs. Sterling."

"Leonore Wakefield; of what place?"

"I don't know that, if indeed any one does. Lisle married her
here, where she was well known and much admired, I believe."

"I once knew a Miss Leonore Wakefield—a beauty so called, but
too much upon the *statuesque* order for my fancy. Is she young?"

"Not one year Lisle's junior, and certainly a beauty."

"And they quite idolize each other, eh? 'Two souls with but a
single thought, two hearts that beat as one.' Is that the idea?"

"How can you speak in that contemptuous tone, Louis? If you
really loved me, you couldn't."

"Pardon me, Julie. Other people's love affairs seem very different from one's own. I'm sure I wish Mr. and Mrs. Sterling much happiness, which is more than they will ever wish me. When will you make me entitled to it, Julie?"

"Oh, not yet, Louis. I do not wish to marry without Lisle's consent, and it is useless to expect it yet. He will change in time; and after all, there is no occasion for haste. We are young, we can wait."

"How coolly you say that! I am not young, I cannot wait,—and such a probation,—stealing into corners, like a thief, for the bare privilege of seeing you! I will not endure it, Julie. If I am not to meet you upon equal terms with your most indifferent acquaintance, I will claim you at once; and if Lisle Sterling interferes, the consequences shall rest upon his own head."

Julie shuddered at the thought of such a collision. Lisle wished for this meeting, was even now doubtlessly looking the city over for him. He was her promised husband, he must not suffer for her. In distress of mind she clasped his arm beseechingly.

"Oh, Louis, go away. Leave the city for awhile at least."

"Not till you give me some definite and satisfactory answer, Julie. I ask you definitely, when will you become my wife?"

"At the end of one year, Louis. Give me this one year in which to win my guardian's consent to our marriage. Were I not to make every effort to gain it, I should reproach myself forever after. Think of all he has been to me, and say if I can uselessly give him pain."

"Let him suffer, if he has that human capability! Others do so. Am I less to you than he, that you thus sacrifice me to a caprice?"

"It is not a caprice. But call it what you will. I am resolved."

"Julie, you do not love me. It is as I prophesied. You have heard me reviled by Sterling and his wife, till your love has quite faded out, and, for all I know, the irresistible Edward is pressing his suit not unsuccessfully. It would seem so."

'How unreasonable and unjust you are!'

"Tell me truly, then. Is Edward only as a brother to you? Ah, you cannot answer! I knew it. Yet you ask me to 'go away' from you, to 'wait.' Like all women, you are a hypocrite!"

"Then you cannot wish me for your wife," she answered coldly.

"'Wish!' Good heavens, Julie! I don't know what I wish, what I say! I am frantic; and you stand there so coldly! Oh, it is a simple thing for you to banish me, and that indefinitely!"

The clock struck ten.   In alarm Julie sprang from his detaining hand.   "Oh, Louis, go! in mercy's name go.   It is ten o'clock!   I am dying with fright!"

"When may I come again?   You will not thus say adieu for a year!"

"Come Friday evening, then, at the same hour as to-night.   I dare not tell you to come sooner.   Two evenings in succession would excite curiosity, as I am *never* out alone.   But do be prudent!"

"Never fear.   Every man in love is either a sneak or a sycophant!   It is a part of the experience."

Julie's eyes flashed resentfully.   But there was no time for protest, and hastily leading him to the garden gate, she would have let him out with hasty hand.   It was locked.   Joseph had carried away the key for the night!   Louis laughed.

"Oh, Louis, how can you?   Do you realize that there is no way to get through this gate?"

"I realize that there is a way to get *over* it.   Kiss me good-bye, dearest, and you shall see how easily I defy locks and bars."

He kissed her, and was gone, lightly scaling the garden paling in his egress; and not till she turned up the pathway alone, did her alarm subside.   Half way between the gate and the house she met Joseph, who, in the dark, was making a tour of the grounds with unusual watchfulness.   He nodded familiarly to her as he made way for her to pass, and said suspiciously,

"It's a oncommon sort o' night for a young thing like you to be out in.   Seems as if you was belated like in your walk."

"I don't see, sir, that you are called upon to make any comments," she replied with cool dignity.

Joseph turned and looked after her as she ascended the steps and went in; then settling his hat more upon one side of his head, he said with a cunning leer,

"There is them as seems to think Joe Perkins is a fool."

CHAPTER XXIV.

THE hours succeeding to that stolen interview, were filled with ceaseless alarm and apprehension to Julie, who started each time she was unexpectedly addressed, and quite trembled whenever she heard Lisle's footsteps. Had he met Louis? did he know that he had visited her under his very roof? Reassured once, her fears continually returned, and she at each instant feared to hear the name, which as yet remained unmentioned, since the day when it had caused such varied emotions. Struggling as she was between inclination and duty, she would have ventured everything for Leonore's advice and sympathy, assured that whatever might be her personal feelings upon the subject, she would respect the confidence and keep it inviolably. But Leonore herself seemed troubled and pre-occupied, remaining much in her own room as a tacit intimation that she desired solitude, and only rousing to anything like animation when Lisle was near. Again and again Julie raised her eyes to her face as if seeking in it courage to commence her revelation and plead for that influence with Lisle which Leonore so perfectly possessed ; but it was not a sympathetic glance that met her own, and the manifest cloud chilled her to utter silence.

Much as Julie felt that an interchange of confidence and sympathy might benefit both herself and Leonore, there was a certain nameless feeling of constraint infused into her very affection for her, which rendered her incapable of assuming the initiative. Even in her most communicative moods there was about Leonore a certain air of reserve and moral fastidiousness impossible to encroach upon, and it is rarely indeed that one woman chooses for a *confidante* another who yields no confidence in return.

What was it that so oppressed her even now? Not one word or allusion gave the slightest indication, and the effort she made to conceal from Lisle the very evidence that she was illy at ease, proved that she desired no confidant. Perplexed as she was with her own interests, Julie scarcely queried over this, only tacitly admitting and acting upon the fact, convinced that there was no one who could aid her to see and do the right in the position in which she was placed.

It seemed that the hours had never passed so slowly as those during which she felt ceaselessly in peril—that the time when, Louis definitely answered and dismissed for a whole year, she should be once more at ease, would never come ! But the day dawned at last, and she counted the very moments to eight o'clock.

What transpires in the parlor is always discussed in the kitchen, and the observing Joseph was not in ignorance that both ladies were anxious and silent when not compelled to exert themselves for others. Drawing in his hollow cheeks till nothing remained but two cavernous recesses, he said to the Infant,

" Old lady, there's things a-brewin' in this here family. There's a smash of a certain natur' a coming, and you'd best stand from under. The madam has got an awful attack of the peculiarities, the young miss is a worriting, and Mr. Edward a-racking of his wits to find out what it's all about. The master's as blind as a bat, old lady, and there is them as is a-calculating on it !"

Mrs. Perkins turned upon him with serious reproof.

" Joseph, it's neither kind nor becoming for a young man like you are, to turn against them as is his betters, not to mention all the years I've served him faithful ! Dear me ! When I think how Master Sterling, which was then but a slim chance of a lad, dear knows I come to the old plantation along with his uncle which was the kindest old gentleman, God rest his soul, though he didn't know but little or nothing about children and their little hankerings, which how should he and he a bachellor? and when I think how Master Louis—which was a sort of relation to both of 'em, being as Mr. Fitzjames was a near being his true and lawful parent, turned out so miserable and ongrateful, handsome as he was—well it a just seems to me this blessed family is my family, and their griefs is my griefs, which dear knows I"

" Well ; then let me tell you, old girl, you've got enough of 'em, and more ! I tell you things is a-working :"

" I don't mind telling you, Joseph, that the mistress has something on her mind as is onhealthy and discomforting to her. I'm not blind, and I see it. Sweet, pretty creature which she is, and gentle as the day is long, she an't just the sort of wife for Master Sterling, who wants one of them *capable* wom n which is gay and rollicking and wouldn't go off with a fit every time he gets a cloud on his face.   The little wife don't belong to the rollicking sort, and she's a-growing further from it every day.   Even maid Margaret, close-mouthed which she is, lets drop a word now and then as shows she's a human, though you wouldn't think it; and he was a sighing only this morning, that her mistress cried more than enough, and didn't take naturally to being comforted.   Poor dear, Lord knows wha' it's all about!"

" Yes, and so does Joe Perkins," ejaculated that personage sagely.

" You, Joseph?   You don't say so, now!" said the old dame waking to active interest, and pausing with her fluting-iron closely clinging to a smoking ruffle.

" Maybe I don't, then, if you say so," he replied aggravatingly.

" But do tell me, Joseph, what should a young man like you know of the secrets of a fine lady like the mistress.   It's impossible, Joseph!"

" There is them as thinks Joe Perkins a fool; but he knows the troubles of the madam, and he knows the worrit of the young mis ."

" For mercy's sake, Joseph!   Well, now, make a clean breast of it, and you'll feel better, dear."

" Thank you, old lady, I feel pretty well now.   I shan't tell you a word, for all the world knows a *young* woman can't keep secrets, let alone an *old* one.   When this one gets ripe, Joe Perkins'll feather his nest, sure as you live, old girl!   I'll blow right out into a gentleman, then, and we'll see who'll kick me down the steps for just speaking to a fine lady!· Great lady she is, too, *I* tell you!"

Kind old Mrs. Perkins was but a woman, after all, and her curiosity was tortured.   Approaching Joseph, she laid her hand caressingly upon his knee decorated with a generous patch placed there by her own careful fingers.

" Come, now, Joseph, make a clean breast of it.   Partners, which we truly are, shouldn't have secrets from one another this way.   It's been so long since I've had a real good secret to keep, that I'm falling off in flesh.   What's the trouble of the mistress, now?   There's a dear!"

Joseph gave voice to a mocking laugh. ●

" No you don't, old lady!   It's along of you the pretty cook was sent off; it's along of you that my speculations is a'most done up, and my step-son in-law likely to come to grief in spite of his step-father-in-law being in a rich place as ought to put hourly money in our pockets.   Poor Melissa han't had a new bunnet since she got married, and she's as slip-shod as poverty!   This place would be something handsome for us, if you didn't just lay yourself out to do me all the damage as is doable."

"Well, Joseph; tell me all this as I'm hankering to know, and I'll give you half my this month's pay to do what you like with."

"Can't do it for that, old lady. I've the feelings o a step-father-in-law in my bosom, and I can't forget as there's a step-grandchild as looks to me to do something handsome at its christening."

"Well, all this month's pay then. The secret's worth it, let alone the grandchild as is my own flesh and blood, if it *is* mixed!"

"And you'll make a big pudding for me to take round to Bill and Melissa as haven't laid tooth to a pudding this long time? a tomato pudding with onions into it?"

Mrs. Perkins rose indignantly.

"That's what I won't, Joseph. Partners is partners, and I'll do what is right by you; but ongrateful offspring isn't to be tolerated, and I'll go secretless to my grave before I'll stew and fry any more for greedy Bill. I'm shut of him, and shut of him I'll stay."

"And the secret?"

"You'll be punished for it, depend upon it. 'What comes over the devil's back, goes under his belly;' which means, as you couldn't have come by it honestly, you'll get no satisfaction out of it."

Joseph laughed. "Well, be consoled, old lady; if I'd told you at all, I shouldn't have told you right and fair. You've only saved me the trouble of fishing up a yarn for the occasion," and plunging his fist into his hat to improve its shape, he tossed it upon his head, and sauntered out.

In serene unconsciousness of the comments so freely uttered, Leonore kept her room, and Julie mused over her unsatisfactory position. There was more of real discomfort than pleasure in such interviews with one, who, dear as he was, caused her all this uneasiness and apprehension, nor could she conceal from herself that her *tête-à-têtes* with Louis were always tinged with some unpleasantness which remained long after the visits were over.

It might be, as he said, that all this which so pained, often angered her, sprang from the very ardor of his love for her; but it lingered disagreebly in her memory, and seemed to her wilful injustice and tyranny. He doubted her, often actually accused her; and her resentment remained despite the tender words with which he strove to allay it. For the first time she now asked herself if dispositions so unattuned to each other were consistent with any asting happiness; and in silent contrast to the violence she deprecated, arose the memory of Edward's invariable kindness and gentleness toward her. She banished the thought as soon as it arose, as if its very existence were a species of infidelity against Louis; but as if in revenge for the effort, it came again and again, linked with many recollections till now unnumbered.

Louis's jealously had suggested the very thing he feared; for it had never before occurred to her to compare the one with the other. Already he suffered by the comparison;—he would continue to do so whenever in the future discord should arise between them, as it so often did, despite their mutual affection.

She was no advocate of "lover's quarrels;" and for the first time her promise of marriage struck her as rash. Free from the fascination of his presence, she reasoned calmly. Perhaps, could she courageously confess her engagement to him, Lisle's most effective argument against a marriage he must detest, would lie in authorizing Louis's visits to her, satisfied that as she knew him better she must like him less. It was a dangerous thought for a *fiancée*, and she felt it a wicked one; but it was with her when Lisle returned home this eventful evening, and but for the mental reminder that her positive promise was beyond recall, she would even yet have given him her confidence, and appealed to his generosity for aid and counsel.

"You are late to-day," said Leonore, going forward to meet him.

"Yes, little one, I was detained. At the last moment, we decided to go in grand party to hear ' Faust ' to-night, and I had to go for the box tickets. Here, I have them; the Venards, Bertrams and Sterlings. Are you pleased, or would you have preferred remaining at home to-night ?"

"I must stay at home, Lisle. I have been ill all day with a headache, and I don't think the ' Soldier's Chorus ' would alleviate it. You must all go without me, please."

"Not to be thought of, child ! Edward and Julie shall represent our illustrious family, and I'll remain as nurse."

Julie interposed, seeking for any excuse that would enable her to keep her engagement with Louis.

"Let *me* stay with Leonore, Lisle. It is more than probable Mr. Bertram will refuse to go at the last moment, and two gentlemen can't be spared. I don't care to hear ' Faust.' I don't like the story, and I've no idea it is improved by being told to music. I would rather not go, thank you."

"Well, Edward, let us hear from you;" said Lisle. "But be sure you decline, for families shouldn't be divided in opinion."

"I should very much like to go," replied Edward decidedly; "but my doing so depends entirely upon Julie, as I certainly will not go without her. Married ladies may be very pretty and agreeable, but one doesn't like always to be confined to their society. Beside, they do such a vast amount of *patronizing* toward young gentlemen, a sort of moral patting on the head, that is trying to the feelings of a sensitive youth! Do go, Julie."

Placed in an embarrassing position from which there was no reasonable method of escape, she felt constrained to yield: but she made amends for it by exclaiming with evident pique,

"Why upon earth, Lisle, can't you gentlemen ever do anything decently and in order! Here has 'Faust' been named for to-night, for days and days, and you say nothing of going till the last hour! These surprise parties of pleasure are seldom surprisingly pleasant. I haven't sent word to my hair-dresser, nor gotten anything ready."

He laughed as he always did when he saw any exhibition of feminine temper; but he answered consolingly,

"Never mind, little sister. You look best with your hair right side out and untortured, and as for 'getting ready,' you are beautiful in anything. Let us come to dinner, and you'll grow philosophical."

There was nothing else to be done; and resolving to leave a note in the summer-house, explaining her absence and appointing another meeting, she resigned herself to her fate with what grace she could summon. She left the table to dress, leaving the others with their coffee, which Leonore rather absently toyed with instead of drinking, as listlessly she poured it out in spoonfuls, leaning her pale face in her hand. Lisle watched her affectionately.

"Poor Leonore!" said he at last. "You are really suffering. You must let me stay at home with you, as indeed I would rather."

She smiled reassuringly. "Oh, no Lisle. I am better than I was; a night's sleep will quite cure me. I won't consent to your remaining."

Lisle stood beside her, gently stroking her hair as she smiled up at him, and only Edward saw the look of anguish that passed over her face as she laid it again and suddenly in her hand. Why, he could not have told, but the conviction flashed upon him that it was a mental ailment from which she was suffering, and that some crisis was impending which she dreaded. Little as he knew of her, that scene with Joseph the evening he had kicked him down the area stairs, had left an ineffacable impression upon his mind, and it came up before him vividly now, linked with her whole deportment.

It was plain to him that, devotedly as she loved Lisle, happy as they appeared to all casual observers, some painful secret existed in her life, which he was not allowed to share, and which at times cast its shadow over them both, strive as they might to resist it. The thought was uppermost in his mind as he noted the tenderness of their parting when the carriage was driven round, and saw again that expression of utter misery upon the face she turned longingly after them as they drove away. In the fresh wind she lingered in the open gate till the darkness rendered each invisible to the other, and then turned wearily away.

She was quite alone now, and, as if goaded by the very demon of restlessness, she paced back and forth with impulsive steps till utter exhaustion forced her to cease; and seeking the sofa, she threw herself upon it and covered her face with her hands. At length she arose and looked around her, as if compelling herself to brave something from which escape was impossible.

The moon was rising, and its soft beams lighted the yard upon which, approaching the window, she looked steadily out. Although it was midwinter, the night was one of those warm, balmy ones which so often light up the southern winter, and, oppressed by her own gloomy thoughts, stifled in the lonely parlor where the gas burned dimly and low, she tossed a light veil over her head as a protection from the dew, and strolled out to the summerhouse, looking so peaceful and serene amid its blooming vines slightly agitated by the breeze. As she entered it thoughtfully and with downcast eyes, some one sprang forward and caught her in his arms. Involuntarily she uttered a suppressed scream. Her lips were silenced with a storm of rapturous kisses, and a laughing voice exclaimed,

"You are rightly punished, little tyrant, for having kept me waiting here a half hour at least! Oh, Julie, how could you?"

Leonore gasped and turned sick as she recognized the tones of a voice not unfamiliar to her ear, and for one instant she was powerless even to move. Then rousing herself, she pushed him from her with a movement of loathing and disgust, as she exclaimed,

"Louis Hartley, what brings you here?"

Seizing her arm with a grasp more eager than polite, he drew her into the moonlight, and gazed into her face, with a mocking smile upon his lips, till, apparently satisfied, he made her a saluta-tion of mock reverence, and said, gallantly kissing her hand,

"Fair Leonore, you honor me. I had not anticipated the pleas-ure of this interview."

Her face actually *convulsed* with the bitter scorn that rendered her speechless, and contemplating the hand he had kissed, she struck it with all her force against the lattice, and turned abruptly to leave him. Stepping before her, he barred her way. Her lips quivered with anger, and raising her hand she would have struck him had he not prevented her. She wrenched her arm from his grasp, and forcing voice she demanded,

"Why are you here, Louis Hartley, and what under heaven do you want of me?"

"I want very little of you, amiable lady. I am here to see Julie."

"What, have you dared to write her? I recognized your writing in a letter addressed to her two days ago."

"If you saw the letter, you doubtlessly know what it contained. You owe me no thanks, though, for my *silence in regard to you*, for at that time I had no suspicion whom Lisle Sterling called his wife. That knowledge came later; but even then I was silent. Not a word or hint has passed my lips."

"Incredible!" she exclaimed, fixing upon him a piercing glance.

"Not at all, when you know the secret of it. I intend to make Julie Kelley my wife, and I can't afford to indulge in revelations."

His mocking manner made her skeptical, and she replied,

"Julie become the wife of such a creature as you! Impossible."

"You are not complimentary, fair lady; but let me remind you that even 'such a creature' has been highly favored in the past. I am not afraid to test the truth by Julie's own reply, and I hope momently, that she may come to give it."

"She is out; gone to the opera. She will not come to-night."

"Then she must have left some message. Let us search."

Leonore stood and silently watched him as he began a search in whose sincerity she did not even yet believe. As she doubted and queried, an ejaculation of delight fell upon her ear. There where they had sat among the shadows when he had visited her before, lay the little *souvenir* he sought, and he waved it aloft triumphantly, before reading it aloud.

"Dear Louis, I am compelled to go out this evening, despite my engagement with you. I am more disappointed than I can express,

for this suspense and ceaseless alarm are terrible. Don't fail to come
to-morrow night, at the same hour as heretofore. If I live I will not
then disappoint you."

He had told the truth then. Julie loved this man who to her was
so utterly hateful and abhorrent! Leonore stood. speechless, convinced. Louis approached her with more gentleness, saying persuasively,

" Now, Leonore, secret for secret. I have yours, you have mine,
or rather Julie's, since she in any event would be the only real sufferer. You cannot take her from me, but you can make her miserable. She has vowed to marry me, and she will keep the promise,
whatever you do."

" She will not, she shall not. If I cannot prevent her, I will tell
all to my husband who assuredly can and will."

" No you won't, Leonore. You will keep silence."

" How dare you, sir ?" she exclaimed, resenting his tone and manner.

" I repeat that you will tell him nothing. You dare not defy me
at the price I will make it cost you. I have not known you all these
years to need the assurance now, that you have not revealed *the past*
to him as I could reveal it—yes, and prove it, too! and I know him
well enough to know he never would have married you had you been
truthful enough to do so. He may love you very devotedly, Leonore
—you have a gift of inspiring devotion when you choose—but he is
not angelic in his disposition, and I hate him sufficiently to drive
him to the madness I can inflict upon him. You had better be prudent, Leonore. You know how much reason I have to shield *you*."

" And because you hate me, you would wreak vengeance upon my
husband ?"

" Ah, fair lady, that is the second time that word has fallen so
sweetly from your lips! To think that I should once have plead in
vain for that enviable title! 'Husband' or not, I hate Lisle Sterling for his own sweet sake, as he knows. Strange that you two, of
all the world, should have married each other! Ah, sweet creature,
do you remember how you hurled me from your door, in one of your
angelic tempers long ago ?"

" I remember too much which I would give my life to forget! But
of what use is all this reminiscence. Say what you really have to
say, and begone. The very air you infest is hateful to me !"

'Then let me assure you of this. As I love vengeance, if you
utter to Lisle Sterling one word concerning me or my affairs, or a

any way arouse his suspicion relative to a matter which I do not at present wish him to know for reasons of my own, I will just so surely tell him what I know of your little life history, and reveal to him that part which you would so gladly wash out by tears of blood could they efface it. You have your choice, Leonore. If you select the path of wisdom and prudence, you have nothing to fear from me, but if you decide for war, you shall have it to the bitter end. We may as well understand each other, Leonore."

"Who will believe the words of a felon, arrested as you will be the moment Lisle encounters you ?"

"Passsion robs you of sense, Leonore. I need not be 'encountered,' to carry my threat into effect. Ink and paper speak at any distance, and even did they not, the law is powerless against me here, save by an amount of circumlocution which Lisle himself would not invoke in so doubtful a case as mine. I shall have ample time and opportunity for any scheme I may design. How have you silenced Joseph Perkins, gossip lovers as all servants are ? What have you done with—"

She raised her hand in mute entreaty for forbearance, and a cold tremor shook her as she sank against the latticework for support. Her anger had subsided, and in its place reigned a dull despair and utter humiliation of spirit. She buried her face in her hands, unheeding the gaze Louis fixed steadily upon her. Some little g eam of compassion dawned within him, for gently enough forcing her to be seated, he said more calmly,

"Why will you inflict all this upon yourself, Leonore ? Heaven is my witness that I never intended to have molested you. You were as one actually dead, to me, and accident alone has thrown us once more together. Even now we need not be enemies. Leave me in peace, and upon my honor as a gentleman I will do the same by you. I know how much you have at stake, and I do not wonder that the sight of me is hateful to you. But be comforted. When I accomplish what I came here to do, I shall go away, and it is for you alone to decide whether you will remain as I found you."

She raised her face and looked at him.

"Tell me, then, what you require of me. If I am to aid you, even silently, tell me what is you propose."

"Why I have told you already. I propose to marry Julie Kelley with her own consent, though possibly without her guardian's. Her little fortune is her own independent of any caprice of his, and with what I have I can support her as is due to her, and I will take

her away, perhaps to Europe, where the sight of us shall afflict no
one. I shall marry her because I love her, and, though you may
doubt it, I shall make her a good husband."

"Louis Hartley, you never loved any one but yourself. If Julie
becomes you wife she will repent it in suffering and humiliation."

"Then congratulate yourself that you are not responsible. However you may believe in your own prophecy, you have now to choose
between her humiliation and your own, or more justly Lisle's. Is
it then so very difficult to keep silence about what, after all, does
not concern you? Julie has as much judgment to guide her as most
young ladies who are suffered to exercise it; and remember, the
very worst you could tell her of me, little favor as you bear me,
would not have the weight with her which it has with you. You
cannot risk so much to gain so little, Leonore, believe me."

She rose slowly and turned away without a word. He caught
her dress in a detaining clasp.

"Your promise, Leonore. I cannot let you go without that."

"Do you not see that you have it? What choice have I?"

"None, in very truth. Let me advise you, Leonore, to remove
those blood stains from your dress, and to make some healing application to that hand which seems determined to tell its own story."

It was true; the blood which had oozed from her wounded hand
had left its stain upon the light silk of her robe. She looked down
upon it indifferently, and upon the hand itself, purple and somewhat swollen; then dragging the veil from her head with an
apathetic force that brought down the whole mass of her hair with
it, she wrapped it round, and walking slowly past him without one
word of adieu.

Standing as she had left him, Louis watched her as she passed
under the drooping branches and at last disappeared. One final
glimpse he caught of her standing cold and white on the moonlit
gallery, her hair hanging heavily down her neck and bust, her
whole attitude one of utter dejection and misery.

A suppressed chuckle fell upon his ear from among the shrubbery
near, and Louis saw the ungainly figure of Joseph Perkins creep
out into the light. With one step he approached him, and laid his
hand heavily on his shoulder.

Joseph raised his hat with a salute of recognition, and, obeying a
mute command, followed him out into the street, and the two went
away together.

CHAPTER XXV.

THE morning sun streamed broadly into the family parlor where
Leonore's favorite seat was unoccupied; the fire, laid more for brightness than for warmth, smouldered and smoked in the grate as if loth
to throw out its brightness with no one to admire it, and the bright
plumaged bird, tired of having chirruped in vain for a familiar face,
now screamed in a fretful tone that added to the general desolate-
ness and discomfort of the room.

It was with a moody and troubled brow that Lisle glanced in
upon his way to the breakfast room whither the bell had summoned
h m, and where Edward awaited his coming, consoling himself with
the morning paper for the delayed breakfast.

Julie entered late, as young ladies generally do, and she laughed
blithely at the two sombre faces which met her view. Scarcely a
word had been interchanged between the brothers, Lisle being in no
humor for conversation, and Edward feeling that he was so. His
eyes were swollen for want of sleep, and his face was pale.

Julie saw this as he looked up in answer to her salutation, and
asked hastily,

"What is the matter, Lisle, and where is Leonore? Isn't she
coming to breakfast?"

"I am tired and ill. Leonore is not in her room, and it is problematical when she will breakfast with us again."

"What do you mean, Lisle?" she demanded in surprise.

Lisle hesitated a moment as if at a loss how to explain, then said
with an evident effort at serenity,

"I may as well tell you once for all, Julie, that when I married
Leonore, I promised to leave her in the fullest possession of her independence, and never to attempt to interpose my will in place of
her own. I knew that she was singular in many respects, quite unaccountably so in some. In short, I knew, for she told me, that
there is in her life some history which she chooses to reveal to no
one, and I certainly claim no right to question her concerning it.

This absence, so unexpected to us, to me as to you, is connected with that history, and for this reason I trust you will allow it to pass without comment. If her absence is suspected by her 'dear five hundred friends,' you will be subject to every variety of social prying permissible in the polite world, and I make you this explanation, that you may know how to receive it."

Too much surprised to reply, Julie bowed in silence, and, seeing that he had quite finished, Edward broached some indifferent topic, and the breakfast proceeded as usual.

As Lisle went out into the hall, he met Mrs. Perkins, who said mysteriously, and with a sympathetic face which she thought proper under the circumstances, little as she understood them,

"If you please, sir, the coachman is waiting on the back gallery; which he wants a word with you."

Turning, Lisle went back to the door, where James awaited him.

"Please, sir, the madam's saddle pony is missing," he said inquiringly.

"Since when?"

"Well, sir, I don't just know. I'm sure he was in the stable when we went out to the opera last night; but the truth is, I took a drink too much while I was waiting, and I can't swear whether he was in or no when I stabled the carriage horses afterwards."

"Did no one saddle him last night or this morning. Mrs. Sterling has gone into the country for a day or two, and probably took him with her. Where is Joseph? He may know something about it."

"No, sir; he don't seem to know anything about it. That's what's strange about it all. I don't reckon the madam would saddle him herself, *would she, sir?*"

"Perhaps so. Many ladies do such things, I believe. It is all right, James, I've no doubt. Nothing else is missing, is there?"

"No, sir. It's all straight as a string touching everything else."

"Very well." Lisle turned away with seeming indifference, and as he passed down the path he saw Joseph trimming the shrubbery. The doubt in his own mind was speedily settled; for calling Joseph, who came shambling forward, he said,

"Are you sure, Joseph, that you saddled Mrs. Sterling's pony securely? I feel uneasy about it, as it is not your usual business."

"I 'an't saddled no pony for the madam nor nobody else. She must have done it herself, if Jim didn't, as he says; for the old girl swears *she* didn't, and I'll swear she *couldn't*, and she knowing no

more about a martingale than the Pope of Egypt's grand carriage!
She wouldn't know the bit from the crupper, nor which went tother-
most. There was queer doings in this here premises last night,
Mister Sterling; mighty queer doings. I'll swear I made the gates
all fast last night; yet this morning the side gate was a-swinging
wide open, and nary a key to be found to it."

"Some of you servants went out early this morning, probably, and
naving carelessly left the key in the lock, it has been stolen. I
should think you had been reproved sufficiently for that already."

"I think, sir, the madam rode out that way, and wasn't able to
fasten the gate a horseback. I see plenty of tracks that way, not to
mention as the verbena border is quite ruinated. I'll swear the
tracks is Selim's own hoofs."

"Very likely," and seeing the carriage drive round, Lisle went
out, smoking his cigar serenely.

Once alone in the carriage, he tossed away the cigar impatiently,
and his heart swelled in bitter protest against what seemed Leonore's
wanton cruelty. If she wished to go anywhere, why could she not
have gone openly, in broad day light, and with due regard for all
the proprieties. What need had she to demean herself by performing the duty of hostler, to steal out of her own grounds like a thief
in the night, and thus to cause gossipping comments in the servants'
hall! Gladly as he would have gratified her every caprice, he felt
wronged and indignant under such conduct. He asked of her no
confidence which she did not wish to give, no restraint of her own
free will; but he protested against this evident duplicity, and want
of dignity toward herself and him. He was displeased with his
very coachman for not having come first to him with his inquiries
concerning Selim. Had he done so, one word would have hushed
the matter so far, as, however much his pride might revolt, a silently offered *douceur* would have taught the intelligent fellow what he
was desired to testify. Leonore had nothing of the 'Die Vernon'
in her, and if with her own hands she had groomed her horse, it
was with the one object of escaping unobserved. Of whom and
what was she afraid? Vain query with which he puzzled his brain
as he rode down to the office, where he must resume his hypocritical manner and seem at ease, suffer as he might.

Edward and Julie were lingering on the balcony when the carriage returned, and in surprise he looked at his watch. "Ten
o'clock! See, Julie, for how much you are responsible! I had an
appointment at half-past nine, from which you have wilfully be-

guiled me. You don't seem to realize that I have become a most
inveterate pill-roller and administerer of hideous compounds in general!"

"Well, some one is under obligations to me for one less mon-
strosity than you intended, then. You won't recall half-past nine by
lamenting it. Tell me what made you fancy that Leonore was
unhappy, and contemplated something desperate, as you said."

"Many small things inquisitress. For more than a week past,
she has been actually suffering, and Lisle himself would have been
the first to perceive it had she not carefully concealed it from him
above all others. I really believe she *fears* him,—why, Heaven only
knows! I never shall forget how she looked as we drove away last
night. The very shadow of death was on her face."

"Oh, Edward, what an imagination! I am sure she loves him
too much to fear him, and it would be a mortal terror which should
overshadow her face."

"Of course it was not terror; it was only dread and self-conscious-
ness. Every one knows that when a woman fears a man, she
merely hoodwinks him. Leonore not only *loves* Lisle, but she is *in
love* with him, which is more. I believe she would have suffered
death rather than to leave him as she did last night, had the
choice been left her."

"How strange it is that he knows so much and yet so little of all
this!"

"Yes, proud as he is, and worshipping her as he does, it must be a
living death to him! If they were politely indifferent to each other,
like most married couples, it wouldn't so much matter. Were it in
my case, I should prefer dying by wholesale, to a small retail business
like this."

"How can you jest!"

"Julie, what upon earth are you two ladies made of, that you
don't get into each other's confidence, if ever so little? She is lovely
and lovable as possible, and you know what I think of you. Yet you
live on together like two polite automatons, when she, at least,
yearns for your affection, whether or not you care for hers."

Julie laughed. "Many men, and some women, might fall in love
with the lady Leonore; but she chills me heart and soul. Why, Edward, she is as cold and pulseless as marble."

"How you women always misjudge each other! She is neither
proud nor cold, and were you faintly to conceive the fire and passion
she veils by pure force of will, you would wonder how she ever a:-

quired such outward gentleness and dignity. You blush, and stammer, and carry each thought upon your little pink and white face; so people give you credit for sensibility. She is calm, and proud in one way, *i. e.*, she is self reliant, and would stand at the stake with a well-bred smile upon her lips; so people say she has no heart. Some day they will see it bleed, and then I suppose they will be convinced she has one. It is you who have no heart, Julie. In proof of it, you hear that poor bird cry, without one effort to comfort him."

"I never cared for a bird in my life. I don't know how. Do you feed him chicken and curry?"

"I will give you a perscription before I go. Here it is. 1 oz. mixed seed (to be replenished when exhausted); 1 leaf lettuce, endive or chickweed. Gravel and cuttle-bone at discretion; 2 ozs. pure cold water (you see it's all pure English), 1-2 pt. or so tepid ditto for bath. Poor Cardinal! One would think you were nursed by expectant heirs! Julie, if I pour calomel down the wrong patient to-day, or order some one's stomach extracted instead of Miss Jones' neuralgiac tooth, you are responsible for having detained me till I've forgotten my calculations."

Seizing his hat he rushed down the steps, waving her a good-bye from the gate, and she went back to the lonely parlor to while away the day as best she might. It passed uneventfully save for a visit from Mrs. Venard, whom Lisle himself received, as he had come home earlier than usual, hoping against hope itself that Leonore might at any moment return.

In answer to Mrs. Venard's inquiry for his wife, he told her frankly and unaffectedly of her absence, and she who understood all, uttered no comment save what was interpreted in the glance she bent upon him—a glance which saw nothing but the calm confidence and faith in Leonore which he had always exhibited. The hand-grasp which accompanied her good-bye might have been more cordial than usual, and his eyes certainly moistened under it; but the whole would have passed unobserved by a stranger, and scarcely attracted Julie's attention, absorbed as she was in her plans for the evening.

It seemed to poor little Julie that her trouble and suspense with regard to Louis were never to reach an end. This was the second time she found herself unable to keep her appointment with him; for, restless and impatient, Lisle wandered ceaselessly about, now in one part of the grounds, now in another, yet ever returning to the parlor from which she would be missed during the first moment of absence. Edward, too, lingered closely beside her, with that contented air which bespoke a whole evening's leisure; and seeing that there was no hope, she took a book upon her knee and in it wrote a note, with as much outward carelessness as she could assume. She begged Louis to go away immediately, assured him that to meet him was impossible, but pledged her word to become his wife at the end of the year upon which she had decided at their last meeting. It was now about Christmas; at next Christmas time he might, whatever befell, claim the fulfillment of her promise; but meantime he must cease to molest her, nor make one effort so see her unless circumstances should accidentally throw them together. Her letter seemed even to herself cold and harsh; but she found nothing else to say, no kinder words in which to say it; and stealing unobserved to the summer-house, she placed it where he had found the one of the preceding evening, and hurried away.

She met Lisle just entering the summer-house, and scarce'y knowing what she did in her alarm, she put her hand upon his arm and drew him hastily away.

He bent an astonished look upon her, and she exclaimed,

"Oh, Lisle, don't go in there. The shadows are invested by hobgoblins! Come back the parlor, and I will sing to you."

"I am in no mood for music, Julie. I am fit company only for hobgoblins. Let us rather come in and keep them company. Why, Julie, how restless you are. Were you really frightened in there?"

"Oh, no. Don't suppose it. Certainly we will go in if you wish; but it seems to me the wind is blowing up cold," she replied with an effort.

"So it is, Julie, and you will take a cold. Let us go back to the house. I am restless as a condemned soul, to-night."

They entered the parlor together, and having opened the piano for her, Lisle threw himself at full length upon a sofa, and, gradually calmed by her sweet voice as she sang song after song, sank at last into a sweet and restful sleep.

So the evening passed away, and with a heart at rest, and mind reassured by the decision she had found means to communicate to Louis, Julie felt happier than she had done for days, despite the disappointment of not meeting him once more before so long a separation. She doubted not that the fiat she had thus pronounced would be received with more displeasure than resignation; but mentally querying if engagement be not the vanishing point to all real happiness in courtship, she enjoyed the sense of freedom left to her for one whole year in prospective, resolving to let the future look out for itself. She refused to admit to herself that her engage-ment no longer afforded her the happiness it had done at first, and attributed her want of content ment solely to the circumstances which surrounded her. She was not one who closely analyzed every pass-ing emotion which affected her; indeed, she never thought of it at all when she could avoid it; and, pre-occupied as she was by the present situation of the little family, she devoted herself to making Lisle forget the trouble that oppressed him, and to making his home as pleasant as possible in the absence of his wife.

Thus passed three days during which not one word was heard of Leonore, and Lisle's brow grew gloomier and more stern with every passing hour. Whereas at first he had seemed merely grieved and anxious, he was now growing angry, not with that violent passion which soon burns itself out, or dies by explosion, but a deeper, more enduring feeling of real wrong undeservedly endured, against which the very soul rebels in bitter protest.

The fourth day of this mysterious absence dawned, and silent and gloomy as he was under it now, Lisle left his room at the usual breakfast hour, till which signal he was always invisible. Face to face on the upper landing he met Leonore, who, calm and serene in her morning wrapper, was descending to join the family at table. She advanced toward him with a bright smile and open arms; but coolly bidding her "good morning," he bowed and stepped aside to allow her to descend before him.

The color fled from her very lips, and she grasped the balustrade for support under the giddiness that overwhelmed her. As she did so, Edward's door opened upon them. Resolutely conquering her emotion, she turned and extended her hand toward him. He clasped it warmly, and involuntarily pressed it to his lips. Her own quivered under the affectionate caress, and tears rushed to her eyes as she followed Lisle down the stair-case.

All that was chivalrous and sympathetic in Edward's heart rose to the surface; and as he passed Lisle in the doorway he said with mingled anger and sorrow,

"Lisle, for God's sake don't be a brute!"

He seemed less than one in anything like human sympathy, as without raising his eyes to his wife's plaintive face, he with cold dignity drew back her chair, and seated her at her accustomed place, with a courtesy that was stinging in its very indifference. She pressed her hand to her eyes, but instantaneously withdrew it as if determined to betray nothing more of the pain she endured;

and as if most opportunely impressed, Julie at that moment came
quickly into the room, tying the tassels of her wrapper as she advanced, in a manifest effort to appear "on time," as she did during
Leonore's absence. She was half-way across the room, before looking up, she saw Leonore, who with apprehensive air waited for her
greeting. With one bound she was beside her, and throwing her
arms around her neck she kissed her again and again amid broken
ejaculations of joy at her return.

The distance which had heretofore separated them, was spanned
at a breath under this joyful surprise, and happy despite the pain
she felt under Lisle's displeasure, Leonore's eyes beamed softly upon
the pretty blonde, who, at last seated with due decorum, chatted
most volubly despite the lowering clouds which kept Lisle cold and
silent. Provoked with him at last she exclaimed impulsively,

"I declare Lisle! Your welcome must quite enrapture your wife.
I never saw so perfect a picture of gladness and content!"

Lisle dismissed the attendant, and then without replying to Julie's
taunt, he asked Leonore,

"At what hour did you arrive?"

"It was about daylight, Lisle."

"How did you get in without ringing? I have heard no bell, and
I was awake long before then."

"I have a key of my own, as you have," she replied quietly.

"I wish, then, that you would make a better use of it than leaving the gates open all night when they are supposed to be shut.
You furnished entertainment for a fine flock of goats the night you
left the garden gate swinging, as your ruined borders can testify."

"But my key unlocks the front gate. I never left the other open,
for I never go near it."

"At least Selim did, for I saw the print of his hoofs, myself. Don't
stoop to so shallow an evasion."

"'Evasion,' Lisle! what do you mean? What have Selim's
hoofs to do with the open gate, or I with either? Explain yourself."

"Thank you, I think that would be quite unnecessary, even had I
finished my breakfast. I shall hear next that you never ride a
horse called Selim; that you haven't been outside the yard for a
month; and various other surprising items. Surprises are not
good for the digestion, and I decline them."

Edward pressed his lips firmly together, and turned upon Lisle
as if to address him reproachfully; but a supplicating look from

Leonore arrested him, and deferentially bowing, he lighted his cigar and went out.

Julie sat one moment in mute surprise at Lisle's humor, and then rising, she said in a distress that was half comical, despite its sincerity,

"Oh, dear, I can't stand this! Do scold, quarrel, or anything else quite satisfactory to yourselves and each other, so that you quickly end it all."

Left to themselves, the two remained in perfect silence, which Lisle, at least, showed no intention to break. Upon the contrary, he walked out into the hall, and reaching his hat from the rack, prepared to go out. Leonore felt that she cou'd not thus see him leave her for the day, and following him she laid her hand upon his arm, and said very gently,

"Lisle, won't you come up to our room a little while before you go out?"

"Certainly, whenever you feel inclined to make the explanation which you must feel is due me. Perhaps you had better wait till you recover from your fatigue."

"Lisle, how can I rest while this cruel coldness kills me!"

"Very well," and he followed her up stairs with the same unyielding manner.

Once in the privacy of their own room, the restraint she had imposed upon herself gave way, and throwing herself impulsively upon his breast, she sobbed,

"Oh, Lisle, Lisle, what have I done, that you treat me so coldly!"

Involuntarily he pressed her head more closely upon his breast; but his voice was cool and reproving as he said,

"That is a strange question, Leonore!"

"I do not think so. As I am now and must continue to be, you married me, in spite of my warnings. Nothing new has come between us. Of your own free will you guaranteed me the perfect liberty of action which is my only cause of offence now. I told you that you would find yourself unable to endure it."

"No, I am not. 1 am as far, now, from wishing to restrain you, as I ever was. But, as your husband, I have the right to protest against your needlessly humiliating me and giving occasion for gossip that might be so easily avoided. Ask yourself if the manner in which you left your home and one who would die to serve you, was kind and considerate, not to say dignified. Not content with leaving without one word of a'lieu, nor so much as a wr.tten line to reassure

me, you carefully concealed your intentions till such an hour as you
could, unseen, steal into the filthy stables and with your own delicate hands perform the service of a common hostler! I thought,
late that night, that I heard the footsteps of a horse along the walk;
but I dismissed the idea, for how *could* I believe that my wife thus
lurked around in darkness, waiting till that mysterious hour to leave
a home of which she is undisputed mistress? Oh, Leonore, that is
the severest sting of all!"

She raised her face and looked into his own in a mute surprise,
quite powerless to check his words which flowed on dispassionately.

"I can understand, Leonore, that not wishing me to know the
precise hour of your departure, you led me to think that it had taken
place whi e I was at the opera which you declined to attend upon the
score of illness, and that having thus deceived me, you would leave
no clue to the real truth, and so saddled Selim and departed as
secretly as possible. Grieved as I was at your cruel lack of consideration for me then, what do you think my feelings would have
been could I have realized the whole truth as I knew it afterwards!"

"Oh, Lisle, is it possible that you accuse me of all this?"

"I do not *accuse*, I simply recount."

"Oh, you are wrong, all wrong. I am not so guilty.

"I can well believe, Leonore, that all this sounds far more harshly
in the cool narration, than it seemed to you while acting under what
I know was strong excitement. See, now, how easily all might have
been arranged as you wished. Had you but told me that you wished
to go upon this errand, whatever it was, you could have gone equally
as well in broad daylight, and my knowledge and sanction of it
would have redeemed it of even eccentricity. Your air of mystery,
and shallow effort at concealment, are the worst features in the
whole programme, and you cannot wonder that I am both wounded
and offended. Believe me, Leonore, it was an insult I do not deserve, and cannot forget."

She had found words now, in which to set herself right, and with
an indignant gesture she closed his lips, and commenced,

"Of all human injustice, this is the worst! Tried, convicted and
sentenced, as I am, I will protest against it. I *did not* lurk around in
darkness, as you choose to express it, after having led you to suppose I had already gone. I *did not* go to the stable for Selim, as I
had no occasion for him, and eccentric as I may be I did not prefer
a night in the saddle to a few hours journey by rail. All your taunts
of swinging gates and ruined borders are as undeserve l as trivi :;

for I *walked* to the depot to meet the ten o'clock train, going out by the front gate which I locked after me. Even then I was not alone; so no impropriety was committed which could shock even your fastidious taste!"

"Who went with you, Leonore?"

She did not reply, and the color deepened and deepened in her cheek, under the injustice she resented.

"Leonore, who went with you even so far as the depot? I want to know upon whom my wife bestows the confidence she denies to me."

"You have no right to ask me, but as you may wish *witnesses to my truthfulness*, I tell you. My maid Margaret accompanied me, and returned when the train left. I imagine that she enjoys little confidence you would care to possess."

He looked at her in utter confusion. He could not disbelieve her.

"What, then, have you done with Selim?" he asked.

"I? Nothing. What should I have done with him, though he was my own if anything belonging to a wife *be* truly her own."

A sudden suspicion entered his mind; a suspicion more unjust and humiliating to her than any that had preceded it. It might have been aroused by the bitter, taunting manner that so changed her from all he had ever known her; but he gave it expression at once.

"Leonore, do you receive less money than you need? If so, tell me. Name any amount yearly or quarterly. It is yours unquestioned."

"No, *my salary* is quite enough. You pay it very punctually, and are more than generous beside. You are liberal with your money, Lisle; I give you due credit for that."

"So I am '*liberal*' with you, am I? 'Liberal' and 'generous;' strange words for a wife to speak to her husband! Henceforth, Leonore, you shall have a bank account of your own. When my wife accepts money from me as an offering of generosity, and liberality, she must feel herself a pensioner indeed! I see now how it is; you have needed more than your pride permitted you to ask of my generosity. Selim was your own, you had a right to make the sacrifice, and you sold him. The next time you wish to dispose of any of your personal property, let me be the purchaser. I will be as liberal in my *deal* with you, as you esteem me in my *benefactions*."

She had resented his injustice, but his sarcasm overpowered her.

and sinking upon a chair she covered her face with her hands, only ejaculating,

"I have done nothing of the kind! I tell you I know nothing whatever of Selim, and I care less."

"Is this true? Have you no clue to his disappearance, which dates from the night of your own temporary absence?"

"I see, what you begin to, Lisle. Since it was not I who carried him off, some one else has done so. He is lost, stolen."

"I never thought of this," he said, coming behind her and smooth`ng her head with a gentle touch. She looked up earnestly.

"I tell you some one has stolen him! Did you not tell me that you heard his footsteps late at night along the path, that you saw his tracks next morning near the gate, found wide open? Through that gateway Selim was ridden out by some one who ingeniously chose that opportunity, that he might be well gotten away before you should learn that he was not with me."

"Then that some one must have been either a conjurer or spy. Leonore, I am much mistaken if Joseph doesn't know more of this than you or I. If he is guilty he shall pay the penalty, and I warn you not to attempt to shield him, as you often do. He is a rascal born and bred, and your interest in him is something that pas es my comprehension."

As he spoke he rang the bell, and Margaret, whose especial duty it was to answer it, immediately appeared.

"Send Joseph here directly," was the brief command Lisle gave as he paced the floor thoughtfully without raising his eyes.

Leonore's heart beat suffocatingly as she realized all that might develop itself in this interview. She knew who had been in the grounds that eventful evening, and it was quite possible that Joseph knew as well, prying and curious as he was. Might he not, if sorely pressed, thus screen himself under the mantle of another, and part cularly of that other who could utter no defence, while naturally an object of suspicion and dislike to Lisle, who little dreamed that interest could have brought him there. Involuntarily she glanced down at the hand she had in her anger bruised against the lattice, and with a gesture of loathing she buried it from sight among the folds of her dress.

CHAPTER XXVI.

Some time elapsed before Joseph obeyed the summons, and Lisle was about to repeat it, when he appeared in the door-way, wiping his mouth with the back of his hand upon which remained sundry fragments of the breakfast he had waited to finish quite at his leisure.

In one hand he carried the battered hat of playful angles, without which he was never fully equipped, and he looked unusually shabby from his faded coat to his self-styled " tropical boots," from which, with their customary eccentricity, his feet had gradually retreated and taken up lodgings in the area, to the utter desertion and prejudice of the wrinkled front. They were twin brothers to divers pairs which had preceded them, and doomed to the same humiliating end. Lisle's provocation against him increased as he inventoried all this at silent leisure, during which Joseph seemed quite unconscious of anything except the battered *chapeau* which he turned and twisted into fantastic shapes from which it emerged more mellow and dejected than before. Lisle's voice aroused him.

" Joseph, have you no better clothes than these, that you are so shabby ?"

" Well, yes, sir. There's my Sunday-go-to-meeting ones as is better, though nothing to brag on."

" Put them on, and give these to the beggars, if you can find one who won't feel insulted by the donation. You are not fit to be seen as the servant of a gentleman."

" I was a-asking of myself only this morning, if it was possible these here duds was a quite done over; but says I to myself, ' Joe, you're a poor cuss of a feller, and don't you say anything is done over, till you're told it. There's them whose business it is to notice it, and they'll tell you.' I han't no sort of gift for knowing when things is a worn out. I'm obleeged to you for telling me," and he turned to go, as if satisfied that the colloquy was at an end.

" Stay, Joseph; it was not for this that I sent for you. Do you remember the evening Mrs. Sterling went away upon the visit from which she has just returned ?"

" Yes, sir ; it was on a Friday. I can tell that by two or three thing I made a note on at the time."

" What were they ?"

" Well, you all went to the opry, and left the madam at home all alone. It was a warm night though the wind blowed fresh, and I see her all a-fluttering in the gate where she stood to see you drive off, as white as a sheet."

" Well, what happened after that ?"

"I had took a note that for a good smart of time the madam had been in a queer way, and I had said to the old girl, said I, 'old lady, things is a-working. The madam has something on her mind '—"

" Why do you harp upon 'the madam' so persistently ? I want to know what took place around the grounds that night; whether you noticed any one lurking near, whether you locked the gates as usual, and who went out or came in after the usual hour."

" I looked all up earlier'n usual that night, cause I wanted to go out; but I didn't go, and about nine o'clock I thought I heered something out in the garden, and out I went to look after it. I made sure I see some one go into the summer-house, and I just put softly along after it."

" Who was it, Joseph? Go on."

" Yes, sir, being as you tell me to. It was only the madam her-self, then, looking as white as a ghost, and just as she got to the door she gave a little screech like she'd met a twin ghost."

Lisle looked at Leonore, who sat motionless, as white and still as the dead. In alarm he laid his hand upon her shoulder, and feeling the shudder which stole over her, he recalled at once the alarm Julie had manifested the succeeding evening when she had avowed that the place was infested with goblins. Curious and interested, he asked with a half incredulous smile,

" What did you see, Leonore ? Was it really a ghost?"

She made an effort to reply, but the white lips only trembled, and were silent ; and fearing that her secret would escape her and thus rob him of his importance as its sole possessor, Joseph hastened to reply for her.

" It wasn't no ghost at all, sir. The wind made queer shadows, and tossed the vines about, and one of 'em struck her in the face. I seen it all, and being as it wasn't my business to say a word, I didn't and kinder shambled off out of sight."

"I hope you showed your good sense by leaving entirely."

"Why, no, I may say I didn't. I felt such a hankering to know what possessed the madam, that I couldn't leave my absence behind me, and I kept an eye on her from that time out. Says I, there's no harm in finding out all a feller can in this world, and so I sot down under the bushes and fell a-thinking."

"You deserve a caning for you impertinence, sir. Who employs you to watch and spy upon your mistress."

"Not you, sir; I says that, and I says it honest. I didn't make very smart for all my watching, though, for after maybe a hour, maybe less, I only see the madam come out and stalk along to the house right through the wet grass, and as bareheaded as she was born, with all her hair a-dangling down her back, and the bushes a-catching at it like mad! I sot a wondering what it all meant, when after a bit I see her come out onto the gallery along with maid Margeret, and away they went together, the madam locking the gate after 'em with a key of her own; and I was that astonished at it all, that I went into the house, and says I to the old girl, 'old lady, things as was a-working is worked.' All I see after that, was maid Margaret come back and rung at the side gate like nothing had happened only a female run out. When I went up to bed, I heered her a-snoring like mad, and says I, it's all right with the madam wherever she is, or maid Margaret couldn't fetch such a snore as that."

"And you heard nothing during the night; you have no suspicion of how Selim was gotten away, nor who took him?"

"Not I, sir, though I mostly has my eyes open. The next morning the madam was gone, and Selim was gone, and you said she'd likely saddled him herself and took him into the country. I couldn't swear she didn't, though I didn't see anything of it; for when people begin to act queer, they go on doing no end of queer things."

"Joseph, if you think this long, wordy harangue has imprsed upon m, you are mistaken. I am more than ever convinced that you know what has become of Selim, and I've a mind to have you arrested upon suspicion, without farther parley. I give you just three days to return him, 'and no questions asked,' or to take the chance of your being proved the thief."

"And won't you offer a reward, sir? something handsome, being as it was the madam's saddle horse by which she sot a store."

"Not a dollar's reward, to you, sir. I won't offer you a premium for rascality. Now go, and remember what I tell you. *Three days.*"

Lisle paced the floor slowly and gravely when Joseph went out, and at leng h said with some bitterness,

"You see now, Leonore, how you incur the criticism, and pique the curiosity of your own servants! The moment a woman really has a mystery in her life, she sets herself to call everybody's attention to the fact. She is like a weak-minded old hen, who, having carefully hidden her nest, makes such a cackling over it every time she drops an additional egg, that one can find it in the dark !'

. The uncomplimentary comparison fell dead upon her ear. She was abstracted, lost, in the realization that she was more than ever in Joseph's power by his knowledge of that fatal encounter upon the very night of Selim's abduction. Should Lis'e attempt to prosecute him, he would threaten her at once with a revelation of what he had as yet concealed, and denounce Louis as the thief. She would not, for a thousand Selims have Louis' presence in the grounds suspected, even could he establish his innocence of the charge. Lisle would never believe that their interview was purely accidental, should the revelations she dreaded be made. The whole truth would kill her, less than that compromise her forever. All depended upon Joseph's silence, which she must purchase at any price. She had endured too much to see all imperilled now ; anything was preferable to this. Lisle was resolute, and obstinate always when so. It was useless to appeal to him upon any pretext ; beside, he had warned her not to attempt it. There remained, then, nothing but to cast aside the frail barrier she had been able to interpose between Joseph and her own dignity, and to purchase his aid and silence upon his own terms. It was not marvellous that a few sarcastic comments fell pointless upon her ear. Her own thoughts were far more bitter than another's words could be.

Dared she but confess all to her husband! She would give life itself to do so. But that was not to be thought of. The consequences of such a confession to one so inflexible as Lisle, were too terrible to think of. Moreover, she had no right to make it, now. Having married him without this revelation passing her lips, she was morally bound to spare him the misery it would now inflict—a misery tenfold in bitterness since it would now be inflicted by his *wife*, instead of by a woman whom he might be at liberty to wed, or leave forever, as he should decide, knowing all.

It was worse than useless now, to deplore the weakness to

which she had yielded in marrying him. If her lot were filled with bitterness instead of the unmixed happiness for which she had hoped, she would endure it patiently; and in the resolution she let her head sink upon her breast in an attitude that was full of unconscious resignation and humility.

"Poor Leonore!"

The wo.ds fell upon her heart rather than upon her ear, and she looked up in surprise and gratitude.

During the five minutes he had watched her, Lisle's heart had bled with pity for her. The expression of utter wretchedness and hopelessness upon her face had touched him as no other appeal could have done, and he yielded unconditionally. He reflected that this was the wife he had won and wedded against her own consent, despite her struggles and warnings, utterly refusing to be content with the friendship she had offered him. He had honestly meant to make her happy. Looking at her now, could he think he had succeeded in doing so? His heart reproached him bitterly, and opening his arms he had exclaimed, "Poor Leonore!"

She sprang into his embrace, and sob after sob heaved her bosom. Struck with remorse, he murmured words of love and tenderness, while inwardly cursing himself for all that was harsh, and resolving never again, whatever the provocation, to address her one reproachful word.

She was indeed innocent of all that had vexed him most—he knew it now—and convinced of that, it really seemed that she was guiltless of all cause of offence. It was no longer he who had any-thing to forgive, it was she; and he told her so with a generous abandonment of pride that proved how dear the reconciliation was to him.

Thus at peace with her husband, Leonore felt strong to battle with all else, even the invincible Joseph, who would not scruple to use any power he possessed for the advancement of his own interests.

It weighed like an incumbus over her, and resolving to end suspense, she improved the earliest possible moment to stroll into the yard, and by degrees approach him at his work, sure that he would be the first to speak, and so give her the requisite clue without her appearing to seek it. But she was not prepared for the vein of confidence and self-satisfied cunning with which he abruptly accosted her, without even the preliminary ceremony of a bow.

"Well; didn't I head him off without his getting much satisfaction, for all his sharpness?"

A shudder of disgust stole over her at the thought of a secret understanding with this untaught boor, and with an effort suppressing her indignation at his presumption, she asked coolly,

"Do you really fancy, that Mr. Sterling has let you off so easily? I assure you he is quite in earnest, and if Selim is not restored, he will carry out the threat he made you."

"If it comes to that, ma'am, *you* know there is them as will be worse off than Joe Perkins."

"Who, Joseph?"

"Well, him as *might* have took the horse, which you seen in the summer-house, yourself, if so be your testify should be called for. Do you think I don't know who was along with you that evening, because I didn't tell it to the master? There is them that thinks Joe Perkins a fool, and likes to put on airs and treat him according; but it won't work."

"Supposing you do know that Mr. Hartley was that evening at the house. Do you fancy that you can divert justice by attempting to throw suspicion upon a gentleman? You are less astute than you think yourself, Joseph, and you had better be careful how you proceed."

"Well, you do put it on brave, I swear!" he exclaimed admiringly, and stopping his work to look at her.

She affected to misinterpret him, and continued resolutely,

"You may think I speak very plainly, but it is for your own good. You know that your reputation for honesty is not very enviable, you know how many times I have benevolently screened you, and assisted you out of difficulty. Ask yourself if you can stand alone when all will be against you, since no one will believe you innocent. What can you do?"

"I may come to a pretty tight squeak if you let the thing go on; I'm free to own up that I'll have a hard row. But what I *can* do, is to tell the whole truth about that there night, and if any one has to account for him a-being there as hadn't ought to have been there, why you can, and you'll have to. You'll be my best witness, Miss Leonore, and I count on you. Lord! only to think, now, as he should a-come to see the young miss, and fall in with the madam! and no love lost atween 'em now, whatever there used to be! I l ave it to you, ma'am, whether a feller mightn't as well be s'ealing a handsome horse as is useful, as one or two ladies' hearts as don't belong to him and as is useless enough, Lord knows! Besides, he might have helped himself to both, you know! 'In for a penny, in for a pound.'"

She saw that he was determined to brave all, that he was fully informed of all that could aid him in that night's unfortunate events; and hesitating how to pr cee l, she affected to brush something from the hem of her dress, and in doing so, displayed, unconsciously, her wounded hand not yet recovered from the violence it had received. Joseph pointed to it warningly.

"You'd best wrap it up in arnica. It was a smart blow you give it, and it may tell more tales than you'll like. I'll have enough evidence without that; that won't help me any, unless I make up my mind to tell the truth for one time, just to see how it will seem. If I'm convicted, I will. I'll have my say if I'm put to it."

"Joseph, you have nothing to gain by telling me a falsehood. Did you take Selim off? and what do you intend to do with him? You can't keep him, of course."

Joseph laughed. "Well ma'am; I don't say I *didn't* take him, and I don't say I won't find him and bring him back for a good price. Do you think the master'll give it?"

"No. He distinctly told you that he would give you nothing. The horse was mine, and if any one makes terms with you for his recovery, it will be I, myself."

His face fell. He had a moderate estimate of the sum under her exclus.ve control, and his speculation seemed less lucrative than he had hoped. However, he would not come down too low, and as a last effort to arouse her fears, he said doggedly,

"After all, where's the use of fooling. Whoever's got that there beast, knows he's worth more than the reward, and it won't cost *me* a c nt to let it come out in court where he is and who put him there. Mister Louis always had a taste for horseflesh, and—'

"Hush; I forbid you to speak his name again. However willing you may be to fix your guilt upon an innocent man—"

"Lord!" interrupted Joseph. "If you call *him* an innocent man, the devil may drink holy water! and as to speaking his name, you'll have to hear it a good many times if I'm put to testify. The whole story is bound to come out then, for when them lawyers get a feller, they're bound to have it all out of him. My gran'father was had up afore the lawyers one time, and he always said afterwards, that he thought to the hokey they'd have drawed his toe nails up through his mouth!"

"All this is of no effect, Joseph. I know what you think, and what you hope to accomplish; and all this circumlocution is useless."

"Would you be kind enough to put it in English, ma'am? I han't a gift for edication, and them long words an't wholesome to me."

"Tell me for just how much money you will bring Selim back. You need not try to extort anything from me. I am not afraid of anything you can do, and unless you listen to reason, the law shall take its course."

"Yes, I know Mr. Sterling said so. But I know, too, that you'd rather lose forty Selim's than one husband, and that you'll never let him unbeknownstly run himself into a lawsuit where even if he gets his property, he'll see his wife so smashed that he won't care to pick up the pieces. You'll never go and trade yourself off for a horse."

Leonore flushed from neck to temple. It was a categorical statement of the position of affairs, and she could not deny it; but with as much firmness as she could command, she said,

"Name you price, Joseph."

"And no trap? You won't spring something on me after it, as will make my profit a sorry one?"

"No. I am dealing in good faith with you. Only you must consider that it is a business affair which concerns no one but you and myself, and you are upon no account to mention it to any one."

"Well, then; say three hundred dollars, and it's done."

"I will give you that."

"In advance, ma'am; cause you see it mayn't look so little when the beast is fairly in the stable again."

"I will give you half in advance. You know I am to be trusted, and I know you are not. I will place this *half* in the hands of your wife, who is honest, and you shall not touch even that, till you have earned it—she need not know how."

Joseph laughed with an agitating chuckle that shook him from his tropical boots to his carroty hair, and said admiringly,

"You're a heap sharper'n you was in them old days, ma'am. Your eyeteeth is pretty well cut now, and no mistake! It's a pity you hadn't 'em when you needed 'em more!"

She made a gesture of disgust and impatience.

"Tell me at once, Joseph. Do you accept the terms?"

"Yes, I accept 'em. I don't want to be too hard on you, and you've managed it pretty sharp, for you."

He was patronizing and encouraging her! Stung with humiliation and anger, she turned away abruptly and went to her own room. Lisle had entered it a moment before, and greeted her with an affectionate caress as they met.

"What an unusual color you have, child. Does it spring from happiness, or excitement? Tell me; *are* you happy?"

" Oh, Lisle, entirely !"

"You pardon right royally, dearest," and he kissed her forehead tenderly.

She raised her finger warningly, as she answered playfully,

"I pardon, but I attach conditions to the oblivion that should follow a disagreement. This time I am mercenary."

"I recollect you displayed a talent that way the day you consented to marry me. Well, what is it now? You shall have it, ' even unto the half of my kingdom.' "

"It is not even the half of your fortune, Gracious Majesty. I want only three hundred dollars!"

"Most extravagant lady! But, seriously, Leonore, I am going to-morrow to open a bank account for your sole benefit. I would have done so to-day, but they prefer to see you as you write your name in their books, as there is so little difference in ladies' handwriting. It is only a safe precaution, and if you will present your checks in person, the extra trouble will be amply compensated for in the perfect security against forgery, etc. This deposite is *your own*, Leonore. Use it as you will, and from this time cease to consider me your banker."

She threw her arms around him, and only kissed him passionately for reply. Tears were in her eyes, and softly drying them he said earnestly,

"I would give anything, Leonore, if I could make you forget this feeling of a separate identity! I do not feel it, I could not with you. I do not believe it is in the power of mortal woman to imagine the oneness of thought and feeling, the perfect blending of identity, which makes a man feel that himself and his wife are literally the same being."

"Very likely not. But don't forget, Lisle, that she is not likely to forget that they *are* two distinct individuals, when half her life is passed in making her own will subservient to his—when it is she who is plastically to bend her own existence into the channel he directs. I doubt if this is ever accomplished so perfectly that some twinge following the sacrifice does not painfully remind her that they are two to all intents and purposes."

There was a regretful tone in her voice, soft as it was, and he answered it with playful raillery.

"Little lady, how many husbands may you have had, to speak so wisely and earnestly upon the subject. I should be sorry to believe that you acquired all this philosophy under my tutorship."

"You are a good husband, Lisle. Have you ever asked one sacrifice of me? If ever wife had cause to be content, that wife is yours."

They were reclining on the sofa, and she was threading his hair with her fingers as she uttered her loving evasion. Suddenly he caught her hand and bent a troubled gaze upon it.

"Leonore, what ails your hand? It has spots upon it as if it had been bruised. Indeed it is scarcely healed. How did you hurt it?"

She snatched it from him and rubbed it briskly with her handkerchief, as if to show that it was not sensitive.

"It is nothing, Lisle; a mere trifle which will leave no trace in a few hours. How easily you are alarmed."

He took both her hands and held them in his own as he said pleadingly, "Leonore, why won't you trust me! This is no recent accident; those green tints are the work of days, not hours."

She did not reply, and he continued more earnestly,

"If you will; not trust me, do at least accord me the right,—or if you will the *blessed privilege*, of protecting you. When you make these journeys in which so many accidents are liable to occur, do not start off alone, at night, and so mysteriously. Only let me accompany you to your journey's end, and I will leave you when you command, without one effort or wish to learn the object which called you. I will, in no way embarrass you; I will upon the contrary do everything in my power to carry out your wishes which you need not attempt to explain or account for. Only grant me this, my little wife; accept my service upon your own terms, and be assured that you cannot realize the favor you will thus bestow upon me."

His lips quivered, and his eyes were misty as he finished his appeal in a voice more eloquent even than his words.

She bent forward and tenderly raised his face to her lips. She had no words in which to reply to such a petition as this, and she struggled with a choking sensation which threatened to relieve itself in tears. Mutely, with his appealing face pillowed upon her throbbing breast, he waited her reply.

A great love swelled her heart to bursting. Whatever motive had led her heretofore to sacrifice herself, every fibre of that suffocating heart cried out against thus sacrificing the object of its love, and clasping him in an embrace whose impetuosity was only equelled by its ardor, she said passionately,

"Lisle, Lisle, I promise all you wish! Let what will happen, I never will leave you again. Never again will I voluntarily absent myself from you for one hour. Oh, Lisle, I would rather die than grieve you, than cause you one moment's anxiety!"

Catching her to his breast he covered her face, neck, and brow, with kisses, while tears of tenderest gratitude beamed in his eyes, and murmured words of love and joy told how deep was his appreciation. Pushing the loosened tresses from how forehead, he looked down upon it tenderly, as he said,

"Remember, Leonore, I ask no sacrifice of you. Go where and when you will; so that I go with you to shield and protect, I care not where it is."

"I will go no more, Lisle. My pilgrimages are done; there is no inducement strong enough to take me from my home, *our* home."

This was more than he had hoped. It was a new lease of life and happiness. He had no more to dread the comments of a censorious world, no longer a secret at his hearthstone. For the past he cared nothing, for the future he was assured.

Leonore was awestruck at the intensity of feeling he displayed. She, who knew him better than all others, had often thought him cold and cynical, always believed him too self-contained to suffer deeply upon any account, to become enthusiastic under any circumstances. A pang of self-reproach and fear darted to her breast, as she mutely ejaculated,

"Should he ever learn all I conceal from him, he will go mad! God help and forgive me!"

The next morning, bright and early, Selim made his appearance, and in her dressing gown Leonore ran down to bid him welcome. He gave a little whinny when led up to the balcony for her caress, as if testifying that his little jaunt had agreed with him, and indeed was sleek and glossy as if he had not been outside the aristocratic precincts of his own proper territory. Lisle looked at him closely, and more than ever convinced that no one but Joseph had ever thus cared for him, ordered him to the stables, and awaited the return of the shambling figure who soon afterward reappeared chuckling with much self-satisfaction. As he came round the corner, Lisle collared him with no gentle grasp.

"You are a conscienceless knave, sir, and deserve a caning before leaving my service. From this hour you leave it, and never do you darken my door again."

Joseph looked around bewildered, but exclaimed with an injured air,

" I thought you said, ' bring him back and no questions asked.' "

" I've asked none. I only tell you to begone. Not a word, sir !"

He skulked around to the kitchen for the double purpose of claiming his reward and taking a marital farewell, and for days Mrs. Perkins was transformed into a well-fed Niobe with a swollen nasal organ which spoke much for her sensibility, if it did not improve her comeliness.

Altogether Joseph's absence was a relief to all ; and having shed some natural and wifely tears, Mrs. Perkins found consolation in philosophy, and thus expressed herself in confidential soliloquy,

" There is few husbands as is worth the having, after all ; and she as gets quit of one without lending a hand, is blessed beyond women in general ! Joseph *is* an unprofitable partner, which it can't be denied. I do wonder, though, how he came to be paid all that money. It's along of some rascality, as I'd be put up to testify !"

CHAPTER XXVII.

AN interval of profound peace and quiet happiness succeeded this first domestic storm; a peace so hushed and serene, a happiness so evidently perfect, that no one could believe it ever ruffled or threatened by one disturbing element. Even Mrs. Venard dismissed the apprehensions that had assailed her, born as they were of her very love for Leonore, whom she cherished as one woman does now and then cherish another, despite the jibes of scoffer and skeptic. Mr. Bertram alone luxuriated in his chronic grumbling, excusing his foreboding under so serene a prospect by the assertion that " Bedlam itself must now and then be quiet while remustering forces for a fresh row."

Lisle, more jovial and universally companionable than he had ever been, bestowed upon his wife the most devoted attentions, while she, usually so calm and undemonstrative, met his glance with radiant eyes, and a soft flushing of the cheek that was the very roseate reflection of the love nestling in her heart. Relieved of her anxiety for Julie by her evident content under Louis Hartley's absense—and it was unmistakable that he was absent—she hourly confirmed in herself the conviction that Julie's good sense and discrimination had led her to dismiss him and refuse his proffered devotion, convinced as she must be that it was utterly impossible that her friends, and Lisle especially, would ever consent to a marriage between them, even were her regard for him unchanged. It was more than probable that she had changed toward him. Observing day by day all that passed before her in connection with Julie for whom her anxiety had been so torturing, she believed that a new love had already supplanted the old. It was impossible she should not see the deep affection manifested in Edward's every act toward her, natural that she should appreciate it, and she was less than woman if she did not in some measure return it. He must indeed be unlovable, or have appealed to a deeply preoccupied heart, whose devotion reaps not some tithe of the reward he would claim for it. Julie was too truthful and honorable to give even tacit encouragement to a love she did not reciprocate, even did she not in a thousand ways evidence that she did so, as was now the case. A conscientious, true hearted woman ever feels herself as fully committed by the silent encouragement she gives to such a hope, as though she had verbally sanctioned it; and either Julie was at war with her own heart, or all danger from her regard for Louis Hartley was over. Thus Leonore reasoned, and was content.

Edward himself was not the least satisfied member of the little family, happy even by imperceptible degrees to approach that one consummation in whose pursuit he had never wavered. Already possessing a fine practice, he was winning at once celebrity and a competence, playfully as he derided his own skill, when, as sometimes happened, congratulations and compliments became wearisome. He had "the real Fitzjames family modesty," he declared in family conclave, "and after a wholesale massacre of the innocents by mistaking measles for scarletina, and teething for cholera infantum, a f llow feels that there is less than a shade difference between extreme politeness and sarcasm." The surest evidence of his skill lay in the fact that his remarks upon it did not weaken other people's faith in it. His instinctive jealousy of Hartley had faded out, as nothing occurred to keep it alive; and indeed his very existence seemed forgotten, so completely unmentioned was his name.

Lisle himself no more alluded to him as heretofore, and if his avoidance was studied, nothing manifested it. His name had proved a disturbing cause—sufficient reason it should rest unmentioned.

Happy in the sunny tranquillity of his home, Lisle gradually forsook the business routine which had before absorbed so much of his
time, and quite surrendered himself to the delights of that lover's
paradise which exists so rarely in married life, even when mutual
regard is most lasting and sincere. So the wintry days glided by,
and the bright spring-time came with its wealth of color and per-
fume, like a natural harmony set to the "love life" of the happy
family.

All day long the birds sang in the blooming shrubbery which made
the capacious grounds a bird paradise, and conclaves were held to
discuss the propriety of nesting in the live oaks that bordered the
carriage drive out to the street—debates settled at last by the more
adventurous actually commencing their labors, with a family gravity
most edifying to behold by those who idly watched them from the
windows. The galleries were strewn with treasures dear to the
heart of the feathered brood, who, exulting over the building material thus provided, and tempted by the choice selection of commis-
sary stores, went and came with a rollicking familiarity that won
for them the title of "little friends." In vain the tidy housekeeper
remonstrated against what she termed "an unwholesome litter."
"The little friends" remained triumphant, and Mrs. Perkins retired
in disgust at "the idle, upsetting ways, which were like anything,
more than like any quality ways she ever saw before." Great was
her relief when a new direction was given to their thoughts by preparations for a summer flitting to the s aside watering-places, Lisle
himself displaying an unusual interest in what he had ever before
ridiculed if not disliked.

Edward alone remained proof against the epidemic raging
through their entire social circle, quite refusing to desert his patients
for an entire summer, but promising the delights of his society by
each Saturday's boat, and even Julie's appealing glances won from
him only the laughing assertion that "there is a charm in chronic
rheumatism, and the dear delights of whooping cough, not to be
rivalled even by watering-place gossip and the snares of beauty."

" I won't hope that you may be afflicted with both for your preference; for I am charitable, little as you may think it," she laughingly retorted ; but after a moment's serious pause she added softly,
"I cannot express to you how much your absence will detract from
my pleasure. I had calculated so certainly that you would be with
us !"

Possessing himself of her little hand, he pressed it fondly, as he asked, looking into her eyes now veiled and downcast,

"Is this verily true, Julie? Am I *just a little* necessary to your happiness? Thank you for the assurance."

She hesitated before she replied with a flushing brow,

"It *is* true, Edward, though I perish for confessing it. I have no right to speak such words to you. Forget them if you will."

"Ah, Julie! If you knew how impossible it is for me to forget the slightest words you ever spoke to me in kindness! If you knew all I have dared to dream of, what I now dare hope—"

He drew her head to his breast, and tenderly kissed her fair hair.

She felt that she should forbid the caress, that strict honor bade her then and there forever crush the hope he avowed. But she had not the resolution, if indeed she had the wish to do so, and she compromised by saying softly,

"Sometime, Edward, not now, I shall tell you something which I feel it is right you should know."

"I do not wish to hear it now, little one. Keep it for some leisure hour when I visit you at your seaside resort."

"So, you still intend *only* to visit us?"

"Julie, I would sacrifice far more to go with you than you would to have me. Think how lonely my life will be here without you. I simply cannot get away, but shall pass my hours among the sick, while you, amid dancing, merry-making, and flirtation, will hardly count the hours that separate us."

"I shall not flirt at all. Of that you may be sure. I only wish I had nothing more serious to trouble me. Edward, I am a wretch; just a conscienceless, miserable little wretch!"

"Yes; but I am in love with such wickedness. Don't protest now. Tell me all about it another time."

Shaking both the little hands he had imprisoned, he lightly kissed them, and smiling brightly he turned away.

It was a large and merry circle, that, flitting in company, took possession of the rooms awaiting them at the chosen resort, where rolling waves dashed upon the beach, and the white spray looked ever fresh and cool despite the burning sun that beat down upon it during the noontide heats when the most inveterate pleasure seekers were fain to remain indoors. Here, fanned by breezes that swept the green waters for many a league before cooling their grateful brows, chosen coteries loitered on the galleries, with many a jest, or more seriously conversed in accordance with the caprice of the hour.

Delicious strolls after sunset, boating and fishing excursions, all the amusements which occupy the passing hours, lured each to his chosen diversion, and care was a thing apparently forgotten.

Master Charley Venard fancied himself seriously enamored with Julie, and favored her with an amount of devotion which was sufficiently amusing to others, however serious to himself, and that young lady showed him a flattering preference over all her gallants, that brought down upon him many a mental anathema from those who would gladly have filled his place, had she permitted. Certainly she flirted with no one if not with Master Charley, and Edward himself must have been satisfied had he known. Like lovers of a larger growth, Charley's devotion was fervent while it endured, and if his vows of eternal fidelity were to be accepted with a mental reservation, it was only carrying out the resemblance. This playing at love was very amusing to Julie, and she rewarded him with bright smiles, and most constant companionship. "The child must learn it at some time," she laughingly declared ; and she corrected and tutored him in a way that was keenest sarcasm upon his elders, when she choose to inflict it.

For one wole month Lisle endured the customary round of watering-place life ; and then his gradually waning patience failed entirely. The tedious amount of dressing, the idle chatter, the weary round of sleepless hours filled up with an amount of labor that rightly applied might have moved mountains instead of merely defining the lines of quadrille and waltz, and, worse than all, the loitering round his parlor of idle ladies whose chit-chat was always the same and never ending, quite depriving him of anything like the society and companionship of his own wife,—all this became unbearable, and his old forcibleness of expression came back upon him, banished as it had been under the happy life preceding this migration.

"Feminine tongues must be made of the very tangible essence of restlessness! and if there were some legal interdiction against all originality they couldn't more carfully refrain from it. I've heard the same things so many times over, that I always know just what the next sentence will be, no matter who utters the first. Aren't you homesick, Leonore ?"

She only smiled and shook her head.

"Haven't sported all your dresses yet, or you would be. How long before you will have paraded the very last one ? I'd like to have some limit named to my martyrdom. Ah, me, who's th t at tho door! 'Better dwell in the midst of alarms than reign in this horrible place!' Come in, Mrs. Bertram. I'm glad it is you."

"Since it must be some one, eh? Well, as I've no husband of my own to growl here, I'm glad to hear some one's else. What upon earth did you come with us for?"

"I wanted to maintain something like social intimacy with my family; but I've been sadly disappointed. See now; here comes at least half a dozen more ladies, and a fashion magazine to be discussed!" So indeed there did; and feeling much in the humor of 'Mrs. Pardigle's' bricklayer, he might have asked 'are there any more of you,' had not politeness triumphed over human nature. Mrs. Bertram fixed a pair of laughing eyes upon him. "You are crying to go back home, I'll wager my last treasure in crochet. Do you cry like the poor starling, 'I can't get out?'"

"With a difference; the spirit is the same. What is the latest thing in bonnets, ladies? for I'm sure all that commotion is due to the all-powerful bonnet, and nothing less."

"I'll be glad to know what could be less, for that has come to be just nothing at all," replied some lady unnoticing the quiet sarcasm of his manner.

"Ah, me; if I were but a member of Legislature now?"

"I'd ask what if you were, if I were not sure you've an impertinence to put forth," retorted Mrs. Bertram.

"Don't ask; I'll tell you without. I want to legislate upon a matter that has caused me many sleepless hours; namely, walking monuments of folly."

"Ah, that's wrong. Never turn traitor to your own sex!"

The bevy of ladies received the *repartee* with much merriment. But maintaining his gravity, he replied,

"Not for my own sex would I stoop to politics. I rise to such a height of magnanimity only for yours. I'd like to see an act passed setting aside about three ladies in every hundred in a community, who should perpetuate the 'gone out' fashions. When the majority prove false to their last 'loves of bonnets' and the rest of the paraphenalia of the same date, let three remain faithful and not leave the old one for the new. I confess I should compassionate tho victims, but it would be a sorry comment upon the taste and judgment which so universally cry 'lovely,' 'splendid,' beautiful,' at each new deformity pronounced *au fait* by fashion makers."

"Don't we hear enough such philosophy as it is? I've yet to learn that any man ever admired his wife the more for looking a dowdy

Dowdiness may be one of the cardinal virtues, but husbands will prefer ladies less perfect in that respect. Isn't it so, Mrs. Sterling?"

"I know I would not put my husband's regard to such a test; and he's a model husband too. You'd better beat a retreat, Lisle. You will find no sympathizers here," Mrs. Sterling replied. It was evident that he represented a minority composed of one; and he leaned back on the sofa in silence.

"Thirteen ruffles of graduated width," read she of the *magazine des modes ;* and Lisle paraphrased sotto voce,

"Thirteen devils of various shades of aggravation! Mrs. Bertram, wave your handkerchief out the window when this cabal breaks up. I'm compelled to desert my home."

"Hush, and be civil. They won't stay long. They never do when you are here, if it consoles you to hear it."

"If every one had a generous husband, like you, Mrs Sterling!" was the next ejaculation that caught his attention. "I haven't asked for a new dress in six months without being treated to a long array of what Henry styles 'facts and figures,' and I'm sure I detest them!"

"So do I," chimed in another. "I never yet saw a wife too well informed upon her husband's business matters, who was not worn out, anxious, and prematurely old."

Lisle laughed his cynical laugh, and took up the retort despite his wife's appealing glance.

"Oh, woman! ' thou help-meet in hours of trouble, thou consoler of our sorrows and divider of our burdens; most soothing companion of the weary hear. and toil-worn brain!' I wonder who invented all that? It couldn't have been a woman, for such an idea never occurred to one. It was probably some imaginative bachelor!"

There was consternation if not displeasure among the coterie who received this moral bombshell, and though she drew a quick breath of surprise and alarm, Mrs. Bertram replied with a sally,

" Lisle Sterling you can't expect to have such sentiments tolerated in this community. Take them back to the shadow of your domestic roof. Go back to the Infant and the invaluable Joseph, and leave us in peace!"

"Alas, Joseph ' has gone, he has left me, I shall see no more' the features that always seemed to me to have been gathered up by handfuls and flung at him. He has gone, tropical boots and all! I don't know how Leonore will exist without him, for he was her factotum. '

Leonore looked so troubled and apprehensive under this banter, which her new acquaintances were at an evident loss how to receive, that Mrs. Venard, who was one of the circle, rose to disperse the assembly, saying as she set the example of going,

"I would candidly advise you to banish that husband of yours, Mrs. Sterling. People will say, next, that he has been embittered against our whole sex by his unhappiness with his wife. The more unjust a slander is, the wider it seems to circulate."

The ladies left, some of them evidently piqued; and Leonore sighed audibly. Women are so quick to catch at anything that can by any possibility be construed as a reflection against another woman, that the sarcastic apostrophe Lisle had uttered would certainly recoil upon herself should she by any chance lose her popularity among them. She did not utter the reproach she felt, but he read it as he did most that she thought.

"Dear little coward, why should you care whether or not they fancy you a model wife, so long as I am satisfied?"

"Ah, you admit then that you haven't given the very highest testimony in my praise!" she said smiling faintly.

"I didn't think of that till this moment. I have no patience with wives who are ceaselessly complaining of niggardliness in their husbands, yet obstinately refuse to recognize his pecuniary position. The marital 'Henry' is my debtor for a lecture, whatever his wife may think of it! But I'll leave to-morrow, Leonore. I don't think this sort of life improves me, and I'll confine myself to weekly visits, like Edward."

Julie entered the room in time to catch the last assertion, and she brightened under it most unflatteringly. Lisle turned upon her with characteristic reproach.

"Glad of it, are you? And why, pray?"

"Oh, husbands are often capital fellows, but it's comfortable to have them out of the way when one loves the wife the better."

"And pray who may be the mysterious 'one' who loves my wife? I don't know that I thank him for the compliment."

"Blue Beard, it is I who dare commit such blasphemy! I don't see enough of Leonore to consider that we are intimate associates, now."

"Nor I. It is for just this reason that I am going. If you gain by it any opportunity to confide to her your wonderful little secrets, you will be more fortunate than I have been in remaining."

Julie laughed. "Mrs. Bertram would retort that people who are in love with each other ought not to go into society together; but one couldn't expect you to turn recluse for life. Don't coax Leonore off with you, for she can't be spared."

"So she thinks. Keep her, and may she be an ogress in her guardianship of you. Hello! there comes the steamer, and of course Edward." Seizing his hat he rushed out to meet his brother, and the two ladies were left together.

Regularly as Edward had made his promised visits, the hour to which Julie's revelation had been postponed had not yet arrived, and week by week she was more loth to tell him of her engagement to another. Unsuspecting the existence of such an obstacle to his happiness, Edward was content in her manifest affection for him, little dreaming of the many sleepless hours during which she looked her destiny in the face, querying if it were indeed inevitable. Not one real thought of breaking her engagement with Louis Hartley had been entertained by her. Never had she been false to her p'edged word, she would have shrunk from being so now. But her weak woman's heart clung to the happiness this new love created in her life, even as it shrank from inflicting a pain which might in some now unknown way be avoided. Thus has many a woman compromised with strict honor in battling against a fate which she prays may be averted by other power than hers. Who shall say that much of what the world terms heartlessness, is but the living essence of divine tenderness and mercy; that many a one who is stigmatized as a conscienceless coquette, is unfortunante only in being endowned with more heart than judgment. Despite the sentimental teaching, love may change its object; and who shall say that one only is sincere and genuine, or both a counterfeit?

CHAPTER XXVIII.

THE departing steamer upon Monday, found Lisle on board, faithful to his word, and Leonore and Julie remained without him. On the very day succeeding his departure, Louis Hartley, still under his *nom de guerre*, appeared at the hotel, and his was the first figure that greeted the eyes of the two ladies as they entered the breakfast room. He looked up and bowed profoundly as they took their places at a table near him. Leonore's head remained uncompromisingly erect, her face unrevealingly calm despite the quick throbbing of her heart, and Julie alone returned his salutation, with an increase of color which she could not control.

Either by accid nt or design, he was seated so near them, and so exactly opposite, that it was impossible to avoid meeting his eyes each time they raised their own, and the triumphant half-smile that fixed itself upon his face proved that he realized the full effect of his unwelcome presence.

Forcing herself to maintain the same outward imperturbability, Leonore proceeded to breakfast silently, and Julie was equally absorbed. Master Charley had habitually sat at their table when Edward did not monopolize the fourth sea*, and Mrs. Venard this morning joined them, though rather late.

"I don't li.e this vacant chair to repro ch me for the advice I gave you to banish its lawful, if sometimes lawless, occupant, so I will fill it myself. Do you already begin to feel forsaken?"

Leonore made an effort to reply in her usual tone; but it was a said failure, and Mrs. Venard noticed it.

"You have taken cold upon that windy gallery, Leonore. You are hoarse, and looking far from well."

She was spared an evasion by an exclamation of Master Charley, who with his customary interest was inventorying the new arrivals. Suddenly his eyes had flashed, and touching Julie's hand to attract her attention, he said with precocious jealousy,

"There sits that fellow we met on the beach the other day! I wonder what he's here for. He is just horrid, with his eternal grin."

Mrs. Venard cast a reproving glance upon him, as she said,

"Hush, my son, you will be overheard. Haven't you been taught never to make remarks upon people in their presence?"

"I don't care if he does hear me. He's a jackanapes," was the rather unfilial reply, but in a lower tone. Mrs. Venard glanced at the gentleman thus apostrophized, and so chanced to meet a most peculiar look bent upon herself. It ceased directly that she so encountered it, but it left an indelible impression, one of those thrills of antagonism which very sensitive people often experience when brought in contact with those who are mentally repulsive to them, though even unknown; and heedless of her recent reproof to Charley she exclaimed involuntarily,

"What a disagreeable man!"

"So you don't think he's so mighty handsome, ma?" Charley suggested.

"Oh, yes, he certainly would be called handsome, by many. Who is he?"

Julie bent a telegraphic glance upon the boy, who too magnani-

tious to reply when he knew she desired him to be silent, hung his
head, while she herself said carelessly,

"He is a Mr. Horton whom I met in the North some time ago. If
Charley knew how little interest I feel in his presence here, he
wouldn't be jealous, as he evidently is."

"And why not, when he kissed your hand, and jabbered all the
time in French so I couldn't understand a word. I don't believe any
man would stand that peaceably."

"Oh, you ridiculous boy!" exclaimed his mother laughing. "Miss
Julie will regret all her condescension toward you if you make such
a return for it as this. It is bad enough when grown-up boys turn
tyrant in response to over appreciation, but worse in small ones.
Recollect people are tolerated only during good behavior."

"I shall discard Master Charley from this hour," said Julie laying down her napkin and gravely rising to go.

The subject of this conversation had meantime departed, much
to Leonore's relief. Glad as she was that Mrs. Venard's attention
had b en directed from herself, it was scarcely better that she was
troubled upon Julie's account, seeing, as she had, that there was
more beneath this chance encounter than met the eye. Faithful to
the instinct of boyhood, Charley had laid a train that he could not
render harmless, and there was so much real displeasure in Julie's
mind against him, that he passed but a sorry day amidst ineffectual
repentance and unabated jealousy.

Leonore followed Julie to their private parlor, an l effectually
bolting out intruders, seized her impetuously by the arm and drew
her to a seat beside her, as she exclaimed abruptly,

"Julie, do, you must, give me your confidence. What is that
wretch to you?"

"How do you know he is a wretch? What do you know of him?"
she asked in surprise.

"Don't question me, Julie, unless indeed you will give me confidence for confidence. Will you do this?"

She shook her head. "It is useless, dear Leonore. All I could
tell you would be powerless to change what is inevitable."

"O , Julie, have I then so entirely failed to win your affection?
If I have so failed, Heaven forgive me, since it was only because I
felt that I had no right to receive it. I will win that right by any
self-humiliation, if through it I can serve and save you."

Julie kissed her very gently as she replied,

"I do love you, dear Leonore. Of this be assured. But you cannot 'serve or save' me. No one can do that. I never knew, before, what it was to wish for any one's death! God forgive me!"

"Then you do not love h'm, Juli·. Thank Heaven for that. Do you know who he really and truly is?"

"Yes. Do you?"

"Too well, too well! How fortuna'e Lisle had gone before he c·me here!"

"He has been near here day after day, Leonore, and you may be su:e he had by some means apprised himself of Lisle departure, before he so boldly appeared. I did not tell him of it, you may rest assured. Why should I?"

"Oh, Julie, ha! we only been the sist·rs we should have been all this time! How could I know that I might aid you, when I so little thought you interested in him! Why does he pursue you if you care nothing for him? Why do you submit to be persecuted by his presence, since it must be you alone who have attracted him here?"

"Ask me nothing, Leonore. I cannot explain."

"You are not already married to him? Tell me, in pity, that you are not."

"No indeed. Don't excite yourself, Leonore. What is all this to you?"

"So much that I would give my life to know it. Oh, Julie, now indeed do I regret the conscientious scruples that prevented me long since from winning your love and confidence! You cannot understand why I have ever restrained my own affection for you; but let me tell you that my own life was so cold and dark and unlovely, cave for the brightness Lisle sheds upon it, that my future is so unassured, so involved in possible misfortune if not shame and sorrow, that I dared not inflict upon you the possible suffering our close affection might entail. The day may come when Lisle will reproach me for accepting his proffered love, for presuming to link my destiny with his. If such an hour should come, enough that he should upbraid me upon *his own* account, without accusing me of dealing dishonorably and selfishly with you, whom he loves as an own sister!"

And this was the woman whom Julie had pronounced destitute of heart or impulse! She reproached herself with the memory of the words, and answered earnestly, ·

"Could I but have read your generous heart! How could I know that you needed my sisterly love and sympathy? you ·o calm and proud, evidently so happy. I was but a guest in the house of which

you were mistress, but a ward of him who is *your husband*. I think
I should never have presumed to kiss you, had not a joyful surprise
impelled me. Do you remember the time?"

"Perfectly! Now let me tell you, Julie; calm and proud as you
think me, I am neither. Happy I am, despite the most dire forebodings that ever tortured mortal. But of the house of which I am
the acknowledged mistress, I feel less real proprietorship than any
being in it. Were Lisle to bid me leave it to-morrow, without a
penny, I should go feeling that I had no right to complain. In
short, nothing is mine save on sufferance!"

"You will tell me next that Lisle himself is not your husband,"
Julie interposed stopping her lips with one hand.

"No, not that, thank God! He *is* mine, by every tie human and
divine. But what would even this avail me were his love to cease?"
She stopped by an effort, and then resumed in a changed tone.
"But don't let us talk of myself. It is of you and you alone I want
to think now. Tell me where you met that man!"

"Leonard Horton, for so he called himself, was introduced to me
the summer I was at Niagara with the Sandfords. I need not tell
you that had I at first known who he really was, I never would have
received him as an acquaintance. But I did not. He was well received in other circles, Mrs. Sandford approved of his attentions, he
certainly was agreeable, and we became very intimate. He told me
the truth, afterward, and certainly there is much to mitigate the
enormity of his crime, even had he not since made a restitution
quite Quixotic in its generosity."

"Which he well knew would cost him nothing, as Lisle never
would have received it, even had not the amount been willed him
by Mr. Fitzjames. It was returned to him through the same mysterious channel by which it was received, so that he has won his laurels cheaply."

"Nevertheless, he made the reparation in good faith, and I exon-
erate him."

"Who knows even how he obtained that money? I have known
him to steal--I believe he would murder!"

"Leonore! You so good and gentle; how can you say such
things? He is nothing to you; you might be generous, or at least
just, toward him."

"I tell you, Julie, he is an adder who should be crushed; a villain
unwhipped of justice, but who will assuredly yet come to retribution.
Years ago I knew him well, better than you know him now, and I
tell you I hate him with all the strength of my soul!"

"See, then, how prejudiced a judge you must be. Do you consider, too, that what one person thinks a positive crime, is to another only a venial error?"

Leonore groaned aloud as she realized how futile were her efforts. As yet Julie had not acknowledged her engagement. How could she account for her own knowledge of its existence without exciting suspicions which even now might be uselessly aroused in Julie's mind against her. Louis' threats rang in her ears menacingly. Suppose, too, she were but to sacrifice herself, and accomplish nothing; since Julie's generosity seemed wide enough to cover all things. Despite her efforts, bordering even upon imprudence toward herself, she had gained at best but a divided confidence, since Julie did not even confess those interviews in the summer-house. There remained but one appeal, and she staked her hope upon it.

"And poor Edward—what of him?"

Her lips trembled but made no reply, and Leonore continued,

"You will not sacrifice him, however you may throw away your own chances of happiness. What will he say if you ever become the wife of Louis Hartley? What must he think of one who would voluntarily sacrifice him to one so every way his inferior. You cannot, Julie, you will not."

"Suppose I had promised, long since—before Edward was anything to me or I to him. Can I be false to a vow voluntarily given?"

"Will you be false to your word, or to your heart? How would Hartley himself receive your marriage vows at such a price?"

The words raised the first dawn of hope. If indeed he were to break the engagement himself when he knew all! She had changed, she loved him no more. She had sworn to him that she would abide by her promise to him; but if he flung it back upon her inconstant heart, she at least was guiltless of perjuring herself to the *letter* of her vow, and certainly nothing more remained.

Leonore saw that her thoughts were running in the channel she so much desired, and did not interrupt them by a word. Julie herself broke the silence with a sarcastic little laugh.

"Things have come to a sad pass when right and wrong are so confused that one can't decide which *is* the right! I suppose I may console myself, that, if there be any truth in Lisle's preaching, *as a woman*, I haven't to sustain any great reputation for either constancy, honesty, or conscience! You don't know, Leonore, how I have always despised those silly, capricious women who never know their own minds two hours in succession; and now to become one of them!"

"I have known people to break their hearts for a principle; but I have yet to learn that the sacrifice proved to their lasting happiness when at best the principle was quest onable. I think that if one is true to one's ownself, one can hardly be false to any real principle worthy the name. When the list of so called 'martyrs' comes to be read over in the grand summing up, many a one will be found to have been only a bigot or a fanatic."

Julie was not in a vein to appreciate philosophy in the abstract, and she broke in upon it with an abrupt query,

"But, suppose, after all, Louis should hold me to my word?"

"He is quite capable of doing so should he be influenced by pique. It only remains for you then to sacrifice a principle of action to a real moral right; for what shall be said in judgment upon a woman who marries without affection, who makes a solemn vow to love, honor, and cherish, where she does not even respect! Rather than see you fall so low as this, I will make *any* sacrifice, even of myself. I will trust everything to your honor, Julie, everything."

Julie answered the earnest appeal with a sisterly caress.

"Let us talk no more of it, dear Leonore. Shakespeare tells of 'keeping the word of promise to the ear, and breaking it to the hope.' I cannot believe that any one would deliberately choose to be so dealt with by another, and I will hope for the best. The most immediate perplexity is how to receive Louis, since he is really here and certainly will seek to renew old acquaintance. I do not ask you anything of your acquaintance with him, except, was it such that you can again meet him without pain?"

"Certainly. I dislike him, but there is no reason why I should shun him. He will assuredly assume the right to visit you, and I have no authority to forbid him."

Later in the day the expected card was received, and Julie descended formally to the parlor. He awaited her, hat in hand, as though anticipating a summons to the private parlor, and when he realized that it was not accorded to him, he said with sarcastic humor,

"I am very happy to be so confidentially received, Miss Julie. I felt assured of a warm welcome, as indeed why not?"

"I regret that you are dissatisfied with your reception. It would, perhaps, have been better to have remained away until you were invited to come."

"That remark is very like you—of late. Thank you."

"Louis, if you really desire a quarrel, I will oblige you. Why do you ceaselessly reproach me without reflecting that you are in the wrong? Why do you meet me with taunts in place of kindness? why do you ceaselessly disobey my known wishes, an I insist upon forcing yourself upon me when I do not choose to receive you? There was a time when you were gentle, kind, and lovable, and then you were always welcome."

"I can hardly recal such a time. It was long ago."

"Have I not met you day after day despite my fear of our meetings being observed and commented upon?"

"I remember you did seem overjoyed the first time I joined you on the beach," he said bitterly.

"I admit that I was not. The surprise was even painful, from attendant circumstances, as well it might be. But this is the first time I ever heard that the way to woman's love and confidence was by ceaseless fault-finding and reproach."

"Admitted; what then? Is a man to endure all things in silence? Do you pretend to tell me that you are unchanged since we parted one year ago at Niagara?"

"No. I confess that I am changed. Does it follow that upbraiding will accomplish anything."

"Oh, Julie, I told you this would follow our separation! Why were we not married when you loved me, or professed to do so."

"Because we had not my guardian's consent, and for one certain reason could not expect it then."

"And now? What can I do that I have not already done?"

"Nothing, as far as he is concerned. The responsibility now lies with me. I have not told you that I will not fulfill my promise to you at the time I named. I meant to do so when I told you I would, and my heart was with my words. But tell me, Louis, how did you think to keep my affection for you bright and warm during the long months of unbroken silence you observed toward me in pique for my failure to keep the last appointment I named in the summer-house, and which you told me recently you believed I intentionally broke? You could have written me one word had you so chosen; I expected this, and should have replied."

"Yet you consoled yourself very happily for my neglect. The new love sped all the faster for the lack of interruption from the old."

"Yes, you *dared* to place a spy upon my actions, maintained with that spy a correspondence you did not attempt with me. It was through this Joseph Perkins that you learned of my very presence here, where you suddenly met me with recriminations, and where you remain despite my protests and the constant embarrassments you subject me to. What do you expect to gain by remaining?"

" The charm of your society, fair Julie, if not that of the most amiable Mrs. Sterling, who may possible aid me in my suit."

" You need not think it. She is the Leonore Wakefield whom you once knew, and she has not forgotten you."

" Did she tell you so?"

"Yes, and much more."

" I am not afraid of anything she can tell, and that it was very little your manner convinces me. Julie, of what use is all this sparring?"

He took her hand as she spoke more kindly, but she withdrew it with a darted glance around the parlor, which chanced to be quite deserted at the moment, the little party who had occupied it having gone out upon the gallery, unobserved by her.

Louis re-ented the action, and murmured bitterly,

" So. Not even your hand, pledged to me as it is. Banished from your society, forbidden even such favors as you would extend to your indifferent acquaintances, you bid me be satisfied and content! Julie, you forget that I am mortal and that I love you!"

"You proved it by employing a spy to watch me."

" You will insist upon this, Julie?"

"I insist because I know it. I knew Joseph was watching me, ceaselessly, and I was foolish enough to think it from idle curiosity. till your intimate knowledge of my movements taught me better, I never will forgive it, never! It was adding insult to neglect."

He saw that he should gain nothing by discussing the subject and he said with paitent resignation,

" Assume what you will, since you delight in being unjust to me. Only tell me what you wish, and see if I can accomplish it."

" I want but one thing ; to be released from our engagement. I cannot ratify it, I have no moral right to do so. Release me and I will be grateful to you forever."

" Julie, has it indeed come to this? You no longer love me!"

She looked her affirmation of the doubt, and for awhile both were silent. Then he said gently,

" Is it that you merely love me no more, or has another taken my place in your heart?"

" What does it matter, since I do not wish to marry you? I am here not to be questioned, but to ask one last favor, the greatest you can grant me. Give me back my freedom, and I will be your friend forever."

" Edward Sterling is very gallant and hand-ome. I prophesied that his suit would not be in vain. But Julie, I will not resign my claim, to any living being. I cannot do it. It is too much to ask !"

She started and her face flushed angrily as she asked,

" You *will not ?*"

" Yes if you insist upon the repetition; I never will release you from your vow, and you dare not break it."

" Do not be too sure of that. I may deem it the lesser wrong of two."

" Never, Julie. You are capricious and fickle, like all your sex. But you will not break a solemn pledge given to one who trusts you implicitly, who believes in your honor if he doubts your love."

It was a direct appeal to the creed that governed her, an echo of the argument ceaselessly urged by conscience, and she was silent under it. Was it not enough that she should be false at heart, without adding real perjury. His words had their effect even while she resented the tyranny that prompted them ; and at last she replied coldly,

" You know that your appeal to my honor and truthfulness is enough. You may thus compel me to fulfill my promise so far as the strict letter of it is concerned, but I tell you its spirit is dead. I can neither love nor respect you as a wife should do, and I leave you to imagine what our home will be without this. If you will be a jailor for life, go learn a turnkey's duties. There is ample time for you to perfect yourself in them, as six months of comparative freedom yet remain to me."

" Be as bitter as you choose, Julie. I endure it now, satisfied that some day you will beg me for pardon. It is not in a spirit of tyranny that I claim the fulfillment of your vow, since I am sure that you *will* love me again as you did when you made it. As your husband I will distance all rivals, even Edward himself. How many wives have you known, indifferent upon their marriage day to the husbands they accepted, yet learning after to idolize them? That is a tale which repeats itself week after week, and year after year."

" I congratulate you upon the self-improvement you must meditate."

" You are pleased to be ironical. Very well, if you were to tell me that you hate me, as I have little doubt you do at times, my resolution would remain the same. You have told me that nothing should prevent our marriage, and I repeat it; nothing shall."

" Very well. But since you so firmly announce your resolution, hear mine. During this half year that yet remains to me, I will not be persecuted by you. You shall leave me to seek happiness in any way I may choose, cease to annoy me by attentions that are disagreeable to me, and above all, our engagement shall remain a profound secret. I will not be tortured by arguments and remonstrances from my best friends which I am powerless to answer or yield to."

"To so much I consent. I will not press my attentions upon you in public, I will assert no claim upon you. But I will not go away from you and leave Edward Sterling to fill my place, however much you desire it. I shall remain as near you as possible, I will know all that interests you, though I will be silent unless you force me to protest. But remember I will endure no flirtations!"

"I never flirted in my life!"

"Well, I admit that where real love exists flirtation does not. I will amend my protest, and avow that I will submit to no lovemaking."

"Ugh! What a detestable wretch!" she exclaimed with a shrug of her pretty shoulders, and a contemptuous look."

Louis laughed. "You are quite bewitching when you are angry, Julie. Blondes are apt to look insipid. For that very reason one of them in a real storm is irresistibly fascinating, from the contrast. Now, since we quite understand each o her, let us chat a little. Who have you here entertaining, beautiful, or witty? Any pretty girls?"

"There are no Miss Phebe Venards, as at Niagara. Heiresses and captivating young authoresses are not met every day."

"By the way, are the Venards stopping here any relatives of hers?"

"The lady whom you saw at breakfast with us is her sister-in-law."

"So I suspected. She looks strong-minded, though decidedly stylish."

"How glad she would be, did she know you so approve her!"

"Oh, I will tell her of it. Never fear. Of course you'll present me?"

"If she so request. Really, 'Mr. Leonard Horton,' you are a most modest and unassuming gentleman, and beyond doubt very agreeable. But you must excuse me for pleading other engagements, as a bar to an extended visit with you, and allow me to wish you a very good morning," and with a mock reverential courtesy, she left him.

Once in the privacy of her own room, her courage and defiance vanished, and sinking upon the sofa she gave way to a girlish fit of weeping. She reproached herself for her weakness in withholding all from Edward, while she had permitted him day by day to win his place more securely in a heart dedicated to another. Had she only confessed all upon that day when she felt the impulse to do so and was too weak to obey it! How weak and wicked she had been, and what a bitter penalty she was to pay for it. Her punishwas greater than she deserved, but she bore it bravely. Leonore turned her eager eyes upon her in vain. She eluded their questioning gaze, and, too delicate to ask what was withheld from her, Leonore remained in ignorance of that ratification of the compact which she knew had become hateful, and believed had been broken. Everything seemed to confirm this belief. Louis Hartley still remained, it was true; but his intercourse with Julie was confined within the bounds of the most formal politeness, while her deportment toward him was one of complete indifference, bordering at times upon actual discourtesy when some little attention more marked than ordinary, was offered by him.

A casual introduction, scarcely to be avoided, had placed him upon speaking terms with Leonore, who till then had not once recogniz d him, but she did not present him to her immediate circle, although bantered to do so by some of the younger ladies who were attracted by his handsome face and figure, and his courtly manners. Mrs. Venard had not ceased to observe him critically, and, entrapped into the presentation despite her resolution to the contrary, Julie had introduced them. A sudden memory had flashed across the lady's mind as she acknowledged his salute, and she said abruptly,

"'Horton.' That is the name of Phebe's husband; don't you remember, Miss Julie?"

"I never heard it. I knew merely that she was married. Perhaps Mr. Horton himself may enlighten us. I remember he was one of Miss Venard's favorites last year, at Niagara."

He bowed profoundly, as he smilingly replied,

"I am one of a numerous though not illustrious family, and it is not impossible that some relative may have received the honor to which I dared not aspire. I should be happy indeed to know it, for I admired Miss Phebe, vastly."

The intended taunt was powerless now; it was a matter of utter indifference to Julie whom he admired in the past and present, and her look expressed it. Bowing his adieu, Louis joined Leonore at the piano where she was about to play in obedience to the usual request. She was thinking of him, even as he approached her, wondering if he would remain and meet Lisle upon his arrival the next

day. As Louis bent over her to arrange her music on the piano
rack, she said quickly and low,

"Lisle will be here to-morrow evening."

"I congratulate you. I have no doubt you are a most affectionate pair."

"Go away, for mercy's sake, go away. He hates, as I detest you."

"You are cruel, fair Leonore; or is this indeed a proof of some
interest in my welfare?"

She struck the opening chords of the music as the sarcastic question fell upon her ear, and her calm face betrayed no evidence of
one spoken word. Louis said softly, again bending near,

"You are wrong to spurn me as you do. It were much better we
should be friends. You cannot afford to quarrel with me, Leonore!"

"I cannot endure your presence. Anything rather than that."

"Well, I shall relieve you of it to-morrow, since you ask me to go.
But I shall return, and I prophesy we shall yet become friends.
Lisle and I seem bound to alternate, 'two buckets in a well.' I to-
day, him to-morrow."

Some covert sarcasm lurked beneath his words, for they stung
her through all her armor of pride, and she bit her lip so sharply
and suddenly, that a red moisture filled the wound her teeth had
made.

Louis saw it, and he said with half ironical pity,

"Ah, foolish bird, that wounds itself with every flutter! Why
will it beat its powerless wings against the hand whose caress it
once suffered, and which at any hour could crush it."

"In Heaven's name what do you want of me?" she asked impetuously, while she mechanically played on.

"I will tell you when I return. Lisle will not remain longer
than usual, will he? When will he leave you?"

"By Monday's steamer."

Not another word passed between them till the music ceased, and
then he politely brought her a chair, and left her with her friends.
She looked after him as he walked carelessly down the room. A
strange throbbing moved her heart. It was a singular effect of his
presence, that rebellious as she was against his power over her,
defiantly as she commenced each conversation with him, he quieted
and subdued her at last, and bent her to his will as he would have
bent a pliant reed in his white hand. Menacing, insulting as he
was, his gentler tones awoke strange echoes in her heart, and she
felt that she was less conquered than yielding. In her most bitter
moments she would have dared even the ruin with which he

threatened her, and she scorned the idea of owing anything to his generosity. Out of the mesmeric power of his presence this was her ruling instinct. Yet when with him, this generosity was not hateful to her, and she supplicated for it.

_____.

CHAPTER XXIX.

LISLE and Edward came together by the next day's boat, and the quiet Sabbath succeeding was one of unmixed happiness to Lisle and Leonore, who met more like lovers than like a married pair who had sedately walked the path of life together for a whole year.

"Have you missed me very much, little fellow?" Lisle asked smoothing her hair with a touch more affectionate than artistic.

She looked up with an assuring smile despite her retort.

"Cruel boy, to ask such a question after having deserted me! Have you missed _me_? and how are they all at home?"

"Wonderfully, and wonderfully well; to answer both your questions in one breath. Selim sent you a respectful whinny of regard, and the Infant, 'which likewise is well, begged to be remembered,' if I may presume to imitate her own phraseology. The virtuous Joseph is petitioning me to receive him back into our service. You'll be glad to know his affection is thus unaltered."

"If he ' _is petitioning_,' I conclude you haven't yet yielded."

"I told him I would leave you to decide; at which his elation was evident. It isn't every man who relies upon a feminine to such an extent as he does in you. Truth to confess, the Infant came at me first with her woman's weapons of tears and protests. 'He is her husband, it is her duty to follow him, she borrows trouble about him,' and all that. Why is it that however wretched a man and his wife may be together, they are more miserably wretched under a separation?"

"Don't ask me. Haven't you been a victim to matrimony as long as I have? What did you learn of Bill and Melissa?"

"More than enough. They are quite worrying the old dame's life out. Bill is more than suspected of knowing too much about certain missing portable property belonging to various citizens, and Joseph spends too much time in the charming society of his step-daughter, to please either the Infant or the marital stepson-in-law—a double and twisted relationship that, but it's one of Joseph's own inventing. You see why poor Mrs. Perkins wants him back under surveillance."

" You won't take him back, Lisle?"

"Yes, I think so, as your especial *valet de place.* You see one is morally responsible for the vagabonds one makes, and as no one else will have him around, I must."

" Lisle, I will not have him back again."

" Oh, indeed, if it comes to that—"

" It has come to that. I never was more in earnest."

It was an unprecedented assertion of her will, and he yielded to it at once.

" I'll crush his hopes the instant I return. I will tell him you have ceased to protect him, and that I am to obey your commands or leave the premises."

She did not so much as smile, and seeing that the topic was distasteful to her, he abruptly changed it.

" Have your fine lady friends forgiven my apostrophe to the sex?"

" I don't know ; I fancy not. It seems to me some of them are censelessly on the watch to discover the secret sins in my character which have so embittered my husband."

" What a guilty conscience you must have, Leonore. Fie, for shame ! However, if you are convinced that this is anything more than imaginary, let them work away."

" I don't fancy it, I assure you ! It isn't pleasant to be considered a persecutor of one's husband."

" Nonsense. If they ever realize their hopes they will all have husbands of their own, and then they'll know that *all* wives are persecutors. I don't want you annoyed, but if they make this an unpleasant abiding place, perhaps you will come back home. I couldn't live here all summer to save my life."

" I've a mind to tell you what Mrs. Bertram said of your chronic restlessness when she found you had really left us."

" Tell it of course. I've quite a respect for that lady's opinions, irreverent as they sometimes are towards those who demand reverence."

" She said, ' if Lisle Sterling had been the scriptural Prodigal Son, it would have been a useless job to kill that fatted calf, for he would have changed his mind and run away again before it could be dished up.' "

" Very likely. I never liked veal, at best. But how long can you content yourself here ?"

" As long as Julie so much enjoys remaining. The close, dull city is no place for her during these stifling months." · .

" I can imagine something how the parents of grown-up daughters

feel, compelled to suffer all sorts of inconveniences till some inexperienced fellow can be entrapped into marrying Eliza Jane who
squints, or Sarah Ann who has a pug nose! Since the day 'tender-
eyed Leah's' governor schemed to get her off his hands, fathers
have diligently practised the same trade, and mothers model their
tactics after those of an old hen, who is forever pecking her half-
grown chickens on the head, to drive them off."

"Oh, Lisle, that's a slander!"

"I wish I thought so; but I tell you this world contains more
'Becky Sharps' than pretty women ever dream of. Of course the
pretty ones never become a drug even in the matrimonial market;
but the ugly ones, whether or *not* they have mothers to help them
off, are like poor 'Becky' who so complained, 'compelled to
scheme for themselves.' As for Julie, she can't do better than to
marry Ed, for whom half the young ladies are doing their prettiest,
and it is strange she doesn't realize it. By the way, she is looking
melancholy. What ails her?"

"Imagination again, Lisle. She is as blithe and merry as possible. She is the life of the drawing-room, and universally popular."

"I suppose, then, she has only formed a sentimental attachment
for some one. This so-called 'love happiness' always seems to me a
most sorry and lugubrious sort. Love is a disease, Leonore."

"Most sage conclusion, and consoling for a wife to hear from her
husband's lips. I should judge the very announcement would prove
a panacea," she replied, a little hurt.

He laughed as he reassured her.

"Oh, I don't mean the tender regard a husband has for his wife,
which leads him to pay her shoe bills without grumbling, and
chivalrously to conceal the fact that half her back hair and several
of her teeth are false, and to love and cherish her through all these
infirmities. I mean the grand heroic sentimental idiosyncrasy, which
prompts one man to worship at the slippers of another man's wife to
the prejudice of his own, or is even more liable to attack the very
young of both sexes. It is the last of a line of ailments of which
measles and chicken-pox are the predecessors."

Few women approve of treating the subject in such irreverent
fashion, and Leonore's serious reception of it proved her no exception to the general rule; and feeling that his philosophy was unap-
preciated, Lisle put himself upon his best behavior for the remainder of the day, though laughingly protesting that it was hard when
a man's own wife couldn't follow the highest flights of his genius
and fancy. They were left quite to themselves as if by mutual con-

sent, even Edward and Julie leaving them undisturbed, and whiling away the day as best they might. At sunset *they* wandered out upon the beach together, and silently watched the fadinu out of the last rose colored and purple reflections from the water which lay unrippled as far as the eye could reach.

Despite the reign of peace and harmony around them, neither face reflected the light of happiness, and the sigh breathed by Julie, was responded to only by a sudden and vigorous launching far out upon the water, of the bright pebble Edward had been carelessly tossing and catching as they strolled along. The action seemed to have re-awakened his power of speech, for he said a little impatiently,

"I must confess that I can't understand the fine points to which you attach such importance. You confess what your manner long since led me to believe. Yet in the same breath that you make the sweet admission, you bid me hope no more, tell me that even this must cease. I will apply for canonization, as a martyr to feminine caprice."

"It is not caprice, Edward. I have told you that I am engaged to another. I have been frank and truthful with you now, as I ought to have been long since."

" And I repeat that were you twenty times engaged, I would not lose hope nor cease to love you. You cannot forbid this, and I don't see why you should protest. You cannot love us both, and I believe every word you ever uttered to me."

"Oh, Edward, I tell you the blessed truth. I love you unto death! Yet the fact remains that I am bound to the fulfillment of a promise from which I have vainly sought a release. Nothing but death can free me; of that I feel assured."

" I'd pray for a second flood if I thought it would sweep him out of existence. But it wouldn't, Julie. The children of this nine-teenth century would ogtwit the deluge itself, and every one be saved—very likely patent the invention, after."

She smiled despite her seriousness, but he was grave and even contemptuous. ' The Fitzjames spirit ' in which his mother had de-lighted, was uppermost, and he was in no humor to kiss the rod.

" Who is this all conqueror, Julie? You haven't told me that. Since I know so much, tell me all."

She hesitated, and then asked, flushing under the evasion,

" Do you remember a gentleman whom you met at Niagara last summer, a Mr. Horton, to whom you were introduced ?"

" I thought so then! It was plain to me that he was your favored lover, but I fancied distance and absence had lent forgetfulness."

"Edward, I must be truthful with you. I am going to tell you something more, if you assure me that you will keep my confidence sacredly."

"Well, I promise you. I have a holy shrinking from all things resembling duty."

"This Mr. Horton is the Louis Hartley of whom you have heard so much."

He raised his eyebrows and gave a little whistle of consternation.

"You are surprised, and very naturally," she said quietly.

"No, not surprised at anything connected with a love affair. The evil one himself has his admirers, and were he dressed in broad-cloth, would be a most successful gallant, I've no doubt."

"Perhaps so," replied she with patient resignation.

"Horton, or Hartley, he is a very handsome gentleman, and beauty goes far towards gaining favor in this world. I make no comments upon his *alias*, as I suppose we both know his reason for assuming it. I always believed him an unmitigated rascal; but he must have redeeming virtues of which I know nothing, or you never would have loved him.

She slipped her hand into his and softly thanked him for all reply. He bent a long look upon her of blended curiosity, quizzical-ness and doubt, then he said dispassionately,

"I wonder how much of your verdict and acquittal were based upon a dispassionate analysis of his character as revealed to you, and how much is due to sweet words and a pleasing exterior. His influence over you must be strong, or the sentiments you hear expressed of him so continually, would awaken real doubts in your mind, and they do not seem to have done so. What has kept you faithful to him during this whole year of adverse influences?"

"'Faithful' is a word most undeserved. But in so far as I am not quite faithless, I reply in one word, Conscience."

"Well it is the first time I ever heard of a young lady's loving with 'conscience.' Give him that as long as you choose, Julie. Only leave me the heart, and I will take the chances of winning over the head. I expected, little Julie, that you would be wooed and won a score of times before you would dream of the mischievous boy who had hung your doll-babies, and practised amateur surgery upon your pets in bygone years. I know now, that I loved you even then, and I can't remember the day when the hope of making you my wife was not ever present."

"Oh, Edward, Edward! I am as wretched as I can live!"

"Two lovers always make a woman wretched! Tell the other to leave."

"I have, and he won't go. But I'll worry his life out if I marry him!"

"Do, and I'll marry his widow. Seriously, Julie, do you think it less than a positive sin to marry in this way? I ask you most unselfishly."

"It is a worse sin to break a promise given as solemnly as mine was. It would be very easy to reap the reward of my own fickleness, and cry out that all else is wrong! I can't do that, Edward."

He hesitated to ask the next question, but after a pause did so.

"Julie, is any time named for your marriage?"

"Yes, in December. I promised that, six months ago."

"I cannot remain to see it. I shall visit my old home then, where I ought to have gone this summer, but could not. Father writes that mother will hardly live till another spring, and is constantly begging that I will go back to her. I believe I am the only one of all her children whom she really loves, and I ought to go if it will give her any happiness. Meantime, Julie, let us go on as we have done. If I am to give you up at last, there is no need to hasten the hour of sacrifice. We are happy together, why should I be banished?"

"You shall not be. If you are content, I am a thousand times so."

"Then let us not so much as allude to your engagement. We shall not be likely to forget its existence, but I don't want to hear it mentioned. I have your love, if I am not to possess yourself; and I would rather have it without yourself, than to marry you without having that. I candidly think, little Julie, that if a man is throughly convince that he possesses, entirely, a good woman's love, he may be content without asking one boon beyond."

"I can't be so philosophical. It is dreadful to be completely wrapped up in one and to belong to another!"

She shivered as she spoke the words.

"Do you suppose Lisle's consent can be won to this marriage, Julie?"

"No; it is useless to expect it, and he will be spared the trouble of refusing. I don't intend to consult him about it. It is simply insulting to ask one's advice when the solicitor doesn't intend to respect it."

The gathering darkness warned them in at last, but not till happier themes had banished the discomfort growing out of the confession she had at last summoned courage to make. Arm in arm they strolled back to the hotel, and from their happy faces no one would have dreamed of the scene that had passed. Even yet Edward did not resign the hope of years. While she was free, he would not, and she realized it joyfully. The few happy months that yet remained to them, were like a new lease of life; and that happy intoxication of heart and brain which is inseparable from an ardent and mutual affection, possessed them both. The door of Leonore's parlor stood hospitably open as the two passed by it upon their way along the hall, and she called them in.

"Come, Julie; add your persuasions to mine, and let us see if we can't keep our truants a day or two longer. Won't you be persuaded, Edward? Why need you hurry back?"

Julie bent her softly radiant eyes upon him, but he resisted their mute appeal.

"It is utterly impossible, pretty sister. Keep your husband if you will. He's of no use anywhere else; but I can't stay. I ought not to have left my patients for even this visit."

Leonore looked disappointed at the reply, but remonstrance was useless. Lisle had a complaint to make, and he advanced it.

"What do you think of a wife who utterly refuses to write to her lord during absence? Leonore outrightly refuses to do so, in punishment for my declining to remain and do penance here. I want you to put her upon a strict regime of bread and water, till she relents and consents to do her duty, Julie."

"Wouldn't bread and honey do as well?" Julie asked demurely.

Edward nodded his approval of the suggestion.

"There are scientific reasons for preferring the latter. You see, Lisle, that upon the sanitary condition of the stomach depends the nervous vigor and healthy condition of the mind, and—"

"Hold on there, doctor. That smacks decidedly of the days when you exercised your budding genius upon poor pussy and chanticleer. It is but one advance beyond 'circulation' and 'adipose tissue,' and not half as intelligible. Besides, I don't want a letter inspired from Leonore's stomach, and nervous paraphernalia. They are no doubt excellent articles to have about one; but as I have never yet had one letter from her, it should come from the heart, like all first love letters."

"I was educated to think the initiative belonged to the gentleman in matters pertaining to the tender passion. How many letters have you ever written to me?" Leonore said banteringly.

"I'll write you one this moment, if you promise to answer it Tuesday."

She shook her head, and with some display of pique he exclaimed, "I declare, Leonore, I never knew you had so much obstinacy." She bent her head upon his shoulder with a caressing gesture that softened him at once, and bending his cheek down upon it, he said,

"What a strange little puss it is. So good and gentle, yet so relentless! You will repent when I am gone, and the white-winged little messenger will come to tell me so." She did not reply, and he left, believing that her silence was a tacit consent.

Left once more to themselves, the ladies "took up the burden of life again," just where they had laid it down the preceding Saturday. Louis Hartley reappeared at the hotel punctually Monday morning, and his presence awoke the same longing wish in the hearts of both, to return to that peaceful home where he dared not intrude.

Julie knew herself the sole object of his persecution, and detested him accordingly. But Leonore wavered between two opinions, sometimes fancying that his sole wish was to annoy and harass herself, sometimes believing that he remained only in the hope of reinstating himself in Julie's favor, and only cared to make her of some service in attaining his object. As yet his attentions had not been sufficiently marked toward either, to arouse that spirit of gossip ever dominant in such an assemblage of idle people as thronged the hotel. But during this second week of Hartley's sojourn, it was whispered among the censorious that he was far too devoted to the beautiful Mrs. Sterling, who had refused to go back home with her husband despite his solicitations, and that her affectation of coldness towards her handsome admirer was only a veil to screen the flirtation, if indeed it were not something **more** serious.

With consummate tact, Hartley had managed to ingratiate himself with all sorts of people there present, and managing m amm is angled for him upon the mere strength of his own assumptions. Julie looked on while the manœuvers proceeded, fervently praying that he might be entrapped by some fair damsel, whom she would have blessed as her benefactress.

Little by little it began to be said that he was rather too fond of play; but brothers laughed to scorn their sisters' consternation, and mothers declared it a mere fashionable folly of which matrimony would cure him. Leonore heard these whispers of him, and they did not increase her pleasure at being the now unmistakable object of his attentions. Yet scheme as she would, she could not prevent them, his seeming complete unconsciousness of her coldness leaving her no choice between them and an open rupture, which she dared not make.

Julie was far from making any such concessions. She knew that he attached himself to Leonore for the sole purpose of being one of her own party and carrying out his threat of protesting should she accept too exclusive attentions from any other.

So the time passed on, cheered for Leonore only by the arrival of the promised letter from Lisle. It was in reality the first he had ever written her, and verified his assertion that as such it came from the heart.

Saturday came at last, and with it he returned, accompanied by several Benedicts. Mr. Venard and Mr. Bertram were among the number, and while Master Charley entertained his papa with boyish loquacity, Mr. Bertram smoked, and aired his heels upon the balcony railing, while his wife flitted and chattered around him as if resolved to extract something resembling conversation from the atmosphere around and above him, through which she now and then caught a glimpse of him.

" What upon earth ails you, Mattie !" he exclaimed at length between two voluminous puffs of cigar-smoke. " You are like a facebewitched fly, with your continual buzzing and setting at one ! One would think you hadn't had a chance to talk for a whole month."

" I haven't to you, and one likes to keep up appearances before people. Suppose I were to leave you out here all day ."

" Humph," was the appreciating rejoinder.

"Isn't it lonely at home, dear ? "she asked with one more affectionate effort, determined not to give way to the resentment that was rising.

" What for, pray ?" He asked the question in real surprise.

" Oh, you must be so utterly destitute of politeness there, judging from the small supply you brought with you," she retorted as she retreated and left him to himself. Truly Mrs. Bertram had not a polite or attentive husband ; but he let her have her own way, and most wives appreciate this as much as they would all the model virtues without it.

Leonore marvelled at the *sang froid* with which they made their adieux when the hour of parting arrived. As Lisle kissed her good-bye, he said gently,

" You don't owe me a letter unless you choose to think so ; but I need not tell you one would be as dear to me as mine could have been to you."

The appeal rung in her ears long after he had left her, and she wrung her hands impotently as she remembered it. "Oh, this hateful, hateful place! I cannot stay here another week!" she exclaimed as she dashed some rebellious tears away. She resolved to ask Mrs. Bertram to chaperone Julie, and to return home with Lisle upon his very next visit; and deriving some comf rt from the resolution, she bathed her eyes for the social review to which she might at any moment be subjected.

Quickly enough following this preparation, the expected rapping was heard at her door, and she opened it smilingly. A boating excursion was being planned for the evening, and a committee were taking the names of those who would form the party, that accommodations might be secured for all. Leonore accepted the invitation with the customary seeming appreciation that was but lip service to the world around her. This should be her last week of so unsatisfactory an existenc ; and strong in the thought, she took her place in the boat at the appointed hour and reached out her hand to Julie who was to follow. But that young lady waxed refractory when she saw that Louis' Hartley was Leonore's especial gallant, and quickly effecting the desired change, she delegated another to the place reserved for herself, and with a nod to Leonore sprang into another boat. In the boat immediately following, two young ladies were discussing her with that confidential interchange of opinion so common among ladies of a certain turn of mind.

"I declare," exclaimed Miss Sophie, "that Mrs. Sterling is too affected to be endurable! She is easily read despite the haughty airs she assumes, and she is as vain as possible. I don't see what that elegant Mr. Horton finds to admire in her."

"Yes, and to leave us to take up with su   as there is left here," and she looked around contemptuou   the collection of young brothers not yet out of their sisters' riding strings, and receiving many a 'snub' from those ladies while practising their juvenile gallantries toward others. The young lady resumed, "I wonder what her husband would say if he knew it. You heard what he said about wives being comforters to their husbands, that morning in her parlor, didn't you? He knows his own troubles, for all he plays devoted to her before people! Another thing, Josie, I've made a discovery that is significant. Do you notice that every time the husband appears upon the scene, a certain gentleman vanishes from it, and no sooner is the husband away than forthwith reappears the certain gentleman ?"

Miss Josie grasped her companion's hand.

" I believe that is really so ! Dear me, how scandalous; and she affecting to chaperone a young ward of her husband's. But she is pretty, to tell just the truth, and she sings splendidly !"

" 'Pretty !' Why she's as pale and cold as a snow-bank ! Just see her there where she is bending over the water. Of course she is quite unconscious that Mr. Horton hasn't taken his eyes off her since she cast herself into that forlorn attitude."

" Sophie, Sophie, lean over here. As sure as you live, Julie Kelley has heard every word we've been saying ! I thought she was going in the other boat. She doesn't look this way, but I know she heard, for her blue eyes are just snapping !"

" I don't care. If she don't like the comments her ladyship incurs let her give her a hint or two. She has the more sense of the two, and a lesson wont do Mrs. Sterling any hurt. When you see these wonderfully perfect women—look out for them !" and with this feminine philosophy Miss Sophie consented to drop the subject.

Quite unconscious of the observation she excited, Leonore retained her position till Mrs. Bertram roused her.

" Come, Leonore ; no dreaming here."

Raising her eyes, Mrs. Bertram saw that they were misty with unshed tears.

" Upon my word !" she exclaimed. " What is the matter ?"

" I am homesick and heartsick," she replied sadly.

" Then in mercy's name go home, and carry the sick heart to its keeper."

" I will if you will be kind enough to take Julie under your charge."

" With pleasure, most assuredly. So you really have a caprice to go home ?"

" It is mor▓▓▓▓▓▓▓rice. I am literally heartsick under this weary separatio▓▓▓▓▓my home and husband !"

Hartley raised his hat as he said with a covert sneer,

" Mrs. Sterling's husband is more fortunate than oth rs. I thought wives quite luxuriated under these separations. Perhaps, though, the flirtations in which they indulge during such tempting opportunities, are only by way of rendering endurance possible."

Leonore did not deign a reply, and Mrs. Bertram took up the gauntlet.

" Mrs. Sterling never did so undignified a thing as to flirt, in all her life. To be sure she has no temptation to do so, for her husband is more loverlike than any one else could be. But I'm far from thinking it singular that most married ladies are somewhat too fond of the nice little attentions and bewitching whisperings called flirtations, bidding farewell to the u, as they do, from the chosen one, from the hour they are married.

Her listeners smiled at her vivacious explanation; and really entertained with her, Hartley exerted himself to please her, knowing that if she should really be left as Julie's companion during Leonore's absence, it would serve his interests to gain her favor. So well did he succeed, that as the two ladies mounted the stairs together upon their return, Mrs. Bertram said, " Why didn't you tell me that Mr. Horton was so entertaining ! I fancied you didn't think him so."

" I don't like him at all, if you wish the truth."

" Why not ?"

" Because he is detestable to me," she replied emphatically.

" Well, that is an all-sufficient reason, I admit," Mrs. Bertram good-naturedly replied.

Julie entered soon after, out of spirits as was evident at a glance.

" What is the matter, Julie ?" Leonore asked in surpise.

" The matter is that I'm disgusted with this place and every one in it. Do let us leave it and go back home."

" With all my heart, little girl. I would have gone ere this had I known you wished it."

Julie struggled with some strong feeling, but directly asked abruptly,

" Leonore, what is Louis Hartley to you ?"

" Nothing but an object of dislike," was the calm reply.

" Has he fallen in love with you, Leonore ?"

" He cares less than nothing for me."

" Well, people are talking strange thi   er that may be. Why does he follow you like your very   d if you dislike him why don't you tell him to clear out ?"   d impulsively.

" Julie, you have heard something unpleasant. Tell me all, please." ·

" I will, for I don't believe in the rôle of silent friendship."

She told her what she had overheard, and then silently awaited her comment. Leonore's color went and came under the relation, but she did not once interrupt it. " I know," said Julie in conclusion, "that he don't thus play at hide and seek with Lisle upon your account, but mine. But I tell you, Leonore, I wish you would coax him to stay and get his head everlastingly broken, as he would were Lisle to catch him here. He won't gain anything with me by staying here, and if you don't like him, I don't see what there is to keep him any longer. He'd leave to-day if we did."

" You don't like him any better than you did when we came here?"

" Heaven forbid! Don't you see I won't suffer him near me? I forbade his attentions long since, and you ought to, if you will pardon my saying so. I don't presume to offer my advice, Leonore, but I do think him less than a gentleman however he is universally mistaken for one. He hates Lisle, and would gladly torture him by causing his wife to be maligned and slandered upon his account."

" It shall stop here, Julie. We will go back home next week."

CHAPTER XXX.

THE week passed, and with Saturday came Edward and Lisle. Leonore looked up with an apprehensive glance as Lisle crossed the threshold, for mingled with her joy at his presence, was the consciousness of her own delinquency. His letter had remained unanswered. Never before had she permitted his slightest wish to pass ungratified. What must he think of her present neglect.

" What's all this? What is wrong, little fellow?" Lisle asked wonderingly.

" Everything is wrong while we are separated. I cannot live away from you! I am homesick, heartsick and miserable. Only take me back home," she said appealingly.

" I dare not, Leonore. The city is one pest-hole of disease. People are all al▓▓▓▓▓▓d rushing away as rapidly as possible."

" Then stay ▓▓▓▓▓f you cannot or will not, I will go back and share the da▓▓▓h you."

He presssed her fondly to his breast, and kissed her again and again delightedly " Inconsistent little mortal," he said at last, " who will not so much as write me one little scrap, yet begs to risk her life for the sake of remaining with me!"

" Mine will be risked no more than yours, and I certainly shall die if you tell me stay away."

" I will do better, dear child, for I will stay with you."

" Will you? Will you really?" she queried earnestly.

" I really will. Why not? If you are tired of stopping here, we will go elsewhere. And Julie, how is she? Still in love with the place?"

"She is tired to death of it."

"So we go; the beloved of yesterday is the detested of to-day, and thank God for change! She isn't to know of the fever, though. If Ed is to have it he won't be a shade the less saffron-hued because her eyes are redder and her nasal organ more prominent with weeping."

"Why Lisle! How can you jest over such a possibility?"

"Only because if worst comes to worst it involves his taking a turn at his own perscriptions. Every doctor ought to come to that once or twice in his life, just to make him merciful. There are no such cravens in existence as a physician, or a clergyman, when in any real danger to life or limb. The trouble is, neither of them believes in his own theory, however he may pat it on the back in hours of security. Edward will vouch for that, as here he comes"

He had overheard the last words, and he nodded approval when thus appealed to.

Lisle turned to Julie, who, bright and radiant, had seated herself beside him.

"Well, Julie, make a report of what you and Leonore have been about during my absence."

"Enduring the malice of the 'dear five hundred friends' whose tongues you set wagging one unlucky morning."

"*Mirabile dictu!* As if they required to be *set* wagging, when they are never anything else!"

"Well, at least you gave them a new impetus and direction; else they never would have attacked Leonore, who is declared guilty of bringing your gray hairs in sorrow thus far toward the grave."

"Well, I admit that a husband who thus causes his wife to be accused, deserves to be sat upon by a coro̶▬▬▬▬est of old women, and condemned to eternal matrimony i▬▬▬▬▬orld with a red-headed feminine and a lap-dog!"

"I'm glad we are to go back home," Julie interrupted with enthusiasm. "If this is what people call going pleasure hunting, I'm sure there's a vast amount of hunting for very little game."

"Nothing of the sort, little sis!" Lisle replied tormentingly. "Two fashionable ladies creeping down the back staircases, and living in the area, lest their neighbors' servants should report them not out of town! I couldn't consent to it."

"I would protest if I believed you in earnest. Is he, Edward?"

"I believe so indeed. I heard him giving orders to good Mrs. Perkins which seemed to indicate that he was flitting for an indefinite time."

" And you, Sir Esculapius ?"

" There were no orders issued, but I shall jog on as usual, I suppose."

" Yes," said Lisle, " Ed has become too big a gun to bear transportation, and will charge around home—I wish I knew his benefactions would half equal the charge—and I've no doubt he'll slay his thousands !"

She looked her disappointment, and Lisle hastened to comfort her. " You are to be led to fresh fields and pastures new, Julie. If any one is devoted enough to follow you, let him come. Otherwise you shall practise your little arts upon an entirely new crop of beaux."

" Leonore wants to go home as much as I do. She would insist upon doing so, too, did she feel any sense of possessorship there, which she doesn't. Come, now, Edward, having thrown this bombshell into the enemy's camp, I'm ready to leave. Let us off to the beach."

" What does the child mean ?" Lisle asked when the two had left them. " I verily believe that she fancies, as I often do, that you think your reign in our house a sort of right upon sufferance. Do be assertive, tyrannical, anything to show that you fully believe in your own rights."

" Why, Lisle, I have none save what your love gives me !"

" And I tell you I protest against this view of it. Why can't you feel that all I have belongs to you in an equal degree! Why, Leonore, you *own me*, body and soul. Don't you know it ? You would, could you know all you are to me. How utterly dark and worthless was my life till you *grew into* it, revivifying and brightening it, and making it for the first time worth having."

" Ah, Lisle, that sounds like your old-time misanthropy !"

" 'Misanthrope well might it have been worse. I was born to a fate as undeserved as bitterly unjust, and I commenced to accomplish it before I was out of my cradle. In my youth I staggered under a burden that would have crushed a full-grown man, and I can remember when I shrank and cowered away from my mother's glance with a trembling awe that was terrible. What should I have become, if not misanthropical ? If such a man ever does learn to love and trust, that love and trust are terrible in their intensity, and she who wins them holds a fearful responsibility ! Why, Leonore, you would be frightened at your own power over me did you realize it ! Yet you shrink from all it gives you, cry out that your rights are based only on my love and generosity, and ceaselessly interpose between us a nameless barrier which I cannot break down. Oh, my little wife, you must feel toward me what I so entirely feel for you, that literal identification of thought and being, that makes us one and the very same. I have nothing in God's world but you!"

He clasped her to his heart with a gesture replete with the very agony of love, and for an instant her heart stood still under it. She was never mistress of herself when he spoke so earnestly, and half unconsciously she murmured, "miserable, guilty wretch that I am !"

"Why miserable ? Guilty of what ?" he demanded protesting'y.

"I tell you, Lisle, it is nothing but my own conscious unworthiness that creates this invisible barrier of which you compl.in. When I am most completely wrapped up in you, I least dare reveal it; and when most I realize your devotion to me, this same self-reproach cries out that I am all unworthy to receiv? it. Banish me, send me away from you at once and forever, and let me die, as I soon should. Then you will be avenged."

"Strange words. Banish you ? Not while life remains, were you as lost and guilty as I know you good and innocent."

"Innocent indeed, if so you could pronounce me! I never sinned against any other."

"Then be absolved for all imaginary sins. I forgive you all; only love me."

"That I do, God knows !" she exclaimed fervently, and then raising herself from his arms, she gazed at him most wistfully. "Suppose, Lisle, just *suppose*, that I had weakly deceived you, led you perhaps to make me your wife, in your confiding trust in me, and your utter ignorance of all I thus refrained from revealing to you while you had the undisputed right to my perfect truth and confidence. Had I thus made good my place in your heart and home, thus won the honors you delight to offer me, would you still say 'you are good and innocent, I forgive all ?' Tell me, Lisle, would you forgive *anything* that thus makes us one ?"

"Ah, Leonore, are the old shadows over you again ? I thought they were banished long ago ! I thought that in making you my wife I had forever dispelled them, as I would. But I answer you thus : If indeed you have done all this which you ask me to suppose, I say never convince me of it. Better to be happy even under a deception, than, in being undeceived, to see one's ideal shattered and peace forever wrecked ?"

"Lisle. Lisle ! I would give my life to make you happy !"

"Well, keep it and pass it with me. This is all I ask. Oh, if I could once weary of you, Leonore ! I am never satisfied with your presence, ever restless out of it! These weeks of separation have been an eternity of discontent and weariness. Let us seek out some quiet little nook of our own, where gossip and worldly vanity come not, and there have a little cottage of romantic aspect where for once the poet's dreams shall be realized. I will transform myself into a wreather of lilies and roses, and deck you with seaweeds, and perpetrate any absurdity supposed to be emblematic of the tender passion."

She smiled her reply, and chanted archly, "'Wreathed with bright seaweed, a mermaid I will be'—"

"And I the enchanted mortal attracted to destruction. Verily, a husband who thus follows into retirement a wife—his own, mind you; not some ones' else; that's different—in whose presence he is content to forget the world, is already under the spell of enchantment. Rehearse your sea-cave chants, fair mermaid; or, better yet, open your piano and sing to me in good sensible fashion."

She smiled compliance with the request; but before she had commenced, a rap was heard upon the door, and Lisle opened it while she kept her p'ace at the piano. Mrs. Venard came in, bearing an open letter from her husband, and her face was anxious and troubled.

"Tell me, Mr. Sterling, just how you left matters in the city."

"Bad enough, I can tell you. There's an exodus of the panic-stricken in all directions. However, Venard is safe. He is acclimated."

"Yes, so am I. I am going back home to-morrow, to do what good I can."

"Mrs. Venard!" exclaimed Leonore in alarm.

"Not in the least Quixotic. Did you ever think how many die in every epidemic without receiving one alleviating care? If I lessen the number of these even by one, it is better than idling here. Will you keep Charley with you, and so leave me quite at liberty?"

"Certainly, unless you will take me with you as your assistant."

"That I will not. Stay with your husband, for I shall have no time to nurse raw recruits, nor power to heal broken hearts should you make one by your imprudent zeal. Mrs. Bertram has orders to remain with you—marital injunctions which she will gladly obey, so you may have quite a merry party yet. I am glad you have formed the sensible conclusion to stay with your wife, Mr. Sterling. She has but a lonely time of it without you."

"Not to mention that gossip-mongers find her name attractive," he rejoined.

"Ah! I hoped she did not know that. You will some day conclude to profess some admiration for the sex, if only upon your wife's account. Unfortunately, people don't all know what a harmless cynic you are."

" I will reform, I promise you. Foolish people; do they imagine that when one really suffers the evils he pretends to lament, that they are thus proclaimed from the housetop ? A man keeps *real* grief in his own heart, and guards it jealously."

" This is not a reflecting world, and it has a truly feminine talent for jumping at conclusions."

" Yes. A man may proclaim his felicity till his lungs are sore, and nobody believes him; but let him drop a hint of 'secret grief and family trouble,' and it flies trumpet-tongued. Don't go, Mrs. Venard."

" I really must. I have all my packing yet to do. I hope, dear Mrs. Sterling, that you may pass a most pleasant summer. If your lord needs any more lectures, let me know. It is such a pleasure to serve him !"

" Your generosity is well known, fair and gracious lady," said Lisle with a profound bow. " I'd like to know when you two or three ladies made this conspiracy to join forces against me. Well may Leonore be a turtle dove of meekness and resignation, when she knows that you and Mrs. Bertram are ever ready to do battle for her !"

Going out, Mrs. Venard met Julie in the hall, and drew her toward her room with her, as she said kindly but with light warning,

" I am to leave you to morrow, little Julie, and I must caution you not to lose your heart to this fascinating Leander of the melancholy eyes and insinuating manners, whom you call Mr. Horton. I can't like him, and were I to use a homely term, I should say he is a humbug. I have written Phebe, asking her if he is one of her new relatives ; for I know that he is laying a desperate siege, and my sympathies are for Dr. Edward. Don't surrender, Julie, till you know what is said of him by those who know him best."

Julie made some mocking reply, and tripped away, mentally glad that Mrs. Venard had shown the good judgment to speak to her alone instead of in Lisle's presence, for she feared each moment to hear that name, which she knew would arouse his curiosity at once. It was from Mrs. Bertram, after all, that the danger was to be feared, and later it came, as that thoughtless lady exclaimed,

" I wonder if the gallant and devoted Mr. Horton will follow us to our new stopping place ! You don't know, Lisle, what a devoted cavalier your charges have gain d here, nor how ho is besnubbed by all but me."

"No, I am still in ignorance of such an important affair. Besnubbed, is he? yet everlastingly adoring. Who is the Adonis?"

"Oh, do make a clean breast of it at once," Julie exclaimed before Mrs: Bertram could reply. "Just own up that he is a favored escort of yours upon whom you have pounced as a successor to Mr. Bertram if he ever does the handsome thing by you and leaves you a young widow! Mr. Horton will find no other defender here, for Leonore detests and I hate him. How dull and mopy we all are. Why don't we play and sing?"

"Upon my word, Julie, your anxiety to change the subject makes me think there's something in it. I must investigate yours and Leonore's doings in my absence." Lisle laughed as he made the assertion, but it was not echoed by either of the ladies most interested, uneasy as they were least the idle gossip that had been uttered should reach his ears.

It was, then, with a feeling of profound relief, that, all arrangements complete, the little party took their flight early in the following week for the fairy cottage of which Lisle had talked, and most delightful it proved. Julie resigned herself as best she could to this lengthened absence from the home to which she longed to return, not a little braced to its endurance by her resentment at Edward's refusal to accompany them, which she had termed "real obstinacy;" and so it seemed in her ignorance of his utter inability to do so. There was an intense satisfaction in the thought that at worst she had defeated Louis Hartley's plans for the season, since he would not, for his own sake, intrude upon them while Lisle was their protector.

Mrs. Bertram and Julie, accompanied by Master Charley, made long jaunts and tours of discovery around the adjacent territory, while, left to undisturbed felicity, Lisle and Leonore lingered together upon the balcony that looked far out over the rolling waters, one reading softly to the other while the fresh breeze fanned their faces, lit up with the very spirit of content. Then when the moon rose bright and cloudless, arm in arm they wandered down the beech upon whose hard and beaten sands the waves broke in rolls of molten silver. Thus peacefully and sweetly passed the remainder of that long hot summer, while in the city they had left, pestilence held carnival. Not till the cold blasts of October swept down upon it from the North, did its saturnalia cease. Then familiar faces

once more came thronging on the streets, and among the first w re
Lisle's and those of his cottage brood.

The Venards, though weary and worn with ceaseless ministerings,
were in good health and spirits, and Edward had passed unscathed
through all the danger round him. Julie wept in very joy at the
realization of so many blessings, and humbly begged his pardon for
all her petulant protests against the "obstinary" she forgave and
respected since she knew its cause.

"Could you really think that I remained away from you so long
just of my own free choice?" he asked reproachfully. "I am not
one of those who take up a cross for the mere sake of bearing it.
How much time we have lost, little Julie! Ah, should it only have
pleased Providence to have called *him* home from this wicked
world! It has been a sickly summer everywhere!"

"Don't hope it. People whose life is valueless, never die. He'll
live till I worry him to death, you may be sure."

"May his constitution prove feeble, and his power of long-suffer-
ing much less marvellous than that of most Benedicts."

Meantime Lisle and Leonore wandered out into the pale golden
sunlight of the cool October morning. From garden to summer-
house, from flower-borders to the sombre shade cast by the live oaks.
Everything seemed to give them an audible welcome, to which
Leonore responded gratefully,

" Oh, I am so happy! This is what it is to have *a home!*"

"You are glad, then, after all, that you married me and thus made
it 'a home' to me as well as you?—for it was not so before," responded Lisle.

"' Glad?' Yes, a thousand times! If I die for it, I have at least
known heaven first! Conscience itself has ceased to reproach me."

"I knew you were merely over-sensitive. See now, how weak I
should have been to allow such a very myth to interpose between us
and happiness! You feared I should tyrannize over you. Ah, Leonore!"

"So you would have done—and gained less—had you not been
the most generous and noble-hearted man who ever lived."

"I'm afraid you have not an exalted opinion of men in general,
and husbands in especial," he replied, smiling.

They were strolling along again, now, and Lisle said, pointing to
a dead vine that clung to the trellis,

"See, child. Your climbing rose is quite dead. Things don't
flourish in Joseph's absence. He is a good gardener."

As if the mention of his name invoked his presence, Joseph him self came suddenly upon them as they turned among the shrubbery.

"Well, Joseph, what now?" Lisle asked, seeing that he waited to be addressed.

"I just come round to find out what you'd concluded about taking me back. Says I to myself, Joe, if you could get to see the madam herself, and have a talk with her, she'd hear to reason; so I came. I know'd, for you told me, as how she'd refused, but she'll think better on't."

She turned without any reply, and picked a bud or two from a blooming branch near her. Joseph's lank face assumed an expression of defiance and bull-dog tenacity, as he said a little louder,

"We was old friends, the madam and me was, and I counts on it. She an't going to say good-bye to the past in that way."

Lisle raised his eyebrows quizzica'ly as this "old friendship" was alluded to, but supposing it was merely a reference to the protection he himself had often rallied her upon, when Joseph had been in their service, he said with a shade of sarcasm,

"Oh yes; I know she treated you with most distinguished consideration. It breaks her heart to refuse you, but she is compel'ed to do so."

"Such friends as we *might* be, too!" Joseph pleaded with a glance at her.

he maintained the same silence, and Lisle who again replied,

"Mrs. Sterling has serious objections against employing her '*friends*' in any menial capacity, and decides to employ less distinguished people."

"*Mrs. Sterling* says so, does she? *Mrs. Sterling.* He, he! Well, now!"

She turned upon him as the taunting words reached her, and holding back the hand Lisle had raised, she stopped the descending blow so well merited for his insolence, and with utter defiance written in every line of her pale face, she said, pointing toward the street—

"There lies your way, sir. *Go!* Into my service you never enter again, come what may!"

Lisle looked upon her in surprise at the anger she displayed. Never before had he seen her so aroused. Joseph, too, stood one moment spell-bound by it, and it was with marked respect and humility that he spoke the next words.

"I begs your pardon. ma'am. I don't want to be one of them everlasting sticktights as can't be got rid of nohow; but poverty

makes a man sharp after every chance as comes up, and since I had
that there yaller job on my hands, I'm poor enough, Lord knows!"

"So you really had the yellow fever, did you?" Lisle asked with
a gleam of compassion for the melancholy looking wretch.

"Yes, and about the yallerest on it, I reckon. Didn't know my
own face from a saffron-bag when I got to see it again. The young
doctor can tell you as I was nigh leaving my absence behind me for
good and all. He's a rouser of a doctor, is Dr. Edward, and no
mistake. The old girl, she wanted to pay him for the dosing he
give me inside, and the mustard pickling he did to my outside, but
he wouldn't touch it. The old lady's fond of me, Mr. Sterling, and
maybe for her sake you'd take me back?"

"You are too fond of horseflesh, and your turn for speculation
isn't appreciated. Tue fact is you are a great rascal Joseph," said
Lisle confidentially.

"I've quit all that, sir. That yaller job is a rouser to the conscience, and I had a mind, then, to make a clean breast of two or
three things; but said I to myself, 'Joe, don't you do that, for if
you get up of this, you'll be persecuted for it and had up afore the
lawyers."

"I will try and do something for you in a day or two," said Lisle
kindly, his passing anger quite forgotten in Joseph's humility.

Without so much as a look toward Leonore, Joseph made his
bow, and left.

Leonore looked at her husband with compressed lips, and he saw
that his relenting humor found no response in her heart.

"He is but a clown, at best, and doesn't mean to be impudent as
he sometimes seems," Lisle said excusingly. She turned and faced
him resolutely,

"Do you intend to take him back despite my prohibition? Is
this the 'tyrannical rule' you wish me to exercise in our house?'

He laughed in real amusement at her anger, but he hastened to
reassure her.

"I did not say I would do so, Leonore, nor do I so intend. I will
place him elsewhere, as I easily can. It would be a pity to nip in
the bud such a sprouting saint, for want of a little encouragement.
Leonore, may I ask you a question?"

"Certainly."

"Did you know Joseph before you found him in my service?"

"Yes."

'Then it must have been in Louisville, for I don't think he ever
was outside the place till he came here."

"I never was in Louisville," she answered briefly.

"I thought he was Louisville born. Then indeed, Leonore—"

"Why *must* you talk of him? He and all things connected with him are hateful to me. He destroyed my peace in our own house, dear Lisle, and I cannot consent to have him here. That is all."

The pleasure they were enjoying in their ramble was destroyed, and by tacit agreement they walked thoughtfully back to the house. Lisle's philosophy soon banished the passing cloud from his spirit, but Leonore's buoyancy did not return at will, and day by day the weight upon her heart seemed increasing, mysterious as was its cause. No less attentive and devoted in her every action toward him, she was pensive, melancholy, and the efforts he made to cheer and enliven her, were oftener rewarded with rising tears than by the smiles he invoked. All his tender questioning failed to clicit the cause, and he was compelled to resign himself to this sudden change in her, in utter ignorance of what caused it. She seemed at times even to wish to avoid him, and humoring the caprice which he pretended not to see, he often watched her pacing to and fro the winding walk that led from the gallery out to the street, her figure now lost, now reappearing through the shrubbery. Thus sitting and watching her one evening at dusk, while he smoked his cigar, an unusual solicitude prompted him to offer one protest. The dew was falling heavily and chill, and he stepped in for a veil to cover her head from its penetrating dampness. Part way down the walk his steps were suddenly arrested by a sight that met him at the gate beyond. The figure of a man was lurking by the entrance. He saw Leonore approach him, linger for one instant as if in colloquy, and then they hurriedly separated, the figure of the man going up the street, and Leonore at first hastening her steps, then resuming her accustomed pace up the walk she had been promenading.

Unobserved by her, Lisle returned to the gallery and resumed the seat he had occupied when last she approached it. Leonore came near again, hesitated, as if intending to join him, then turned and went away once more. An impulse of bitterness sealed his lips when he would have called to her in that undecided moment. "If she would thus expose her health, and sacrifice her own inclinations, for the purpose of more thoroughly deceiving him as to the real object of those twilight promenades which he had heretofore attributed to mere restlessness, let her accept the consequences. If she was chilled and weary he was not responsible! Who was this other for whom she thus toiled and waited?" The next instant he reproached himself for these thoughts, and conquering his rebellious impulse, he sprang down the steps and overtook her. Casting the veil over her head, he said gently,

"The dew is very heavy to-night, Leonore; are you not chilly?"

She thanked him for the act, and said something about 'going in directly,' which he did not catch. He took her hand and drew it through his arm, saying lightly,

"Are you really forsaking your own roof and turning into a sort' of elegant 'tramp?' Five-and-fifty times you have paced up and down this path to-night. I wonder if you have peas in your shoes, like a real penitent?"

"I shouldn't feel them if I had."

"Oh, the peas are in your conscience then! Well, Leonore, one of the pilgrims thus condemned, *boiled* his peas before he commenced the expiatory journey. There is an example for you."

Resolved not to annoy her by any seeming observation of her movements, from that evening he went out upon the other balcony to smoke his cigar when he saw her ready for her solitary stroll. Evening by evening she returned more composed and serene, and satisfied with anything that made her so, Lisle said nothing of the scene he had witnessed, and she was far from suspecting it. Thus affairs stood when a river excursion was planned by an ever restless party of pleasure seekers, who insisted that the Sterling family should accompany them. As usual Lisle declined the invitation for himself, but urged its acceptance upon Leonore and Julie, who were compelled to assent, though Leonore's reluctance was evident. But one day intervened before the anticipated excursion, and that, till late into the evening, was monopolized by guests never done with important plans and suggestions relative to it. Restless and nervous, Leonore's eyes turned ever toward the theatre of her evening walk, and Lisle pitied her while powerless to relieve. It was ten o'clock when the last enthusiastic chatterer left, and with a heavy sigh, Leonore went up to her room.

The excursion day dawned bright and cheery, early November as it was. Leonore looked wearily out upon the waving treetops " ' in o the distance, hazy with the delicious purple glow of autumn. Julie accosted her gayly as she entered the breakfast room, asserting that married people were never good playfellows. She had no spirit to reply, and Edward changed the subject by an announcement quite unexpected by all but Julie herself.

"Next month I intend to make an excursion compared to which this is but a babe in arms. Do you know, Lisle, I'm really going to visit the old people?"

"In midwinter? I wish you joy of the tempting excursion. I hope you don't style it *pleasure* excursion."

"No. Duty excursion would be more literal. You know I am mother's Benjamin, and my presence must be urgent to her, when father has really expended twelve cents in postage to tell me so, as he has done in the last few weeks."

"Hush, Ed. You won't give Leonore an exalted opinion of our family, if you go on. I haven't told her its peculiarities."

"Never told her that you are the grandson of a poetess? You can't have forgotten 'Poor lady, poor lady, you're always undone,' and the rest of it. But you know mother used to affirm that the old lady had more sense than all the rest of the Sterlings put together, crazy as she was."

"'*Crazy!*' repeated Leonore bending forward breathlessly. 'Crazy!'"

"Yes, and I'm sadly afraid it may prove hereditary," Edward replied gravely. "Insanity crops out so unexpectedly, when it runs in families this way—almost certain to reappear in the third generation, with the least disturbing cause. Any great grief or disappointment, being crossed in love, or having a troublesome wife—Why what's the matter, Leonore?"

Pale and breathless she leaned forward upon the table, never raising her eyes from Lisle's face.

"You have frightened her to death with your crazy stories! Come, Leonore. Don't think of what he says. It is pure nonsense."

As he spoke Lisle raised her and led her to a sofa.

"Lisle, Lisle, if I drive you into insanity—oh, good heavens!" she exclaimed in terror.

CHAPTER XXXI.

GLAD in heart at the evident change for the better in Leonore's spirits, Lisle soon dismissed from his mind the anxious queries that had harassed it, and believing that once more the ever recurring clouds were banished for an indefinite period, he was satisfied and content. Convinced that he possessed her entire and undivided affection, why should he complain that there was in her inmost soul one little recess into which she could not suffer even him to enter? Had he, who had maintained toward her a silence upon one important topic, which seemed even to himself bordering upon dishonorable, of all others, the right to complain of want of perfect confidence? Lisle was just, even where he felt most strongly. He had asked himself the question before he ever made her his wife, he had no occasion to answer it differently now. And content with the measure of happiness bestowed upon him, he sauntered out with his cigar, upon this, the first evening of his temporary desertion, and made a leisurely tour of the grounds which were of remarkable beauty.

It was quite dark when he at last turned to go back to the house, and he quickened his steps as he approached the main pathway up and down which Leonore had pursued her restless promenades. Their recollection caused him to turn toward the gate where he had once surprised her in a stolen interview. As if invoked by the act, there, where it had stood then, stood now the figure of a man, as if waiting for some one who now came not; for in his impatience he moved ever and anon as if hesitating yet wishing to enter the gateway.

For some moments Lisle stood still and watched him. It was impossible to examine him in detail at such a distance, and with as much caution as possible Lisle approached him. Simultaneously, wearying of his watch, or feeling that he might be observed, the figure glided away. Hastily Lisle reached the gate and stopped to listen. A light, fleet step fell upon his ear. What gentleman would thus lurk around another's house, what common man could have any errand which rendered such caution necessary? This mysterious being, whoever he was, could be none other than Leonore's unknown visitant; he was ignorant of her absence from home, of which she had had no means of informing him, and doubtlessly this was the subject of her restless anxiety during the company be-tortured evening preceding, when it had been impossible for her to steal out to her tryst. The conviction was not a pleasant one to Lisle, despite his philosophy.

Lisle lighted another cigar as he resumed his favorite seat on the balcony; but his serenity was ruffled, and nothing pl ased him. The air was chilly, and he shrank from it; the cigar its lf seemed of another brand, and he threw it away in disgust. The figure at the gate came between him and all peace, and under the sudden impulse he sent for the servant who filled Joseph's old place in the grounds.

"James, see that you keep the gates well locked while the family are away. This shrubbery furnishes too good a lurking place for thieves and vagabonds." ,

" Yes, sir.   I kept them always locked when I first came, but the
madam told me not."

" The madam is gone now, and there are too many prowlers
around."

" Yes, sir, I was watching one myself these two days, and he left
here only a bit ago."

" What was he like ?"

" A regular rough, sir.   That's what I'd call him.   Anyway, he's
a poor man, and poor people an't safe to have around unless they've
business."

Not stopping to analyze if his own prejudice were not about as illiberal as James' philosophy, Lisle intrenched himself behind his
plea of " common prudence," and at length reasoned himself back
into something like philosophy.   Resolved to avoid a similar annoyance the succeeding evening, he went out directly after dinner, and
having spent the whole evening away, returned late, and went to
sleep in serene unconsciousness of a letter awaiting him upon the
dressing table.   It was the first thing he saw when he arose next
morning, and as he leisurely dressed he thought idly of the strange
address scrawled upon its face.

" For L. Sterling," and hardly curious as to it, he left it till quite
ready to descend to breakfast.   " For L. Sterling," he said half
audibly as he at last raised it and broke the seal, and read,

" I asks pardon For writin' to yu at All, but bein' that for 2 dais
i hev wated Hopin' to se yu, and To-day likewise wated Hopin' in
vane til Pitchdark, I cum this mornin' to ask for yu, an the Poarter
div me off; i wan to tell yu as him as was sic is dangcruser agen,
an' yu'd bes cum out fur a day or to, es ther's no Knowin' what may
hapen', hee is at the Time askin' fur yu, an' won't rest Easy til yu
cum.   With mutch respec, tho Writ very poor, this is From your
Facthful Tom."

Lisle read this half illegible scrawl the second time, unable to
make anything of it, before the idea flashed across him that it was
not intended for himself.   " L. Sterling " was an address no less
applicable to Leonore, and strange as it seemed, it was but in keeping with the letter itself manifestly written by an unready pen.   How
came the letter here at all ?   Some one about him knew, probably
James, whose business it was to answer the bell.   He was busy at
the moment upon the gallery, and stepping out Lisle raised the
letter before him.   " James, did you take in this letter yesterday ?"

" No, sir, Mrs. Perkins took it herself, as the man who brought it
wouldn't give it to anybody less."

" Who brought it ?"

"That fellow who's been hanging round here for a day or two."

"So, this man was but an emissary between her and another," Lisle said to himself as he went in to breakfast. Mrs. Perkins was waiting to do the honors of the table, according to the old familiar style which she remembered in Fitzjames' time, and during Lisle's young bachelor days, and she looked up in surprise as he entered with more of his old time misanthropy expressed on his face than she had seen since his marriage. "I found a letter in my room, this morning, addressed in a rather peculiar fashion. Did you put it there, and do you know who brought it?"

"Take the letter I did, but as to knowing who he was which brought it, I'm glad to say I don't. I'm an honest, respectable woman, and always have been, as you, which have known me so long, can testify. Him that brought it may be honest, too, but he wasn't wholesome company for the likes of you or me. What he'd wanted a-prowling round the house these two days, Lord knows! which it's my opinion he brought the letter at last just for an excuse, though he made such a fuss about who he'd give it to, and who he wouldn't, making me promise over and over to give it just according to the directions as was on it."

"And didn't he ask to see me at all?"

"Laws, no, sir, being as it wasn't you he wanted to see, if anybody. The way of it all was this. Day before yesterday when cook went to the garden for the salad, she saw this man a-hanging round the yard like as if he was looking for somebody. Cook thought it strange, but being as she is a modest, quiet-spoken young woman, she didn't let on about it. Afterwards, James, he saw him, too, walking around on all sides of the house and looking up at the windows anxious-like. Two or three hours he staid a-questioning of the house as never answered him back a word, and James got worried like and came out on him of a sudden. All he said back, was, that he was waiting to see the madam, and when he was told she was gone off a pleasuring and wouldn't be back under three or four days, he went away, and James thought that was the last of him. But no, back he came again yesterday, and nothing would do but he must see me. So I s'eeked my hair and put on my new cap, and out I went to the gate, for he didn't want to come in, then. Says he, 'You are the housekeeper, Mrs. Perkins, be you?'—though, how he knowed my name I don't know — and says I, 'yes, of course, who else? which Mrs. Drew was once my name, and as Drew and Perkins I've been Mr. Sterling's housekeeper many a year, young as I look.' Then said he, 'I don't care nothin' about that. I only want to know if you are true and faithful to the madam, and can be trusted!' I said, 'I'm a Baptist Christian which does my duty by the madam as is as sweet a lady as you'd wish to know.' He seemed kind of touched when he found I was a Baptist and spoke a kind word for the lady, and said he, 'so she is sweet, ain't she.' Then he showed me the letter, and says he, 'Here's a letter as I've writ for her, and though its writ too poor for her to look on, she ought to get it the minute she comes home;' and say he, 'will you see she gets it all safe, madam?' He gave me the letter when I said I would, and sure enough the directions on it was her's. So then he went away for good, and I put the letter on the dressing-table to wait for her coming home. That's the whole story."

"Very well, Mrs. Perkins, but in future when letters are handed you for any one, keep them yourself till you give them into the very hand of the one to whom they are written. This letter was directed merely 'For L. Sterling,' and I might have read it by mistake."

"Which it's little Mrs. Sterling would mind if you had, the sweet lady as loves you ten times better than herself!"

Not caring to prolong the conversation, Lisle went out, feeling that no further light could be thrown upon the subject, which nevertheless tormented him during the succeeding days. Who was it whose illness had caused her so much anxiety? this invalid who was pronounced "dangerouser" by the writer of the letter so evidently in her confidence. *Who* demanded her presence and could not be comforted without her? With whom should she remain for "a day or two," forsaking him, her husband, and their mutual home? Having learned so much of her secret, what might remain for him to learn? For the first moment his brain reeled at a wild, terrible suspicion that crossed it. Impossible, she could not be faithless to him, could not abuse his unlimited trust and confidence in her, by wronging him under the very armor of security such faith gave her! Yet impossible as he pronounced it, the doubt remained.

It was with mingled emotions that he received Leonore, when at the close of the week she returned with the gay party of which she was at once the leader and the delight, and with the announcement that it lacked but half an hour of dinner-time, he left her to make her toilet, sure that the waiting letter would consume a portion of the time.

That it had done so, was evident when she descended in demidress, her face haggard and anxious, and traces of tears in her eyes. The furtive glance Lisle turned upon her awoke his pity. Gentle, tender, loving as she was, she *could* not be the guilty thing he had

dared to think her. Oh, why would she not trust and confide in
him! how could he win her to do so! All that was possible to
mortal, he would do for her would she but permit him; but if she
thus sealed her lips and would not confide in him, what could he
do? Would she obey this summons and add one more to her several mysterious departures? What now would become of the
promise she had voluntarily given to leave him thus no more!
Could he, if he would, restore it to her, without awaking her suspicions that he knew more than he wished her to believe? Did
generosity itself require that he should be thus tender of her feelings
while his own were lacerated? But one conclusion was arrived at.
If she desired his generosity in any way, she knew she had but to
claim it. He would wait for her to do so; and day by day he offered her every tacit encouragement to ask it. But she remained
silent, pensive, sometimes serious. She would keep her promise
to him; that was evident, if she really felt any desire to recall or
violate it; and Lisle's heart beat reassuringly.

It was Edward's departure that became a daily topic now, and
while others wondered that he should have chosen the dreariest
time of the year for a visit he could pay at any time, Julie kept her
own counsel, and if she sometimes wore a serious, troubled air, not
habitual to her, none thought anything of it. The tender relationship between herself and Edward received the natural construction,
and while each knew it, neither cared, only wishing that for once
public rumors were true. Hartley's name was unspoken by all,
Leonore herself at ease about him so far as Julie was concerned, and
Lisle quite unsuspicious.

In such a position were affairs, when Lisle was suddenly summoned to Louisville on important business. Loth as he was at all
times to leave home, he was doubly so now. He felt instinctively
that some impending calamity threatened him, yet reason urged
him to resist the presentiment. Despite his efforts, the foreboding
remained, and he made an effort to induce Leonore to accompany
him. She shook her head and smiled as she spoke the negative he
anticipated. He urged the question, and she burst into tears.
Pained beyond expression, he took her in his arms and soothed her
as one soothes a child, and said tenderly,

"You can well understand that I dread to leave you in such a
state of mind as this. Is there any place you would rather stay than
in this great, lonely house, if indeed you will not go with me?"

She shook her head and strove to recall her smiles.

"Think again, Leonore. I will take you to *any* spot this side the grave—blindfold if you wish me to be so—or you shall go alone, and when you send me word that you have arrived in safety, I will start upon my journey with a lighter heart."

"Where should I wish to stay except here in the only home I have ever known—here where all the happiness of my life is centred? Lonely I certainly shall be, but not more unhappy than I must be anywhere."

"So you admit that you are unhappy? Oh, Leonore, why won't you trust me? You have not so true a friend in this wide world, nor one who would believe in, and trust you so implicitly, however circumstances might seem to condemn you."

She bent her face in her hands and murmured brokenly,

"Oh, stop, stop. Leave me to my fate; I am not worth one heart throb!"

"Yet God knows every throb of my heart is yours, every tear you shed is wrung from its core. Oh, Leonore, I too suffer, but only through you. You do not know what storms you set raging in my soul, what battles I fight with my own terrible fancies!"

"I will weep no more, dear Lisle. I am, as you said, nervous and ill, and if I am silent when you would have me speak, it is only because nothing I could ask or you can grant, would make me any happier. I tell you, Lisle, I am paying the penalty of a mistaken past, and it is as heavy as I can bear in silence. *To speak it would kill me.* Bear with me, dear Lisle, and above all love and trust me."

He did, supremely, as he folded her to his breast, and his heart reproached him for the base suspicions he had harbored against her. The few days that intervened before his departure were passed as usual, all seeming cheerful and happy.

"What are we to bring the ladies on our return, Lisle?" Edward asked upon the last morning they breakfasted together. "I believe that since the days of 'Beauty and the Beast,' he who departs is expected to return with welcome gifts. I've no idea what is certain to be acceptable to a lady, except a box of gloves. What is Leonore's number?"

"I believe she wears sixes now, though before she was married she revelled in five and three-quarters. Halcyon days, those 'before I was married,' of every woman's memory! The fatest one who walks abroad, could be spanned round the waist by one's two hands, and the foot which now aspires beyond No. fives, was at ease in one and a half, all 'before I was married,' if one is to credit the self-made statement. One is inclined to believe that matrimony must have most prodigious effects. What *did* you wear in the glove department, Leonore? Fives, wasn't it?"

"For shame, Lisle. I wear now just what I always did. Plain sixes."

"Wondrous development you must have had as an infant, as you say '*always*.'"

"Thank you, I didn't cut teeth in 'Alexander's best,'" she said smiling.

The morning flew rapidly by, and the hour of parting came all too soon.

"Be as happy as you can, Leonore, and be assured I shall return to you at the earliest possible moment!" Lisle said cheeringly as he clasped her in his arms at parting.

Edward awaited him on the gallery, having spoken his adieus, and Julie was nowhere to be seen. But a handkerchief waved from her window as they drove down the street, evidenced that she was not unmindful of the departure she could not summon enough courage to face.

Left thus to the silence and loneliness of the great house, its very space and grandeur possessed a sort of terror for Leonore in the nervous, unstrung state of mind she was in. Creeping shadows seemed to lurk in each obscure corner, and every noise from without startled her like a dreaded presence. For the first time she realized how much there was around her to tempt the avarice of thieves and burglars, who of late had perpetrated many acts of unprecedented boldness, and escaped unharmed.

While Lisle was with her she had turned a careless ear to these reports; but now each casual creaking of a staircase, every swinging door, alarmed her, and at least a hundred times during that first trying night she sprang up in terror at the images her fancy had raised. The morning found her pale and weary, and disinclined to rise; and Julie took her breakfast alone with no one to remark her own pale face and swollen eyelids.

Leonore came down to the parlors towards noon, somewhat refreshed by her morning sleep, but painfully nervous, and starting violently at every unexpected address.

Soon after she came down, James sought her, hat in hand, and dressed as if to go out. He had received word that his only child was dying, and asked permission to go it. She had never thought before, whether or not he had a family, and the appeal struck now upon a tender cord. "Your child is dying—dying! Yes, go at once, poor man! Can I do anything for you?"

"No, ma'am, thank you, unless you'd be kind enough to let me stay and comfort my poor woman for a day or two. There's Joseph Perkins, the housekeeper's husband, will be glad to take my place while I'm gone. He's just lost his last place."

"Oh, yes, let him take it. He will do well enough for a day or two."

How could he think of such homely details while his little child was dying? Her morning indolence had perhaps robbed him of the li tle thing's last smile of recognition and love! The self-reproach tortured her as no words could have done, and it was well for her that coming gu sts forced her thoughts into another channel, and as the day went by her spirits rallied, and as she and Julie mounted the staircase, together upon their way to their rooms late in the evening, they were chatting once more naturally. The two sleeping-rooms were contiguous, and leaving open the door between them, they talked for a long time after each had retired, mutually feeling the comfort of such companionship. Sleep overpowered them by inperceptible degrees, and at last all was silent, while the low burning gas threw a dim light over the rooms, just relieving them of total darkness.

Leonore could not have told how long she had slept, it seemed not many minutes, when a faint noise in her room aroused her. The floor creaked under a cautious tread, then all was still, next followed that indescribable rustling felt rather than heard, so startling to one whom it awakens to a real sen e of some strange presence near. She strove to rise, but a deadly weakness enthralled her ; she would have called aloud in cha lenge, but the same deadly nightmare hushed her voice beyond her own control. Physically powerless as she was, mentally she was as self-possessed as ever, and with a desperate courage she watched and waite I for what was next to come. Reassured by the breathless hush around him, the intruder moved toward Julie's bed, and c utiously peered through the curtains. Evidently she was quite unconscious of everything, sleeping softly and profoundly ; for Leonore saw the intruder's hand s eal under the pillow and withdraw the tiny watch nightly placed there, and with his clumsy fingers he pushed and crowded its dangling chain and little "charms" into his pocket. Not a motion escaped her as she lay watching him, and even before he turned toward the flickering light, she knew that the ungainly figure and unagile, if stealthy movements, were those of Joseph Perkins.

Even as he thus turned, the strange spell that h d bound her was dissolved, and with one bound she was upon her feet in the centre of the room. Not a cry broke from her lips, though as she thus sprang up a quick hand had turned the gas quite off and an inky darkness veiled everything. A firm hand seized her neck in threatened strangulation, and a voice that certainly was not Joseph's, said warningly,

" You'd best be quiet now. If you don't screech out, nothing an't going to happen to you. Tell a feller where's your money and your little traps, and we'll clear out respectable when we've took 'em."

Her only reply was a sudden spring from the detaining clutch, and a scream that rang out clear and piercing. Julie echoed it as she sprang up in terror, but the door was quickly shut and securely bolted b tween them, and while his comrade uttered maledictions, Joseph said to Leonore,

" You mind now what Joe Perkins tells you. If you've seen what you'd no business to see, keep mum about it, or it'll be the worse for you. If you peach on me, I'll peach on you ; and you know you can't stand the damage, or you'd have screamed when you first see me here ! Slide down the gallery pillars, Bill ; you'll be caught if you don't."

" You're a pretty feller to be speaking out names, on such a trip as this ere !" was the surly retort as the injunction was obeyed.

At that instant voices were heard in the hall. and Mrs. Perkins ejaculated, " Lord bless us and save us !" Leonore sprang to the door leading into the hall, and opened it wide, as she called hurriedly,

" This way, this way ! Look to the man who is on the gallery."

There was no one to be seen, but a shouting on the street was heard, and a policeman's voice called distinctly, " I've got him, I've got him," while on all sides the sounding of the policemen's alarm rattle proved that they were on the alert. There was no chance of escape for Joseph, now mingling with the excited household, if indeed he meant to have attempted one ; and Mrs. Perkins plucked him anxiously by the sleeve, as she asked suspicion ly,

" How did you come to be on hand so quick ? which its slow enough you are in general, and you not in bed this bles-ed night !"

" Why you see the way of it is this. I'd been out on a bit of a ' tear,' to tell just the truth. old girl ; and just as I let myself into the house, I heard somebody a-moving up in the hall. I made sure it was you a-waiting up for me, and says I to myself, Joe, you're in for it now, sure, and so I stood a-thinking what I'd best say to save a-going over,—for you're a strong one on going over, old lady,—and then all of a su lden I h-ered a screech in the madam's room, and a screech in Miss Julie's as was worse, and I made straight bolt, up here. It was as dark as pitch, and the doors was all bolted so I couldn't get in to see what was up, and him as was up to mi chief bolted over the gallery and off, and the police has got him now, and serves him right?"

Leonore deigned no reply. She had hastily wrapped herself in a dressing-gown, and reassured Julie who understood nothing that had occurred, and she calmly dispersed the little assembly to talk it over among themselves, Mrs. Perkins starting at once upon a tour of the house to see what depredation had been committed.

As might have been anticipated under such circumstances, nothing was missing beside some valuable articles of jewelry, the principal object of the marauders having been to gain possession of these, which Joseph well knew were kept in the rooms where he had been surprised. Most of this was found upon Bill's person when arrested, and having been duly identified, was restored, Leonore by some means having added the watch in Joseph's keeping, to the other articles returned. Bill was fully committed for trial, and Joseph, unsuspected by all save Leonore herself, who had her own reasons for protecting him, remained at large, though strictly forbidden the premises. Learning what had occurred, the faithful James returned at once to his post, and quiet was restored. As if her nervous terror had only warned her of this one attempted violence, Leonore's courage and calmness returned, and she resumed her usual avocations serenely.

And now again she commenced her restless walks at dusk along the pathway to the gate, and again the waiting messenger delivered his intelligence and mysteriously departed, though now with less danger of observation than when Lisle's attentive eyes followed her every moment.

CHAPTER XXXII.'

ONE night during the second week of Lisle's absence, Leonore came at a late hour to Julie's bedside, and bent over her. The action woke her from a sound sleep, and she started in surprise. Leonore placed her hand gently on her shoulder and said,

"Don't be frightened, Julie. It is only I."

Very ghost-like she looked in her white robes, and, but half reassured, Julie exclaimed,

"What is the matter, Leonore?"

She bent her face upon the pillow beside Julie's own, and suppressing a sob, said low and earnestly,

"A great sorrow is slowly falling upon me—greater, heavier than I can bear, as I have tried to bear it, silently. Julie, Julie, my very heart is breaking hour by hour. I can stay here and suffer it no longer—I must leave you for a time "

"For what, Leonore? Where will you go?"

"Where duty and affection call me. Ask me nothing. I have violat d every instinct of my heart till I can do so no more. *I must go*, but I shall return in a few days at most. I shall lose my reason if I am compelled to stay."

"Then go at once. Don't think of me."

Leonore silently kissed her in reply, and after a little time said,

"I hope to return before Lisle; but if he should come first, give him the letter I have already written for him and which you will find upon my table. I shall leave before you are awake. And, Julie, if Lisle is very angry, very bitter against me, very doubtful of all he ever believed good in me, be to me the sister I shall so much need. I don't know what may happen—I dare not think of it. I only know that I have no choice—that I *cannot* longer support the existence I am leading!"

"Hush, Leonore; don't talk of dying in that bitter way. Only tell me that *you* forgive *me* for all my errors past, present, and to come; for I am treating you like a hypocrite, Leonore!"

"Not so, Julie. You are lovable and good—as I would be had I the power. Only let us promise to love and cling to each other whatever may happen us. Do you promise this, Julie?"

"It is I who should ask that were I like you. 'Promise?' Yes, forever."

With a last embrace, Leonore left her as noiselessly as she had came, and through the remainder of the night busied herself with the preparations for her departure.

Later in the morning Julie unclosed her eyes, heavy from want of sleep. It was one year this day since Louis Hartley had made her that visit in the summer-house, during which she had named the limit for his patient waiting, and two letters had lately reached her, reminding her of her promise. He would come to claim its fulfilment, of that she had been assured. There was not a hope left; and wearily she rose and descended to the deserted parlors. She was not even surprised when she received a tiny envelope in his well-known direction. In response she briefly named an hour for an interview, and for the first time Louis Hartley crossed Lisle Sterling's threshold. The interview was but brief, and at its close Julie threw her mantle around her and hurriedly sought Mrs. Bertram. She would not leave the house quite solitary at Lisle's arrival, should he reach it before Leonore's return, and Leonore's letter to him *must* be left in trusty hands, and her wishes obeyed by one who would do all in her power to soften the double blow thus inflicted upon him. A few forcible words made Mrs. Bertram acquainted with the whole condition of affairs, and Julie would not suffer her to protest.

"'Wait till Lisle at least returns?' I can't. It would only make matters worse, and they are bad enough already. I won't insult him by being married under his roof. I suppose people will call it an elopement; but I don't care. I'm only glad Leonore, too, is absent. Since it is enevitable, all has happened as smoothly as possible. A little ride to the regular city 'Gretna Green,'—you know where that is,—a clergyman in want of a fee, and that is the last of me!'"

Mrs. Bertram took her by the arm. "Julie Kelley, I've a splendid dark closet, just *made* to receive bad children! I've a mind to shut you in it till your senses return."

"I never had any. If I had I shouldn't be in my present position."

"Julie, do you remember Phebe Venard, who married nobody knows who, despite the remonstrances of her friends? She is a poor deserted woman, her fortune already squandered, and hourly expected back here to claim the protection of her brother, her father being dead."

"I am sorry, but I can't weep over trouble in general when I've so much in particular. I'll risk my husband squandering my fortune, for it is too small to be noticeable; and if he deserts me, all well."

"What a crazy creature!"

"There is so much method in my madness, that I shall send you my valedictory address to Lisle, whom I never expect to forgive me. Leonore will, and I shall write her when all is over. Now say good-bye, for I must be off. Go to Lisle the hour he comes back, and do what you can to make him hear to reason."

She was gone with no more formal leavetaking than this. Plainly she expected neither sympathy nor forgiveness for herself.

An hour later a carriage stopped at the gate, and Julie was helped into it by a gentleman who raised his hat in mock salutation to the house as they were driven away. James noticed it and thought the action strange, and the maid, Margaret, upon entering Julie's room found her trunks packed and labelled "to be delivered according to orders when given." But neither said a word of it, and there was nothing suspicious in the mere fact that she had gone out for a drive. If Margaret stood aghast one moment at her discovery, and was fully five minutes recalling her imperturbability, no one knew it. Scarcely had she succeeded in doing so when the gate bell was rung violently, and Mrs. Bertram rushed in, inquiring eagerly for Miss Julie. James was about to carry her a note which Julie had instructed him to deliver, and he handed it to her for all reply. The enclosure to herself contained but the one word, "good-bye," the other was for Lisle.

Mrs. Bertram threw up her hands with a little gesture of consternation and despair, and then rushed out as rapidly as she had entered. James saw her hasten down the street toward the Venards, and then wonderingly relocked the gate. But it seemed the bell would never cease ringing to-day, as just at dusk it pealed forth another summons, this time for the master of the house himself.

"How are you, James?" was the cheerful salute he received as Lisle hurried up the path to the house. Bursting open the door rather than swinging it back, he came full against Margaret, who fell pale and breathless against the wall. What a series of calamities was here—the mistress absent on one of her mysterious journeys, the young miss gone no one knew where! Margaret felt herself unequal to the emergency, and uttered not a word. Lisle threw open the parlor door. "Shut up, of course!" he soliloquized, and turning, ran up stairs. His wife's room was solitary and deserted also, and opening the doors, he called her name. Still no reply, and with a sinking heart he rapped on Julie's door, then opened it. Still no one! He rang the bell, and Margaret summoned courage and appeared.

" Where are the ladies, Margaret ? Where is my wife ?"

" Not in, sir. Shall I see if she is at Mrs. Bertram's ?" for Margaret had a woman's talent for putting another in the breach, and felt instinctively that Mrs. Bertram must know more of this household flitting than any other. Reassured by the evasion he did not remark, Lisle dismissed her upon her errand, and awaited her return. She came, and silently handing him a sealed envelope, left him. He broke the seal impatiently, and read. It was from his wife.

" Lisle, dear Lisle, forgive me, however you may at first blame me for what must seem strange if not heartless in my conduct; I am called away from our home, dear Lisle, and I *must* go. I can refuse no longer, I can no longer stifle the voice of my own heart. When you so generously offered to take me to any place where I might prefer to pass the weary hours of your absence, I told you, truly, that I was better in my own home and preferred to remain in it. But other circumstances now exist, and *I must* go. Do not say that I thus break my solemn promise to you. Were you here now you would restore it to me, as you tacitly did when you told me to go *anywhere* this side the grave, that I might choose. Believe me, my ever beloved husband, wherever I may be, and whatever I do, I am yours most entirely and devotedly. You see I *would* not leave you this time in the 'utter silence' of which you once complained. I would not go at all could I refuse without being an unworthy, heartless wretch ! Yours with an aching but loving heart,

LEONORE."

At first he was not even surprised. Her affectionate adieu, that " first letter " for which he had vainly plead—was his at last, and he regarded it again with loving interes'. A sudden cloud darkened his brow, and hastily tearing open his wallet he drew forth that long-preserved envelope addressed to his uncle, Mr. Fitzjames, which he had once produced for family inspection, declaring it would yet give him a clue to the writer. Laying it upon the letter just received, he compared the chirography of the two. It was one and the same—there was not the shadow of a doubt. His heart beat suffocatingly as he realized the fact. *This* was why she had never dared to write him one word, despite his pleadings ! What was the reason for all this mystery ? What could she have had in common with Mr. Fitzjames whom she professed never to have known, and how was it that after so much duplicity she should have betrayed herself at last ? What was the secret in her life so continually interposing its hateful presence between them ? If she was indeed the innocent creature he had believed her, why was she not frank with him, and just both toward herself and him, instead of thus wringing his faith in her ?

He did not hear the bell ring, and he went down mechanically when told Mrs. Bertram was waiting to speak with him. She sprang forward, seized his hand, tried to speak, but burst into tears. He saw that she was terribly agitated, and controlling his own emotion he led her to a sofa and sat down opposite her.

" What's the matter, Mrs. Bertram ? Do not distress yourself, I know all."

" No, no. I kept back the worst, hoping to spare you the knowledge. I have another letter which I had not the courage to send you with Leonore's. It is better you should learn all from Julie herself, than to hear it from others. Read." -

She handed him the brief letter Julie had left for him,

In the fewest possible words Julie told him that she was going away from his house to become Louis Hartley's wife, confessed her long engagement and her reasons for having concealed it. She asked no forgiveness, for she felt that she deserved none, and so bade him a last farewell. The letter dropped from his nerveless fingers, and he uttered an audible groan. It was incredible, even though she herself had written it; and he begged Mrs. Bertram to tell him all she knew of it. She did so, but it was little beyond what he himself knew. He only learned that under his *nom de plume* of 'Leonard Horton' he had followed Julie in her wanderings, carefully keeping out of *his* way. As for Mrs. Bertram, when she learned of him that this Mr. 'Horton' was the Louis Hartley of whom she had heard so much, but never known, her surprise was unbounded. Julie had not hinted this. Had Leonore known it, and was this the secret of her dislike toward him when they were all at the seaside together? She asked Lisle the question, but he shook his head. There was a pause, and then she resumed,

"I told you there was a bare hope that this marriage might be frustrated. Shall I tell you all?"

"Yes; though let me tell you in advance, that I am hopeless."

"There is an impediment to this marriage that will invalidate it even if consummated. Mr. Venard knows it, and he went in pursuit of them within an hour of their departure."

He was so utterly without hope, or power of connected thought, that he hardly heard her words—asked no explanations; and seeing it was so, she left him to himself.

He threw himself into an arm chair by the fire, and refusing to have the gas lighted, gazed into the glowing embers with his brain on fire. Thus sitting in darkness by his solitary hearthstone, he looked the past and the present in the face. The clock chimed eleven, sending its metallic ring out upon the wintry air with a clear resonance that roused him from his reverie. With an involuntary shiver he rose and looked around him. There was scarcely enough light in the room to illuminate its objects, but the outline of a human form, heavily draped in black, was leaning against the half-open door which it had just entered noiselessly and secretly as the shadow it seemed. With a chill as though he had seen an apparition, Lisle hastily turned up the gas jet and looked again. Pale and cold as the apparition she had seemed, Leonore stood still and waited for him to speak. She had returned home at this late hour, and letting herself in with her private keys, was ignorant that he had returned before her, brief as had been her absence, and coming suddenly upon

him thus sitting like a reproachful shadow at his deserted hearth,
s e stood in mute alarm, not knowing if it were indeed his living
self that met her eyes. Lisle's face was more cold and unpitying
than she had ever seen it, and with a little cry she raised her hands
imploringly. He only took them both in one of his, and leading
her forward to the fire, for she was shivering with cold and fatigue,
said calmly,

"I am not going to reproach you. I have perhaps no right to do
so, certainly no wish. There is too much between us now for mere
protests to avail anything. First of all, I have two questions to ask
you. Did you write this, and this?" and he held before her the
letter she had written him, and the ill-starred envolope of years
before.

"Yes," she gasped rather than said.

"So you confess it?"

She summoned dignity under the tone, and replied firmly,   .

"I *admit* it, Lisle. 'Confess' is not the word."

"A distinction without a difference, under existing circumstances."

"Lisle, if I had not resolved to tell you all, at my cost, I never
should have been thus seemingly entrapped. What could it matter
whether you suspected something of what I had resolved so soon to
tell you? I can endure my tortured existence no longer. Better go
forth into the wilderness, like Hagar of old." She struggled suffocatingly to undo her wrappings, and with the gallantry natural to
him, though without one impulse of affection, he removed them
for her and cast them aside. He noticed then that every article of
her attire was of the deepest black, and he marked the shuddering ·
gasp with which she herself looked down upon the robe that hung
pall-like around her.

"Do you know what has become of the orphan girl commited to
our care, the little sister for whom *you* and I are responsible, strive
as we may to ignore it?" he demanded. She looked up bewildered,
and he resumed,

"I will tell you, Leonore Sterling. Faithful, conscientious
guardians that we are! She is, ere this, the wife of Louis Hartley!"

Leonore uttered an ejaculation of surprise and horror, and leaned
back trembling among the cushions. Unmoved by her anguish,
Lisle continued,

"She has become the wife of a scoundrel whom I would have
whipped, a thief whom I would have spurned from my threshold had
he dared to cross it. A living curse on the face of the earth, I hate
him and all who ever called him theirs!"

'Stop, Lisle, for God's sake stop. You are *cursing me!* God
pity me, *I was once his wife!"*

Lisle stood as transfixed by those incredible words. He had no
power even to utter an exclamation, and he turned fairly giddy
where he stood staring down upon her. Shrinking and shuddering she had buried herself among the sofa-pillows till only the outline of her figure was visible. For a space, not so much as a breath
broke the dead hush in the room. Lisle was the first to move, and
in a voice hoarse with emotion he spoke her name. "Leonore!"
She did not look up, or seem to hear him, and again he called her.
"Leonore, look up at me, and let me see your face. Is it indeed
your very self?" Bending over her, he lifted her head with gentle
hands and turned her fair face toward him. Then indeed he realized
that she had fainted. Her face, which had grown sadly thin and
sharpened of late, was as hueless and fixed as marble. A divine
pity swelled his heart as he looked down upon her, so forlorn and
helpless in her wondrous loveliness, and lifting her tenderly in his
arms, he bore her to the window and threw open the shutter. The
cold air revived her; and opening her eyes she gazed round her,
bewildered. Recollection came back to her with a sudden pang,
and burying her face in his breast she shivered from head to foot.
Caressingly he laid her back among the cushions, and knelt beside
her. The pitying eye of Heaven only marked the storm raging in
his soul. Not one word, not a gesture revealed it. Was he indeed
wifeless? Yes, by the creed in which he believed. He who had
ever denied the legality of divorce, could not profit by it now. This
was that obstacle in the way of their union which she had not
possessed the strength to confess to him, often as she had essayed
it. He saw it all, now, and minor troubles were forgotten in the
one annihilating feeling that she was his no more, that he must give
her up forever! Every selfish passion faded and died out before
this one bitter, overwhelming grief. Half frantic with grief and
despair, he groaned aloud.

The sound roused her to speech and action, and with a caressing
gesture which she in the same instant repressed as though feeling
herself unworthy to offer it, she said,

"Let me tell you all now, Lisle; all this which I have hidden in
my heart till it was like to burst."

He would have protested, for he saw that she needed rest and
quiet; but she hushed him by a gesture.

"Stay near me thus, Lisle, but in pity turn your eyes aside. I can never tell you what I have to tell, if you turn that wistful glance upon me."

She hesitated a moment as if doubting how to commence, and then said,

"I never have told you much of my life, because while there was nothing in it which I could recall with pleasure, there was much that was too painful and utterly humiliating for me to confess. My father died before I was born, and my mother, a gay, handsome, worldly woman, yet in the prime of her youth and beauty, looked upon me as an obstacle to all her pleasure and enjoyment in the life she led, and a serious impediment in the way of a second marriage. Her ruling ambition was to be wealthy and a leader of fashion, and she was far from being either when I unfortunately was born. As a handsome young widow she might aspire to most anything; but as a mother who upon a limited income was to support herself and a little daughter, the case was very different, and she made me feel and understand it most precociously. We lived very quietly, and she was the only companion of my most favored hours, if that can be termed companionship which was all power and selfishness on one side, and shrinking dread and obedience on the other. When I attained the age of fourteen, she sent me away to a Seminary for young ladies, partly that I might be fashionably educated, but *principally* because being a well-grown girl for my years, I was a serious inconvenience to a yet husband-seeking widow, whose age could illy bear the suggestions my appearance caused. I hailed my deliverance from home with a joy I cannot express to you. I was remarkable only for my aptness in music, which I had always pursued at the expense of everything else, and this gave me the *entrée* into certain social circles from which my youth and inexperience would otherwise have debarred me.

"Beyond the customary supervision of our teachers, no one held any rein over us, and it was quite impossible for them to know the sentimental nonsense so ceaselessly indulged in by young beaux and belles. So it was, that, meeting Louis Hartley, who was pursuing his collegiate course, I received his gallantries and fine speeches without attracting any especial observation. He was then in the senior year of his course, handsome, genteel, and quite an authority among us all. Meeting him often and being always the object of his undivided attention, with the usual precocity of girls in all love matters, I soon came to fancy myself violently in love with him, as he professed to be with me. Of course we made a marriage engagement. At first it was for an indefinite length of time, he not

yet having so much as chosen any profession in life, and I being a
mere school-girl. But one romantic episode followed another, till
at last the suggestion of a secret marriage was made, and my heart
fluttered at the prospect of becoming one of those heroines of which
I had read so much in the novels my mother loved and wept over.
Having thus decided, the opportunity soon came, and one evening
we slipped out from a social gathering and rode out of town un-
checked, to the house of an ever ready 'Justice,' who for a handsome fee risked being compelled to suffer the legal penalty, and we
were married. Thus at the age of fifteen I was made the wife of a
youth of nineteen !

"Looking back upon it now, I can hardly realize the total eclipse
of reason that must have come over me ! That I was alarmed when
I coolly reflected upon what I had done, is true, and my first repentant tears proved to be anything but the sweet showers of sentiment
I had pictured them in my fancy. Louis, too, became alarmed at
the possible consequences of the step he had taken, should Mr.
Fitzjames, whom he regarded as his guardian and mentor, learn it.
All the happiness I had enjoyed in my modest belleship, was destroyed by the sight of his gloomy brow when we met in the little
circles that had before been so delightful, and shunning them more
and more, I gave way to apprehension and discontent, till even the
stolen hours we passed together were embittered by it, and mutual
recriminations made a real breach between us. This was bad
enough, but worse was to follow. I discovered—I found that——
Oh, spare me, Lisle, and guess what a terrible alarm I felt.

"It was impossible for me to remain longer in the Seminary—
where could I turn ? Louis was about to graduate—he dared not
go away with me before ; and I wrote to my mother as the one refuge left me. Casting aside the fear and restraint I had always felt
toward her, I wrote her all, concealing neither my error nor my repentance, and assured that she must respond to my appeal, I packed
my trunk in readiness to go to her at once. Imagine, if you can, the
disappointment I felt when she coldly wrote me that as I had chosen
my destiny I must abide by it ; that my husband, not she, was the
one to whom I should look for protection. She bade me appeal to
her no more—and from that day to this I have never addressed one
word to her, nor she to me.

"I showed Louis her unfeeling letter, and his only remark was an
oath—not that she had outraged me, but that he knew not what to
do with me, helpless as I was. His total lack of anything like manliness toward me, angered me, and in a rage I demanded that he

should avow our marriage and place me in some quiet lodgings, where, my rights as a wife allowed, I would ask for nothing more. The result of a long and warm discussion was a compromise. I was received in the house of a poor widow who would keep the secret of my residence, in exchange for a price agreed upon; but he steadfastly refused to confess the marriage till he should be established in some buisness, and away from the college companions whose ridicule he dreaded. A few weeks afterward Louis received his diploma and went home for a visit.

"I waited hopefully for the letter that was to announce to me his plans for the future. It came at last, telling me that he had accepted the position offered him *as your private tutor;* that as he was to reside in Mr. Fitzjames' house, with you, it was utterly impossible to have me with him.

"All my protests were in vain. The widow with whom I lived had evidently begun to suspect that I was deserted, while my unfortunate situation was more and more apparent, and at last came the warning to seek other lodgings. In despair I wrote Louis everything, and he appeased the widow's virtuous indignation by sending her his first quarter's salary, and a letter acknowledging me as his wife. Whether or not she believed the assertion, she was more respectful to me, and I remained under the roof where I had been *insulted,* simply because I knew not where in the wide world to seek another! Here in due time my little boy was born, and nursed by such unloving hands, I came back to the life I had nearly lost forever."

Sobs choked her utterance here, and for a moment nothing else was heard, while Lisle sat in silent agony, his face buried in his hands, which trembled with the emotion that shook him as an ague. She felt instinctively all that he suffered, and she appealingly exclaimed,

"Oh, Lisle, do not shrink from me in pitying contempt! I was so young and friendless—barely yet sixteen—misguided, foolish, but nothing worse!

"Even then, Louis refused to come to me, basing his refusal upon grounds all to trivial to conceal the fact that he did not care to see me or his child. My first storm of passion passed, I turned to the little one as the only comfort vouchsafed me, and I loved it with an intense devotion. My half-deserted position was more endurable now, and for awhile I ceased to protest against it. So months passed by, during which I did not once see Louis, hardly received a word from him. Then my conquered pride again blazed up, and I wrote him an impetuous letter in which I threatened to reveal all to his benefactor, Mr. Fitzjames, to take my little boy in my arms and force him to acknowledge its paternity. I asked nothing of him now, I only threatened, but those threats effected what tears and prayers had failed to attain. He wrote me for heaven's sake not to execute my threat, promising me that he should soon be able to declare all and take me home with him as his wife, and announced that he should visit me at the end of the first year of his tutorship, now near.

"He came as he had promised, and fully aware that I could influence him only through his fears, I practised upon them to such good purpose that I went with him from the cheerless prison I had so long occupied, and he established me as a boarder, *and his wife*, with a respectable woman in a little town near Louisville, where he could often visit me without attracting any attention from his nearest friends. This woman, who was kind and motherly, was the mother of Joseph Perkins, then a half-grown lad whom I paid a weekly stipend to relieve me in my care of my child, and I devoted the leisure thus secured, to the most diligent study and practice of my music, too long neglected.

Thus passed two years more, not unhappily, and during the third a new hope arose in my heart. Mr. Fitzjames had decided to provide for both his protegés at once, by uniting them in a business house with himself; and I looked forward to assuming my proper place in the social world. Judge, then, of my disappointment when, the business arrangement completed, Louis refused to fulfill his promise, and defied me to prove our marriage. His former fear of Mr. Fitzjames had vanished, since his business prospects were assured, and upbraiding me for the very claims I had upon him, he accused me as an obstacle in the way of his success, and plainly told me that but for me he might make a marriage every way advantageous to himself. He offered me—me, the mother of his child, a sum of miserable lucre to forever renounce my claim upon him; coolly proposed that I should seek a new home far away from him, and with the money he would give me, commence life anew, as a young widow, and leave him free and untrammelled.

"Snatching my little son to my indignant heart, I vowed that not one cent from him should ever contaminate either of us, but that by my own labor I would rear my boy to avenge his mother's wrongs. I scorned to hold by a legal tie one who was not willingly mine, but I dared him to attempt to set it aside. Bound to me by every legal tie he should remain; having thus deserted me he should not profit by it; and having told him this, I opened the door and actually hurled him out it.

"The next day I left the place with my child—that child so like his father in every feature that I often involuntarily thrust him from me, worshipping him as I did, conquered by an impulse, as in t summer at the seaside I was often conquered by the father whose every look reminded me of the child for whom I yearned most passionately, forced as I was to keep him far from me! In the new home I sought, my musical proficiency soon enabled me to gain a handsome support. I lived quietly and secluded, carefully avoiding all cause for remark, and feeling no care for the future. But for my child I might have lived and died thus. But impertinent curiosity left him no enjoyment among his playfellows. I had uncompromisingly called him by his father's name, but of that father he knew nothing, and his dim recollection was but just enough to make his queries unanswerable. I had told him that he whom he thus remembered, was dead; for his careless prattle of him was unendurable; but older tongues took up the burden tossed and parried by the younger, till it became evident that unkind suspicion was fully aroused, and I could submit to it no longer in silence. The poor child himself seemed sinking under the ceaseless taunts cast upon him, and delicate as he was, I feared even for his life.

"In the midst of my trouble, Louis Hartley suddenly appeared before me. I know not what late coming compassion had at last stirred his heart—perhaps it was only a recognition of the power I held over him—but he offered once more to take me and the child under his protection, and with us forever leave the country. Even now I do not know what it was that aroused my suspicions again t him, but a sudden inspiration seized me that he was a fugitive, and I demanded of him of what he was guilty. He told me with a shameless desperation. He was disgusted with the business in which he was a co-partner, jealous of Mr. Fitzjames' manifest and open preference for you, tired of everything in the life he was leading, and so had ended it at once for all. 'An adventurer going out to seek his fortune,' he declared himself. Such was the destiny to which he invited me and my innocent boy, such the ill-gotten gains upon which he proposed to prosecute it. A *thief*, as well as a shameless ingrate! I despised him, and I told him so as I drove him from my sight.

"Never till th n had I cared for the legal freedom to which I was entitled. But I despised him so thoroughly that the very thought of any tie between us, however ignored, was galling to me, and I took steps at once to free myself forever from it. Little time was required fo. this, and all legal formalities being observed, I was once more free and unshackled, and I resumed my maiden name, as entitled to do. Now indeed curiosity had found something tangible upon which to feast, and in the midst of its clamors I suddenly disappeared to return no more. Now it was that I wrote that letter to Mr. Fitzjames which has kept your interest aroused till this day. I wrote him the whole story of Louis' unworthiness; told him my wrongs and how I had at last avenged them, and vowed to him that in time Louis' son should repay him all that he had lost by Louis crime. I never thought that the blow I thus inflicted could strike his heart. Assured that he must bitterly resent Louis' ingratitude, I only thought to add utter detestation to indignation, and not even anticipating any reply, I left the place where I had written the letter, and went back at once to good Mrs. Perkins. Here, during my brief stay, I by chance took up a Louisville journal containing an account of the dear old gentleman's sudden shock and death; and I stood appalled as I realized that my letter might have caused that stroke. I suffered the mental agony of an actual murderer, at the very thought, and you may imagine what I felt when long afterward your lips confirmed the fear! Do you remember handing me the envelope to that letter, one morning at the table? I could have dropped when I recognized it!

"I stayed long enough with good old M s. Perkins, now become a widow, to mature a plan I had conceived, and leaving my little boy in her care, I came to this city alone, and fortunately made a most advantageous engagement in the Wheeler family, which enabled me to put my plans into execution. Poor Mrs. Perkins', bereaved of her husband, had also lost her son, Joseph, who left her in anger for some well deserved reproof, and had for some time been in the city of Louisville; and quite dependent upon her own labor for support, the modest income I was able to offer her to keep my child and care for it in my absence, seemed to her a handsome competence. I had saved enough during these years of labor and close economy to rent a quiet little house in a place a little way on this city, and here I established her with a faithful man servant whom she knew to be as zealous and secret as herself. It was my absence upon this mission that brought upon me my disgrace with the Wheelers, and almost exhausted as my little stock of money was by these heavy demands upon it, I was in real despair when Mrs. Venard chanced upon the scene, and so nobly befriended me.

"Of course frequent visits to the poor child were quite impossible. Even were it possible to fly to him for a few hours, and back, a

dared not risk such chances of detection, and I contented myself
with the frequent reports brought me by the faithful servant,
Thomas, and with the letters I sent back to the little fellow who,
with a precocity far beyond his years, understood the whole position
of affairs, feeble as were the words by which I strove to explain it to
him.

"At last the little fellow fell violently ill, and too anxious to
observe his customary prudence, Thomas was seen by Mr. and Mrs.
Venard to give me the letter Mrs. Perkins had written begging my
immediate presence. I went in response, as you remember, and for
the days succeeding I never left his bedside. Fortunately the violence of this attack abated so that I dared leave him and return in
time to spare Mrs. Venard the embarrassment she must otherwise
have suffered from so apparently eccentric absence. Unfortunately
I missed the train I intended to have taken, and when at last I did
arrive, so late at night, I felt positively guilty, and afraid to look
her in the face. She received me as only *she herself* could have done;
and I went down to the parlor, later, reassured and at ease.

" *You* met me there, I never shall forget how ; and I realized then,
what I had not before suspected, that you loved me. I had known,
before, that *I loved you ;* but the very hopelessness of such a love
had kept me within the bounds of reason and common sense.

"You were not the stranger to me that I was to you. For years
I had known your very eccentricities, and harshly as I heard them
criticised, I was irresistibly attracted by them and by you. An
overwhelming presentiment of all the evil to come, swept over me
as I felt how powerless I was to struggle against your love and its
pleadings, and I seriously contemplated flying from you forever.
For even this I had not the moral courage, and I remained to be
tempted by a power which I knew would conquer me. I had not
forgotten your peculiar creed relative to marriages annulled by
legal power. You know how I strove to do what I knew to be
right and just under such circumstances.

"In a weak hour I yielded to your suit. I told you that 'a mere
conscientious scruple ' separated us, and when you waved it aside I
determined it should be forever. In becoming my husband you
were making no sacrifice of conscience, violating no principle even
of your own illiberal creed, while in resigning you *I* was giving up
more than life itself. With such thoughts I married you, and God
knows I meant to make you happy.

"As if to convince me that no real and lasting happiness can proceed from a wrong act however glossed over by argument or sophis-

try, one cloud after another darkened the horizon where I had expected only sunshine. On the very threshold of our new home, I met Joseph Perkins, and the impudent leer he cast upon me told me plainly that he recognized me, and believed me *not your lawful wife.* Of course I could not stoop to explain, and the ceaseless dread I suffered lest he might reveal all he knew of the past, made me a slave to him and his demands, however unreasonable. You know now upon what was based the protection upon which you so often rallied me.

" When I had resigned my child to the care of another, I had vowed to myself and him that *once every year* I would go to him for a visit of at least twenty-four hours. It was little enough, not more than the holiday to which even the worst tasked governess is entitled. This right I had mentally reserved while claiming none other beside the ' salary ' which was to be my own, unquestioned, needing it as I did for the maintenance of my child, and which you awarded me in that contract whose playfulness did not impair its good faith.

" As the period for that visit drew near for the first time after our marriage, I was half distracted. I could not disappoint the poor child, of whose delicate health I heard infrequent reports. I could not well tell you that I was going away upon a mission not even your protests could have forbidden—I dared· not leave you one written adieu with any excuse, for the reason you know. I went silently, and heaven knows sadly. I ceased to reproach myself for going, when I looked upon the poor child's delicate face, hardly life-like even under the glow of joy with which he sprang into my embrace. Though ailing he was not really ill, and though anxious about him, I was no longer alarmed.

" I came back to you from that first visit since our marriage, and our first misunderstanding arose from it. My first thought was one of resentment, but I accepted your anger as a justice bestowed unawares. Selim's abduction I traced at once to Joseph. He had known of Louis' presence in the grounds that evening before I went away, and I saw that he had timed the doubtlessly long contemplated theft accordingly. He knew I could not brave a prosecution in the case, which would inevitably lead to a knowledge of that other hated presence ; and that he defied me to do so, was the secret of my firm resolve that he should not be received back in our service after you had, to my joy, discharged him. I confess to you, now, that I bribed him to restore the horse, since I dared not do otherwise.

"Our happiest hours followed his departure, and I shall ever regret that we disturbed them by that sojourn at the watering-place during the summer. Here Louis Hartley reappeared. I believed all was over between him and Julie, and I attached little importance to his presence in such a resort, till gossip led me to think that he was deliberately avenging himself upon both you and me, by making my name a subject of scandal as connected with himself.

"We returned home in October, and the first news that greeted me from the cottage so long unvisited, was the serious illness of my child. I dared not go to him, the very promise I had given you under an impulse too strong to be resisted, forbade me to do so. But I ordered a report to be brought me daily, and I met Thomas at the gate to receive it. For some time the little fellow wavered between life and death, then rallied. I was forced to go away upon that excursion you remember. I had no opportunity to warn Thomas not to come during my absence, and I was compelled to rely wholly upon his prudence and natural shrewdness. When I returned I found a letter written by himself and given into the housekeeper's charge, telling me the boy had suffered a relapse, and begged for me continually. I forced myself to remain here as I felt I ought, though health and nerves gave way beneath the task. You went away for a time, and the temptation I had so long resisted came over me with irresistible power. They told me he was dying, and I flew to him by the first train—too late—he was dead when I reached him!"

Her voice broke, and utterly failed her, and she wept convulsively. Moved by profoundest pity, Lisle caressed and soothed her till her self-control returned, and she resumed briefly,

"I returned home directly from the funeral, hoping to reach it before you. I had written you at last, careless, in my suffering, what danger I incurred, resolved as I was to tell you all and so end the feverish life I endured. I thought when I came so unexpectedly upon you, that your very ghost had thus appeared to taunt me, and I was terror stricken. You were very angry, Lisle, but I know you will deal justly. I have told you all, at last. Condemn and sentence me as you will, but remember my temptation. *I loved you!*"

Yes, with a love beyond all price! He knew it, but the fact remained, pitiless, inexorable? She was no wife of his by any law he recognized. But one course remained to him in honor—renunciation! Bigoted, fanatical he might be, but conscientious; and he bent over her in a silence that sent the bitter truth home to her heart. White and still she rose before him. Roused by the action he sprang to his feet and caught her to his breast in one impetuous, passionate embrace, uttering only her name again and again. She was not deceived by the act, not one false hope dawned in her heart, but her very woman's pride died out of it, and she murmured,

"Do not, do not send me from you! I *am* your wife, I could enforce the title if I would. Well, I resign it; I will adopt *your* conscience, and never speak the word. Keep me upon your own terms, I have none to make."

He would have been more or less than mortal had not he hesitated. The Saviour himself was tempted, but less insidiously than this! Heart and brain reeled under it. But the next instant he put her from him shudderingly.

"No, no, a thousand times no! Ah, Leonore, I love you too well for this. *Wife*, my true and lawful wife—or nothing!"

"How *can* I leave you!" she uttered despairingly.

"That you shall not," he answered resolutely. "This home is yours by the law you recognize; half I have in this world would be accorded you, to-morrow, were I never again to look upon your face. Keep it and use it. No one need know the insuperable barrier between us; as my wife you shall be recognized by all, and if the day ever come when Louis Hartley's hated life is stilled, a secret marriage known to none save us shall legalize the name you never ceased to bear so that *my* heart and soul are satisfied. Leave me? Never!"

CHAPTER XXXIII.

THE remaining hours of that eventful night which had so revolutionized his life, Lisle passed in restless, ceaseless pacing across the floor, insensible even to fatigue, under the mental torture he suffered. Under such a renunciation there was faint consolation in the thought that he should not be entirely separated from the wife he could not acknowledge or believe legally his, that he should meet her day by day in such social converse as was rightfully theirs whatever the tie between them. After all, was this a principle for which he was sacrificing so much? Was it not, rather, a prejudice, as she had termed it? Whatever might-have been his decision had he known all before the actual marriage had taken place, had he any spiritual right not to be granted him legally, to annul it now?

Reason triumphed over prejudice, at last, and he blushed as he remembered the terms upon which he had bidden her to saty, generous and just as he had deemed them when proposed. Proud and uncompromising as she was, how had she not rejected them at once ; how not refused thus to temporize with her lawful rights ? What he had offered her was a living death to a proud woman who *knew* herself his lawful wife, and who loved him with more than a wife's devotion. That love itself had sealed her lips under his mockery of justice, as it had prompted her humble offering of herself and her life, even though he ignored their marriage. Such love as theirs would have sanctified most any tie between them—yet she had meekly yielded and conceded all.

Day had dawned ere reason thus declared its sway, and he glanced up at the rosy eastern sky that seemed to smile approvingly upon this second renunciation, not of his love and happiness, but of a bigotry that had presumed to say *the law had power to bind, but not unloose.*

With the glow of happiness upon him, he stole to his wife's door and listened. Not a sound reached his ear, and glad that sleep had overpowered her despite her misery, he went cautiously away. Recalling how wan and ill she had looked when he parted from her, he left her till late in the morning, hesitating to arouse her even to happiness. His impatience became uncontrollable at last, and resolving at least to look upon her as she dreamed, he softly opened the door and entered. She was not there, the room was quite deserted, and evidences of hasty packing showed how she had passed the hours during which he had battled with himself. He stood appalled by the shock of the conviction that rushed upon him. She had fled from him forever ! He threw open the *armoirs*, dreading to find that in the usual style of ' heroines of romance ' she had left behind her all for which he was supposed to care, her wardrobe and the jewels he had given her. The bitterness faded from his mind the instant it had swept across it, for this insult had been spared him. With her exquisite sensitiveness for *his* feelings, she had thrown back upon him nothing that was hers by any generosity of his; and he mentally thanked her.

She was gone, this bitter truth remained ; and pressing his cheek upon the pillow where her own so often had lain, he gave way to the utter desolation of soul that racked him. Where had she fled, to whom would she apply for the protection she thus refused to accept from him ? Suddenly he remembered that little cottage of which she had spoken. Could he find old Mrs. Perkins, he should learn tidings of his wife ; and he rang the bell for Margaret, who was more in her mistress's confidence than any other. Not she, but

James, appeared in answer to the summons, and Lisle eagerly demanded,

" Where is Margaret ?"

" She went away with the madam, before daylight. I took them and their trunks to the depot for the four o'clock train."

So, she had gone up the country; this was some clue, but where ? This he might learn of the ticket agent, and he hurried out. No. The agent had seen the lady and her maid waiting for the train, but no tickets had been purchased, nor had Leonore ever procured tickets when making her former visits as confessed. Strange fatality that had kept unnamed this little village of her pilgrimages, when she had so fully revealed all else ! Disappointed but not discouraged, he returned home.

" Mrs. Perkins met him at the threshold, unusually disturbed ' " Please, sir, would you mind giving my Joseph a hearing, being as he's come this early to ask it ? Though he won't tell me, which am his lawful partner, anything about it, I'm sure it's about the dear lady he's something to tell."

" Send him to me at once," he exclaimed as the idea flashed upon him that more was probably to be learned of Joseph than from all others combined; and soon that worthy individual appeared.

" Well, what have you to tell ?" Lisle abruptly demanded.

" A good deal first and last, as is worth a heap of money, sir."

" I make no bargain with you, Joseph. Tell me first, and if you are really useful to me, you shall be well paid."

" I can put you on the madam's track, if you think she's worth the following. You see, a long back I han't had right smart of business, and I know'd there was more to be made a-keeping watch on her, than in any other kind of speculation. She was always full of secrets, was the madam, and some of 'em I know'd."

" Well, go on, and tell all you know as briefly as possible."

" Well, I know where the madam used to go when she went away so mysterious, and I know what she went for. I suspicioned it all at first, and to make sure, I followed her. I don't mind owning up that I was hired to watch both the madam and the young miss, by one as had an interest in 'em both. The party as hired me to watch 'em, wanted to know the whereabouts of another party—a small party tother one was—because he thought it might come useful to him if the madam set herself agin him in a certain projec' which he had, which I don't mind telling you was a-marrying of the young miss herself. There wan't no love lost atween him and the madam, but she set a s'ore by the small party, and there he had her if he once found the small party. So, as I say, I followed her, and I found out what he wanted to know. It turned out he didn't have to use it, but'that an't neither here nor there. Only just it was this way I come to know what I do know about it; and enough trouble she give me with all the twistings and turnings she took to go twenty odd miles straight into the country, and I seen her into the very door of the nest she'd got hid away so knowingly, and I seen it was my own old mother as kept the nest warm for her while she was away from it so continually. I was just struck of a heap when I seen my old relation, for I hadn't a idee she was down in this country. I know'd then where she went, and I know'd as the servant man I'd often seen a-coming to the gate here, brung her news of the small party. Well, time went on, and nothing happened till now. The party as hired me is married with the young miss by this time, and ı spose he had the same right to take another wife that the madam had to take another husband—for he *was* her husband, and the small party was a boy as was had atween 'em six or eight years ago. The boy is dead these two days, and the madam come home all in black from his funeral."

"You are wondrously well informed, Joseph. All this I knew, before. Go on."

"You know'd it, sir ! Then, by gumbo, Joe Perkins was the fool some people took him for. I'd a sworn all the madam's trouble was to keep it from you ! And you know'd it ?"

His surprise was genuine, and under less painful circumstances would have invoked laughter. Obeying a gesture, he conquered his loquacious surprise, and resumed,

"Maybe you know all I'm going on to tell you, then ; but I'll tell it. Yesterday was a busy day round this house, and I couldn't just make out all as was going on. I hated to give up beat, and I hung round till nigh eleven o'clock, when just as I'd made up my mind to knock off, who should I see leaning up agin the gate but the madam herself come home from the funeral. She looked clean beat out, and as I know'd you was setting up in the parlor almost in the dark, I know'd as there'd be a time atween you, and I clumb the fence and come up under the window. All of a sudden the shutter flung open, and I was nigh being hit by it ; but you hadn't seen me at all, as I was afraid, and I see you a-holding the madam in the air, and she fainted dead away. I know'd then as something uncommon was up, and I hung around to see what'd come next.

"Just afore daylight, around come the carriage, and James and Margaret brought out some trunks and piled them on as best they could, when out came the madam herself and got into the carriage with maid Margaret. I'd seen the madam go off before, but never like this in grand style, and, said I to myself, she'll quit it when they get to the depot. Sure enough, there I found 'em, and the carriage left, empty, while she and Margaret went on the cars. Knowing, as I did know, that the small party wasn't calling her off now, I just took a back seat on the same train, and I stuck by 'em till we got into the same town she'd always gone to before, and here off they got, bag and baggage. So back I come on the next train, and says I, if there's money to be made out of *any* one, now, the master himself is the one."

" Give me the name of this town you speak of, and directions by which I can find the cottage, and I will pay you liberally."

Joseph's eyes brightened as he complied, and having carefully written them down, Lisle fulfilled his promise. He stopped with a strange expression on his face when he had reached the door upon his way out.

" There's another thing I could tell, as might interest you. When I said I ' hung around here,' it didn't just mean that I stayed every minute. I went and come, and once when I went I hung around the city prison for a bit. It was long after dark when I see a carriage come up, and out got a police feller with Mr. Louis Hartley at his heels."

Lisle sprang up electrically, doubting if what he heard were indeed real, and Joseph answered as though interrogated,

" Yes, sir, it's the Lord's truth. I asked some folks standing round talking it over after they two went inside, what was up, and they said ' the cuss had been marrying too many wives.' "

" And did you really see Hartley lodged in prison ?"

" Well, sir, I didn't see him lodged, nor yet fed, cause I hadn't time; but I see him took in, and then I come away. The young miss wasn't with him, and I don't know yet *where* she is. I'll find out all about it, and save you the trouble, if you'll come atween me and the state's evidence my step-son-in-law is threatening agin me in a piece of business."

" Take yourself off. If you've been in rascality together, I hope he will turn state's evidence. I thought you had reformed."

" I did, but I kind of backslewed—I believed they call it in the meeting-house. I'll serve you faithful if you hush the madam's lips, being as she's the only one can hurt me. I wouldn't risk your find-ing her if I didn't put trust in the gratitude you'd both ought to have towards me, when you come back together like two turtle doves."

Feeling that his anxiety was not appreciated or sympathized with, Joseph turned away, and Lisle was left to himself.

Relieved as he was by knowing where Leonore was to be found, hope brightened within him, and he went cheerfully in to breakfast, despite the uneasiness he suffered upon Julie account. She was in safety among the friends who had rescued her, probably under Mr. Venard's protection. Before he had carried out his intention of seeking her at Mr. Venard's house, that gentleman himself appeared, and briefly as possible related what had transpired leading to Louis Hartley's arrest.

Sooon after Julie's departure from home the preceding day, with Louis Hartley, Mr. Venard's sister Phebe had arrived at his house, her suspicions excited by a letter Mrs. Venard had written her mon hs before, but whose reception had been delayed by Phebe's absence from home upon a search for a Mr. Horton, whom she had married the preceding summer. Mrs. Venard's description of tho Mr. Leonard Horton stopping at the watering-place, awoke the deserted wife to the conviction that this gentleman must be the identical one for whom she was seeking, and she had come to her sister-in-law immediately upon receiving the letter. The gentleman was fully identified, the only question being where he might now be found; and Mrs. Bertram, who opportunely came in to relate the morning's interview with Julie, whose result would be no secret, was electrified into announcing the whole truth in a manner more convincing then soothing to the feelings of the injured wife, while Mrs. Bertram hastened away to discover whether tho lovers had indeed quite departed. They were indeed gone, and nothing remained but to pursue them as quickly as possible. Taking a warrant for the arrest, Mr. Venard started at once, the city "Gretna Green" being too well known to render any error possible, and ho reached the place scarcely an hour later than the pair whose waiting carriage still stood at the clergyman's door. The marriage ceremony was but just ended, and Mr. Venard made no apologies for his abrupt appearance npon the scene. The warrant he brought was for the arrest of one "Leonard Horton," but the *alias* was too manifest to be quibbled over, Julie herself establishing the fact, and while the newly made bride who was not a wife returned to the city in Mr. Venard's charge, Mr. Louis Hartley, *alias* Leonard Horton, returned with a policeman and took bridal rooms alone in the parish prison.

It was late at night when Mr. Venard and his charge reached home, and he had prevailed upon her to wait in his house till morning. She was mortified, pained and embarrassed, and ashamed to look Lisle in the face, but resolved to end it all at once, she had accompanied Mr. Venard home. Shown into a room where Julie sat alone, she met Lisle suddenly and without warning. She ran toward him, then stopped and hid her burning face in her hands. Lisle looked at her one moment in silence, and then his heart softened. She was paying a sufficiently heavy penalty for her *escapade*, without one word from him; and taking her hands from the flushed face, he kissed it very gently. She looked up at him in glad surprise, and threw he arms around his neck in speechless gratitude.

" Come home, Julie. The house is sad and lonely enough now. I will tell you all that has occurred during these eventful last twenty-four hours."

As they were going out the door Phebe entered it. She and Julie had already had a long interview in which everything was discussed and explained, and it was Lisle whom she now addressed.

"He married me just for my money, after all," she said. " He is welcome to it all if he would only be the husband he vowed to be. I gave him ten thousand dollars the week we were married, to ' help him on in his business,' whatever that was; and I'd have given as much more any time he asked for it. He didn't ask ; he only made debts I was forever paying, and I sent him bank checks all over the country to ' enable him to come home,' and he never came but once. He did stay with me on the plantation from Christmas till June, and then he left to follow Julie to a watering-place *where I paid his bills.* It is shameful !"

Lisle affirmed her verdict with more of good faith than he was wont to show her, and she continued,

" They say I can prosecute him for bigamy, and have him shut up in State's Prison, fined, or something, the *very fine* to come out of *my* pocket ! I don't see where I'm to get any comfort in that. The law hasn't any comfort for women, and wont give me even a decent revenge on him. It would shut him up longer for having stolen a horse or fired a barn. But I *will* prosecute him."

They left her weeping and storming by turns ; and taking Julie back home, Lisle told her all Leonore's wrongs and sufferings inflicted by this rascal who would have been *her husband* had not an actual crime prevented.

As she plead her own defence, Lisle read the whole state of affairs, and Edward's visit North was accounted for. Knowing all as he had done, Edward had no cause to feel aggrieved, and knowing that he would not linger an hour away were he apprised of the *denouement*, he left to Julie the slower medium of a letter and telegraphed him to come back at once, and then took the next train in pursuit of the wife so soon to be restored to him, as he fondly believed. The events of the day had so delayed his departure, that it was quite dark before he reached the cottage, and having knocked loudly, he stood impatiently awaiting admission. In that one waiting moment a dread presentiment rushed over him shiveringly. Here, upon the threshold, his hope deserted him, and a dire foreboding fell upon him in place of it. The door opened, at length, and the homely, honest face of the servant Thomas met his eyes.

"My wife," he exclaimed as he took one step forward.

Thomas comprehended who and what he was, at once, and with visible embarrassment he hesitated to reply.

"Come in, sir, come in, the wind is sharp and cold enough," he said evasively, showing his visitor to the fire.

Lisle's impatience was torturing, and he said again,

"My wife, Mrs. Sterling. Is she here?"

"Well, no, sir. She were here, but she went away hours ago."

"Where has she gone? Tell me in heaven's name."

Again the faithful Thomas hesitated, but compassionating the torture he recognized, he answered respectfully,

"She sailed for Liverpool three hours since; she and her maid."

Lisle groaned in agony of spirit.

"Gone, gone! sailed for Liverpool, did you say? How do you know it?"

"I will tell you all about it, sir. This very morning, afore we were astir, the lady and her maid reached here, and sick and pale she were. Dame Perkins warmed her and comforted her the best she was able, but the little creeter's heart was that broke that she only sobbed and cried the more for all the kindness as was showed her; and then she told the Dame that all was over between herself and you forever and ever, and that she was going away, *any* where out of America. She wouldn't consent to stay here, spite of all we could do, and when maid Margaret was to have been left behind, she went on her knees to the sweet lady as couldn't deny her, and off they went together. I went with them and see them both aboard the ship as was already weighing anchor, and they'll touch land no more till they reach Halifax. There they'll touch, and the lady promised to write a line back to the Dame, who loves her like she was an own child, however humbly."

"What ship did she go on? Do you remember the name?"

"The 'Flying Scud,' bound to Liverpool. Here I have the clearance notice just as I cut it out of a city paper. 'Flying Scud, Guble, master.' You're welcome to it, sir."

Words were not necessary to interpret Lisle's hopes and fears, and wringing the faithful servant's hand he rushed out and away. Too late, too late! How every hope mocked him! Still one was left, he could reach Halifax before them, by rail; here he would claim his wife and bring her back to their home, for all time. Never again would he lose sight of her. Hope though deferred was strong within him as he returned to his cheerless home where Julie waited for him anxiously.

The next morning a messenger came from Louis Hartley, who, unable to procure bail, awaited his trial in the prison. Julie had firmly refused to see him or hold any communication with him, and it was to Lisle he now addressed an appeal for one moment's interview. Thinking it better to hear what Louis had to say, he granted the request, and he and Louis met for the first time in years.

With a weak appeal for compassion, Louis told his story with such excuses as he could frame, and complained of Julie's heartlessness and cruelty to him. "If I did wrongly it was for her sake I did it, and she owes me appreciation at least," he said when all was told.

Contempt sealed Lisle's lips. He had no words for such a proposition as this, and he turned away disgusted. He had expected defiance, but not such unreason as this. Louis stopped him with a gesture.

"Lisle Sterling, you of all men owe me justice, if not some generosity. You stand in my place as master of a fortune which you kept me out of by your schemes and wheedling of a weak old man, who was *my* guardian long before he became yours; *all* I ever lost, you have gained. Yet now you turn your back upon me. Well, go, but at least, grant me one interview with Julie. I ask nothing more."

"A modest request, most truly! Will you receive her here?"

"What does it matter where? If she loved me she would come; if she does not, let her tell me so. I can die but once, and that as well first as last."

"If such is really your intention, let me suggest that 'procrastination is the thief of time.' Julie not only does not love you, as you well know, but she *despises* you, and were you free to day she would never look upon your face again."

"Then my death will be upon her soul," Louis tragically exclaimed.

Lisle smiled ironically. "It is too unimportant a matter to lie very heavily upon it. I applaud your resolution, certainly the best one I ever knew you to form. If you were capable of anything praiseworthy, I should advise you to live and become a better man for the sake of your wife, who even yet would forgive you. But you are not."

Louis' lip curled contemptuously. "My death may touch her temper, but not her heart, for she has none. She'll make the whole story an episode for one of her astonishing novels, and so give them a touch of the real they never before possessed. I am her benefactor."

"May the consciousness of your benefactions abide with you!" and with such a benediction, Lisle left him.

Unwilling to leave home while matters were so unsettled, Lisle resolved to remain till the last day he could do so and still reach Halifax before the ship could possibly arrive there. Each hour he dreaded the public *exposé* of the incident in which Julie had been so important an actor; but if it was known among the knights of the quill, the high position of the parties connected with it screened them from public comment, and as yet nothing had been said. So another morning dawned clear and bright. Glancing over the columns of the morning paper, Lisle uttered an ejaculation that startled Julie from a similar occupation opposite him. "Louis Hartley is dead! Committed suicide, last night, in the city jail!" Incredulous of what she heard, Julie sprang to her feet with an eager exclamation. Lisle handed her the paper, pointing out the item, and she read,

"Louis Hartley, *alias* 'Leonard Horton,' awaiting trial upon a charge of bigamy, committed suicide last night in the jail where he was temporarily confined. It is hinted that 'disappointed love,' under the scorn inflicted upon him by the lady fair whom he had done the honor of making his second wife while the first one was yet living in the flesh, was the direct cause of this rash act, which, if it has not gained heaven a saint, has certainly relieved earth of a rascal. We give no names, as we would not willingly offend."

The red blush of shame and chagrin swept over her very forehead, and she dropped speechless upon the sofa. Lisle smiled.

"You won't wear widow's weeds, little Julie? Foolish girl; thank your lucky stars that you have escaped so easily. I advise you to hush the clamor of busy tongues by the ringing of marriage bells. Society dearly loves sensation. Have you written Edward?"

"Not a word! How could I?"

With a quizzical look he took his hat and walked out. But a great relief had come to them both in this last, best act Louis Hartley had ever perpetrated. Each was free from the blight his living presence cast upon them, and to Lisle especially it was as the dissolving of a nightmare. Ah, if Leonore in this hour knew it, how gladly, joyfully, would she return! No fear, now, that, distrusting the enduring force of his own arguments over himself, she would dread to put them to such a test as he would have insisted upon! She could come back to him with an assured heart, a conscience free from one self-reproach, untroubled by one foreboding. His heart beat lightly under the consciousness.

The hours flew by till that one arrived for which Lisle waited, and as he sat alone late at night, expectantly, the welcome ringing of the bell greeted his ear, and Edward was with him.

Till among " the wee sma' hours ayont the twal," the two brothers sat and talked together, discussing lastly Edward's visit home.

Old Mrs. Sterling had died while he was with her; this Edward had told him earlier; but neither had cared to discuss the details till other engrossing topics were disposed of. To Lisle she had never been a tender mother, and Edward himself, her best beloved of all her children, had shown her duty rather than affection. Of all nearest her, the husband whom she had so bitterly wronged was her sincerest mourner.

" Did she speak of me ?" Lisle asked with a fear at his heart that shook his voice.

" Much and often. It really seemed as if avenging justice rebuked her cruelty to you through all these years! She was the most unhappy creature I ever saw, if not quite a maniac. She had a most singular fancy concerning you, Lisle."

" And that "—Lisle suggested breathlessly but with forced calmness.

" Was that you were the son of Dr. Kelley. She asserted it again and again, urging the poor old man to disown you in his last will, and leave the property to me. I think she would have disowned all her other children for the accomplishment of this one wish. 'Twas strange !"

" And the old gentleman, what did he say to this strange fancy ?"

" Just what you might anticipate, knowing how much he always loved and respected her, aggravating as she was toward him. His only fear was that malicious tongues might repeat her ravings, to her prejudice and yours. It was fortunate for us all, that her life

was too full of all the homely virtues, to leave one spot for scandal
to fix upon ?"

Lisle breathed more freely under the reassuring words.

"Poor old father," he said compassionately. "He never ceased
to feel flattered that a Fritzjames had stooped from her high degree
and deigned to become his wife! I've no doubt he mourns her
more deeply and sincerely than many a husband mourns a wife who
embodied all the virtues and devoted her very life to his happiness !"

"Yes, indeed. He has never in his whole life so rebelled against
the will of 'a Divine Providence' as now when 'it for some wise
purpose, though a hidden one, permitted the last hours of so good
a woman and Christian to be troubled so mysteriously.' Of course
I tried to teach him something of the diagnosis of brain diseases, and to account learnedly for aberrations of mind; but it was
useless. He couldn't have looked more pained and shocked if I had
suddenly professed and expounded our old grandmother's theory
about people being 'let down out of the fog.' Mental aberration,
diseases of the brain, and total lack of brains, are all promiscuously
hustled on to the broad shoulders of Providence, till the load is prodigious! Will the reign of common sense ever come?"

So, his mother was really dead, with her secret and his unknown,
narrow as had been the escape from its shameful exposure! It was
dreadful in the abstract for a son to feel a sense of inexpressible relief at the death of a mother; but dependent upon her strength of
mind, as he had been, to guard that one bitter shame of his life, it
could not be otherwise. The curse under which he was born had
been bitter enough upon his life to exemplify the wording of the relentless text: "For I am a very jealous God, and visit the sins of
the fathers upon the children, to the third and fourth generation;"
words to which Christians bow the head, which childish lips are
taught to utter, as if they shadowed forth God's own justice and
mercy to erring mortals!

Lisle had borne this curse, but he endured it as of human, not
divine origin. It was lifted from him at last. He alone knew it,
and for the first time he tolerated it. No more of the secret dread
of that hour when he should hang his head in the presence of his
fellowmen, feeling that an impostor's mantle had been stripped from
his shoulders! Unutterable relief! He was half mad with the delicious intoxication of this first feeling of security from all that had
hung like a pall around his life. Sleep and he were strangers
through that night; but the spirit within him had found a sweeter
rest than " tir'd nature's sweet restorer " had power to give.

CHAPTER XXXIV.

JULIE'S good genius inspired her to unclose her eyes at an unusually early hour, quite unconscious as she was of the arrival upon the preceding night, and having run down to the parlor, whose brightness and warmth were most grateful upon this wintry morning, she came unexpectedly upon Edward himself, who, unable to sleep under the spurring of a busy brain, had risen as soon as the fires were lighted. She uttered a little cry, forced from her by the very intensity of joy and surprise, and darting forward he caught her in his arms.

No need of explanations here, where nothing had been concealed, and Lisle had the night before related all that transpired in Edward's absence. It was a happy hour that followed, and Lisle's advice relative to the "marriage bells" was advocated by Edward with lips far more eloquent and persuasive.

"This is the very season of holidays, Julie. Why not thus celebrate a 'merry Christmas,' and send Lisle on his way rejoicing. He vows he will resign his guardianship before he ever again trusts you alone, and I don't know who would more joyfully assume it than I."

"But, Edward, how will you endure all the gossip of which I am sure to be the object of this disgraceful *denouement* of bigamy, suicide, and the rest of it, spread abroad! Are wives, like 'hearts, caught at the rebound?'"

"Now and then, by those who have skill and good fortune. I should have waited for the widow, you know; so this is my good fortune. I am quite content with it, believe me. Do you remember how many years I have waited for this hour however it might come?"

"Yes, I remember. But, Edward, this is serious. Don't try to laugh me out of the conviction that society will demand the fullest penalty for my mistake. If this is being something like 'a heroine,' I certainly don't feel very heroic; and I don't want you to come in for a share of what doesn't belong to you."

She looked very serious, but he laughed.

"So it is *society* you are afraid of, is it? May I never be guilty of setting up a golden calf and then falling down and worshipping it! As father would say, 'there's teaching against it.' What, after all,

is society, but a golden calf? probably the very one figuratively mentioned in the incident referred to."

She shook her head dissentingly, and he continued more seriously,
"Tell me if you can, who, and what, is 'society.' Is it, or is it not,
a collection of individuals, each one of which is entitled to the rights
and privileges guaranteed by the Constitution—'life, liberty, and
the pursuit of happiness.' It is a very good brotherhood when all
its members agree ; but were I one of its law givers, I would utterly
refuse to bow down and do reverence to the edicts I had helped to
frame *for others* to follow.

> 'As some tall guide-post stands upon the down,
> Its hands still pointing to the distant town,'

I'd point out the way to others, but I wouldn't be forced to pursue
it myself. Just assume the right to revolt, once, remembering that
numerically you are as strong as any among the fellowship, and
though to-day you may constitute a minority, to-morrow some other
unlucky wight will stand in the breach, and you can be relentless
with a majority. As the French say, '*chaque un a son tour.*'"

She laughed at the irreverent philosophy ; but not a difficult convert to any creed which her own heart favored, she gave assent to
his project, and the gratifying intelligence greeted Lisle, who soon
after descended. She had dreaded many sarcastic comments not
serenely to be borne,-but he made none. He was gentle even to
pensiveness this whole day, and as much rejoiced as surprised at it,
she felt herself supremely blessed.

Of course those who dared, protested against so quiet a wedding,
insisting that it should be deferred till Mrs. Sterling returned home
from the visit she was supposed to be making out of the city, when
they should make amends for Lisle's fraud upon society in his own
quiet marriage, while everybody was out of town.

Edward put such protests laughingly aside, affirming that he
dared not give the bride elect time to change her mind, and the marriage was solemnized amid only the little circle that had so long
been almost like one family.

Too supremely happy to care what might be said of this second
marriage ceremony within one week, Julie bade a light farewell to
the old guardian in accepting the new, and Lisle left them upon his
journey of so many a weary mile of rail, to intercept at Halifax that
wife whom the good ship was hourly bearing to meet him.

Only one item rippled the serene domestic life of the newly married lovers who kept honeymoon in the quiet home. Poor Mrs.

Perkins fell under misfortune. Alarmed at the probable result of the ungrateful Bill having actually turned state's evidence, Joseph evaded arrest by dodging the minions of the law, and so flying the country, taking with him as the divider of his troubles and the doubler of his joys, the faithless Melissa, whose tender offspring had first been conveniently and ingeniously sent round to pay a visit to its grandmother. A lengthy visit it bade likely to prove, and the old dame was wroth.

"It is bad enough," she sobbed indignantly, "to be deserted in my old age, and that for my own daughter which was always a trial to me, but to put a teething little beast as is its father's very image, off on me, and that father just sent to the Penitentiary for Lord knows how long, is a burning shame! I only wish 'em joy of each other, for a shiftless couple they are, and shiftless they'll be."

It was a sad state of affairs truly; but there was a tinge of the ludicrous in it that made it less affecting to others than to herself, as is often the case in this vexatious, irreverent world.

———————

Blow, blow, blow. What a screaming of the tempest let loose over the earth, what wrenching and racking of the tortured objects that offered an unavailing resistance to its rush and whirl!

All night as Lisle pursued his journey upon this the last end of its course, the fearful storm kept company with the shrieking engine that struggled pantingly forward with the lumbering train, cowering before the dangers that beset its progress, without a hope of a coming lull, or defence and protection from the storm. Now and then branches wrenched violently from the overhanging forest trees were hurled against the closed carriages, while here and there some rugged member of the fraternity lay prostrate by the hurricane, and its fellows held wake over it with arms tossed frantically in air, and their angry voices lending their clamor to the unearthly shrieks that rushed on into the inky darkness as if to announce the approach of the adventurous train that dared this night invade their territories.

Blow, blow, blow. While the wind swept over them, the wayworn, terrified passengers huddled together in the coaches closed to stifling and heavy with the foul air of many breaths, and talked in hoarse whispers of the dangers by land and sea, while the more courageous told fearful tales of flood and field, and hair-breadth scapes that startled the crying children into breathless silence.

Ever and anon nervous hands wiped from the windows the wintry sleet that dimmed them and trickled down in little rills under the influence of the warmth within, and eager eyes strained themselves to pierce the blackness beyond. Vain effort. Nothing could be distinguished under that inky sky, and the heavy, clinging dampness, directly reobscured the window pane whose momentary clearness had but rendered the darkness beyond more visible. Blow, blow, blow. All the crime and wickedness that ever stalked the earth, were holding high carnival this night, shrieking their frenzied mirth into the startled ear of Heaven, huzzaing with wild glee as some exploit more terrible than the rest was proclaimed abroad. Wild under the reign of anarchy, staid old monarchs of the forest that had for half a lifetime swayed their sceptres right royally over their peaceful subjects, now cast aside their crownly pomp and dignity, and joined in the mad revel with savage glee. It was a fearful night, and all creation seemed but a handful of clay to be whisked about at will by the warring elements that battled and wrangled over it. Even when the cold, gray daylight dawned, the heavy clouds fought inch by inch as they were driven back, and ever and anon fierce blasts not on duty at the grand assault, pounced down upon some unoffending atom and annihilated it at one sweep, heralding its triumph by a rushing hiss, and gusts of rain and hail followed in its train, wreaking their impotent malice upon whatever had survived the general wreck.

Thus the belated train arrived at last at the seaport which had been the haven of Lisle's hopes through so many weary hours; and racked with anxiety at the inevitable danger to all who were ocean tossed under such a tempest, he hastened to learn if the ship 'Flying Scud' were yet safe in port. His heart stood still under the answer he received. The ship had touched there long before she was expected, having made the quickest time on record, and had proceeded on her way to Liverpool. Disappointment rendered him speechless, and he leaned against a pillar for support under the mortal weakness that overpowered him. Again too late, despite the wide margin of time he had allowed for all possible detentions and accidents! It seemed as if the powers of earth and heaven had combined to baffle him; and a superstitious thrill ran through every nerve. For the first time he lost all hope; and staggering into the street he wandered up and down, lost to all sense of time and place. Suddenly the import of the news cried through the streets flashed through his benumbed mind, and he snatched eagerly at the 'extra' in a newsboy's hands.

"News by telegraph. Shipwreck of the 'Flying Scud,' Guble master, bound to Liverpool. Stranded off Cape Race, during the storm. Loss of life not yet known. Survivors being taken off by the 'Sea-Bird.'"

Such were the items Lisle comprehended as he glanced through the extra; and learning that a steamer was about leaving for the scene of the wreck, he hastened on board, with many others.

The storm had quite abated now; but the wintry air was bitterly keen, and the waves rose and fell angrily as they ploughed through them. It was easy to imagine how greedily they had snatched at their prey during those fearful hours of tempest-tossed peril, how they had gathered in white-capped majesty and dashed themselves against it as it struck the reef. They seemed now like a horde of murderers exulting over their work, and sick with horror Lisle turned his eyes away, and, struggling against the madness that threatened him, tried to fix his attention upon the conversation around him. There were many passengers on board, called out by the usual variety of emotions, some tortured with anxiety for loved ones thus imperilled, others forced by mere love of excitement, or by *ennui* to visit the scene of the catastrophe. Their remarks would have waked a smile in one quite unconcerned; but Lisle looked with a species of horror upon one man who seemed more heartless than all others; a tall, spare person, who as he incessantly chewed his tobacco, discoursed upon the chances of the wreck.

"I had a mother-in-law on board that ship," he said, "who owns a good bit of property first and last, that'll come to my wife if the old woman is drowned; and I thought I'd just come over and see. If it is so, I'll go back to Jersey and set up a grocery I've got my eye on. I don't wish the old woman any harm, but she is getting on in years, and we all *have* to give up sooner or later. Mother-in-laws are mostly easy spared."

The idle knot around him laughed carelessly, and kindred jests were told by one and another of the crowd.

It seemed too terrible, this jesting with death under so frightful a form, and under existing circumstances. The very waves were less cruel, and bending over them Lisle gazed down upon them till a wild fascination possessed him.

They soon reached the wreck. There it lay, pounding on the reef, the waves breaking over it at every surge, but not a soul to be seen. The Sea-Bird had finished her work and departed, bearing the rescued to the shore. Thither they followed her, and the search for the missing commenced.

With an aching palpitation of the heart, Lisle flew from place to place, longing yet dreading to find her whom he sought. How would he find her; dead, or yet alive? He dared not think. In the midst of his search he met the man who had come over to look after his mother-in-law. Lisle would have passed him shudderingly, but his steps were stayed by the man who, after all, seemed to have some compassion in his nature, stirred by Lisle's wistful eyes.

"Looking for some one, stranger?" he asked not unkindly.

"Yes, my wife," he gasped in reply.

"Young and handsome woman, with a black-eyed maid?"

"Yes, yes. Have you seen them?"

"Well, I guess so. There's the likes of them in that little house yonder, where I found mother-in-law as hearty and sound as ever."

Without hearing another word, Lisle rushed away to the indicated spot. Leonore was indeed before him, but pallid, inanimate apparently dead, with the faithful Margaret weeping over her as she strove to recall life and animation. Dashing everything aside, Lisle clasped his wife in his arms. Not dead, not dead! Oh joy unutterable!

Margaret stood and gazed at him in mute astonishment, unable to comprehend what she beheld. With many a murmured word Lisle laid the fainting form back upon the pillow, and shutting out all intruders, nursed her back to life. Once more the dark eyes opened, wonderingly, but with a blessed light in their depths as they fixed themselves upon his face.

"Leonore, my wife, my little wife!" he exclaimed as tears of love and joy fell from his eyes.

She raised her hand caressingly to his face; but a deadly weakness was upon her, ill as she was from long endured excitement culminating in this catastrophe that had nearly torn her from him forever. That feeble, loving touch was dearer to him now than any caress of the past, mute assurance as it was that she accepted, unquestioningly, the name and title he thus restored to her.

The long hours he sat beside her while life and strength were waved back to her, were perhaps the very happiest they had known together. The blessed interchange of thought and confidence, the loving protest she offered when he accused himself for all the suffering his bigotry had caused her, these were grateful enough to each; but when he told her of that suicidal death which lifted the last

cloud from their united lives, she only said, "thank God," and
nestled her check in his hand, too grateful to express her joy.

Lisle carried her to New York when returning strength permitted, and from here he wrote the joyful letter so anxiously awaited
by Edward and Julie in their southern home, where he hoped so
soon to join them.

"How sweet it is to feel that there are no shadows or secrets between us henceforward and forever! How can any true wife and
true husband fail to realize that perfect happiness *cannot* exist, except with perfect trust and confidence in each other? The lips that
smile over an unuttered secret but mock at married happiness."

"Hush, Leonore," he whispered, conscience stung.

"How can I 'hush' when my very soul is so full of happiness!
You cannot realize what it is to cast such a burden from one's conscience—to feel that one is no longer a hypocrite and a living lie to
all one loves best on earth."

"*I will* know it, Leonore. I have the same need to learn it that
you had. I have erred toward you no less than you toward me.
Pride and shame both kept me silent when I should have spoken,
before I dared to make you the wife of such an unfortunate as I! I
had no right to wife or child, Leonore, for I had not so much as a
name to bestow upon them. Cursed in my birth, I am a living example of woman's treachery and man's selfishness. She who called
me son, hated me for the one fact of my existence; he whom I called
father, owned no drop of kindred blood with that coursing in my
veins. An illegitimate son, the very name I bear is false, the name
I dared impose upon you as my wife. Forgive me if you can! How
could I tell this to the woman I loved, before I had bound her to me
as with bands of steel!"

She bent her head upon his breast in sublime pity and affection,
but did not interrupt him by a word. Soothed by the action, he
said more gently,

"Had I been the unfortunate proof of an unwise love, I could forgive even the curse thus forced upon me, in very pity for the sufferings of those who called me into being; but even this is denied me.
Without one consolation I have endured this deadly burden, crushing down my very manhood at times, and the hourly dread of a
shameful revelation has been with me for years. Twice I have by
the merest chance escaped it, and the death of my m th r left me
sole guardian of the secret. For the first time I breathe freely, for
the first time I am *a man!* Do I trust you, Leonore?"

" As husband never trusted wife before ! Oh, Lisle, Lisle ! And you were *afraid* of me !"

"I *was*, but I *am not*. *My wife* cannot harbor one injustice against me in her heart, my life's secret is her own. Have I won the right to that divine happiness of which you spoke—the blessed consciousness of ' perfect trust and confidence '—that my ' lips mock at happiness by smiling over *no* unuttered secret ?' "

" Oh, Lisle, there never was an hour when you might not have told me this ! *Could* I have loved you less, in realizing that you needed it the more for your very misfortunes ? No, no. Why should I lament that in being the son of *a gentleman* you are all I love and admire as thoroughly as I respect, while the son of Miles Sterling might have been an object of utter indifference to me ! Oh, Lisle, you are not ' cursed,' but blessed. Whoever your father was, God bless him."

" I am sure he did long since. He deserved it, for he paid as bitter a penalty for his fault as I have suffered from it. *I* blessed him and forgave him, and God's justice is tenderer than man's."

A solemn silence reigned between them when Lisle had spoken these words ; but cheek to cheek and heart to heart in a fond embrace, each felt all that the other thought ; and so tenderly and reverently they buried the mutual secret in their united souls, murmuring only " *Requiescat in pace*."

What need to follow them farther, to go back with them to their southern home henceforward blessed and hallowed by that pure and enduring affection born of mutual trust and sympathy, that oneness of heart and soul which is the only true marriage. Why depict the joy of tired and faithful friends over this reunion of two beings who had leraned to understand and thoroughly appreciate each other only through such trials and sufferings as mocked their efforts to comprehend. Deeply buried in his heart Lisle kept the secret of his wife's flight and his own pursuit, nor would she herself confess it when giving to her faithful friend, Mrs. Venard, so much of her confidence as she felt belonged to her in return for all the affection and perfect faith reposed in her when circumstances had so condemned her. Even the faithful Margaret lisped no word of that eventful journey which had so nearly been their last, and none suspected it. Thanks to the fair Melissa's fascinations over the absent

Joseph Perkins, no one remained who had the power or wish to annoy Leonore with memories of the past, and even the Wheelers who had watched her suspiciously, forgot their vigilance when nothing occurred to keep it alive.   Mr. Bertram himself, having seen his prophecies *reasonably* fulfilled, ceased to croak of future misfortunes here, and transferred to his business the energy heretofore expended in grumbling and foreboding, much to his wife's peace and enjoyment.

How little the world suspects the tragical inner lives of those whom it delights to honor; how little society dreams of the aching, weary burdens borne by many of its idols and votaries! O'er many a life some curse hangs, dread and heavily, and blessed is the veil that screens it from unpitying eyes.

THE END.